Also by Jessa Hastings

The Magnolia Parks Universe

Magnolia Parks

Daisy Haites

Magnolia Parks: The Long Way Home

Daisy Haites: The Great Undoing

Magnolia Parks: Into the Dark

Never

Never

THE CONDITIONS OF WILL

JESSA HASTINGS

Bloom books

For all my fellow adjectives…
keep modifying those nouns.

Published by Bloom Books, an imprint of Sourcebooks
P.O. Box 4410, Naperville, Illinois 60567-4410
(630) 961-3900
sourcebooks.com

Cataloging-in-Publication data is on file with the Library of Congress.

Printed and bound in the United States of America.
LSC 10 9 8 7 6 5 4 3 2 1

1

IS THERE A GOOD WAY to find out bad news? I guess, probably yes? Just...regular, I suppose—nothing scarring or dramatic.

My sister has been calling me around the clock for about a day and a half, and I haven't been answering her calls because I never answer Maryanne's calls because she has an undiagnosed narcissistic personality disorder and also, she's a bitch, and also, I just don't answer her calls. Not that she calls particularly often, but if and when she does, they mostly always go unanswered.

Now, admittedly, half of the reason I don't answer them is because I know that it gnaws away at her—every time the phone rings out, her eyebrows would lower, her eyes would pinch a little, and her jaw would jut forward as her bottom teeth touch her top ones, quietly seething. If she was trying to call me in front of anyone else, she'd just flick her eyes with a demure little roll and tell them I'm impossible sometimes, but if she were by herself, a puff of air would escape her flared nostrils. She'd give her head a slight shake and her chest would go tight because Maryanne Joy Carter cannot *not* be in control of a situation.

Me, my brothers, and my sister are victims of that God-awful trend Pentecostal parents all seemed to fall into the trap of in the nineties. You know—the naming their children after Christian-adjacent words?

I never tell anyone my full name because my middle name feels like a smear on my forehead that tells the world where I'm from, and I don't want to think about where I'm from, but here it is:

Georgia True Carter.

Oh my God, I know. *True*. It's painful.

My oldest brother is Tennyson Honor Carter.

Maryanne Joy Carter (a year and a half younger than Tennyson) is whose calls I avoid, but that's not entirely her-specific (while also absolutely being entirely her-specific). Admittedly, I avoid almost all calls from my family except those coming from Oliver Just Carter. My youngest older brother—one year older than me, two years younger than Maryanne.

It was one hundred percent our mom who picked out our middle names, no doubt about it.

To be fair, it was probably pretty edgy of her for Beaufort County back in the late nineties—I'm sure she felt cool doing it, but I've never felt cool having it.

I've always wondered whether she meant to do it too…

Tenny and Maryanne, the Nouns… Me and Oliver, the Adjectives.

Even by the pure function of what a noun is as opposed to what an adjective is, she likes nouns more, I know she does…

A noun is specific.

Adjectives? Their main syntactic role is to modify a noun, and that just isn't something you do in South Carolina.

There are lots of things you don't do if you're from South Carolina, though.

You don't disobey your parents.

You don't skip church.

You don't be gay.

You don't look like a blond Stephanie Seymour from the nineties. Which I do, apparently.

Always have, even when I was far too young to look like Axl Rose's troublesome girlfriend, that's for sure.

I get it all the time. And it's nice, because she's a bombshell and I guess

I can see it... The way my hair tends to fall, the milky skin, the rosebud lips, the big blue eyes. I have all those things, so sure—I can see what people mean. But don't you think her eyes look sad? I've always thought that maybe it was the way her eyebrows were shaped or how she holds her mouth in photographs. I can't say for certain without seeing her in real life, which I never have, and even if I did, I look like her *then*, not *now* (or so I'm told)—but it was back then that I looked like her, and back then she looked sad.

So then, sometimes I wonder whether that means I look sad too.

Maybe I do. Maybe sometimes I am.

Not consciously though, and there's a difference.

Conscious feelings are present on the surface, and you make decisions around them, but subconscious feelings exist under the surface, and they dictate your decisions too, arguably even more so, but often you only realize that in retrospect.

Befriending Hattie and Bianca? Retrospect.

Staying in London? Retrospect.

My sexual choices between the ages of fifteen and twenty-two? Retrospect.

What I study? Retrospect.

Anyway.

I've gotten about fifty calls from my sister on this very regular Saturday night in April, and I've ignored them all. Primarily because I thought that if there was something I actually needed to hear, they all would have the good sense to get someone else to give me a buzz after the first five calls went unanswered.

I don't know why it wasn't Violet who called me. Besides Oliver, my aunt Violet and her husband, Clay, are the only ones I talk to if I can help it, but she didn't call.

I think maybe she didn't want to hear the indifference in my voice if she told me.

Or maybe Maryanne just plain old didn't let her.

My phone rings again and my housemate, Hattie Ramsey, glares at it on the breakfast counter.

"Fucking answer it, would you?"

I give her a steep look. "You answer it."

"I can't listen to the CTU ringtone one more time, Georgia—it's been ringing since last night—"

"I know," I sigh. "You think she'd get the hint."

She lifts her eyebrows. "Maybe it's important."

I shake my head. "It's never important."

Hattie doesn't believe me, but she's never met my family.

There's a certain brand of crazy that's reserved special for the American South, and people who aren't from there just won't get it.

There's no doubt in my mind that my sister thinks what she's calling me about is important, but it wouldn't be beyond her to have seen me write something anti-Trump on social media and feel like it was a personal attack, which is a thing that's uniquely American, in case you didn't know. The way people there conflate their political alignment with their personal identity. Being a Republican or being a Democrat in America is for so many people akin to racial identity. Now that I don't live in America anymore, that strikes me as so weird. Because—honestly—neither party is great these days, and when you personalize something to the extent many people do in politics, any time anyone questions something the party does, it can feel like they're questioning you, and that's just plain unhealthy. I'm saying all that to Hattie for the millionth time when my phone pings with a text message. Finally.

I stare at my phone for a few seconds, just sitting there before I eventually reach for it, and in that space of time, Hattie—so over it, so desperate for the ringing to stop, apparently—she grabs my phone and checks the message.

Her hand that isn't holding the phone clenches a little, just quickly, half a second. At the same time, her bottom lip pulls and her brows knit together in unison before they quickly shoot up, eyes dragging behind them a fraction of a second later.

Quick inhale of air.

Sadness and surprise.

Something bad's coming.

She hands me my phone, brows still low, chest rising and falling quickly.

MARYANNE:

Dad's dead.

I stare at the screen for a long time, blinking.

It whistles around my clinically inclined brain that it's not a positive sign that all I felt was a twinge of sadness. Not much more or less than a feeling of inconvenience.

I know how you're supposed to feel when a parent dies.

People often experience a loss of identity, a crisis of self. They question who they are and their place in the world as though their parent themselves anchored them on to the planet.

GEORGIA:

What?

Nothing.

I don't feel anything.

That could be shock, I know. I could be going into shock.

But why would I be going into shock at the loss of a parent I lost so many years ago already?

MARYANNE:

Dad died.

I tried to call you.

Heart attack.

GEORGIA:

When?

MARYANNE:

Yesterday.

"Are you okay?" Hattie asks. She hasn't stopped looking at me since she handed me my phone.

She's frozen up the way some people do around death.

It's a natural fear, I get it. All humans, whether they know it or not, are profoundly impacted by their imminent deaths. Mortality is unbearably confronting, so much so that lots of people spend their whole lives trying to live as though it doesn't chain them like it does the rest of us.

We do all these things to avoid the ephemeralness of ourselves and the people we form attachment bonds with around us, but there's nothing any of us can do about it...

One day I'll die. One day you will.

Hattie Ramsey and I met about four years ago but have only been roommates for a bit more than a year, when her best friend moved out of their Blandford Street flat to live with her boyfriend. Now it's our Blandford Street flat.

Hats comes from a wealthy family, born and raised in London. Her mother is a successful artist and her father is an environmental lawyer. They are very in love, a rare and bizarrely functional parental unit who are highly supportive and passionate about the rights surrounding their daughter's sexual orientation, which is bisexual.

She has one sister, whom she shares a close and delightful relationship with, and the expected frictions that life affords us all, which are essential for tenacity and personal growth, have been provided exclusively from sources outside her immediate consanguinity.

Hattie Ramsey is sheltered. Sheltered as fuck, one might almost put it.

Death is confronting for sheltered people because it fractures realities.

To be fair, death is confronting for all people, probably. Sudden deaths, anyway. But the idea of death, when we look at it square in the eye, it unsettles us all.

The idea that it ends—that it all ends—that everything you spend your life doing and building toward one day amounts to actually nothing the second you take your last breath.

It's why people have children. To exist beyond their existence.

So here's Hattie, standing in front of me, jaw agape, eyes round with horror, projecting the eventual looming death of her own very good father onto the death of my very shit one.

She's devastated for me; She is more devastated for her though; she just doesn't realize it.

"I'm okay." I give her a reassuring smile.

It's not a Duchenne smile. My orbicularis oculi muscle doesn't move at all—there's no eye crinkle, no crow's feet in the corners of my eyes that shows it's genuine, but she won't notice it because most people don't and I don't want her to anyway. On a different day I would have thought to crinkle my eyes to make it more believable, but my father just died so I give myself a break.

She nods quickly; it's a nervous nod.

She's going to call her parents within the next ten minutes and tell them how much she loves them. She'll stay here with me until I give her a signal that I want to be alone, and then she'll excuse herself. I know she doesn't like it when I read her how I do, and I try my best to placate her, go the long way around with things normally... Pretend I don't notice when she's attracted to someone or when she's had a fight with her best friend.

I talk to her about those kinds of things in the slow, boring, drawn-out way that allows her and all other people to feel like they're a mystery, because feeling like you're mysterious seems to be something humans value, maybe because people don't like to feel exposed, but I don't have it in me to appease her in this way today.

"You can go," I tell her.

She frowns a little more. Bottom lip sucks in a little. I've offended her a tiny bit. "Are you sure?"

I give her another smile again, but this time I think of the Dachshund puppy that the owner of the café down the street just bought, so my smile looks more genuine, and then I tell her that I just want to be alone, but I touch her arm as I do because I know it'll put her at ease. It does.

She nods, relieved, and goes to her room.

MARYANNE:
His funeral's next Friday.

GEORGIA:
Okay.

MARYANNE:
Can you tell Oliver?

GEORGIA:
Why haven't you told Oliver?

MARYANNE:
None of us have his number.

I glare at my screen.

How is that possible?

How do none of them have Oliver's number?

Violet has his number, but she probably doesn't want to call him for the same reason she wouldn't want to call me.

GEORGIA:
I'll call him.

MARYANNE:
Good.
Thanks.
When will you fly in?

God, I hate South Carolina.

2

OLIVER AND I HAVE THIS rule with phone calls where we never call more than twice unless it's an emergency.

We (and by we, I mean I) established this rule when he moved to California nine years ago, and because of the time difference of me living in London, I'd wake up and have nine hundred missed calls from my brother when it would have been at about 2 a.m. LA time.

He moved there when he was eighteen and fresh out of St. Benedict's Military School. Our parents sent him there when he was sixteen to avoid facing what they had long suspected.

Los Angeles was in many ways both a wonderful and a terrible move for my brother.

It was the first place where Oliver ever really felt at home and accepted. It was the first place he was ever fully himself. It was the first place he was ever afforded the space to feel the weight of the life he left behind in Okatie and breathe in all the ways our family failed us.

It also swallowed him whole. The lights drew him in like a moth. It consumed him.

He fell in with not even the wrong crowd, but just a crowd without limits, and Oliver's not so good with limits anyway. He has ADHD, and—I probably don't even need to explain it more than that—obviously he has inherently lower levels of dopamine, and so he's always mining for it. There are parts of life in LA that would feel like you've struck oil if you're an emotionally dysregulated neurodivergent, which he is.

It didn't take long for him to blow through the money I gave him and crash-land into a pile of sugar daddies and alcohol.

The alcohol wasn't LA specific. He started drinking well before I left, and I was fifteen when all that happened, so I think he probably started drinking maybe when he was fourteen? God, fourteen. You're just a baby when you're fourteen.

He's doing better now, I think? That's what he tells me. He's in AA again. Sober four months this time.

We went different ways, me and Oliver. Like, literally and metaphorically.

They sent us both away: him to Georgia, me to the UK. Around the same time, a few months apart. Me first, him after.

I will say this though: sending a gay teenage boy to an all-male military boarding school isn't the punishment they thought it was. Sure, homophobia might run rampant there at times, but it surely wasn't any worse than what Ol was getting at home, anyway. And at least he made friends there who kind of got it? Who were sent away for the same stupid reasons.

I think he was just glad to be away from the rest of Okatie.

And them sending me to England? That was like they were setting me free.

I think they thought I wouldn't want to go, but I wanted to go so badly, even though I also didn't.

Cawthorne Grammar School felt like a safe haven for me, and I knew that was true. I was safer in Bath than I was in Okatie... Happier too.

But there's always that niggle, sometimes conscious but most often not—that the people who made you, the ones who created you, your own flesh and blood, the ones who are genetically wired to want you—they didn't want me. They didn't want Oliver either.

Not really, anyway—

Not the way they wanted Maryanne and Tenny.

And I knew that Oliver knew it too.

You can tell yourself you don't even really want to be wanted by people like them anyway, but it isn't true because the same way parents are supposed to want their kids, kids have a genetic predisposition to want to be wanted by them.

I mightn't like my parents, I mightn't like what they stand for or what they've done or how they've behaved, but they're my parents and they sent us both away because we weren't like them. That pulls a number on your psyche when you're growing.

I don't actually know whether they did it to punish us, hide us, reform us, or avoid us.

That was a hard thing at first, the not knowing why.

I mean, with me at least there was a catalyst they masked as the why, but it wasn't the real why...

It took me a while to land the thought, but eventually I decided I'd never know why, and I'm mostly sure, most of the time, that even if I did know, it probably wouldn't justify it much anyway.

Oliver struggled with the why. Struggles—present tense. Can't blame him; it's a really normal thing to struggle with. He looked for the answer at the bottom of bottles and in the beds of men old enough to be our father. That was probably our first and biggest divergence.

He tried to smother the memories of our childhood. I tried to pull them apart.

I know what he's doing the second he answers the phone.

Sweaty and breathless, as though he's answered midthroes.

"This better be an emergency," he pants.

He did. Midthroes! For what? Who honestly answers the phone in the middle of sex? Just stop or call me back when you're finished. "Fuck—Oliver—why did you answer?"

"This is your third call! That's an emergency—"

"I think we should talk about maybe—in emergent situations—you just stop what you're doing to take the call, not keep on keeping on until—"

"Is this the emergency?" he asks, impatient. "Because this doesn't feel like an emergency."

"Call—her—back—" Someone breathes heavily in the background.

"Gige, I'll call you b—"

"Dad's dead," I tell him unceremoniously.

Oliver's breathing stops, but the sound of him getting pumped does not—all the rustling of sheets, the strained breathing of his partner, that sort of skin-slapping-on-skin sound of sex... I'm guessing—hoping—that the guy he's with can't see his face, because if he can, the guy's an asshole.

Oliver does like assholes sometimes though, so maybe he just is one.

I wait—don't say anything—what else could I say, really?

I hear some movement and the sound of a door closing.

"What?" my brother asks me eventually.

He's twenty-seven, but he sounds sixteen again.

"I'm sorry—" I press my hands into my forehead. My Social Psychology teacher would have had a stroke at the shit I just pulled. "I should have made you call me back—have I broken sex for you?"

My brother sniffs a laugh.

"We'll see." He blows air out of his mouth. "How?"

"He had a heart attack?" I offer. "I don't know anything else. The funeral's Friday."

"Are you going to go?"

I feel my depressor supercilii muscles pull in toward one another at his question, which means I frowned. I frowned at his question. "Yeah—aren't you?"

"I guess." He sighs. "Fuck—"

"Okay, so you fly out of LAX tomorrow at 2 p.m. Then you have a one-hour layover in Dallas—"

"What?"

"I bought your ticket. It should be in your inbox."

He pauses. "You didn't have to."

I pause. "How else would you have gotten there?"

Pause.

"I would have figured it out," he tells me, and I think I can hear a tiny bit of resentment in his voice.

I swallow uncomfortably because I hate this money shit. "I figured it out for you."

He breathes in and out of his nose once. "When do you get in?"

"Monday morning. Couple hours after you."

"If you were a better sister, you would have booked it so you got there before me."

"If I were a better sister, I would have booked us two tickets to the Grenadines."

He sniffs a laugh again. "I'll see you Monday."

"Okay."

There's a pause.

"Are you okay, Gige?" he asks.

"Are you?"

"I guess," he says, and I need to see his face to know how true that is.

"I love you," I tell him.

"Love you too." Then he hangs up.

3

DO YOU WANT ME TO come with you?" Hattie asks as we stand outside Heathrow the following night.

I shake my head.

"It's not a hollow offer," she tells me as she pulls me in for a hug. I knew it wasn't because her eyebrows were raised in earnest, lips parted the slightest bit at the middle, a little hopeful I might say yes because Hattie's love language is being needed.

I'm not always like this, by the way.

Well, I am—but I try not to be.

I do try to switch it off, try look at everything like a person who hasn't taught herself to see the world stripped back to its sinew and bones, but sometimes it's hard. It's hard not to keep seeing things that are there in plain sight once you've taught yourself to see them.

"I know, but—" I shake my head as I squeeze her back. "My mom would spend the whole week convincing you to take your nose ring out and trying to convert you into a heterosexual Pentecostal."

Hattie smiles, amused. "Will you be okay by yourself?"

I take a big breath and offer a smile that's so transparent anyone could have seen through it.

She takes my hand and squeezes it. "I can fly out tomorrow, meet you there—"

"Oliver will be there."

She pauses. "Are you sure he'll turn up?"

I give her a look. "Yes."

But no.

I'm not sure he'll come, actually.

I've booked him two flights to London, and he's not come either time.

He wasn't sober though, so maybe things will be different now that he is?

I haven't spoken to him since yesterday though, and I wonder if that's negligent of me?

Telling my alcoholic-brother our dad's dead and then not checking in on him?

There's arguably a duty of care there, and I arguably have dropped the ball. Not even because of any complicated parentification relationship that may have developed between us because we didn't have anyone else so we had to be everything to each other, but just like, you know, basic human duty of care that I've failed here, and I hate failing Oliver because too many people have already.

I can't even text him now because he'd be in the air. And if he's not in the air, then I can't know that now because the idea of being in that place without him is enough to convince me not to get on that plane myself.

Fuck.

I breathe in through my noise, give Hattie a brave smile and a nod. "I'll be fine. I promise."

"If you're not—" she starts.

"I'll tell you."

She gives me one last squeeze and nods, resolute.

British Airways flies Heathrow to Charleston, direct. Nine hours.

I took an Ambien on the flight so I slept all the way, but as soon as I landed, I was tired.

Okatie tired, not regular tired.

Have you ever dated someone you fought with a lot?

A couple of years back I sort of dated this guy, and he was super hot and nice and smart and well-read, but we fought like mad.

And I liked him, I actually liked him a lot.

I liked the buzzy electricity around us, the surge of adrenaline I'd get every time we'd start to argue, but after about a month, before I'd see him, I'd feel tired.

Like, I knew what I was getting into before we got into it.

And we'd get into it, fall into it like a dance.

We'd have peaks and troughs, peaks and troughs and peaks.

We always ended on a peak; it's why we'd keep coming back to each other.

The peaks were the sex. Everything else was a trough. Everything else made me tired.

That's how I feel as I rent the charcoal-gray Land Rover Defender 110 at the car place by the airport... Tired already.

Tired like I'm saddling up to go knock around with JT Riley again, but at the end of it all, I don't even get to bang it out. I'll just leave more tired and more empty than I arrived.

I could have had someone pick me up, but the thought of sitting in a car alone with my oldest brother or my mother or my sister's husband or worse—my sister herself—makes me want to cry on the spot, so I just drive. It'll be good to have an escape route anyway. I like the safety net of being able to drive away if I need to. And I suspect I will need to.

The last day and a half have been a tremendous mind fuck, I'll give you that.

I slept on the plane because I drugged myself, but I didn't sleep much the night before because my mind couldn't switch off.

I play the loudest songs in the National's catalogue the whole drive there, so my brain never has the chance to lull into silence and feel the full nervousness I refuse to acknowledge.

God, it's like my stomach's swallowed rocks.

And I know why I'm nervous; it's normal, completely normal—my coping mechanism was to never come back, and I never did except for one time when I was nearly nineteen, and that was nearly seven years ago.

But now I have to.

You would have thought I'd processed it…

Parts of it, I have. There are other parts though… I don't know—I think I've done a fairly good job with grappling with what was mine to grapple with. Those first few years after they sent me away, I got real good at staring what happened in the eye. And then the rest of it I knew I was avoiding, but the farther away from it I was, the easier it was to ignore.

But that's not how pain works… You ignore it and it just sinks down deeper. It lodges itself in the corners of our memories, hangs off tree branches on Callawassie Drive. It hides under the pews in the back row of the church. It gets caught in a pile of sheets no one knew what to do with.

I pull into our long driveway and park.

There's one other car out front. A rental too.

A little Ascent.

Neither of the Nouns would be caught dead driving that car, so I know it has to be Oli's.

I sit in the car a second longer, wondering whether maybe, hopefully, no one's home except for Oliver, and maybe I'll have a minute to hug him and catch my breath before Hurricane Maryanne.

I walk into the foyer that's more a part of a big open living space.

Vaulted ceilings, exposed beams, light pouring in from the floor-to-ceiling windows that line the whole back of the house. Not a lot of art, actually. I've never noticed that before. There's a mirror above the fireplace, and this big painting of a plane, but now that I'm thinking about it, I think that's all? A lot of flowers, though. Not just "sorry for your loss" flowers; there's always been flowers here. I think that's maybe why I'm not a massive flower girl? It's strange how you can long for a place to be your own and hate it so much in one breath.

My eyes fall around my childhood home, trailing from the right of it to the left, and it's over there, in the far left, that I see a person I've never seen before.

Very tall—spends a lot of time in the sun with that tan of his, and brown hair—that's what I can see from this far away. That, and he's leaning against the wall by the fireplace, watching me, saying nothing.

I walk toward him. I take it back: his hair's not brown. It's not quite blond either. Maybe it's brown but it goes golden in the sun?

He's wearing light washed blue jeans with the knees all ripped, a white T-shirt, and no shoes. He's got rings on his fingers and a few necklaces tucked away, and he is—without a doubt—the most attractive man I've ever seen in my entire life, so much so that I am immediately sure he is gay. That's just the way the world works.

He's Oli's latest, obviously. Good for Oliver—what a pull!—and good on this little (big) guy, coming to his fuck-buddy's dad's funeral. I like that in a fuck-buddy. (For my brother. I don't like that in a fuck-buddy for me; that's way too involved.)

The beautiful gay man tilts his head to the side when I approach him, and he peers down at me.

Blue eyes. Very blue. Like, should-have-spotted-them-from-the-other-side-of-the-room blue.

For a second I think I see his pupils dilate, which is often associated with attraction, but if he's dating Oliver, that could mean literally nothing because maybe he's just high.

"Hi." I smile up at him warmly.

I'm warm for two reasons. One, this poor man probably has no idea of the dumpster fire Oliver's just dragged him into, and two, my social inhibitions melt away quickly around gay people because I trust them more than straight ones.

He cocks a half smile as he peers down at me. "Hey."

There's an accent, but it's hard to tell what from just a single word.

God, he is tall though.

I offer him my hand. "Georgia."

"Thought you might be." He nods coolly—Australian accent—then he takes my hand in his. And he has to be high because his pupils are definitely dilated.

"Sam," he says. "Penny."

I nod once, looking him up and down.

His feet are squared toward me, but I wonder whether he's just trying to prove something.

"Sam Penny." I frown a little bit as I stare up at him. "God, you're so attractive," I tell him.

His face twitches with a smile. "Thank you."

With my other hand—the one that isn't still in his—I tap the top of my head and reach up to his, trying to measure him.

"What are you—? Six-three?"

He squashes a smile. "Four."

I look down at my hand that he's still holding, noticing the sporadic tattoos on his arms.

I flip his wrist over. "And what do these mean?" He stares at me while I ask that, stares at me a few seconds longer than he needs to—maybe he's bi?—then glances down at his arm.

"Ah, well, this one"—he taps on the heart with a dagger through it with the words *death before dishonor* wrapped around it—"I got at the original Sailor Jerry's parlor in Honolulu. This one"—he points to a flower—"is a magnolia, because there's a song that changed my life. This one"—he points to a ship—"is a ship." He grins up at me. "Doesn't mean anything, really. I just like it."

His talking voice is stupid sexy. Deep but so personable. Maybe he's not Oliver's plaything. Maybe they're in love, and Oliver is going to tell me about it on this trip. I hope they are in love; there's something about him. I don't know what. A warmth, maybe?

"This one"—he keeps going as he taps the one that says *a place where you found you were human*—"is a line from my mum's favorite poet."

"Who's Catherine?" I tap the name scrawled near his elbow.

He sniffs a laugh, but it's genuine. It reaches his eyes. "A girl I slept with a long time ago when I was really drunk."

So, definitely bi then...

I push his sleeve up farther, because this feels a bit like an Easter egg hunt through my brother's boyfriend's psyche.

I feel his bicep through his T-shirt and flick my eyes up at him. "Whoa—" I squeeze his arm again. "You're like—this is—wow—!"

His head's still tilted, pupils dilated, brows up, and mouth a little parted, and I think perhaps, objectively speaking, I should have been becoming less and less confident in my diagnosis of his sexuality by the second, but I'm a sucker for the benign flirting that happens between a gay guy and a straight girl, so I don't want to notice what I should be noticing.

"Well, hi," Oliver says, stage left.

"Hi!" I grin over at him and squeeze his boyfriend's other arm just for show. "I'm just feeling up your boyfriend—" I grin up at the boyfriend before I give my brother a look. "God, Oliver, he is so handsome—"

Oliver bats his eyes at him. "Isn't he?"

"Tell me about it!" I squeeze both his arms up toward his shoulders, so broad and taut, and Sam Penny is just standing still, smile maybe a bit apparent on that exquisite mouth of his.

"He is gorgeous, isn't he?" My brother smiles, nodding. "He's also not my boyfriend."

I freeze.

"He's my sponsor," Oliver keeps going—shit. "And he is, unfortunately for me—and possibly you, considering...this"—he waves his hand in my general direction—"very straight."

The best way I can describe my recoil from Sam Penny is, it's like he's a hot element that my hand is touching.

I yelp as I yank it away.

Sam Penny tries to squash a smile, but it's unsuccessful because it hits his eyes, which crinkle at the edges.

Oliver bullrushes me—thank God—and picks me up and swirls me around in his arms before placing me back down on the ground.

He looks okay, I think? Maybe even good—? Handsome as ever. His hair's shorter now though; it's tousled. Eyes are big and brown, but they're not sunken—neither are his cheeks. I breathe out a small sigh that I didn't know I'd been holding in, waiting to see if he really was okay.

"I love this—" he tells me, as he tugs my hair. "So cute." He fluffs out my fringe the way he thinks it should look. "Yes. Love it. So adorable. This length, I'm dead—wait, is your hair virgin?" He feels it between his fingers. "Virgin hair, who are you!"

He stands back so I can look at him.

He hasn't changed much. It's funny how people freeze in your mind.

His hair is pushed back and styled to disheveled perfection.

A little bit of facial hair that's trimmed down neat and tight. I touch his face.

"You lost the beard." I smile at him, my heart swelling with fondness.

"You like?" He grins at me proudly.

I nod. My brother has always had an immaculate jawline but it's really on display at the minute.

He rubs his hand over his chin mindlessly. "So you've already met my poor sponsor, who you've probably set back several years of sobriety with your vulgar display, Georgia—my God, have you no self-respect?"

"I thought he was gay!" I cover my face with my hands. "It's a tacit agreement straight women have with gay men—I know you know about it"—I point to my brother—"Don't pretend you don't. I know you do—"

Oliver rolls his eyes and I glare over at Sam Penny, the straight sponsor, that traitor.

"You know, you could have told me…"

"What?" Sam scoffs, taking a step closer to me. "And ruin all that fun you were having objectifying me?"

I scoff.

"I wasn't objectifying you, I was..." I trail.

"Objectifying me?" he offers.

I hang my head. "Yeah."

He smiles at me. Duchenne smiles at me. Eye crinkles, cheeks up, no bottom teeth showing.

Pupils still dilated.

Interesting.

"Where is everybody?" I glance around, my cheeks feeling a tiny bit pink.

"Mom's at brunch with her church friends and Maryanne. They'll be home in a minute, and Tenny is—I don't know."

"Tenny is here," my oldest brother says, walking in the back door. Shirt slung over his shoulder, hair pushed back like he walked right off the page of an Abercrombie catalogue in 2008.

He opens his arms wide for me and I hug him.

I don't know why I do it.

We've never really hugged before.

We're not close.

He and Maryanne are close; me and Oliver are close. Or were. Are? I don't know.

It's been that way since forever, them and us. Even before anything happened. Nouns versus Adjectives.

The hug is forced and uncomfortable, and my brain throws a rapid-fire pop quiz to understand why he initiated a hug in the first place. I land on this:

Dad is dead. Tennyson is the man of the house now. Men of houses comfort their house in times of distress. Physical touch is an outward symbol of emotional intimacy, which Tennyson and I share none of, but baser people believe intimacy can be fostered through touch. Sometimes it can, but only for a second. It's pseudo-intimacy. He wouldn't realize that's why he's doing it, but I think that's why he's hugging me. A hollow attempt at a relational closeness we've never had.

"How are you doing? You okay?" He grips my shoulder, his eyebrows slanted upwards in concern, and I think his mouth pulls down, which would be a sign of genuine concern for me, but since fucking when? It doesn't compute.

"I'm fine." I give him a weary smile, because my smile would be weary if it was authentic (which it isn't, and I don't even really believe in a weary smile anyway; it'd be more aptly called a "controlled grimace").

Fine is a dead giveaway word for not being fine, we all know that—but it's enough to placate Tennyson, and even if it isn't, that's the moment my mother swans in.

"My baby!" she coos.

I glance over my shoulder, confused. Who's she talking to? Did they get a dog, or something? And then her hands are on my face.

"How are you, my baby girl?" She pulls me in tight for a hug. "Are you okay?"

What the fuck? I mouth at Oliver.

Oliver discretely nods in Sam's direction, and I roll my eyes, getting it—and honestly a bit put to shame that Oliver understood it before I did.

Margaret Carter is nothing if not a showwoman. I've never been her baby girl a day in my life, even when I was quite literally her actual baby girl.

There's a series of family photos that definitely aren't on display; they're just tucked away in an album somewhere—they were taken right after I was born. It's our whole family, the six of us, and the series starts out with my mom holding me, and Maryanne's right next to our mom, staring at me. A photo later, she's having a blue fit—completely scream-crying. The next photo, Maryanne's run out of the frame. The next photo, my mom dumps me in the arms of my father, and half her body's in the shot as the rest of her darts after Maryanne.

I don't know who was taking the photos—maybe it was self-timer—I always thought it was so strange that they kept taking them. I guess back then you didn't know what photos were being taken. You couldn't delete them how you can now, not print the shit ones. They were all shit ones, is the point. Maryanne made sure of that. And sure, she was four, so it probably wasn't on purpose. Except I'm pretty sure it was on purpose.

My mother pulls back. "How are you doing, my sweetheart—look at you! You're just skin and bone. Rita!" she yells out into the abyss of our family home. And you can be sure of that, it is an abyss. "Georgia's home and she's thin as a rake, would you mind fixin' her a plate?"

"Oh—" I shake my head. "I'm not hungr—"

"You'll eat," my mother tells me, pointed, as her eyes drop down my frame.

I flick my eyes over to Oliver.

There she is.

4

THE HOUSE IS FULL OF people; they come in and out like our family home is the Information Center for Beaufort County.

It's a lot of women with really blond, really big hair, who are all starting to dabble in the world of Botox, which I personally hate because it makes their faces harder to read—a lot of the perfunctory sorrys, some crocodile tears followed by the pinching of my cheeks, saying things like, "Well, I haven't seen you since you were knee-high to a duck," which are expressions you don't hear in England, thank God.

The ones who think they're really cultured ask while winking and nudging me with their elbows if I spend all my free time with Will and Kate, and I say no but I do spend a lot of time with David Brent, and they look confused and say, "The old prime minister?" And I say, "Sure."

No one seems to be talking about Dad.

My mom is like a bee flittering between flowers, too buzzy and busy to slow down or stop, and I think it's on purpose to avoid feeling what she's feeling.

My mother doesn't have the capacity to be weak in front of people; she'll be together until it kills her and she'll finally fall apart in death.

After about half an hour or so, my sister swans in with bags of groceries and her new Realtor husband behind her. She doesn't have an old husband, by the way. He's just her new husband to me. New since I last saw her.

"I'm here!" she announces, carrying the bags just far enough into the house for us to see that she's brought them in herself before she drops them. "Take those to the kitchen will you, baby?" She nods at Jase, her husband.

She herself refers to them as newlyweds, even though they've been married for a year and a half.

I was not in attendance.

"I didn't see you at Maryanne and Jase's wedding?" one of Mom's friends asked before my sister arrived.

The hot sponsor was watching me when she asked that, and I wondered how much he knows about our family. There's every chance in the world that Oliver's told him a lot—he should have, for a sponsor to function at his optimal level of purpose.

I like how he watches me. I couldn't tell you why yet. I'll be able to soon once I've been alone with him again.

"I had a dissertation," I told the nosy lady.

"A what?"

"I was busy."

"Too busy for your own sister's wedding?" She gave me a look that I got from about nine other women throughout today when they asked me a version of the same question, as well as my mother over FaceTime when I told her I wasn't coming ("—After all you've put her through?").

If someone asked me to help them tie their shoe, I would have used it as an excuse to be too busy for my sister's wedding, but the dissertation was real, actually. It was a few months away... But it was real.

"Yep," was all I said before turning away from Mom's friend.

She was disgusted by me. Brows pulled together, whole face pinched forward. You turn up for your family where we're from.

But turning up is a two-way street.

My sister's husband isn't a stranger; no one in Okatie is. Jason Devlin was my sister's high school boyfriend's best friend, which I think is kind of weird, but then—small town?

Truthfully, I wasn't all that surprised when they got together; even from years before, I remember how he used to look at her when she was with Beckett.

Jason's standing on the other side of the room with Tenny and a super uncomfortable Oliver and he's watching me, eyes pinched together with a perfectly precise mixture of suspicion and judgment. But that's like a lot of eyes here.

It wasn't a secret.

Maryanne made sure it wasn't a secret.

Maryanne was the victim and she made well sure that the whole fucking world knew it.

"Georgia!" she calls out in this breathy cry and sweeps toward me.

Everyone parts like a sea for her to get to me, and then she wraps her arms around me and the room lets out a collective sigh.

She's such a good sister, they whisper.

Look at that—

Bless her heart.

Not my heart—no one's blessing that. My heart is fucked.

Maryanne pulls away and strokes my face tenderly. Her eyes are wet, but I see no tear tracks. Her cheeks are pulled up, but there's no movement in the eye area.

She's not happy to see me.

Everyone else in the room would have missed it, and it's only for less than a second, but the same moment she strokes my cheek—the unconscious tightening of her orbicularis oculi and pars palpebralis muscles—that, ladies and gentlemen, is contempt.

That's Maryanne's starter-pack emotion for me. Contempt is our baseline.

"So pretty," she tells me with her head tilted, which sounds nice, but it's not, and I'll tell you why.

Before, when Sam Penny tilted his head at me, it was head back, neck exposed, his smile genuine and his pupils dilated.

Here, with my sister, her jaw is clenched, her chin is tucked, her shoulders are squared, and her nostrils are flared all while she says a nice thing to me.

"Jase!" she calls, taking me by the arm and leading me over to him. Every time she touches me it feels like the kiss of Judas. "This is Georgia. Do you remember Georgia?"

"Sure I do." He flashes me a smile, but his eyes are still pinched.

"Be nice." Maryanne smacks him in the arm heroically. "Don't you pay any mind to him. He's just protective of me how husbands are, you know?"

Everyone is watching us with invasive fascination. The conversation in the room's simmered down, and maybe all of South Carolina has taken a breath to see if the Carter sisters are going to pitch a fit.

This kind of attention is my sister's bread and butter.

I give her a tight smile.

"I'm not married, so." I say that because it's exactly what she wants me to say. It's important for her that our power dynamic feels to her how it's always felt.

She gives me a tight, sad smile, edges of her mouth turned down, but crow's feet appear around the edges of her eyes. She's happy she's married and I'm not.

She gives me a magnanimous shrug before she says, "Maybe one day."

And then I walk outside.

I grab a bottle of wine on the way.

I don't know whose it is or even what it is. Something white.

Hattie would kill me. She says we aren't poor enough to ever drink wine that doesn't at least cost thirty pounds, and we should always know what we're drinking so we can pair it properly.

Her sister is a sommelier, so Hats doesn't fuck around with wine, but my sister's a narcissist so I absolutely do.

Sorry Hats, desperate times…

I sit down on the steps out back.

I can't call it a yard; it's a little estate. Nearly six acres that back onto the water.

A pool, a tennis court, a prayer chapel, hot tub and outdoor bar, a wharf and a boathouse, a separate guest house that had been converted into my dad's home office with a home movie theater—

It's excessive, but that's my mom.

It was the best house out of everyone we knew, and when we moved in here, Maryanne's popularity status went through the roof.

In a lot of ways, I think maybe this house is the reason why what happened happened.

It's a show, all of it. Everything here's a show. Everything's in place, everything's perfect.

Even in the wake of a dead husband, not a single dishtowel has fallen to the wayside.

Consider me officially Okatie tired.

"You okay?" says that Australian voice from behind me.

I look back at Sam Penny, and then without invitation, he sits down next to me, pushing his hands through his hair as he does.

I like the way he moves, how big he is.

His shoulders seem bigger than he realizes. Like one day he accidentally grew up and no one told him.

And his face is interesting to me because he looks young and old at once.

Old is the wrong word. Wise, maybe? Young and wise. It's paradoxical.

There was genuine concern on his face as he asked me that. He meant it: am I okay?

I give him a small smile and nod once. "Yep."

"Aren't you supposed to be some sort of—lying wizard?"

I give him a tired look. "Is that what they're calling me these days?"

He laughs and leans back on his arms, face to the sky, and holy fucking fuck, he is divine.

He has to be a surfer—those shoulders, that tan. He still has bare feet now, even though we're outside. That's so Australian. They're big feet too. Up close and a few hours later, I can now conclude that his hair is in fact brown after all, but it's a bit gold when the light catches it, and I feel like you could maybe even say that about all of him. His mouth is surprisingly rosy and maybe the tiniest bit bottom-heavy. And I'm really glad he's not gay.

"That's a simplified version of what your brother told me." He smiles.

"So what did my brother tell you?"

He rubs his hand on the back of his neck, and I can't tell whether it's a manipulator or if he's just sore from his flight.

"He said not to bother lying to you because you'll just know the truth anyway."

I squash a smile.

"That true?" he asks, interested.

"Ah—" I purse my lips. "No." I shake my head, and he waits for more from me by saying nothing at all.

"Well, you can know someone's lying and still not know the truth... But sure, most of the time I can tell—"

"How?"

"You can ask questions and then the body gives you the answers even when the person doesn't."

He squints at me, a little dubious. "So, what is it that you do?"

"I study." I lift my shoulders breezily. "Both literally and professionally. I'm training under the director of the Emotional Intelligence Academy Group and I'm three-quarters of the way through a double master's."

He straightens up. I've impressed him. "In what?"

"Behavioral science and clinical psychology." I nod.

"Whoa—" He sits back. "Where?"

I pause. It always seems so braggy, but I sort of love it. "Cambridge."

"Well, shit!" He laughs. "Your parents must be so proud of you."

"Come on." I give him a look. "You don't have to be a body language expert to know that's not true."

His eyes look sorry, and I want neither for him to feel bad nor his pity, so I flash him a smile. "Don't worry, I've adapted to coexisting with their disappointment."

He sniffs a laugh. "What made you get into this?"

"Oh—" I give him a playful look. "If you haven't figured the answer out yourself by the end of the week, come back and I'll tell you."

"Yeah, all right." He nods once, eyes smiling even though his mouth isn't. "Deal."

"What about you? What do you do?"

"I own a few coffee shops back in California."

"But you're Australian," I tell him, as though he didn't know.

He nods again. "I moved over from Sydney when I was eighteen."

"And what are you now?"

"Twenty-eight."

I look over his face. "What was in LA?"

He nearly smiles.

"A lack of supervision." Then he laughs once, how people sometimes do at the memory of their former selves. "That's what I was after."

I have more questions and I have a feeling he has more answers—but I decide not to pry too much right now.

"So cafés, like franchises?"

Sam shakes his head. "Sister stores. One in Balboa, one in Los Feliz, and another one in Echo Park. Different names, same level of artistry in the coffee."

"Artistry?" I smirk and his brows lower in defense; then he points at me.

"You've never had good coffee."

I frown a little, not liking the idea that he might think I'm uncultured. "That's not true, I have."

"What's your order?"

"Black, normally."

He arches his eyebrows. "Do you like it?"

"Mmhm," I hum.

He cracks a grin. "Liar."

I am lying. I ignore him though. "What made you get into cafés?"

"Well—" He purses his lips. "The coffee in America is—" He pauses,

I think for diplomacy, and then flashes me an apologetic smile. "It's so good back home. Our café culture is unparalleled. And then I went to Nepal and tried Sherpa coffee. Then Italy and Guatemala, but here, it's just shit… It's always burnt and bitter. So I started roasting my own beans, then I started selling them to friends, and then at markets, and then it kind of—got away from me?" He shrugs. "I had some cash from some modeling, and I just thought—fuck it."

"Why coffee?" I ask him as I watch his face closely. I ask it, even though I'm pretty sure I already know the answer. I just want to know if he knows the answer.

He gives me a long look. "I was sober by then. I think I just needed something else to be hooked on." He tacks on a guilty grin at the end.

He's self-aware. I didn't realize that I thought that was a sexy thing till now, but it's so sexy.

I look at him a bit longer than I should…drinking him in again because he sort of demands it; he's that kind of beautiful. He doesn't look away either, just stares back, chin in his hand.

"You don't look how I imagined a sponsor to look," I tell him.

"Yeah?" He blinks. "How do you think they look?"

"I don't know—you know how Ben Affleck can look sort of weathered? Like, handsome, sure—but weathered? But you don't look weathered."

Sam gives me a look. "He's not a sponsor."

"Just weathered?"

He sniffs a laugh. "I'm weathered." He sounds tired. "Just not in ways you can see with your eyes."

I press my lips together and peer over at him sheepishly. "I'm sorry about before."

He fights off a smile as he shakes his head. "Don't be."

His pupils dilate again, and he looks at his hands.

"You're attracted to me?" I technically ask him, but it's more of a statement because his body is already giving him away.

He scoffs and looks over at me. He looks pained for a second, like he's working out how to proceed.

"Fuck—" He smiles tightly, then laughs again. "Yep." He nods, then shoves his hand through his hair uncomfortably. "What gave me away?"

I scratch my wrist, make it look absent-minded—except it isn't—it's called a manipulator. And I'm not being manipulative to him doing this; I'm humanizing myself. I'm doing an action that would imply to him I feel nervous, and I want him to think I'm nervous because he'll find it a bit disarming, and I want him to stay attracted to me and sometimes men are weird about power dynamics like that.

"Um." I take a breath. "Dilated pupils, genuine smile." He tries to squash his smile. He's amused. "You keep wetting your lips, and you pushed your hands through your hair twice." He starts chuckling. "And your feet—"

He rolls his eyes, exasperated. "What about my feet?"

"They're as pointed toward me as they can be. Even though you're sitting square on, they're pointed in my direction."

He looks down at them and then back up at me, giving me a fake glare before pressing his tongue into his bottom lip. "Can you teach me?"

"Teach you what?"

He waves his hand in my general direction. "How to do your… thing?"

I think it's cute. I think he's cute, all of him, everything about him.

I like how optimistic he is about himself.

"Yeah," I smile up at him. "I can teach you a few basic things to look out for…"

"Like what?" He tilts his head and I wonder what his mouth tastes like.

There's a school of thought that suggests we taste pheromones though kissing.

"Like smiles. How to read smi—"

"There you two are!" Oliver says from behind us, and in a rare moment for me where I'm not in control of the way I allow my body to be seen, I unconsciously shift a little but away from Sam Penny. Oliver doesn't seem to notice that nor what it may tacitly imply as he trots down the back steps and stands with his hands folded across himself. "So, Gige—how are we doing back in the Hellmouth?"

"Well, it took Maryanne a full two minutes of being in the same room as me to give me a passive-aggressive insult, so I think she's getting soft in her old age."

"Oh my gosh, Maryanne will fuck you up and eat you for breakfast if she ever hears you refer to her as old."

"She's twenty-eight. That's nearly thirty." I shrug, just to be petulant. "That's kind of old."

"I'm twenty-eight," Sam tells me.

"Then you're kind of old..." I bat my eyes playfully, then lean over to him and say quietly, "Please don't fuck me up and eat me for breakfast."

"Maybe I will, maybe I won't." He grins.

"Uh-uh—" Oliver shakes his head dramatically, pushing my face away from Sam's with theatrics akin to those you may find in a seventh grade musical theater production. "No way. You find your own sobriety coach."

"I don't have a drinking problem." I frown.

Oliver's eyebrows get tall, and he crosses his arms over his chest. "Well, Georgia, that's your fault, not mine."

"So who's the poet in your family?" Sam asks, I think trying to change the subject.

Oliver looks at him, confused. "What?"

"The poet?" Sam glances between us. "In your family?"

"What are you talking about?" Oliver tilts his head, hands on his hips.

Sam looks at me specifically, but I shake my head. "No poets."

"One of your parents loved poetry though—"

I press my lips together and shake my head.

Oliver raises his eyebrows in expectant confusion.

"You're all named after poets," Sam tells us.

I frown.

"Well—" He considers. "Most of you. You—" He looks at me. "I haven't worked you out yet."

I give him a dubious look.

Oliver shakes his head. "What are you taking about?"

Sam glances between us. "Tennyson…obvious." He points to Oli. "Mary Oliver. And Maryanne… How does she spell it?"

"M-A-R-Y-A-N-N-E."

Sam Penny thinks to himself for a minute. "Marianne Moore."

He raises his eyebrows in victory.

I shake my head. "Our parents were engaged-to-be-engaged fresh out of high school—I don't even think Mom went to college—" I look at Oliver to verify, who shakes his head to confirm that she didn't. "And our dad is the least creative man on the planet."

"Econ major at Cornell." Oliver tells him, like it should explain it all. "He's a real 'shredded wheat bran cereal' for breakfast kind of guy, even though he doesn't have a fiber problem. He ate it for the taste." Oliver eyes widen for the sake of drama. "For the taste, Sam."

Sam chuckles.

"We aren't named after poets." I tell him decidedly. "It's too romantic."

Sam shrugs, unconvinced. "Maybe your mom's a romantic…"

I turn to Oliver. "Didn't Mom say Valentine's Day was a fine day for the devil to stretch his legs?"

"Yeah," Oliver concedes. "But I think that's because I was trying to send a love letter to Josh Hartnett."

"Well—" I cast a look between the two of them. "One could hardly blame you."

"Dad blamed me." Oliver nods as his mouth pulls tight across—AU 14—he's harboring a side of contempt with that specific memory.

"Yeah well, Dad was a bit of a dick sometimes," I say really off the cuff, and Sam goes quiet, unsure of what to say. He just flicks his eyes from me to Oliver.

My brother clears his throat uneasily as he bows his head. "May he rest in peace."

5

THE DINING ROOM IS SO big you could fit twenty people comfortably, thirty if you wanted to push it, but tonight there are just nine of us.

Me and Oliver.

Sam Penny.

Mom.

Mom's best friend, Debbie.

Tenny and his girlfriend, Savannah Ren.

And my sister and her husband.

We're all bunched in at the center of the table, too much space on either end of the room for anyone to ever feel at ease, but the proximity of everyone is good for me because I can see all their faces.

I don't like my mom. I never really have, not for a long time, and you'll get it eventually. It sounds callous to say it now out of context, but context is everything. I love her, sure—an abstract love that stems from a place sadder and deeper and more desperate for acceptance than I care to acknowledge exists within me, but I don't particularly like her.

All that's to say, even without an affinity toward my mother, I have to admit the amount of despair she's unconsciously displaying on a microlevel is like a stab in the guts.

Every smile is laced with heartache; every blink is edged with loneliness.

I don't even know if she knows she feels like this. I don't know if she would have let herself actually be alone since Friday to feel any hint of loss, but she'll learn quickly that losses sneak up on you no matter how many blankets and smiles you throw over them.

My sister is anxious.

My sister is always something... Controlling, mostly, but around me, a heightened sense of anxiety tends to creep into her.

It's because of what happened.

She's just waiting for me to fracture her perfectly constructed world all over again.

Oliver is on edge and alert.

His defenses are high and he's watching for criticisms and attacks. He perceives all things anyone from here says to him as underhanded, which is a mostly-safe assumption, but it's tiring for him, and I can see it in the way his cheek muscles sag. It makes him sad to see the world how he has to when he's with our family, but it's the only way he's learned to survive.

Tenny's easy to read and it's always disappointing.

Disappointing because he's not an idiot, but he acts like he is.

He's more aware of what's going on around him than most people, but he doesn't have the stones to do anything about it. I watch him watch Debbie make a weird comment about Oliver's rope bracelet from Dolce & Gabbana, and all Tennyson does is watch, even though I think I might have seen a flicker of contempt on his face. It's there for a second and then it's gone.

I tell her it's chic and on trend, but Okatie is so far away from the normal world she just wouldn't know it, no more Oliver's fault than it is hers. I say it with a sweet, hollow smile on my face, and I know it unsettles her because people find those kinds of smiles unsettling, but good, because I want her to be.

Tenny's girlfriend is infatuated by Oliver because she's never met a real life gay person "that she knows of," but I get the feeling he's right up her alley, like she's waited her whole life for a gay BFF. This girl is an Instagram sensation waiting to happen; she's bouncy and cute and bright-eyed and I feel like she's probably kind of stupid but hopefully in an endearing, naïve way.

To her credit, she doesn't actually ask him any of the kinds of questions I've come to expect from people here, which are usually so absurdly grounded in what they perceive to be as current queer culture, but are maybe like 2008 queer-adjacent at best (e.g.: "Do you love Ellen?", "Will you audition for Queer Eye?", etc.).

Tennyson's girlfriend immediately compliments Oliver's hair—touches it, even—which he loves, so starved of affection and acceptance all his life—he's so thrilled to have a friend. I don't think Tenny's thrilled though, which I love, but it does add another layer of complexity to the situation because for all our lives, for as long as I can remember, Oliver has been trying to win the approval of our older brother, and buying matching Golden Goose sneakers with his girlfriend won't get him the affirmation he so desires.

Jason Devlin sits beside my sister staring at his plate of food, and I wonder if he hates his life or whether I'm just projecting that on to him. It is a regret of mine, admittedly, with missing (read: avoiding) their wedding, that I didn't get to see their faces leading up to and surrounding it. I'll know by the end of the week whether she loves him and he loves her, truly, or whether they married because that's what the trajectory of their relationship called for them to do.

He's checked out of the dinner conversation, and fair enough, because it's weird.

I know it's weird because I can see it all over Sam Penny's face.

It's like Dad's dead body is on the other end of the table and we're all avoiding looking at it or talking about it. They're all speaking about him like he's still here.

"Daddy likes the Beach Boys."

"Dad likes whitewashed woods."

"Dad likes finger sandwiches." As though as he'll be there to eat them.

"Dad likes open collared shirts," Tenny tells the room, and my mother points a condemning finger at him.

"Boy, I will lay a hurtin' on you if you show up to your daddy's funeral with your shirt buttons down."

"Yes ma'am." Tennyson nods, smiling tight.

"A funeral." My mom sighs. "Good gravy, where do we start?"

"Mama, we're going to sort it," Maryanne tells her, holding her arm. "I don't want you to worry about a thing."

"Sweetheart." Mom pets her hand tenderly. "This is a tough time for us all. I don't want you carrying more than your share—"

Maryanne shushes her. "Don't you lift a finger, we'll do it all…"

Oliver and I trade looks.

I hadn't really planned on doing anything. Like, maybe getting drunk the night of the funeral and having it out with my sister so I don't have to see her for another six years—something like that—but that was the height of my plans.

"So." My sister claps her hands together to get my attention. "How's London?" Her eyebrow is curved upward. It's more of a challenge than a question.

She's daring for my life to be better than hers.

"It's good—"

"Are you dating anyone?" she asks, eyebrows unmoved.

"No."

"I thought you were dating someone," she tells me in a weird tone. Like she's annoyed that she doesn't have the most up-to-date information on my life.

"We broke up."

"When?"

I sigh, tireder than I mean to sound, and I chastise myself for doing it because she'll take it as a tiny victory. "I don't know—four or five months ago?"

"Why?" She blinks, and everything about the conversation has a passive-aggressive undertone, and I don't fully understand why Oliver isn't saying something to save me until I clock him and see he's texting someone.

"He..." I trail because I don't want to tell her anything. Maryanne doesn't know about my life for a reason. Also, I don't want to keep talking about my ex-boyfriend in front of Sam Penny because—no reason. I just don't want to.

"Was he an asshole?" Maryanne cringes sympathetically, but it's fake, because she quite likes the idea of someone being an asshole to me.

"No," I say sincerely, because I can't say anything bad about Anatole Storm, and I hope my face doesn't look pained the way I think it might because I don't want Sam to think I'm still in love with him or unavailable or whatever. I'm not; it was just sad what happened, that's all.

He is watching me closely, by the way. Sam Penny's watching me very closely. His eyebrows are furrowed. He's quite stoic.

"Are you still living with that"—my mother drops her voice so as not to summon more of them—"lesbian?"

Debbie and Mom trade ominous looks.

I try not to smirk at their despair. "Yes."

My mother rolls her eyes a little and sighs.

"You live with a lesbian?" Savannah asks pleasantly. Kind of the same way someone might say, "Oh, you live with a doctor?"—pure interest.

I tilt my head to clarify. "Well, she's bisexual."

"Are you a bisexual?" she asks brightly.

Oliver chokes on his sparkling water and my mother drops her fork, as though the mere thought of having two children on the LGBTQ+ spectrum might kill her dead on the spot.

"Um." I give her a big smile. "No—I wish—"

"You wish?" Debbie blinks. "What in tarnation are you talking about?"

"Well, it's just that when you're bi, the world is your sexual oyster, plus my housemate is super hot, and—" My joke does not go down well with my mother, so I purse my lips and change tactics. "I was joking. I'm happy with my sexual ori—"

"So, London," Sam Penny butts in from across the table from me, catching my eyes. "You've been there a while?"

I flash him a quick, grateful smile. "About ten years."

He nods, and his eyes flick right and upward as he tries to do the math of it all, which I imagine is rather difficult because he doesn't know how old I am.

"So when did you move away?"

Maryanne and I catch eyes.

"When we made her." My mom laughs airily, as though it was nothing more than moving the little silver dog from Park Lane to Mayfair.

"Made her?" Sam blinks, glancing at me, confused.

Oliver cracks his back and stares at his plate, having just tuned back in.

My mother squares her shoulders and, using both hands, pushes her hair behind her ears, which is a form of upregulating. She's asserting dominance; she feels threatened by the question—why would a mother make her own child move to another country? What does that say about her? What does that say about her child? All questions I've asked myself a hundred billion times, but I dare say my mother's probably managed to sidestep.

"There was an…incident," my mother says delicately.

"She was sleeping with Maryanne's boyfriend," Tennyson announces unceremoniously.

"Tennyson!" My mother overenunciates his name with a growl, but not because she's defensive of me, but because she's ashamed of me. She doesn't want people to know her daughter's a whore, but everyone here already does. Except for Sam. Until now.

I can feel his eyes on me, and I hate it. Staring at me like I'm the kind of girl who sleeps with her sister's boyfriend.

The kind of girl I'm not.

"Bygones." Maryanne flaps her hand.

"Very gracious of you, Maryanne." Debbie nods at her from across the table before throwing daggers at me with her eyes.

My mother pats my sister's hand. "Such a good heart, my Maryanne." She looks at her proudly and then over at Sam. "It was a mistake," my mother tells Sam, then eyes me down. "Wasn't it, darling?"

I press my lips together. It's a self-hushing technique, but no one here knows it, thank God.

"It happened one time, and it was a mistake." Maryanne gives me a tight smile across the table. "They both said sorry." Her smile grows as she shrugs. "Like I said, bygones."

I drop my eyes to my plate. A pile of food I've barely eaten, just shoveled around with the good forks, reserved strictly for the best company, the queen, and dinner parties for when Dad's died, apparently.

And do you know what, my eyes are glued to the table, my breath is tucked in under my chest, and I'm still as a stone, because it's not true.

My mom's telling the only story she knows.

Maryanne's telling a lie.

"Excuse me." I push back from the table. "I'm going to start cleaning the dishes."

"Oh—" My mom swats her hand. "We have Rita for that."

"I'm going to help her," I say, already walking away.

"So sensitive," I hear my mother say under her breath, but loud enough for us all to hear.

"Yeah, well, some people don't like their past dug up at dinner, Mom," Oli tells her.

"Oh, Oliver, she's hardly the victim here—" And I can just imagine it, my mother leaning over, squeezing my sister's arm. "Maryanne thought she was going to marry that boy—and we're so glad she didn't!" she declares loudly for Jason's sake. "Because then we wou—"

And then I'm too far away to hear any more.

I don't need to hear any more, I've heard it all before. And part of me is dying that Sam Penny's hearing it right now: Maryanne, good. Georgia, bad.

6

THERE WERE SO MANY HORRIBLE things about the way it all played out on that day.

The way my dad's face fell like a crushed paper bag when he flung open the door and found Beckett Lane with his hand up the shirt of my Christian school uniform, his pants down, my plaid skirt up, and our bodies pressed against each other.

My father roared in this angry kind of way I hadn't heard before or since, and my mother clasped the doorway as though it was her life that was about to be torn apart.

Beckett was ripped off of me and shoved to the other side of my bedroom, and then Maryanne filled the doorway.

She and I held eyes, and I wondered how this would go—what direction she might play this. There was a fraction of a second when her whole face was calm, and then like a switch was flipped, she launched at me.

Even then, before I knew about anything or understood any of what I do now, I knew the way she got angry in that moment was strange. She called me every name and cuss word under the sun, lunged for me again.

Beckett grabbed her, pulled her out of my bedroom, begging for her to forgive him, it wasn't his fault, she knew that, right? She was crying these incredibly believable tears, and I remember wondering even then, what she was crying about—? I don't even know if those tears were real. They looked real—they weren't instant how they often are when someone's putting them on. Was she sad? Had this hurt her? Had I hurt her? Beckett—he was shaking his head wildly, saying everything he could to keep her on his side—he never meant to hurt her, he just got seduced by me—I don't think he needed to try that hard, as I suspected, actually, she was always on his side…

I remember Maryanne sort of collapsed into his arms, wailing like her heart was broken.

"God, Mer, I'm so sorry—I don't know what came over me. It's her—you know that, right?"

Little old me. All of fifteen years old. I did bear the weight of that for a long while, that it was me… My fault, I did it, I seduced him—

My dad was absentmindedly taking off his tie, sitting on my bed, staring off into the distance the way you might expect a man to do when he's just seen his kid getting fucked in the bed he built her. I didn't like how he looked—it scared me, the detachment, how quiet he was.

But not my mother. My mother rushed me.

"How dare you," she spat.

I remember what she was wearing; it's one of the most vivid things about that night, actually. A salmon pink boatneck dress. I hate that color now. I don't even really like to eat salmon, if I'm honest.

She grabbed me by the arm and dragged me to the bathroom, shoved me toward the sink.

"How could you, Georgia?" She was horrified, truly, properly horrified. "How could you do this to her?"

I wasn't sure why we were at the sink. I'm still not really sure.

She ran the tap too hot and washed my hands with soap, both hers and mine, like it would make me clean again, and her by proxy. Then she shoved me into the shower and turned it on—cold. I don't know whether that part was on purpose.

"This is unforgivable—"

Oliver rushed into the bathroom, eyes wrought with confusion and fear and maybe, in retrospect, probably a hint of betrayal.

I used to tell Oliver everything—why wouldn't I have told him this?

"Oh my God." Oliver blinked, staring at me blankly as I shivered and cried silently in the shower.

She made me stand there for probably half an hour.

Oliver sat on the sink, watching me, waiting for me, and even though Mom told him to go, he wouldn't.

Maryanne was wailing somewhere in the background. I heard things in my room smashing. I knew even then, whatever was breaking was exclusively the things I cared about most at the hands of my sister who cared about me the least.

My mom banged the faucet off and flung a towel at me. "Get out."

She grabbed my brother by the hand and dragged him out with her, slamming the door to my bedroom behind them.

They stripped my bed that night. All the pillows, the fitted sheet, the flat sheet, the quilt cover, and the comforter, strewn in a pile on the floor.

They left the window open, airing out my sins, I think.

That night I slept on my bare mattress in my wet school clothes because all my drawers had been emptied.

When I woke up the next morning, my bags were packed and waiting by the front door.

It happened silently.

No one said a word.

Maryanne stood at the breakfast counter, both hands gripping the marble, eyeing me down in a power stance. Tennyson leaned against the fridge, watching with a slight frown on his face, and no one woke Oliver. He's always had to be woken up. Alarms don't work for him; he sleeps too deeply. He was completely out to the world, and it all happened so quickly.

I don't know how I knew before I'd spotted the man I didn't know out front, but I did. There are bounty hunters for teens, did you know? Wayward teens, which I was, apparently. Maybe my family were too still, and it made me nervous. I don't know—but I had a feeling something was amiss.

I tried to run up the stairs to Oliver and I made it as far as the hallway we shared, but my dad caught me and scooped me up in his arms, lugging me toward the door, and I screamed out Oliver's name.

He didn't hear it the first time, but the second time he came barreling down the stairs. He tried to grab me from our dad, but my dad pulled me harder and shoved me backward into the Escalade that neither of my parents were in.

Oliver ran after the car, crying.

I banged the windows, crying for him.

My parents stood there, watching, arms around each other, stolid and assured in their decision. My sister stood in the doorway, and maybe it's my mind embellishing it over time, but I swear to God, there was a hint of a smirk. I'd swear it.

I was taken to a private plane where I was flown to Gatwick Airport. I cried half the way there, mourning no one but Oli.

Tennyson's godfather was the principal of Cawthorne. He was doing my dad a favor when he took me on as a boarder.

I cried a lot at first. I didn't really know where I was or what was happening, but Cliff was a good man, and patient in a way I'd never really experienced. I think he expected me to be a troublesome student, the menace my mother had surely painted me to be, but I thrived there and he gave me room so I could.

It's a funny part of growing up, actually... Accepting that things that are better for you, healthier—they can still be painful. That the worst, most shameful day of my life to date would in turn become the most defining.

There's a knock on my bedroom door and I sit up bolt right, my reverie completely interrupted.

It's the same bedroom they dragged me out of ten years ago. They put me back in here like nothing happened at all. Like there aren't still the indents of my nails on the doorframe from when they began to drag me away.

It's the dead of night, about 2:00 a.m. I grab a nightgown and throw it over myself and scurry to my door, heart pounding and racing because I don't have a good association with people who arrive at my door. I creak it open and peer out.

Sam Penny.

I relax a little and open the door a bit more.

I'm so glad to see him—like, so glad. Gladder than I want to be. Because I was so mortified at dinner, and I liked talking to him and I liked him being attracted to me, and I don't want that to stop because he heard a botched-up version of a story that happened a decade ago.

I raise my eyebrows, waiting like I'm annoyed that he's there because I want to throw him off. "Yes?"

"Well, hi to you too." He smirks.

I purse my lips and smile at him, even though I'm not sure that I should. "Hi."

"Lord Byron," he says, pointing at me, then nods, pleased with himself.

"What?" I blink.

He shakes his head at himself. "It was tough—that was pretty sneaky of them—"

"Of who?" I frown.

"You're named after Lord Byron," he tells me.

"How?"

"Well, Cambridge..." He gives me a look. "His name wasn't Lord—it was George Gordon Byron."

I squint and smile at him, a little in disbelief.

"That's who you're named after." He shrugs like it's absolutely true. He flashes me this look—he's proud of himself, and he wants me to be proud of him too. I can tell in the squaring of his shoulders. "You're all named after poets."

I sigh and roll my eyes. "That's just a coincidence."

He snorts a laugh at my apparent silliness. "Your brother is called Tennyson."

"Do you know how many Jacksons and Braxtons and Masons there are in the South?" I fold my arms over my chest. "The South loves a 'son.'"

"Know a lot of other Tennysons?"

I pinch my eyes, refusing to give him the satisfaction of a "no" aloud, and Sam Penny smiles, once again pleased with himself, as though he's won the argument—if that even was an argument.

"I just wanted to tell you," Sam says, tilting his head to catch my eye. "Because I was pretty sure you'd be awake, obsessing about which poet was your namesake."

I give him a smarmy look. "Well, you were so—"

"Yes." His face softens a little as he nods once. "I was."

He stares at me for a long few seconds, and fuck—I like him how he is. In the dead of night, in a white T-shirt and black Calvin Klein pajama pants. A bit disheveled, a lot perfect.

Sam swallows once and it's heavy, his pupils dilated again now, and I want to reach out and take his pulse, but that would be weird if I did, and no one likes to feel see-through, particularly when you're in your pajamas, so I try my best not to feed the dragon in my mind that sees everything no one wants it to see. It's hard not to feed him, though; he's learned to live off the crumbs of people, and people leave crumbs everywhere.

"Are you okay?" Sam asks as he watches me. I don't answer immediately—not because I'm trying to be mysterious, but because I am, in fact, trying not to feed the dragon at this very moment, trying my absolute best not to let the dragon know that he's just pushed his hands through his hair (again) or that our proxemics are way off for two people who only met today—but in doing so, I don't answer, and so he tilts his head, makes us eye to eye, and the way his brows pull together into a frown, his bottom lip puffing out—God, he's so sincere, and it's so sweet.

"Yeah." I nod (lie), and then I feel something wet slip from my eye. I wipe it away quick.

His frown spreads and he tilts more. "Are you crying?"

I breathe out a tired laugh. "Yeah."

Sam nods to my bedroom behind me.

"Do you want me to come in?" he asks, eyebrows up, hopeful. Still sincere.

Do I want him to come in?

Him with the eyes that look worried for me and about me, him who's been lying awake at night at two in the morning to solve a riddle that he invented about my family in his mind, him who's kept my brother sober and safe—yes, I want him to come in, because look at his eyes in the moonlight. It somehow seems to shine on him from nowhere—there are no curtains open, he's not under a skylight—my bedroom is barely lit by a lamp from Pottery Barn's 2014 fall catalogue, and yet his blue eyes look iridescent. And don't even get me started on the angles of his nose.

"Yes," I say. It comes out all solemn.

His cheeks twitch—AU 12—it's a blink-and-you'll-miss-it pulling of his zygomaticus major muscle on his left-hand side—which is all to say...he's pleased.

"Okay." He goes to move toward me, but I block the door, shaking my head.

"But you shouldn't," I say, because I'm worried that this room is cursed.

His bottom lip tugs downwards now in disappointment. "Why not?"

I try to keep it light, flash him a playful look. "You've got Catherine on your arm already, you don't need a Georgia—"

"I don't know." He shrugs, holding my gaze. "I could need a Georgia."

"Trust me." I lift my eyebrows. "You don't. They're not worth it."

"I'm pretty sure they are," he says, but in the context of everything, I'm pretty sure they're not, so I just give him a tired smile that matches how my heart feels.

"Good night, Sam."

And fast as anything, the inner corners of his eyebrows draw in and then go up—he's disappointed—but then he smiles at me anyway.

"Good night, Lord Byron."

7

I WAKE UP A LITTLE SHY of six the next morning. Not because I'm super Zen or focused or have a killer morning routine or anything, but because it's eleven in London and the jet lag is real.

I walk downstairs as quiet as I can and into the kitchen. I open cupboards and drawers in slow motion because if Rita, Mom's housekeeper, hears me, she'll wake up and make breakfast for me and I think the woman probably needs a good lie-in.

I perch on the kitchen counter with a bottle of water and tuck my feet under me. Childhood homes are weird. It's mostly the same since I left it.

Though it's newer. Parts have been updated. My room is a tiny bit different, not really enough though. Oliver's is a full-blown generic guest room now and mine is halfway there, and if that isn't a metaphor for how our parents feel about us, I don't know what is.

I used to spend a bit of time in the kitchen, actually. When Oliver began sneaking out and I was worried he wouldn't come home, I'd stay up in the kitchen and wait until he did, because it seemed like a better idea than being in my room.

Oliver's blossoming sex life had a high correlation to the expansion of my baking prowess. I started with cupcakes and eventually baked my way around to soufflés.

I didn't eat what I made much. Maryanne would bring them to school the next day, give them to her friends. I think they thought she made them, because one day she came home asking me to bake her a birthday cake for someone, but I said no because I had a biology test the next day that I needed to study for and she was fit to be tied.

I didn't do it though. Even when Mom tried to make me.

Dad told her to leave me alone.

I don't have a lot of positive memories of my parents. Dad telling Mom and Maryanne to leave me alone is one of the few.

"You're up early," Sam says quietly, watching me from the doorway.

He has a croaky morning voice, and I don't know why this happens or even how, but before I can get a hold of the thought, it's away from me and rolling down a hill: how nice it would be to wake up in the mornings to that voice.

I smile at him, tired, even though now he's here I feel a bit bright inside. "So are you."

He stretches. "I try to get up with the sun."

"Oh." I roll my eyes. "You're one of those?"

He chuckles softly and walks over to me. He's barefoot again.

I find it personally offensive that men look effortlessly sexy in the mornings, I really do. It's a great unfairness and an uneven distribution of power. The division of power says that women get sex and beauty, and if that's the case, and it's our commodity—we should have it at the ready, twenty-four seven.

He's just in a gray sweater. Hair's all bed-heady. Mouth a little puffy from sleeping. Same black pajama pants from last night.

He stands in front of me, eyes flickering down from my face then back up again, and then, holding my eyes, he takes the water bottle from my hand and takes a sip. "How'd you sleep?" he asks, not looking away.

And I swallow heavily. There is something about him, isn't there? Like, beautiful and fascinating, and so much bigger than me.

When I was a teenager, I went with my friend's family over the Easter break to the Dominican Republic (because otherwise, I was absolutely just going to stay in England)—and I don't think you're supposed to now, we'd probably get into lots of trouble for it these days, but fuck it, I was sixteen—we swam with humpback whales.

It was crazy, actually. Behind them and beside them. It was this almost otherworldly feeling, where you're so small, but not in a way that's degrading or upsetting, but the fact that you're on the planet at the same time as something so big and so significant, I don't know—it was strangely life-affirming? Like you're not alone in the world.

And I get that same feeling when I'm near Sam Penny.

Other feelings too, like this buzzy electricity. And it's there, all thick in the air, us trying to learn about the other. It feels like we're cramming for an exam, studying like maniacs the night before a test on a subject we've half-listened to all year. The content isn't unfamiliar when you read it; it's like you've read it before. Sam feels like I've read him before, but I haven't.

He feels like the kind of memories I wish I had but don't. He's like déjà vu. And you know how when that happens, your brain is like, "Wait, we've been here before," and you're watching everything unfold and you're waiting for the next thing to happen and you're like, "I knew that," and then the next thing happens and you're like, "I knew that too," and every time something happens that you've been waiting to happen because you feel like it's already happened even though it hasn't, you feel this floaty sense of delighted satisfaction—that's what it feels like to be near Sam Penny.

I give him a smile as my answer because I don't want to lie to him and I don't want to say "bad" either.

"Isn't that your bed?"

I tilt my head. "Frame, not mattress."

I'm not sure why my mother hadn't burned that bed frame along with my mattress the day I was shipped off to London. I think she left it there on purpose, some sort of reminder that what happened happened, and it will have always happened. A monument to the sinfulness of her youngest.

"What about you?"

He shrugs. "A bit cold."

"Oh my God." I sniff. "My mom would be mortified."

He smiles. "Don't tell her, then."

Then we just look at each other for a bit. I like the way he blinks. It's long and slow. Shorter than Bambi's, longer than mine. Like he's in no rush, nowhere better to be.

He takes another sip of my water.

"Are you calm right now?" I ask him.

He nods, a little confused.

"Relaxed?" I clarify.

He nods again, smirking a little.

Then I reach over and press two fingers against his carotid artery.

He freezes.

"...What are you doing?" he asks after a pause, and I hold up a finger to silence him.

"Six...seven...eight...nine. Nine." I nod to myself.

His face falters a little. "What was that?"

"When you're calm, your resting heart rate is fifty-four. Very healthy." I nod approvingly.

He smiles, confused. "Okay?"

I shrug, fingers still touching his neck. "Just establishing a baseline so I can tell when you're nervous later on."

He tilts his head playfully. "What's going to make me nervous later on?"

I open my mouth to say something, but—

"So are you two sleeping together?" Maryanne asks, walking into the kitchen, shifting her long cardigan around her body. She looks at me disparagingly. "Honestly, Gigi? Already?"

"We met yesterday." I roll my eyes, and sidestep that I absolutely have—on occasion—slept with a man the night (nay, once the hour) that I met him.

She lifts her eyebrows, gives me a look like that's her point exactly, and then I feel Sam shift a little next to me. Actually—if I'm dissecting things—I believe he shifted a tiny bit in front of me. Minuscule in action, quite loud in intent though. (And my heart rate might have elevated a little itself.)

"What are you doing here?" I ask my sister.

She rolls her eyes. "It's my parents' house too, remember?"

I give her a look. "If not more so."

She folds her arms over her chest and looks Sam up and down, then looks back to me. "You didn't answer the question."

"Neither did you." I glare over at her, sliding off the bench and pushing some hair behind my ear, upregulating.

"I stayed here last night." She eyes me.

"Where's Jason?" I ask, just being pleasant.

She arcs her head to the side. "Wouldn't you like to know."

I roll my eyes.

"Hey," Sam Penny says, stepping forward and looking back at me. "We were just about to go grab some coffee. Can we bring you in anything?"

And then he gives my sister this look... Assertive and silencing all at once. Like he's daring her to say something else. I don't know why he does it, but it works, and I'm grateful.

"A caramel latte." She gives him a sugary smile.

He nods. "Where's good around here?"

"Hmm." Maryanne purses her lips in thought, eyes flicking upwards and left—she's thinking, properly, trying to recall, so it would seem—and then her eyes flicker straight at me, just for a second, so quick I could have missed it but I don't, I never do, not with her—then her eyes flick back up and left for a moment, and then she shrugs. "Only decent coffee house around Okatie is Stomp."

Sam nods, writing it down in his phone.

She looks at me. "Over on Sergeant William Jasper Boulevard. The Del Webb end. Only a five-minute drive," she tells Sam.

I nod, already walking out of the kitchen.

"Oh great," sings Sam merrily as he walks away, just loud enough for my sister to hear. "Maybe we'll have time for a quick fuck in the car after all."

8

SAM CLIMBS INTO THE PASSENGER seat of my rental Land Rover, gives me a look out the corner of his eye, and thumbs back toward the house.

"Real breezy sister you've got there," he says, that Australian accent perfectly thick.

I snort a laugh.

His face gets a little more serious. "How was it like growing up with"—he pauses, thinking—"that?"

I stare over at him, dumbstruck. I'm not sure why he feels like he can ask me that—? And I know that sounds hypocritical because I ask people invasive questions all the time, but I think I do it (mostly) in the name of science. Sam Penny's doing it in the name of…something else. And yet…that old connection we don't actually have (but somehow we do?) leads me to answer with: "Complicated."

He just nods and looks out the window.

"Sun's not up yet," he says.

"We can go watch it?" I offer, happy to extend my time out of the house. Happy to be alone with him, really.

He looks over at me, eyebrows up. "Yeah?"

"Yeah." I shrug all airy, because unlike my sister, I am breezy. Well,

I'm not really breezy, but I want him to think I'm breezy. "Sure, if you want to."

He swallows—which, as we all know, can be a sign of an intense emotion. It also can be a sign of saliva buildup, so a bit inconclusive there.

He gives me a barely there smile. "I want to."

And then *I* swallow, which feels embarrassing, so tighten my grip on the steering wheel, because I clearly don't have one on this situation.

"So." I stare straight ahead as we drive to Hilton Head Island. "You're a sponsor..."

He nods once, eyes staying on me.

"Alcoholic?" I ask.

He swallows again, and I'm confident that was an emotional response. He's still watching me—maybe even closer than before—and I wonder if he's trying to gauge my temperament. Whether I care, whether I judge him...

Answers I honestly haven't decided yet.

I keep my face neutral.

"And user," he adds.

I glance at him. "Cocaine?"

He nods again. Maybe a flash of shame? His eyebrows twinge together for a second, lip pulling back and a little down. But then it's gone. "Among others."

I nod, looking at the road. "So you and Oliver have a lot in common then."

"Had," he clarifies.

"Had," I agree. "Sorry."

He shakes his head, looking out his window.

When we stop at a red light, I look at Sam and ask, "Is he doing good?"

His eyes and lips pinch together quickly, but he smooths them away as he presses his tongue into his bottom lip.

"You'd have to ask him," he tells me.

"So no."

He swallows. Confirmation.

"It's hard to lose a parent." He shrugs. "No matter what."

"Thank you, I know." I give him a look. "Psych major with a dead parent over here."

He squashes a smile. "You seem to be holding it together okay?" It's a statement, but there's an upward inflection at the end of it.

I sit up a little straighter, proud. "I do?"

"Seem." He gives me a pointed look and I like him a little less. "You and Oliver kind of have a weird relationship with your parents, hey?"

A little puff of air escapes me before I glance at him. "We don't have a relationship with our parents."

He looks over at me. "Why?"

Now, if he was me, watching me, he would have seen it, a micro-expression of anguish flashing across my face, but he doesn't. He misses it because he's a normal person.

"Because they're..." I trail. "Terrible."

"In which ways?"

That question throws me—I don't know why; I guess I just thought it was plainly obvious, but maybe it isn't?

"Um." I take a breath then accidentally sigh it out. "Oliver and I aren't like them. There's them, our parents, and then there were the Nouns—"

His face pulls. "The what?"

"Maryanne and Tennyson. They're—" I roll my eyes. I've had to explain this so many fucking times in my life, and every single time, I've hated doing it. "We all have these stupid middle names. Their middle names are words that are nouns; Oliver's and mine are words that are adjectives."

He looks both confused and intrigued. "What are the adjectives?"

I sigh again. "Just and True."

He watches me for a second; a bit of a smile crops up. "Are you 'true'?"

I glare at him a little. "Maybe."

Sam presses his lips together, looks like he's fighting off a smile.

"What?" I say pointedly, eyebrows up.

"Nothing." He gives me a restrained smile, then shakes his head. "Just—that was sort of insightful of them, all things considered, right?"

I feel my mouth turn into a bit of a pout. "I guess." I've never really thought of that before. That's annoying of him. I feel a bit on the back foot now and I don't like it too much.

I stare back at the road. "What part of Australia are you from?"

"New South Wales." he says. I say nothing and I know he'll say more anyway. "Palm Beach?"

I nod, eyes still straight ahead. "But you live in LA now."

"Corona Del Mar," he clarifies, and I have to admit, that's way better than LA.

"So why are you an addict?" I look at him quickly to try and catch any emotional leakage.

He stares at me for a couple of seconds, and really honestly looks pretty unfazed. "Well, I'm really good at drinking," he says, and he says it so brazenly and with such a confidence that it makes me laugh, so he laughs. "No, really, I am. I'm fucking good at it. And I'm fun when I drink."

"Are you?" I smile, playfully.

"I'll do anything, kiss anyone, climb anything."

"Like what?"

"Like, trees, and telephone poles and cliffs—"

I interrupt him at that. "Cliffs?"

He smiles at me, and I know he can see I'm a bit horrified, and I can see that it pleases him.

"Cliffs." He nods. "I'm fun when I drink...but I'm a fucking idiot."

"How old were you when you started drinking?" I ask.

"Like, normal." He shrugs. "Fifteen? Sixteen?"

"So then what happened?" I glance at him. "What was the escalation point?"

His nose lets out this little puff of air and he glances at me, a hint of a smile. "I was in a car accident when I was sixteen. It was pretty bad," he says, watching me, but then looks out the window to say the rest. "My mum died."

I stare over at him. "Oh," I say softly, and he looks at me again, gives me this tiny smile.

"You would have liked her."

"Yeah?" I smile, but he just nods and then he looks away again.

"She was teaching me to drive when it happened—"

"Oh, shit," I interrupt him.

He glances over, flashes me a quick smile. His eyes look sad now.

"I was in a lot of pain," he says. "Like, physically, mentally—and my heart was all fucked up too because it was a drunk driver who crashed into me, but it was m—" He catches himself, his chin angles upward, as though he's about to shake his head—he's self-correcting—and then he swallows. "I was driving, you know?" He looks at me, and I think I do see some guilt weighing his perfect eyes down a little bit. "I thought for a long time it was my fault."

"It wasn't," I tell him quietly, for good measure.

Another quick smile from him.

"That was sort of my first taste of..." He pauses to choose his words carefully. "Pain numbing."

I nod, following.

"I liked how the medicine stopped all the ways everything was hurting me." He says that with a sense of ownership that I actually find rather astounding. "I liked how it made everything go quiet—but they cut you off eventually." He shrugs. "Then after that—I don't know. My dad didn't know how to deal with it—he's not a bad guy; he's actually a good guy, he was just sad." He pauses. "Still is sad, I guess."

I wait for more.

"Anyway, I never really liked school, and it felt dumb after Mum died, like everything stopped making sense. So I left in year eleven, and pretty much straight away, I got scouted for modeling." Which, I mean, of course he fucking did, look at him.

"And then—you know—" He shrugs again, like it was inevitable. "Coke's such a normal part of that world. And it was fun, and I like having fun. It made shit quiet too, and I liked that." He looks at me, but I mean, really looks at me—like there's subtext.

"When I like something, I just like it," he says.

And it's me. I'm the subtext.

I swallow and drop his eyes because as we turn into Dune House Lane to find a park to watch the sunrise, my heart is bucking like a bronco out of the gate.

I don't like people very often. You can call it self-preservation, call it a defense mechanism, call it being able to see through people and not liking what I find—I don't know, whatever—I just don't get crushes very often, and I can feel one brewing in me right now.

I find a park.

"We're here!" I sing, avoiding his eyes because my cheeks are pink and I know he can see it, so I barrel out of the car and onto the beach, walking quicker than a normal person would, which is as good as yelling from the rooftops that I have a big stupid crush on him. But then, I always wonder if everyone notices these things or if it's just me.

Sam walks up behind me, stands there, and wordlessly, we watch the horizon get lighter and lighter by the second. I think there's something romantic and poetic about how the light creeps up on the darkness that's buried the horizon and blasts it away all gentle and blushy pink.

I cross my arms over my chest, not because I'm uncomfortable, but amidst my effort to get away from Maryanne as quickly as possible, I forgot to bring a sweater.

Sam notices. "Are you cold?"

I shake my head. "I'm fine."

He pulls off his sweater and offers it to me.

"No, I'm okay." I push it back toward him.

"You're not—you're cold."

"I'm fine!" I insist, cheeks getting pink again. I worry that if I have a thing that smells like him wrapped around me, it might kick-start a want in me that I won't be able to curb.

"Here." He tries to put it in my hands.

I fling it back at him.

His brows furrow, annoyed. "What are you—?"

"I don't want it!"

"Would you just—?"

"No!"

"Why?" He makes a frustrated growl—then pauses, clears his throat, and composes himself with a tight smile. "Georgia." He peers down at me. "What is the psychological reason behind why I want you to have my sweater? And why am I so annoyed that you won't take it?"

If I could right now, I'd cover my face with my hands and melt into a puddle of goop, but I can't, so I do it internally instead, because oh my God, he's perfect, and fuck. I don't have a crush on him. I like him. I think like him a lot. I also think I should definitely not like him a lot. It's been about thirty seconds since I met him, and I'm enamored with him.

I take one breath through my nose that's a little too ragged to be normal, but I hope he doesn't notice, and then I glance up. "It's likely one of two reasons."

Sam lifts an eyebrow, waiting.

"Reason one: you could be territorial. We're in a public place, you might want me to wear your sweater so you can prove that I'm yours, or that I'm with you."

Sam's eyes pinch and he glances around us at the entirely empty, still-dark beach.

"There's no one here," he whispers softly, and a bit like he thinks I'm silly, but the thing is—he does it closer to my ear than he needs to. I turn and look at him, and now our faces are closer than they should be too.

I whisper back to him, "People can be irrationally territorial."

Sam presses his lips together before he shakes his head, a bit rueful. "Not really a territorial guy."

I look away from him, hope that the flash of disappointment that I felt doesn't show up on my face.

"I don't know." I give him a little shrug. "I kind of like that primal protectiveness of men being territorial sometimes."

"Okay." Sam nods, squashing a smile. "Noted. What's the second reason?"

"Well, because there's no one around, and because you're not really a territorial guy"—I give him a look—"it's probably most likely that you want me to have your sweater because you want to prove that you can provide for me—like, you can fix me up and you can make me feel better, and that you know what I need."

Sam's eyes pinch, and a smile's playing about his mouth, but he doesn't quite let it land.

"And you're angry," I keep going, "that I won't take it, because you think it's a commentary on how I feel about your ability to provide. Like me not taking it means that I don't think you can."

"Well, I can, so if you'd just put on the fucking sweater—" He gives me a look and I laugh. He nudges me with his elbow. "So, what does it say about you that you won't take my sweater?"

I scoff and roll my eyes, and he does this showy, cocky-little-shit thing with his eyebrows, waiting for my answer.

I swallow.

"Either that I'm romantically disinterested in you and want to establish a clear emotional boundary, or..." I catch his eye, hoping he knows that the *or* is the part that applies here. "...that I value highly being able to care for myself and I'm too stubbornly independent to accept help."

"Right." A smile breezes across his face. "So which is it?"

I bite down on my bottom lip and fake glare up at him.

"Oh," I growl as I snatch it from his hands. "Just give me the fucking sweater."

I hear him laugh as I pull it over my head.

It smells how I'd hoped it would. Peppery, a bit like a fire. Earthy, probably from coffee. And like whatever cologne he wears, which, I'm not a perfumer so I can't be wholly sure, but I think it's something Tom Ford.

He grins as he hands it to me, and then he looks back at the sun.

"Is it hard for you being back here?" he asks eventually, not looking at me.

"What do you mean?" I ask the sun.

"With everything with your sister." He shrugs. "It seems like they hold it over you."

I stare straight ahead.

"You were a kid. It was a mistake."

And then suddenly I feel alone again. I feel my walls come up, the lights go off.

"We all make mistakes," Sam keeps going. "And as long as we're sorry, we—"

"I'm not sorry," I tell the ocean.

"What?"

I look up at him, daring. "I'm not sorry."

"For sleeping with your sister's boyfriend?" There's a mixture of confusion and some surprise on his face.

I raise both my eyebrows in tacit defiance.

He cocks an eyebrow in disbelief, maybe disgust. "Really?"

I nod once. "Really."

Eyebrows up, lips twinging downward—AU 1 and 15: surprised and disappointed—he nods a few times slowly. "Okay."

And then I'm already walking back to the car.

My seat belt's on and the keys are in the ignition before Sam even gets in. I back away from the beach and gun it down the 278.

The silence is equal parts deafening and devastating.

I have been judged about what happened that night for almost the last ten years—I'm used to judgment. People don't get it, no one gets it. There are three people in the world who truly *know* what really happened; one of them is me and the other two are liars.

I don't like his judgment, though…I don't want Sam Penny's

judgment. Not because I think I'm better than him—actually, because I'm quite sure that I'm not. My whole adult life, I've taught myself not to give a fuck about what other people think about me, and I met this stupid guy yesterday, and it feels like a boot is stepping on my chest when I think about him thinking less of me.

He looks over at me staring for a few seconds, trying to figure me out. "You're not sorry at all?"

I shake my head, incredulous. "What's it to you?"

He looks a little pained. "You fucked over your sister and you're not sorry?"

"We don't have to talk anymore," I tell him. I use a gestural emblem tacitly telling him to stop, and he does.

People respond better to nonverbal cues than to verbal ones most of the time. Most people anyway. And when they ignore your nonverbal cues, as I've learned the older I've gotten, they're ignoring them on purpose.

"Forget about the coffee," he tells the road.

"No." I grip the wheel tighter. "You don't want to be the reason Maryanne doesn't get what she wants."

Believe me.

Maryanne was right; as soon as we walk in, I knew she was right.

This place is substantially cooler than anywhere else in a fifty-mile radius. Most other cafés in Okatie, the menus are written in Bradley Hand ITC. Sometimes Papyrus. (If it's ever Papyrus, just walk away.) Here's cool, though. Helvetica, sans serif vibes. Exposed beams, brick, and cement floors. Lots of corners and flat surfaces. It'd slot right in back in Shoreditch.

I can tell Sam Penny is impressed too, and relieved, because I think he was jonesing real bad for a coffee after our nonlovers' spat in the car.

I myself was jonesing for something a little more Irish, but it seems distasteful in front of an addict, and also it's only about seven thirty in the morning, and I don't want the addict to think I'm an alcoholic as well as a whore, so.

There's only one other person in front of us, and the service is quick.

A pretty girl who looks half-Asian smiles at me as I step up.

"Hi." I smile at her, then barely glance at Sam. "What do you want, Penny?"

He flicks his eyes at me, jaw tight, then over to the girl, whom he makes a conscious effort to be warm toward. "Do you do V60?"

"We do, yeah."

"Two of those, please."

She nods and smiles, and glances at me.

"A caramel latte and a cold brew, thanks."

She punches it through and I toss her my card before Sam even thinks about trying to pay for it. I don't want a single thing from him.

That's a lie, but now that he thinks I'm a slut like everyone else in this Podunk town, I don't want to want a single thing from him anymore.

"Penny?" he whispers tonelessly as he stares straight ahead. "We're doing last names now?"

"We don't have to do any n—" I'm saying when someone interrupts me.

"Georgia?" says a voice and my stomach drops ten floors.

I go still. Totally still.

If I was observing me, things I'd notice: thc upper whites around my eyes are showing; my lower eyelid is tense and maybe drawn upwards, my upper eyelid raised; my lips are slightly parted; my eyebrows are sort of raised up but make, for the most part, a flat line. My skin's dropped about ten degrees in temperature.

If I was observing me, this would be my observation: I am afraid.

I brace myself.

"Georgia Carter?" He says my name again as he walks over to me, arms spread open wide, and then he wraps them around me. "My God," he says as he holds me.

I swallow once and consciously slow down my breathing. I can't see Sam's face. I'm glad I can't. I'm more glad he can't see mine.

"Let go of me," I tell Beckett Lane in the quietest, calmest voice I have.

He holds on for just a second longer, and might even grip me a tiny bit tighter as he does actually, and I know it's to prove something, and then he pulls back, cupping my face in his hands and smiling down at me.

He looks about the same. Blondish messy hair, oozing the same Southern WASP-y vibe he's had all the time I've known him. Eyes are too blue though. His eyes have always been too blue for the rest of him. That's what Maryanne loved about him… It drew her in. Even before they'd even started dating, she'd talk about the blues in Beckett Lanes's eyes. She was as annoying about them as Anne of Gables is about—I don't know—fuck me, pick a topic—everything? She spoke about him with that sort of blinded, gooey admiration, always.

She loved him from the second she saw him, which was the first day of junior high for her, and she pined for him every day until she had him.

I'm searching Beckett's face, looking for clues to predict what will come next and what to do, but I'm broken. I'm fucking offline.

I think he's smiling genuinely. Why is he smiling genuinely? Is he happy to see me? He couldn't possibly be happy to see me. Is he surprised to see me? I want him to be scared to see me, but if he is, I can't read it on him.

He just shakes his head like we're just a couple of old friends who the world didn't fall in on ten years ago. "I hadn't even thought about you being here, what with your daddy—" He looks up at Sam, who's staring at me. Just at me. Brows low. Assessing.

"Hey, man." Becks reaches past him, offering him his hand. "I'm Beckett."

Sam takes it mindlessly, still staring at me. He says nothing.

Beckett pulls his hand away slowly, then glances at me.

"This your boyfriend?" he asks with a bit of a smirk.

"No." I answer quickly. Too quickly—it was instinctual, I'm trying to keep him safe—well, not safe, but you know, out of it—but then I wonder if it might sound like I'm eager for Beckett not to think I have a boyfriend, and I get that vomit taste in my mouth. I'm wilting over here like a cut flower.

Beckett moves his head so he catches Sam's eye. "I didn't grab your name?"

Sam finally looks over at him, stone-faced, shoulders square. "Sam."

Beckett clasps Sam's arm with his hand. "Good to have you in Beaufort, Sammy."

"Sam," Sam repeats.

Beckett's mouth twitches in smirky amusement. "Okay. Just in for some coffee, then?"

I give Beckett a look to show him I think he's stupid. "Obviously."

"You know, this is my store," Beckett says, watching me, and my stomach churns.

"Is it?" Sam says, eyebrows going up, and I can feel him looking between Becks and me, but I can't meet his eyes. "Heard it's the best coffee around."

"Yeah." Beckett gives him a warm smile. "You're going to love it," he says, but he's touching my arm—lightly grips my elbow, to be more specific—as he does.

"Your coffee's up," the server says from the side, offering Sam a tray.

I take them before he does and turn on my heel, walking away.

"I'll see you around, Gige," Beckett calls after me.

I climb into my car and hand Sam the tray of coffee, peeling out of there before either of us have our seat belts on.

My chest is heaving too much. I'm obviously upset. My body's giving me away, like I'm just some sort of pedestrian human idiot who wears all their feelings on the surface of themself. I can't remember the last time I couldn't get a handle on myself and my emotions, but the lid is slipping.

Something about the slipping lid feels like it's Sam Penny's fault. Like he broke the seal and he's slowly opening me up. But I haven't been studying what I've been studying for six years to be undone by some Zen reformed coke addict with a savior complex.

"What was that?" Sam asks, watching me.

"Nothing." I shake my head, scrunching my face up like he's stupid.

He shakes his head. "That wasn't nothing."

But I don't speak and stare straight ahead, not focusing on Sam because Sam is a chink in my armor, and if I think about him and how his face looks, I'll feel sad, and I don't want to feel sad, because sadness is a loose cannon, and what I need right now is control.

I need anger.

She did it on purpose.

I know Maryanne did that on purpose.

"That was him, wasn't it?" Sam leans forward, looking for my eyes. "The guy you—"

I snap my head in his direction so fast it silences him. It's a yes, obviously.

I pull into the driveway and storm into the house, my sister sitting serenely at the dining room table with our mom.

I slam her coffee down in front of her. "You're a cunt."

And there it is: a flash so quick, but I catch it. Satisfaction. The faintest hint of a smirk that's quickly concealed by faux concern. Her eyes go round and she turns her lips down, bringing her hand to her mouth.

"Georgia!" My mother gasps—literally gasps—sitting back in her chair, genuinely horrified.

I've actually never said that word before, not in my whole life, but it's the most severe and harsh word that I have in my current vocabulary and believe me when I say, that was the time to use it.

"Oh no," Maryanne sighs, but it sounds like a cry. "Georgia, I didn't even think—" Her mouth shrugs. "I'm sorry—I can't believe you'd think I'd do that on purpose, but I didn't even think about the implications—"

The mouth shrug is a gestural slip that, in this specific instance, indicates that my sister has no confidence in the lies she's telling.

"You didn't even think?" I repeat back to her. "Are you fucked in the head?"

"Georgia!" my mother yells, angrier now, and she stands, looking between us. "Now, what are you two talking about?"

"She wanted coffee." Maryanne looks at Mom. "I told her the best in town is Stomp."

"Maryanne," Mom sighs, nostrils flaring for a sliver of a second. Anger, I think—that's interesting. It can't be on my behalf, couldn't be. Public perception, probably. Could be contempt, I suppose. That feels believable.

"It is, though!" Maryanne's eyes go wide.

"You did that on purpose," I tell my sister, eyeing her. "I know you did."

Her jaw drops. "I. Did. No such. Thing." But she punctuates her sentence with micro-nods.

So she did.

"You're unbelievable," I tell her.

"Take that back!" Maryanne demands.

"No." I shake my head. "Because I know that you did."

My sister clasps her chest in horror. "I'd never—"

"Georgia." My mother points a finger in my face. "No one made you do with that boy what you did except you. You did this to yourself."

Maryanne swallows heavily but copies Mom's stance. Head tilted, eyebrows arched. She even folds her arms over her chest. A physical barrier between us.

I glare over at Maryanne, and—without thinking, really—I smack over her coffee so it spills over the table and down onto her lap. "Fuck you."

9

CHILDISH.

I know. So, so childish.

But there's something about being around your siblings that makes you regress.

I had to push past Sam to get up the stairs to get away from them and I wish I didn't. I wish he wasn't in my way, but he just stood there, watching.

He's watching too much. Seeing too much. I hate it, even if I don't necessarily *really* hate it. I am scared of it, though.

You should have heard my mom and sister hollering after me once I spilled her coffee.

Sometimes it's easier to play the characters we've been assigned.

Maryanne is the Madonna. I am the whore. These two characters can be and have been fleshed out in a multitude of ways.

Maryanne went to Bible school. She got married when she was twenty-six to a good Christian boy from their church. She "didn't have sex till she was married," apparently. (Though, TBC as far as I'm concerned.)

She waited. She wore a purity ring.

She only wears boat necks and high-collared shirts.

She always sides with our parents, especially our mom.

She's never questioned a thing a day in her life.

None of those things are bad if they're true. Nothing about my sister is wrong if it's authentic but, as I told you at the beginning, my sister has narcissistic personality disorder. No part of her is authentic except for that part.

Whereas I, the whore, did everything wrong. And by wrong, I mean wrong according to them.

I didn't "wait." I went to Cambridge. I studied science. I believe in science. I never side with anyone in my family except Oliver, which is problematic for my family in and of itself. I only question things.

And I don't think any of the above makes me inherently good or inherently bad either. The same way I don't think studying science and believing in it precludes me from believing in God if I want to, but my mom says you can't serve two masters.

I take a shower after the coffee incident to wash off my sister, Beckett, my mom, and perhaps most pressingly, the smell of Sam Penny, which seems to have latched itself to me and dug in under the skin of my mind.

I fold up Sam's sweater and leave it outside the door of the room he's staying in, which is Oliver's old room right across from mine. (Oliver's in Tenny's room. Tenny lives out of home now and certainly not with Savannah, except it's worth noting that it's one hundred percent with Savannah.)

I go back downstairs, bracing myself for some sort of verbal onslaught from my mother or sister, but neither are to be found.

Sitting in an armchair in the corner of the room, however, is Sam Penny.

He's reading—probably Jack Kerouac or J. D. Salinger, because his hair makes me feel like he's the kind of person who thinks reading books like that makes you cool even though everybody's read them.

Poor Kerouac and Salinger. They've been Kurt Cobain-ed. None of those people would have liked to be what they've become, yet they've become it anyway. Icons for a generation thirsty to be both defined as individuals but wholly and utterly accepted and palatable to their peers.

Sam looks up at me, lowers his book. *Make Something Up* by Chuck Palaniuk.

Fuck. I hate being wrong.

He puts his book down, resting it on the arm of the chair, and stands, stares at me.

We're a few yards apart and it feels strange and tense. I feel exposed by the weight of his eyes. He nods his chin toward me.

"What happened?"

I keep my face calm, no reaction, no emotion—not that he can see, anyway. I bend my brows on purpose, hoping that it looks like this conversation is inconvenient for me. "Nothing."

He crosses his arms. "What actually happened?"

I rush toward him and glare up. "Nothing!"

He gives me a look. "You're lying."

I scoff. "So what, you're the expert now?"

"No." He shakes his head apologetically, looking for my eyes. "I just—" He gestures vaguely toward my face. "You're sad."

"No." I give him a curt look. "I'm not."

"Yeah, you are," he tells me like he knows me. Like he's known me longer than—what?—the fucking twenty-one hours he actually has.

I feel hot and clammy both on the outside and on the inside, and I don't know what it is about him that gets me so riled up.

The only person I've ever felt transparent to in my whole life was my second-year psychology professor. She called me out on a bunch of my shit and then set me on this path of reading people, though that itself wasn't her specialty—psychoanalyzing people was. And it was as unnerving as hell freezing over. She looked at me like I was completely see-through. Read me like a road map. Guessed my entire life, my whole backstory, explained to me why I was in her class and why I was learning what I was learning. I hated her at first. Sometimes I still do.

We have lunch once a fortnight.

Sam Penny's watching me, not like I watch people, but how people who care about people watch people. Like he's noticed a crack. Not in the construct of who I let the world think I am, but in who I actually am, and he's not staring at me to open it up wider to see what's inside like I would... I think he's staring at me like that so he can work out how to fix it.

"You are sad," he tells me with a small nod—he's decided—and he steps toward me.

"So what if I am!" I yell at Sam. "My dad just died."

He gives me a long look again and then shakes his head. "That's not why you're sad."

I bellow, "Who the fuck asked you!"

He shrugs gently. "I don't know, Georgia—I think maybe the more important question is, who didn't ask you?"

I feel like someone dropped a piano on me.

I don't want him to see that or see me how he seems to, so I glare at him.

"Do not"—I place the tips of my fingers on his chest—"speak to me again." And I shove him away.

He doesn't move. Doesn't even sway.

He swallows heavily once and looks at me. His eyes are weighed down. I've hurt him for some reason.

"Everything all right here?" says one of my favorite voices in the universe, and I turn on my heel and spring myself across the room and into her arms—bury myself in her neck probably more than I should, but I want to hide in her, not feel the strange sort of naked and afraid that Sam makes me feel.

Violet pulls herself away from me to look down and inspect me, her face contorted in unconcealed concern. She can't do what I do with faces, but she does know me.

"You okay, baby?" She glances at me and back up to Sam.

I missed her Southern twang. Everyone else's accent around here annoys me, but not hers.

Her eyes are rimmed red, and she looks like the first person I've seen who's really grieving my dad. She puts an arm around me and pushes a hand through her long, strawberry-blond hair. She's upregulating as she approaches Sam, extending her hand to him. "I'm Violet, who are you?"

He gives her a warm smile and shakes her hand. "I'm Sam."

"He's—" I start.

"My sponsor," Oliver says from behind us. He looks tired, like he's just woken up.

Violet gives Sam an appreciative look—that won him some points—then glances over at Oliver. She gives him a pained smile as she walks over to him, dragging me with her, and squeezes us both together.

"My two favorites! Back home." She offers us a sad smile, puts a hand on each of our cheeks. "How are y'all doing? Are you okay?"

I flick my eyes over at Oliver, and in my peripheral, I catch Sam leaving the room. I don't know how to answer this question, and the lagginess of both my and Oliver's answers is bad.

Violet is my dad's sister, and they had a complicated relationship, namely because she doesn't like my mom. She's never really liked my mom, and I get it, so I can't hold it against her—but I guess it made things difficult for her and my dad. But Violet loved him and he loved her.

She knows Oliver and I didn't have ideal experiences with either of our parents, and I think in a lot of ways, she and her husband Clay stepped in and filled the gap whenever they could, even though my mom tried her best to hedge them out.

I can't tell Violet I don't think I care that my dad's dead. I can't. She won't get it. And it's a sad thing to say. It doesn't feel real yet. But right now, any offerings of grief I have are false.

"I'm okay," I tell her, plastering a manufactured look of strain onto my face.

Violet glances at Oliver, who mimics me. "Me too."

"You guys." She sniffs. "You don't have to be—"

"How are you doing?" I interrupt.

A rueful smile flashes across her face. The smile is for us; she's trying to be strong but it loses its validity in the way it pinches at the end and how she has to steady her breathing.

"It was a surprise, you know?" She wipes her nose. "I just—I wasn't—" She shakes her head. "God, I haven't cried since Friday until now, and then I see you two and just—" She lets out a tiny sob. "He loved you two so much—"

Oliver peers over at me with cautious confusion.

I look at Violet carefully, tilt my head down to catch her crying eyes. "Are you drunk?"

She snorts a laugh and gives me a playful glare. "He did," she tells me, I don't know why really. I guess it's just what you say to kids when their parent died, even when you know it's a lie.

And I give her a look. "We don't have to do this right now—"

She nods quickly, pushing her emotions down and away, folding them neatly up in a drawer to take them out and wear them at a more appropriate time, say, in front of the children he actually did love.

Tenny walks in behind Violet and gives her a hug.

"Where've you been?"

"Hidin' out." Violet shrugs. "Thinkin'..."

Tenny looks at me. "Heard you were in a mood this morning." He has a tray of fresh coffees and a smug expression.

I flash him a dark smile. "Bite me."

Oliver looks between us. "What'd I miss?"

"Oh, nothing much." My sister flaps her hands as she walks into the room. "Just Gigi being Gigi." She gives me a curt smile.

Violet licks her lips and eyes my sister, one brow raised, top lip curling a little—definitely contempt. Vi's never liked Maryanne, not a day in her life, and Maryanne knows it. Actually, she obsessed over it for a long time, but all the things Maryanne could have done to warm Violet to her, Maryanne's incapable of.

"And what, pray tell"—Violet folds her arms over her chest—"does that mean?"

"Oh, you know." Maryanne swats a hand and flicks her eyes over at me with the hint of a smirk. "Running around town before sunup with Oliver's sobriety coach, turnin' up at Beckett Lane's coffee store, throwing coffees in people's faces—"

Anger flashes across Vi's face. but she gets a hold of it real quick.

"Oh, Maryanne!" She steps toward her, touching her arm. "I've been meaning to ask you—" Violet looks over her shoulder at me and catches my eye with a clear message: *Go*! "Where are you getting your hair done for the funeral?"

I grab Oliver by the hand and pull him out the back of the house, running down the steps.

"This is not a drill!" I tell him. "I repeat, this is not a drill!"

10

I'M NOT EVEN REALLY SURE where it came from or when we started doing it, but sometime very early on in our adolescence, whenever things got shitty at home, whenever tensions rose or Mom or Maryanne came out to play, Oliver or I would yell "THIS IS NOT A DRILL!" and then we'd run out of the house and down to the dock, to this white wooden rowboat that we assume our dad must have won in a raffle or something.

One day it was just there. We never saw him on it, though a few times I went out to use it myself early in the mornings and I'd see him sitting in it by himself, a big old book in his lap. I'm not religious how my parents are but I thought it was sort of sweet. Him out there alone with his Bible.

On the side of the boat, it reads *Saint-Émilion.* I saw him paint that on himself—I'm not sure why. Maybe he liked the legend of him, or something.

He and Mom had a fight over it because he wasn't all that handy around the house, I guess? Mom asked why he was painting our stupid boat when the garage door needed to be painted for like a year and a half, and then dad told her she could hire someone for that, and then she told him he could hire someone for the boat painting, and he gave her a strangely stern look and said, "No, I couldn't."

Then she told him to get rid of the boat and Dad said no.

She said he had to because Oliver and I used it to avoid our problems, and he said he thought we used it to avoid her. She was so angry she made him sleep on the couch that night and sulked all the morning through, but even still, he wouldn't cave.

Like I said, I don't have a lot of great memories of my dad (and I don't even know if that can count as a great one? Him not letting our psycho mom throw away our boat like she wanted to?), but the bar was low, so it's at least in the wheelhouse of positive.

Anyway, Oliver and I coined it the *SS Avoidance.*

"I hate it here," I tell my brother as we lie on the floor of the boat, staring up at the sky.

He sniffs a laugh. "Do you? I love it."

I give him a look, then prop myself up on my elbows and watch him. "Are you okay?"

He props himself up too. "About Dad?"

I nod and Oliver shrugs.

"I guess," he lies. "Are you?"

And I hate this. So much, I hate this… It never used to feel hard to talk to him. It was the only thing in the world that made sense once upon a time, and I want it to feel the same; I want to be able to step through this magical doorway back in time to the place where we didn't have distance and mistakes and drugs and shit between us, but that place doesn't exist anymore. All we have is this. The bones of a close relationship and the smoky memory of how we used to be and might not ever be again.

I put my hands on my cheeks and stare back up at the sky. "It's so hard to explain to people how bad they were."

He looks over at me. "Do you think they were bad parents?"

I frown a bit. "Do you not?"

"Bad is the wrong word," he tells me, and I'm not surprised he does, because he's always defended them in one way or another, even though they've never deserved it. Even though they've been worse to him than they have been to me. Oliver can't look the fullness of how bad they were square in the eye, at least not yet. And that's fine—well, it's not really fine, it's incredibly invalidating of his life experience, but I understand that acknowledging the fullness of something then requires you to feel the consequences of it with a fullness too, and I don't think he has the bandwidth.

I purse my lips.

Oliver shrugs. "They should have just stopped at Maryanne."

"Oliver—" I prop myself up again and sigh. "God—you thinking that makes them bad parents."

He shakes his head, which—of course he would. "They just didn't know what to do with us." He shrugs, like that's a legitimate excuse.

I sigh to the clouds. "That sponsor of yours has turned you soft."

Oliver sits up in the boat. "So, what's up with you and Sam anyway?"

I mirror him because I want to fast-track us to an emotional connection, which we already technically have, but he seems prickly, so I want to remind him of it.

"Nothing." I keep my face straight, because I think if I attach any emotion to the words, even surprise, it'll give me away. "He's kind of a know-it-all."

Oliver sniffs a laugh. "I was surprised you guys seemed to get along so well." He shrugs airily as he lies back down. "I thought you'd drive each other stupid mad."

"Why?" I ask super casually, like I'm not a little disappointed that my brother didn't bring Sam here thinking maybe we'd be soulmates.

Oliver takes off his shirt and uses it as a pillow to rest his head on. "Because he's so calm and balanced, he already knows who he is—he's so self-aware already, and you like to read people, not be read. There's just nothing you could bring to the relationship—he already knows all the ways he's fucked up."

I frown. "That's not all that I bring to a relationship…"

"Listen, Gige—" He swats his hand dismissively. "Sam is like, this reformed bad boy turned easy, breezy yoga queen, who loves transparency and balance and wholeness, and you like pushing people's buttons to make their heads pop off so you can see how their brains work."

That isn't true. I don't like pushing buttons; that's such a cheap explanation. More than anything, I just like knowing why people are the way people are, and I see a high value in being able to predict what comes next. Now, sometimes to do that, do I have to push buttons? Maybe, but I'd like to think I'm not unnecessarily antagonistic. I just want the truth at all costs. That's not very breezy though. I'd like to be breezy, I think. But I'm too clever to be breezy. Breezy doesn't get you into Cambridge. Breezy doesn't get you a job at the EIA.

"Anyway." I clear my throat. Breezy. "Are you okay? Sober-wise?" I pause. "Sobriety-wise? Sober-wi—are you sober?"

"Yeah." He props himself up as he eyes me playfully. "Are you?"

I roll my eyes at him. "Why did you bring your sponsor home for a week if you're okay?"

He leans away and points at me. "Don't do that to me." The point is a gestural emblem. He means it. He wants me to stop.

"Then don't lie to me," I tell him, my eyes flickering from his eyes to his mouth, watching for muscle twitches, but there's nothing. Literally nothing, not a thing—neither a twinge nor twitch of emotion.

I lie back down in the boat and look up at the sky again.

We lie there quietly for about twenty seconds, long enough for him to subconsciously let out a sigh of relief, which is when I ask—

"So when did you start using Valium?"

He laughs and groans all at once. "When my little sister started turning into Nancy fucking Drew."

"Does Sam know?"

I don't see it, but I can hear it in his voice, the eye roll. "Yes, Sam knows."

He drums his hands rhythmically on his chest.

"How much are you taking?"

He pauses. "More than I should."

I sigh and sit up, hugging my knees to my chest. "Why?"

He mirrors me and shakes his head. "You wouldn't get it. You don't have an addictive personality."

"Yeah, well, neither do you. It's bullshit," I tell him.

He gives me a dubious look. "What?"

"There's no such thing as an addictive personality; it's a psychological myth and a nice way of saying you struggle with neuroticism and that you have poor impulse control."

He looks at me straight in the eye. "I hate you."

I sniff a laugh and rub my face, tired. "Sorry."

My older brother holds my eyes for a second and a crack of a smile shows itself. "I've missed you."

I nod. "Me too."

He lies back down. "Play the song."

I smile and find it on my phone.

The same song we always played on this old thing, the song that we felt a deep kinship to and many years ago, divvied up the parts to:

"Teenage Dirtbag."

11

WHERE HAVE YOU TWO BEEN?" our mother asks, rushing over to us as soon as we walk into the house. "Were you on that stupid boat?"

"We were just catching up," I tell her.

"The guests will be here any minute." She shakes her head, looking between us.

"What guests?" I blink.

Maryanne walks out carrying a cheeseboard. "We're having some people from church over to celebrate Daddy's life."

"Isn't that what the funeral's for?" Oliver asks.

My mom gives him a sharp look.

"The two of you just go and get changed. Georgia, please can you wear something respectable"—I take a measured breath. She keeps going—"Oliver, try not to look too…" She leaves it open-ended.

"Gay?" he offers.

She rolls her eyes and we walk upstairs.

Oliver kisses me on the cheek as he goes off to get changed. "I love you, Gige. OG BFF."

I give him a small smile as I turn away.

I pass Sam as I do, and I consciously don't meet his eyes. I don't want to. I don't know why I don't want to (yes, I do), but I don't want to.

Twenty minutes later and I'm downstairs and the Hellmouth has opened up in the living room. There are about thirty people in there. Has no one here heard of arriving fashionably late?

In their defense, I suppose there's not a lot to do here, so—

I've trotted down the stairs in this black Versace dress that's practically a shirt but has long sleeves and a big white collar—it's a bit Wednesday Addams-y, and I was going to wear it to the funeral, but I hadn't thought to pack for any of my mom's stupid fancy parties, so I'll have to buy something else this week.

It feels like the whole room turns when I walk into it.

Not in some magical Cinderella-y, slow-motion moment...more like how the Munchkins all turn in horror every time the Wicked Witch of the West lands in.

I pick up a glass of wine from the server in the corner—why are there servers here? I see with Dad dead, there's no one around to curb Mom's spending—and I down it quickly on the spot and pick up another. Half because I've been typecast and I'm happy to play into it, and half because I need it around these clowns.

I need it because normally at these things I'd stick to Oli like a tick on a hound, but he's with Sam and I can't be with Sam around Oliver because Oliver will be able to tell I like Sam, and if you recall, I don't like Sam.

Beckett's here, talking to Tenny in the corner. They're talking, totally comfortable, head-thrown-back laughing, and I blink away the contempt that I know is on my face.

How does he get out of it scot-free? Where's my head-thrown-back laughter with my oldest brother?

I want to talk to Violet, but I know she'll be in the kitchen. I'm about to make my way there when I spot her husband, Clay, talking to Savannah.

She is really pretty... I can see why my brother's into her. She's got the big, doe-eyed thing happening. Eyes a greenish brown, teeth so white and so straight it's nearly offensive and absolutely very American, but I think I like how she holds herself. You know how some young people go weird around older people? She seems super normal around Clay. But that could be less to do with her and more to do with Clay being the best.

He's handsome, if weathered. But being a progressive in a small town can render that same effect.

"Uncle Clay." I smile up at him when I reach his side.

He grins down at me and hugs me off the floor. "My favorite niece." He plants me back down and looks at me. "Come, hide with us."

I look between them, intrigued. "Who are we hiding from?"

Clay gives me a look. "Who do you think?"

I'm not surprised he's hiding from Maryanne, but the girlfriend? That's interesting, and I can't help but eye her suspiciously. "Really?"

Her left zygomaticus major muscle tugs—it's a confession she finds awkward, but it's true.

I cross my arms over my chest. "Am I to understand then that I am your favorite Carter sister, then?"

"By a mile," she says with a steep look.

I look from her to Clay. "What am I missing?"

Then Savannah and Clay exchange looks, and he laughs heartily, shaking his head.

"Nothing," She rolls her eyes in a way that tells me it's not actually nothing to her. "Not a big deal."

And I'm nearly about to tell her all the ways her face just told me that what she's saying is, in fact, not true, but then she reaches out and touches my arm. "Hey, I really am so sorry about your dad. He was a good man."

I breathe in and smile at once. *If you say so.*

"Are you doing okay, kiddo?" Clay asks, holding my shoulder.

And I know this is a question I'm going to get a million times through the duration of my stay, but I wish I could mute it, because I know I have neither the preferred nor the perfunctory response.

I'm fine. That's not a fine answer, though—frankly, it's unacceptable.

And sure, maybe I'm in denial? Maybe I haven't thought of it properly yet. Maybe it hasn't sunk in that my dad dying is the closing of a chapter in my life I'd honestly barely read yet. But there are too many people filling the rooms, filling up the space my mind would need if I wanted to feel the breadth of death in the way it demands to be felt.

"I'm okay," is my answer, and I throw him a weak smile to sell it like I'm not sure I'm actually okay, because that's how I should be responding.

And then I overhear this: "—believe he brought his boyfriend to his dad's funeral?"

"Oh my God, I know."

"I mean, the funeral's going to be in a church—and like, have some respect."

"His dad hated that he was gay. Maryanne told me."

I tense up.

Clay tenses up.

And curveball: Savannah tenses up.

"Are you talking about my brother?" I pop my head into the conversation the three women are having, and the vultures freeze and all display some variant of the same microexpression: eyebrows up and a little drawn in, lips parted in the center, the whites around their eyes showing.

"Yes," says the blond one with the bigger hair. "We were. It is a sin, you know."

Savannah sidles up next to me, folding her arms. "So is gossip."

I look her up and down, impressed. She holds my gaze, and I like her more by the second.

"Leviticus 18:22 says—" the brunette starts to say, but I cut her off.

"Did you know that the word 'homosexuality' didn't appear in any Bible until 1946 when the Greek word Arsenokoitai was mistranslated—"

"No." The girl with the floral blouse shakes her head. AU13—her levator anguli oris muscles pull up. "We don't need your new age, topsy-turvy translation around here. We believe that what the Bible says, and has always said, historically speaking, is what the Lord m—"

"Actually, in a lot of the European Bibles from the seventeenth, eighteenth, and nineteenth centuries, both Leviticus 18:22 and Leviticus 20:13 said a version of 'man will not lie with young boys as he does with a woman, for it is an abomination.'" The women (except Savannah) stare over at me a bit blankly—which, I don't think is technically an invitation to keep going, but I do anyway. "They were talking about pederasty, not homosexuality."

The big-haired blond one crosses her arms over her chest—she's putting a boundary between us. She's uncomfortable. "What's your point?"

"My point is, if you don't like gay people, just say that." I flash her a non-Duchenne smile. "Don't weaponize the Bible for your own gay agenda."

"Savannah," the big-haired blond one says. "This is the girl who ruined Beckett's life, did you know?"

I lift both my eyebrows at her. "Slander is also a sin."

"So is premarital sex," she bites back, pointedly. Clearly a friend of Maryanne.

"So I've heard." I nod, pretending to be rueful. "It's very fun though. Have you had it?"

Her mouth goes tight and she swallows quickly.

I gasp and point at her with a wink. "How salacious! In a town like this?" I take a tiny step closer to her and she takes one back. "How many sexual partners have you had? One?" Nothing. "Two?" Nothing. "Three?" She swallows. I spin back around to her friends. "Three! She's had three sexual partners. Now, I know that in the walls of your small-town church, that probably sounds unbearably scandalous, but in the scheme of other things, like life and death—it's really not a big deal."

The girl is glaring at me, eyes ragged.

"What's going on over here?" Maryanne asks with a big hospital grin that looks a little threatening. On her flank is a pretty girl with brown hair and brown eyes who looks familiar to me, but I can't completely place her.

"Nothin', Maryanne," says the brunette. She looks nervous. I can't tell whether it's because of me or my sister. "We were just talking about—"

"Oliver," I interrupt, giving my sister a chance to defend her little brother.

She presses her lips together and says nothing, nodding once.

"Did he really bring his boyfriend here?" the brunette presses.

"Girls," Savannah sighs.

"Well, actually." Maryanne leans in. "He's his sobriety coach—"

"It's called Alcoholics Anonymous for a reason, dumbass!" I growl, and Clay steps behind me.

Maryanne tilts her head. "What'd you call me?"

"*Dumbass.*" I overenunciate it.

Clay's hand squeezes my shoulder.

"Wait," says the brunette one. "So there'll be two gay guys at your dad's funeral?"

I let out a groan. "Like it matters! Who gives a fuck?"

"You really do have a whore's mouth," my sister says with the politest smile in the world.

"Well." I mirror her smile and give her a little shrug. "Takes one to know one."

Her eyes go wide; her jaw goes tight. Anger. She looks between her friends. "Here's a shocker, girls. Georgia's been running around town with Oliver's sponsor..."

I look at her, annoyed and confused. "You know we literally went to town for like an hour this morning. To the coffee shop that *you* sent us to." I flick her an unimpressed look. "Why are you making it sound like it's something it's not?"

I know why—I don't know why I posed it like a genuine question.

"It's always something with you, Georgia. We all know what you're like." She gives a small shrug.

"At least we know he's not gay," says the brown-haired girl.

I give her a mean smile. "Maybe if we give him five minutes with you, he'll jump the heterosexual ship."

She glowers up at me. "You stay away from my boyfriend."

"I'm so sorry," I say, completely not at all sorry. "Who are you?"

"I'm Beckett's girlfriend."

"Ah." I nod, once. Though I'd be lying if I said that my heart didn't trip a little at the mention of his name. I actually recognize her. Tinsley something. Went to school with Maryanne. "Yeah, you can have him."

I turn back to Clay and Savannah.

"I'm sorry." Savannah frowns, and it's genuine.

"They go to your church?" I ask.

"Um—" She cringes. "I mean—we go to the same church." She pauses. "I don't think we know the same God."

I purse my lips in contempt. Think about how being a "Christian" has so little to do with acting Christ-like now, especially these days, and especially in America.

And I don't know what I believe. I think I believe in God, but not the one people like Maryanne and my mom claim to know. I don't know if there's a PR team in heaven, but can you even imagine the crisis management team they'd need these days? What with people like these idiot girls with bright eyes and dull hearts, not a hair out of place but hearts in the wrong one. Girls like them who bat their eyes as they pick and choose from the Bible to create a world they're comfortable to exist in.

"I really am sorry," Savannah tells me again.

"It's fine." I swat my hand, even though it's actually not. "Tell me—do you have any dirt on those girls that I can use against them? Make them psychologically sweat?"

Savannah smirks.

"We can hear you!" Maryanne huffs.

"Fuck yourself!" I say cheerily, but probably a bit loudly because my mother hears.

"Georgia True Carter!" she bellows and points to the back door. "You get that wicked tongue out of my house right now."

I take a deep breath and roll my eyes, grabbing another wine and trotting out to the back porch.

My sister is smug and gleeful, which is actually just her everyday demeanor. She does a hair flip and her friends crowd in around her, petting her arm and smoothing her hair, congratulating her on surviving a torment like me.

I sit on the step, chin in my hands. Tired. South Carolina tired. Regular tired. Maryanne tired.

And then I hear shifting behind me.

I look back and there he is, filling the doorway with his shadow. I sigh at the sight of him. I don't know why (yes I do).

Black jeans, white T-shirt. Black denim jacket. Still no shoes.

He stands there for a while, watching me from there, his face bleeding concern, and he's so annoyingly disarming, because it's all authentic. How he's looking at me, the worry that's written all over his body...the head tilt, the downturned mouth, the low brows drawn together—he is genuinely sad for me, and it's possible I've waited my whole life for someone to give a shit like he seems to, but nothing makes sense because I'm a fuck-up no one wants and he's an alcoholic and my dad is dead somewhere in a cold room, and something about that makes me feel sick.

Sam Penny holds my eyes for an age that lives inside ten seconds.

"You can ask me," I tell him.

A microsmile surfaces, then dissolves as he licks it away. "Are you okay?"

I just stare at him for a second, saying nothing, and then I stand up and walk over to him, tiredly. I take in a shallow breath and breathe it out my nose. "No."

His face falls a little more and my heart mirrors it.

I touch his chest—I don't know why I touch his chest, it's so intimate, but I do it anyway, and it doesn't look jarring at all when I do.

I blink a few times before I say, "I'm sorry about today."

His eyes catch mine, breath caught in his chest. He gives a little frown and tiny shrug. "No—you don't have to—"

I sniff a laugh.

He frowns a little. "What?"

"Nothing." I shake my head, because Oliver said I'd bring nothing to the relationship, and I don't want Sam to think all I am capable of is seeing through him, but Sam shakes his head, smiles this gentle, encouraging smile.

"No, tell me."

"Your, um—your body language says that you do think I have something to be sorry for, and that I should be sorry about it."

And then he lets out a laugh, properly—his whole face lights up—and that makes me smile back at him.

"Okay," he concedes, and then he tilts his head again and asks a question I knew he would: "What happened before?"

And suddenly, I'm naked once again as he stares, waiting for an answer I don't actually owe him but desperately want to give him anyway, and I feel myself dig in, decide not to let myself run.

I squint up at him. "You make me uncomfortable."

"Oh," His brows furrow. Microfrown. Not the answer he was looking for—not the implication he wanted.

"I think I mean it as a positive."

His brows lift. Microsmile. "Oh."

"I feel like I'm see-through when I'm with you, and I hate that—I think," I add as an afterthought. "I never feel see-through and I never feel readable. I never feel like that, but with you I do."

He lifts my chin with his hand, his eyes flicking from my eyes to my mouth, and I wonder whether he's going to kiss me.

"Georgia, I want you to know," he starts, swallowing heavily. "You are—easily!—the most complicated person I've ever met."

My face lights up, completely elated. "Thank you."

He chuckles, shaking his head. "You're welcome?"

I purse my lips, take a breath, then hold it. "You think I'm a bad person—for the stuff with my sister?"

"No." Sam shakes his head. "Complicated, that's all. You're a puzzle, and I don't have all the pieces yet."

I stare up at him. "What if you don't ever get all the pieces?"

He nods, thinking. "That would be frustrating."

I nod back. "I've been told I am frustrating before."

"Yeah." He presses his lips together, squashing a smile. "I believe that."

I laugh and his smile grows to full size, and I feel this sort of lightheaded hopefulness.

"I don't want you to not speak to me," I tell him, my voice a bit quiet now.

"Yeah." Sam shrugs. "I know."

12

I TAKE A PILL THAT NIGHT so I'll sleep a little better and longer. I wake up a little after 8:30 and spend the next twenty minutes opening the stupid, old brass doorhandles in the house at a glacial pace so no one knows I'm awake so I can get quarter-ready before I head downstairs.

You know "quarter-ready"? The kind of ready that requires you to slink out of bed and silently ballerina-leap across the loud floorboard that would otherwise creak, so that the beautiful boy across the hall thinks you just wake up looking fresh as a daisy and bright as a button?

When I walk into the kitchen, Oliver's already dressed. Tenny's here too. Sam looks up from the breakfast counter and gives me a crooked smile, but looks back down when my brothers notice me.

I lean on the counter. "And where are we off to this morning?"

"We're all going to the cemetery," Oliver says, folding his arms over his chest. His chest is puffed up a little, feet are squared. Head level and tall when often he'd naturally tilt it.

This is Oliver around Tennyson, all our lives. Tennyson never gave Oli the time of day even before he came out, but never ever in a million years after the fact. Even still, any chance Oliver gets to be around his big brother, he's trying to prove himself to him. Like, going to a cemetery? Oliver hates cemeteries. He and I watched that old *Pet*

Sematary movie when we were like twelve—scared the shit out of him. Scarred him. When my dad's aunt died a year later, Oliver wouldn't step in the cemetery.

So him going today? Huge deal.

"Wanna come?" Tenny asks, turning around.

I scrunch up my face. I don't really want to come, to be honest. And Ten's only asking me because he feels uncomfortable about being with our brother alone. And I was really hoping to be alone with Sam, because right now my funeral priorities are really in order like that. "Who's 'we all'?"

Oliver gestures to himself, Sam, and Tennyson at the same time Tenny says, "Maryanne's not coming, don't worry."

That's weird—I think to myself. He's never said anything like that to me before.

I purse my lips, thinking, then shrug. "Sure."

Tenny nods, pleased. "We're leaving in five. Hustle."

Hustle? I frown at him for being unfathomably lame as I trot back up the stairs. "Whatever you say, Captain America."

A few minutes later I come back dressed in just some loose-fitting jeans and a plain white tank, which sounds boring, but honestly, I do look really good when I'm dressed down.

And it works. Sam's pupils dilate and he bites down on his lip, and then he looks away from me because I know he's in his head about me knowing he thinks I'm attractive.

Tenny catches it (somehow?) and he's smirking at me, but Oliver misses it all because he's got the fabric of my top between his fingers and his thumb. "Is this cotton or wool?"

"Cotton."

"Love." Oliver nods approvingly then walks ahead. "Shotgun."

I climb into the back seat, and Sam climbs in next to me. Tenny looks back at us through the rearview mirror. He wiggles his eyebrows and I kick his chair.

"What are you doing?" Oliver turns around.

"Nothing." I shrug. "I just like to kick Tennyson sometimes because he's…a jack-off."

"Well." Oliver nods somewhat sympathetically, but not too much so. "Maybe you should rein in your crazy in front of company."

"Yeah, Georgia." Tenny catches my eye again in the mirror, smirking again, that prick.

"Who wants to stop and grab a coffee?" Oliver asks brightly, trying to change the subject.

"No!" Sam and I say in unison and, without a doubt, pitched in a frequency that begs for questions to be asked.

Oliver glances back at us, frowning, then says specifically to Sam, "You don't want a coffee?"

Sam doesn't know it, but a microexpression of contempt flashes across his face, and then he scratches the back of his neck in a manipulator. "Nah."

Oliver frowns, confused. "You always want coffee."

"We're in the middle of fucking nowhere. No one does good coffee here," I tell him, trying to sound bored.

"Hey," growls Tens.

"Yeah, that V60 yesterday was pretty good!" Oliver looks between the boys for backup.

"I don't know—" Sam shrugs as though he's indifferent. "Thought it was kind of bitter."

"I bet you did." Tennyson smirks from the front, and I flick him in the back of the neck.

Oliver looks at Tenny, confused. "What?"

And somehow, in an unforeseeable turn of events, I find myself actually quite grateful that Tenny's here, because normally Oliver is so tuned in with me, he'd be able to sniff out my weirdness, but when he has an in with Tenny, he's all in, so he doesn't have any brain space to focus on me.

"Because it's—um—bitter," Tennyson—surprisingly—tells him. "Shit coffee, they're right."

Which, I mean, first things first—that was some pretty terrible lying. But also—I don't know why he did that, covering for me. Not that there's anything to cover, but you know what I mean. He's not really like that. Not to me, anyway.

"So." Sam leans forward, propping his arms up on both my brothers' seats. I like how he fills in spaces. "What are you doing, anyway?"

Tenny glances back at him. "We're picking Dad's coffin and then his gravestone..." He pauses. "Gotta tell 'em what to write on it."

I scrunch my nose because I don't like the sound of any of that. It sounds way too high-pressure and far too hands-on. "And what am I doing?" I ask in a tall voice.

"I don't know." Tenny clocks me in the mirror. "Standing there, looking pretty?"

I scoff as I sit back in my seat, crossing my arms over my chest. "I'm literally the smartest person in this car."

Tennyson snorts a laugh. "I went to University of Georgia."

I roll my eyes. "That's a party school."

"I graduated with honors in an econ degree!" he tells me.

I slow-clap for him. Sam snorts a laugh then looks out the window to cover it.

"Hey, queen." Oliver turns around, giving me a pointed look. "Don't be a B."

"Hey, Oliver." And he looks back at me again. "Don't—" And then I make a sucking off gesture, and he reaches around and smacks me in the leg.

"You're so immature sometimes." He rolls his eyes.

Tennyson scowls at me. "That's disgusting, Georgia."

I blink at him a lot, and I feel like being annoying. "You're honestly going to sit here and tell me that you don't like blow jobs?"

"No one said that," Oliver says at the same time as Tenny says, "Not from him!" which is the same time Sam says, "I like them."

I clock Sam—amused, because no one's talking to him and what a fucking time to chime in—and he just gives me a dumb smile. That happens all within the space of a second and a half before I whack Tennyson over the head.

"Gross! Who said anything about Oliver giving you a blow job?"

"You!" Tenny yells at the same time Oliver yells, "Stop talking!"

"No, I didn't!"

"Yes, you did! You made the—" Oliver reenacts me.

"Ugh!" I roll my eyes. "I just meant, like—you're kissing his ass!"

"Then why didn't you do that?" Tenny asks, wide-eyed.

"I—I don't know." I shrug. "That's so—like, how would I even mime that?"

Tennyson rolls his eyes. "Why do you need to mime anything?"

"Because it's a lost art?" I shrug again, and I know I'm being petulant now. "Maybe I was just trying to bring some culture into the car."

Sam's gone still, but he's staring at the floor of the car, the faintest hint of a smile. I don't even realize that we've stopped driving until Oliver gets out of the car and slams the door super extra loud and glares at me, arms folded, pouting like crazy through the window.

He's twenty-six. I just want to remind you that he's twenty-six.

Tenny climbs out of the car and opens my door, puts his hands on the roof, and leans down. "You're being an asshole."

I frown up at him. "Fuck you."

He gives me a tight smile, kind of smug, like I've just proved his point. "Why don't you just wait out here?"

"Dad's been dead for like a day and a half, Tennyson... Don't have to pick up the mantle just yet."

Contempt flashes across his face, and he glares at me as he slams the car door. "You know, you don't have to be a bitch all the time," he says as he walks away.

"You kiss your mother with that mouth?" I call after him.

My eldest brother flips me off without turning around.

And I sit back in my seat, arms folded across my chest, frowning.

Sam shifts uncomfortably next to me, still nearly smiling but not quite.

To be honest—and until now I'd have thought it impossible—I sort of forgot he was there, and now that I've become reaware of his presence, I'm conscious that I perhaps wasn't presenting as my absolute best self.

Sam gets out of the car and walks around to my side, waiting for me to climb out.

We walk wordlessly toward the graveyard, away from the offices my brothers just went into—Sam's call, not mine. Probably a good one. He glances over at me, and he touches his mouth absentmindedly. A self-hushing emblem. He has something to say, doesn't know whether he should say it.

We walk a few seconds more in silence, him pressing his mouth together, and I wonder for a second what it would be like to have it pressed against me, but he's not thinking about kissing me—he's thinking about saying something.

I look up at him. "Spit it out, then..."

He lets out a single laugh and stares at me, a bit bemused. I widen my eyes, impatient.

"You're funny around your brothers," he tells me with a nod.

I frown a little. "What do you mean?"

"I don't know. You're obviously their little sister." The way he says "obviously" makes me feel like I was *obviously* just an idiot. He doesn't seem to mind, though—his countenance is open and warm still, even though he shakes his head. "It's funny. You're so—I don't know... You analyze the way faces twitch and pull the truth out of people in these crazy ways, but—" He laughs again. "You just called your brother a jack-off in the car."

I frown again. "He is a jack-off."

He smirks, like I've played into his hand. "I'm the same with my sister. You think you'd be different because you're grown-ups, but—" He shrugs. "You just fall back into old patterns."

I squint up at him, thinking. "Until this week, I haven't been in the same room as all my siblings since I was...sixteen?"

He blinks, surprised. "Whoa."

"We didn't actually grow up together." I shake my head. "Our relationships never really evolved past the ages we left each other behind."

Sam gives me a subtle wink as he pokes me in the arm. "There she is."

"So." I take a breath. "How old's your sister?"

"Thirty-one."

"Do you like her?"

"Yep." He nods once. "One of my best friends."

I feel a twinge of jealousy and wonder what that might feel like, but I don't want him to see that feeling on my face, so I cover it by quickly thinking of a baby duck going down a slide into a pond, which lights my face up a little.

"She's one of the main reasons I'm sober," he says to me even though I didn't ask, and it makes me feel floaty. It also really makes me like his sister. "You'd like her—you'd like my niece too." He smiles—Duchenne—his niece is special to him.

"How old's your niece?"

"Four. She's so fucking cute and funny and smart and—" Then he suddenly stops talking and stares at me for a second before he pokes his finger into the corner of my big, dumb, smiling mouth. "That's a real big smile you've got there."

I drop it and turn my head away from him, straight to the ground—fuck! "No, it's not." I start walking ahead quickly.

"It's pretty big!" he calls after me.

"I'll call you a jack-off too!" I yell back.

He laughs as he catches up to me. "I'm sure you will."

"Come on." I give him a look. "I made a promise to my dad I need to keep."

I find the gravestone and stand in front of it, frowning.

"Is this your grandfather's?" Sam asks, looking at the name.

Brick Carter.

I nod.

"'Loving father, grandfather, patriot, and friend,'" Sam reads with a respectful nod. "He sounds like a good man."

"Yeah." I clear my throat. "Which do you think sends a stronger message—spitting on a grave or dancing upon it?"

"Uh—I—" Sam's face falters. "What?"

"Spitting or dancing?" I repeat.

He gives me a cautious shake of his altogether too-perfect head. "I don't—understand the question?"

I nod to myself. "Dancing on it probably."

"I mean—" Sam grimaces. "Yeah, probably?"

Then he looks for my eyes, finds them, and holds them as he waits for an answer.

"I promised my dad." I nod. "I told him that if I was ever back at this cemetery again, I'd dance on his father's grave."

"That's a..." Sam trails off before he blows some air out of this mouth. "Fucking weird promise, Carter."

"No." I shake my head. "He was an asshole."

"Your dad or your grandpa?"

"Both." I purse my lips. "My grandpa more, though."

Sam looks at me carefully. "What did your dad say when you said that?"

I purse my lips; my eyes flick up and to the left, which is what happens when you recall a memory.

I look up at Sam. "Nothing."

He didn't say a thing.

In fact, if I were to pull apart the memory how I remember it, I think, if I'm recalling it correctly, my dad's mouth was pulled tight, and there was the slightest hint of a nod before he said nothing, and that's when I walked away from him and everyone else besides Oliver and Vi and Clay until now.

It was the last time I saw my dad, actually, the day they read my grandfather's will. It was the last nail in the coffin for me.

I can feel Sam trying to peek through my memories, and I'm so glad that I'm me and he's not because I don't want him to see right through me, but I'm also glad that he's trying to. I don't think I can remember the last time someone tried to.

Sam takes a step closer to me and his head tilts a little as he looks at the gravestone. "What'd he do?"

I sigh.

"When he died, he left all his grandchildren three-point-six million each."

Sam pulls a face, mock-horror. "...What a fucking monster."

"Yeah—everyone except Oliver," I say, and Sam breathes loudly out his mouth, jaw going tight. I lick my bottom lip. "They didn't invite Oliver to the funeral, actually. They didn't even tell him he died." I shake my head. "I didn't know till I got there. They said Ol's lifestyle and choices would disturb my grandfather, and I said, 'But he's dead,' and they said, 'All the more reason to respect his wishes...' And then I looked at my dad and asked him if this is what Grandpa really would have wanted, and he said yes."

I think my dad looked kind of sad as he said that though, which, you know, I guess is the appropriate paternal response when one of your children is being grossly mistreated, but my father's possible hypothetical displeasure in the situation never actioned beyond that. It's hard to be sure of emotions in retrospect unless you catch them on camera. The slightest shift in my memory of how a muscle twitches could rewrite everything I think I see. So was my dad actually sad? I don't know. Maybe I just wanted him to be.

Sam sniffs a shallow laugh and gives his head a little shake. His jaw's gone tight thinking about Oliver being treated that way. Then he nods once. "Right."

He takes a step away from me and onto the flat burial stone—it feels like he looks at me in slow motion—and then he offers me his hand and I take it and he pulls me in toward him and spins me.

Then he pauses and glances down at me, each of us still frozen in our dance stances, and I hope the universes freezes and I'm forever stuck in the arms of the world's hottest alcoholic, dancing on the grave of a bigot.

13

WE GET BACK TO THE car and my brothers are waiting for us. Tenny has a dipshit smile like he's in on some secret because he thinks he knows I'm into Sam, but Oliver's face looks a little dark. Brows low, mouth stiff.

"You sit in front," Oliver tells me, and a flicker of disappointment breezes through my bones.

I try to sidestep it. Tenny probably said something assholey to Oliver inside the funeral home and now Oliver just wants to be away from him.

"You gonna play nice?" Tenny asks as I climb in.

"Yes, Dad." I roll my eyes.

"Georgia, stop." He looks at the road as he peels out. He shakes his head a tiny bit. "It's too soon."

And then I feel bad. Out of all of us kids, Dad dying would hit Tennyson the hardest. Maryanne might milk it the most, but Ten's the one who'll feel it most. They were inseparable. Tens was his mini and his pride and joy. Tenny worked for Dad straight out of college, and nepotism was certainly a part of that, but the business is half run these days by Tennyson, or so I'm told. Wholly run now, I guess. They sell civilian aircrafts. And for all the shit I was giving him before, besides me, he is the second smartest kid in our family.

Oliver just never applied himself. He could have done anything in the world if he wanted to, anything at all—still could—but he sort of fell into event planning. He partied real hard, that was his job for a while, and then somewhere within the midst of that, he began to plan parties for people, which turned into planning events for people.

Maryanne fell into her MRS.

But Tennyson works hard. He didn't always, which is why he only got into UGA, but he applied himself once he was there, I suppose.

I poke Tenny in the leg and give him a long look that's an apology with my eyes, which I hope he'll accept because I'm not going to say one with my mouth.

He holds my gaze, doesn't say anything, and his face doesn't give me any clues as to whether I'm forgiven or not.

"Where are we going now?" I ask.

"I'm meeting Violet at Stomp, so you're dropping me there," Oliver says from the back.

"Oli," I whine. "Why?"

"Because she and I are picking out the floral arrangements for the funeral, and I need caffeine to think."

"No!" I pout.

"So you fucked an inappropriate man, Gige." Oliver shrugs. "Who hasn't?"

"I haven't," Tennyson says at the same time as Sam says, "Me."

I spin around to face Sam. "What about Catherine?"

He grins and shrugs. "Not a man."

"Who's Catherine?" Oliver asks with a frown.

"No one." Sam rolls his eyes.

"The girl whose name he got tattooed on his arm after sleeping with her once," I tell Oli.

Tennyson chuckles. "How good was she in bed for that to happen?"

"Yeah!" I turn back to look at Sam. "One-to-ten it for us—"

"I don't know." Sam laughs, shaking his head. "I was drunk!"

"Alternative adjective: clingy," I offer.

Tenny laughs more.

"Oh, you guys have in-jokes now?" Oliver asks, eyeing me and Sam as though he's playfully mad, but behind the playfulness I'm sensing the smallest bit of genuine contempt because his mouth tightens a little bit. And Sam's mouth—that perfect mouth—is a dead giveaway when he chews on his bottom lip and looks out the window.

"Oh, I bet those two have a lot of secrets," Tennyson says, and I thwack him in the chest with a *shut up* glare.

"You want to play the secret game?" I give my oldest brother a look and do my best to divert all our focus away from his comment. "How about how Mom believes that you don't live with Savannah?"

Tennyson presses his lips together. "I don't live with Savannah."

I point to his mouth. "Yes, you do."

I hear Sam sniff a laugh from the backseat.

"No"—his fists briefly clench the steering wheel a bit tighter—"I don't."

"Yes"—I point to the hand of his that's closest to me on the steering wheel—"you do."

Tennyson makes a noise from the back of his throat.

"Georgia," Oliver groans. "Leave him alone."

"Tennyson." I blink over at him playfully. "Do you want me to leave you alone?"

He blinks back a lot, emulating my tone. "Yes please."

I roll my eyes at him, and he snorts a laugh and eyes me like we're pals, and I'm confused by the warmth I think I'm feeling from him, so I look out the window.

"So," I say. "Oli, what are you thinking for flowers?"

"Lots of green," Oliver says, looking out his window. "Ivy, leatherleaf fern, lemon leaf. Maybe some honey bracelet? And then something like...bells of Ireland. Delphinium, probably?"

"Are you just making up words?" Tenny interrupts him as we pull up in front of Stomp.

Oli glares at him, then gets out of the car, slamming the door loud on purpose.

I breathe out my nose, a bit annoyed at Tennyson for not just letting Oliver prattle on about flowers and making him feel stupid for knowing the names of them.

Sam glances at me uncomfortably, then begins to get out of the car too, and as I reach for the door handle, Tennyson says, "Wait, I want to talk to you."

Sam looks back at me, pausing halfway out of the car.

"She'll be all right, man." Tennyson eyes him like he's being ridiculous. "Go on inside, we'll see you in a minute."

Hesitation is ripe on Sam's face as he glances from me to my brother and back to me again. My eyes are round and big as I try to give Sam a look to tell him I'll be okay. He climbs out of the car.

"Never pegged you for the strong and silent type." Tennyson watches after him, then looks back to me.

I roll my eyes.

"You're really going to try and tell me nothing's going on?" He raises his eyebrows.

And I feel confused. We've never had a relationship like this. He's never asked me these questions before. Normally it's Oliver pulling me into corners and asking me questions and telling me secrets. And when I say normally, I mean like a decade ago.

I squint up at my biggest brother, a tiny bit happy to have someone to talk to but not prepared to give him an actual smile. So I shrug dismissively. "He just thinks I'm attractive."

"Yeah, Gige." My big brother snorts. "You didn't have to go to Cambridge to figure that one out."

"It's nothing." I shake my head. "Nothing's happened, nothing's going to happen—"

He gives me a look. "Yeah, if you say so…"

Then Tennyson's eyes pinch together and he bites the tip of his tongue, which is the same thinking face he's made since we were tiny. He doesn't believe me. I wouldn't believe me either, but he drops it anyway. "So, I want to talk about the will…"

I drag my eyes over to him. "What about it?"

"I don't know." He sighs. "What if it's the same?"

I frown a little. "Well, have you seen it?"

"No." He shrugs, helpless. "But I mean, you know Dad. He was so weird about Oliver..."

"You really think he'd cut him out of his will?"

My big brother shrugs again, helpless. "Grandpa did."

I give him a look. "Yeah, I mean, Grandpa had a framed Confederate flag over his fireplace and was a terrible misogynist, and I'm not Dad's greatest defender, but even I know he wasn't like that—"

He sighs. "I guess you're right."

Then he rubs his mouth, tired. Or at least, that's what he thinks he does. I tilt my head to get a better look at his face. Elevated breathing, brows low in consternation, mouth set. Thumb pressed into his mouth absentmindedly.

"What?" I ask him, watching his face.

"What *what*?" He blinks, looking sprung. "Nothing," he says with a mouth shrug. Then he scratches the back of his neck.

"What aren't you saying?" I ask.

"Nothing—that's all. I'm just worried Oliver'll be left out of the will again—" Another sliver of a mouth shrug.

I raise my finger to point to his face, but my brother smacks my hand away. "Don't do that shit with me."

"Then don't lie to me!"

"I'm not lying to you!"

"That was another lie!" I yell.

He sighs out a big breath and presses the tip of his tongue into his top lip, nostrils the slightest bit flared—he's annoyed with me but he's cracking—I love it when they crack—his hand is balled into a loose fist and he unconsciously taps his mouth.

"That"—I point to his hand—"is called a self-hushing emblem. It means you have something to say but you're not sure you should say it."

My big brother looks at me with ragged eyes. "You're fucking annoying."

"Yeah, so everyone keeps saying." I roll my eyes. "But spill it anyway."

He licks his lips as he rolls his head back. "A couple years back, I was looking over some numbers and noticed these regular payments were being withdrawn from some rental company in New Orleans." I frown a little. "Nothing massive. Just couple thousand dollars a month, but when I looked at it—it went back years. So I asked him about it, and he went real weird. Clammed right up. Said it was for an office space and that he'd been thinking about expanding the business."

"In New Orleans?" I clarify with a frown.

Tennyson gives me a weighted look. "Then the payments stopped, but I'd written down the details, so I did some digging. It wasn't an office space. It was some girl's apartment." He raises his eyebrows.

I blink a few times. "You think dad had a mistress?"

Tenny shrugs, but his whole face pulls. Yes. Because, I guess, what else could that mean?

"And then," he keeps going, "a few months later, the same amount of money started being deposited into an offshore account."

I frown. "Well, maybe he was doing it as a tax write-off?"

"Sure." Tennyson nods, and he looks like he's trying to believe that himself. But then his face tugs and I know he's concerned. "Either way, I don't know what's going to be in the will on Monday."

My car door swings open and Oliver sticks his head inside the car. "You girls done gabbing in here?"

I jump out of the car and Oliver links his arm with mine, pulling me over to the entrance of the café where Sam's standing, watching us.

"Gige, I need your help," Oliver says solemnly.

"What's up?" Tenny says, squaring up. "I can help."

I roll my eyes without looking at him.

Oliver pauses dramatically, glancing between the three of us. "I need you to tell me whether the guy at the register is gay."

"I can't help," Tenny says with a headshake, taking an unconscious step back.

I roll my eyes again, but this time it's at both of my brothers. "I can't tell whether someone's gay or not—"

"Of course you can." Oliver frowns.

I point at Sam. "I thought he was gay."

Sam bats a smile away and then gives me a subtle wink, and my heart is a drum inside my chest right now.

"But what about your magic?" Oliver pouts.

"Can we just—stop calling it magic? I've studied people's faces for like eight years. It's not magic. I had to learn this."

"What, you think magicians are just born with magic?" Oliver pulls a face. "They have to train too."

"That's what Hogwarts is for," Tenny interjects.

"They were wizards?" I look at him like he's an idiot.

"It's the same thing!"

"Oh my God!" I yell. "Tennyson, if you think Harry Potter is the same thing as a magici—"

"Harry Potter was a magician!" Tennyson interrupts.

"He was not!" Me.

"Guys." Oliver.

"Mate, have you seen the movies?" Sam.

"Guys." Oliver.

"Did he, or did he not do magic?" Tens.

"Not a magician!" Me.

"Ah." Sam considers. "I sort of see his point—"

"Guys!" Oliver stomps his foot, but I ignore him.

"The most famous line from the book is 'Harry—yer a wizard,'" I interject.

Oliver gives me a silencing look. "Georgia, can you or can you not tell me whether this cashier is gay?"

I take a long-suffering breath, but then give Oliver a gentle sort-of smile. "I can tell you whether he's attracted to you."

Tennyson ducks his head, peering into the store. "Are you talking about that cashier?"

"Yeah." Oli nods.

Tenny shakes his head. "That's Avery Cleanth. He's not gay."

I frown. "How do you know?"

Tennyson shrugs. "He was in my class at school."

"Oh, right." I nod sarcastically. "Your heterosexual-only class."

"No." He rolls his eyes. (But probably "kind of, yes" is the truth.)

"So does he have a girlfriend?" I press.

"No," Tennyson says.

Oliver stands up a little straighter, eyebrows raised in expectation. Sam folds his arms over his chest.

I crane my neck. "Then how do you know?"

"He doesn't look gay!" Tenny shrugs, helplessly.

Sam's face scrunches up. Microexpression: contempt.

"What does gay look like in 2024?" Sam Penny asks.

Tennyson presses his tongue into his top lip. He does this semi-shrug and nods somewhat subtly but not subtly enough in Oliver's direction.

Oliver sniffs out an offended laugh and walks inside briskly.

"Nice." I glare at Tennyson before I follow Oliver in.

I don't know why we do that, because the four of us immediately gather again in the same circle just inside of the café.

"For the record"—I look at my oldest brother—"Oliver's in regular black jeans, amazing loafers, and a short-sleeved button up shirt, so—"

"It's pink!" Tenny blinks.

"Fuck you!" Oliver spits. "It's a dusty quartz—"

"Okay! That's—" I interrupt him, shaking my head because that's not going to help. "I've got it from here, thank you. Ol, why don't you go into the line so I can watch for a second, okay?"

Oliver gives Tennyson one last death stare before he saunters away.

"He's not gay," Tennyson tells me decidedly as we watch our brother walk toward Avery Cleanth.

And I hate to say it, but I think Tens is right. Nothing about Avery's body language makes me think he's attracted to Oliver, and Oliver is catnip for men who like men. If you're gay in Oliver's vicinity, you're hitting on him—it's like he's a homing beacon, and so he should be, because he's beautiful and funny and witty, but this guy is giving him nothing, and I don't even know why Oliver wondered whether he was gay in the first place? He's normally sharper than this himself…

Only one way to be sure, though.

I adjust my dress a little—tug it the top part of it down, catch my hand on purpose in the hem of the skirt so I can hike it up a little shorter—and then I go sidle up next to my brother as he's squinting with a perfectly pouted face at the baked goods.

"Hi." I grin at Avery.

"Hi." He smiles back and his eyes drop south of mine. Boobs. Straight men love boobs. I glance back over my shoulder at Sam—his jaw's clenched—and I get a jolt of happy.

"Have you ordered the coffees yet?" I ask Oli.

"Just me and Sam's."

"And three cold brews, please."

Avery Cleanth subconsciously licks his bottom lip before he gives me a cool nod and little smile. "Sure thing."

My older brother walks over to us.

"Told you," he whispers to me before he hugs Beckett Lane, who's appeared at my side. "Becks." He grins. "How's things?"

"Good, good—they're good." Becks taps me on the arm. "Hey, Gigi."

I look up at him, my face emotionless, and flash him an empty smile. "Hello."

"What's good?" He subtly thrusts his chin at me, which is interesting because it's a sign of repressed anger.

"I met your girlfriend last night," I tell him.

He sighs and plasters on a practiced smile. "Isn't she something special?"

"Oh," I nod. "She's something…"

Tennyson pinches me and I wriggle out of it.

"Bring our coffees out," I tell my brother and walk back to Sam, who's now sitting at a table outside in the sun—it's worth noting: in an extremely noncovert way—leaning forward to watch us.

I sit across from him.

He scratches the back of his head, then looks at me for a couple of seconds. "You okay?"

I pinch my eyes, heart beating faster, feeling annoyed that he knew to ask that. "Why wouldn't I be okay?"

Sam gives an unconvincing shrug. "You tell me."

I roll my eyes and look away.

"Do you like your brother?" he asks, glancing over at him.

"Who, Tennyson?"

He nods.

I shrug. It's not a nonanswer, it's just that I've never really thought of it before. "I guess—I don't know. Sometimes?"

He nods a few times, thinking. "What'd you do?"

My face flickers, confused. "When?"

"With your inheritance?"

"I, um—" I breathe in and out and give him a tight smile. "Gave half of it to Oliver, kind of cut out my family for not batting for him, and haven't been back here till now."

He sits back, blinking a few times. "You gave Oliver one-point-eight million dollars?"

I give him another tight smile.

"What's that mean?" Sam presses his index finger into my fake smile and for a second, my brain goes gooey. He's touching me. It's playful and frivolous and it could mean nothing, but also, it could mean something. Frivolous touching coupled with his dilated pupils and how often he clocks my mouth implies it means something, and just at the thought of what it could objectively imply, oxytocin is released into my system, and if we weren't on a main road in the middle of Beaufort, I'd grab him by the collar of his white T-shirt and kiss his perfect face right off.

"Well, well, if it isn't my favorite girl in the world and the handsome boy I keep seeing her with," Violet says, appearing at our table, a big, dumb grin on her face.

I look up at her. "Your top's on inside-out."

She glances down at herself. "Oh—that's embarrassing." She shrugs. "Had sex as I was leaving the house. Nothing puts the fear of God in you like—"

"Sex?" I interject.

"No!" she scolds me. "Death! And sex is the antithesis of death." She leans down close. "Y'all should have it. It's so good when you're hyperaware of the impermanent nature of everything."

I squint at her. "Are you drunk?"

She makes a tiny space between her finger and her thumb. "Little bit."

Sam sniffs a laugh.

Oliver comes out carrying our coffees. "Verdict?" His eyebrows are arched up in a wasted hopefulness.

I shake my head ruefully. "Sorry..."

Oliver's face falls. "How do you know?"

I open my mouth and close it again, confused. "Are you asking for the exact science of it?"

Oliver nods.

I purse my lips. "He clocked my chest within two seconds of me standing there, and then his gaze shifted from my eyes to my mouth constantly until I walked away. He likes girls."

"Maybe he's bi?" offers Violet. Then she claps both her hands on Oliver's face. "The boy's a damn fool if he doesn't like you, honey—now let's go."

14

HOW'D IT GO WITH THE flowers today?" Mom asks Oliver at the dinner table.

It's just us tonight. Mom, the Nouns and their respective partners, the Adjectives, and Sam.

"Good." Oliver tilts his head proudly. "You're going to love them."

"I want no color in there," she tells him sternly.

Oliver pauses. "You might not love them."

"Oliver." She sighs. "I don't want my husband's casket to look like a gay pride float."

"Wow!" I say loudly before Oliver has to respond. My mother throws me a warning look.

Oliver shakes his head a tiny bit. "It's just some baby blue and a lot of green. It's—I can change it."

My mom watches Oliver, tongue pressed into the inside of her cheek. "Show me a sample tomorrow, okay?"

Oliver nods, then looks down at his plate. He's just shoveling the food around with his fork now.

"Sam," my mom says, looking at him. "How's Oliver doing with his sobriety?"

Maryanne glances up, interested.

"Mom." I frown.

"Great," Sam says quickly. "Really well. I'm really proud of him."

"Oh," my mother says, and then she smiles. "How wonderful. Not as wonderful as if he'd not become an alcoholic in the first place, but wonderful considering—"

"Fuck me." I drop my head into my hands, exasperated.

There's a clang of cutlery, and even though I can't see my mother's face, I know it's horrified.

"I beg your pardon!" She blinks.

"Give him a break!" I shake my head at her, incredulous.

Maryanne's eyes are lit up with the prospect of an unfolding conflict.

My mother points a finger at me. "We don't use such profanity under this roof."

"It's a word, Mom." I roll my eyes.

She gives me a pointed look. "It's a sin, sweetheart."

Jason and Savannah shift uncomfortably in their seats. Sam, however, just watches.

He's been just watching me all night, actually. He wasn't seated next to me at dinner—we had assigned seating. Mom and Maryanne, they love assigned seating because they love controlling dynamics. But joke's on them, because not sitting next to him means I get to stare at him, and that might be better.

"Of all the sins that have taken place in your house, I promise you, me saying 'fuck' is like, absolutely the least of your concerns."

She arcs up, pushing her hair behind both ears. Power move. "As far as I'm concerned, there's only ever been one child of mine who's sinned under my roof." Her eyebrows twitch in condemnation.

"Okay." I straighten up. "Quick show of hands if you haven't had sex in this house?"

Sam puts his hand up without a second thought, but everyone else lags on their response time.

Maryanne and Jason are the first to raise their hands next.

My brothers raise their hands next. Then Savannah.

"Liars." I point to both my brothers. Oliver gnaws on his thumb and Tennyson scratches the back of his neck. I look at Savannah and flash her an apologetic glance. "I don't want to drag you into this, because I like you, but you're lying too." I look at Maryanne, then over to Jason.

Jason swallows nervously, but Maryanne is cool as a fucking cucumber. He's had sex here and she hasn't. I feel my chin tuck a bit—I'm genuinely surprised.

"You've had sex here before." I point at Jason and Maryanne snaps her head in his direction—so does my mother for that matter—both of them are surprised to hear that, but only really Maryanne should be.

"What?" He blinks, shaking his head quickly, but for the splittest of seconds, that shake of the head was preceded by a sliver of a nod that no one else would notice. "No, I haven't." He swallows.

"When?" I ask.

"He said he hasn't," Maryanne says loudly.

"Have you cheated on Maryanne?" I ask.

"Georgia," Tennyson says, frowning at me sternly.

"No!" This time Jason's head pulls back. He's affronted. Truth. Interesting.

I nod as I piece it together now.

"So in high school, then?" I offer.

His mouth does an involuntary twitch. Truth. "No." He glances at Maryanne, nervously. And fair play to him, I'd be nervous with Maryanne right now too.

"With who?" I ask, but he says nothing, which obviously leaves me no choice. I lean forward, my chin in my hand so I can watch his face closer as I rapid-fire throw names at him.

"Amber?"

Nothing.

"Ashley?"

Nothing.

"Sophie?"

Nothing.

"Tinsley?"

Jason's face twitches.

"Ah." I snap my fingers and point at him, feeling a victorious little smile appear on my face because I love the truth and I especially love it when I find it, and then I realize—"Gross! You guys swapped?"

"Shut. Up," my sister growls, and then she slams her hands down on the table. "Shut up! No one gives a shit about your stupid little freak show act. You think you're clever, but you're not. You don't have any skill; you're like a card reader at a carnival, what you do means nothing, and you're not even good at it." She glares. "Because you're wrong. I've never had sex here."

I didn't say she had, by the way—it felt like that was worth clarifying somewhere, but I decide to let it slide just so I can say this: "Not for lack of trying though, right?"

I arch my brows, glaring across the table at her.

Mom shifts uncomfortably in her seat.

It flashes across Maryanne's face. Deep hurt. I've struck gold.

"You bitch," she spits, shaking her head and scoffing a laugh. "You fuck my boyfriend, you tear my entire life apart, and then you—"

"You're on wafer-thin ice." I cut her off and point at her. "Wafer-thin."

Mom sits back in her chair, looking somewhere in the middle of intrigued and annoyed.

"If you've got something to say, Georgia, go on and say it," my mother tells me, eyebrows arched.

"Yeah, Georgia," my sister dares me. "Say it."

And I can't. I can't say it. I've thought about saying it 140,000 times, and every way I play it out, it doesn't undo it, so what's the point? All it'll do is raise a bunch of questions I've already waded through with a therapist, and I don't need to do it all over again just to take Maryanne down a peg. I won't say it, and she knows I won't say it, so I turn to my mother and say this instead:

"Your eldest daughter has an undiagnosed narcissistic personality disorder with sociopathic tendencies."

Maryanne laughs hollowly. "Fuck you."

My mother lays her hand on Maryanne's, gives her a look to gently quiet her—the look speaks volumes—and it says, "I've got this, leave it with me." I've never received such a look from my mother.

"And what, pray tell"—she glances at Maryanne and gives her a tender look, then pats her arm to placate her—"does my youngest daughter have?"

I push back from the table. "PTSD."

15

I WAS ONLY JUST FOURTEEN THE first time it happened.

Maryanne had her friends over—the popular kids; she'd been trying to get in with them since day one, but she was a straight-A goodie-goodie and that wasn't the thing back then, not in South Carolina anyway.

I knew she liked Beckett Lane; it was as plain as the nose on her face—and, sure, my sister is a master manipulator, but with Beckett Lane she was clear as glass.

She was seventeen when she finally got in with that crowd. Dad got her a Range Rover for her birthday and let her take the house up in Sullivan's Island for the whole Fourth of July weekend with all her friends, no parental supervision. My mom said it was a recipe for sin, but Maryanne talked her around. After that, these seventeen-year-olds were around our house like a bad smell.

All of them were nice enough. Beckett was particularly nice.

There's a prickle you get. You feel it on the back of your neck and your forearms, when you're in danger.

He walked past my room that night and stood in the doorway. I felt the prickle. He stood there too long, watched me all too focused or something, I don't know.

"What are you working on over there?" He nodded at me, walking into my room uninvited.

"I have a paper on the Constitution due tomorrow."

"Oh." He nodded again. "Yeah, I remember that. I still have mine—if you want it, I can send it to you?" He gave me a warm smile.

I flashed him a quick one in return. "N-no thanks."

He shrugged. "Up to you." He didn't leave. "I like your T-shirt." His hand grazed my white T-shirt, but it was close to a place I didn't want him touching me.

"Thanks." I jumped up and walked out of my room quickly, down the hall and toward the door to Oliver's bedroom. I could see that the lights were on and so was his music, so I walked faster, but even then, I had a feeling Beckett was following me.

I burst into Oliver's room because I knew I'd be safe in there.

But he wasn't in there.

His window was open. Curtain flapping in that South Carolina breeze. José González blaring loud.

In that moment, I was sure of two things. One, Oliver had snuck off again with the new guy in his class from New York, and two, I was about to have sex for the first time, and it wasn't going to be my choice.

I didn't fight him so much. I wasn't sure there was much use?

My parents were out. They were at a gala, staying up in Charlotte for the night. Tennyson was with his girlfriend in his room, and they for certain were not coming up for air for hours. No use in me screaming either, because Oliver's music was loud, but Tennyson's music was louder.

Oliver might have stayed out for the whole night with that guy, I didn't know... That was the beginning of Oliver's sporadic phase that he is arguably still in to this day.

My only hope was Maryanne, but Kayleigh Stevens was downstairs, whom she'd been trying to win the approval of for months, so I didn't feel bright about my chances there either.

I did tell him no, and I asked him to stop, and I do wonder sometimes in retrospect if I had cried or screamed if he would have? I didn't, though. I just lie there with my wrists pinned and my eyes wide open.

And then, about halfway through, my sister walked in. Maryanne froze like a deer in headlights. Beckett looked back at her, a hint of a frown on his face at the interruption. He didn't climb off me. He just stared at her.

Her eyes fell from his to mine and it was all in slow motion.

I stared at her, not blinking, waiting for her to panic or scream or run for me and tear him off, but all she did was this slow blink, and then her eyelids fluttered a few times and then she backed away. She just closed the door.

Maryanne was his girlfriend by the time we got home from school the next day. She was over the moon and didn't look me in the eye for a week. And then, after that, I guess he took it as permission or something? It happened again and again. I don't know how many times. I don't know if it was the no-fighting thing that made him think it was okay, or the fact that Maryanne walked in and said nothing, did nothing—I wondered if both those things combined sent him a mixed message.

I was confused about it for...geez, I don't know—six years or something. Was it even assault? It happened so many times... So many times before my dad walked in on it, which was the last time and about a year after the first.

He never threatened me. I never had a bruise. He never made me bleed. He never even hurt me, not like that—so what was it? Was it my fault? Did I let it happen? I'd just lie there—I never fought him off.

Did I kiss him back? I think about that sometimes. Sometimes I wonder if I started to, toward the end? I think for a while I tried to change the narrative in my mind that we were a thing and he loved me. And do you know what? He actually was so good to me, all the time, in front of everyone. At school, everyone thought he was the best guy, and sometimes I thought he was too, and that fucked me up because I could never tell what that meant. Not then, anyway.

It was guilt or grooming or something fucked up, I can see that now—but then, I wasn't so sure. I wasn't even sure it was assault back then. I stopped telling him no after the third or fourth time—I'd just lie there, frozen and still.

Then we began to study cognitive function in university and the minute my professor mentioned "tonic immobility," I knew it...knew it in my bones.

Beckett Lane raped me for a year, and my sister knew it too and did fuck-all to help me.

16

I WANDER DOWNSTAIRS THE NEXT MORNING, and the house is eerily quiet.

Mom's car's not in the driveway, and neither is Tennyson's, Maryanne's (thank God), or Oliver's. I wonder where they've all gone without me but feel in the same breath an air of gratefulness to not have to deal with anyone's shit first thing.

I round the corner, and sitting on the kitchen bench with a bottle of water in his hand is Sam Penny.

He has bedhead, messy and inviting, and the way his shoulders fall forward in the mornings when he's tired is so attractive to me. I think because I can tell he's entirely unaware of how beautiful he is—which is endearing, because it might be the only thing he isn't aware of. And I do mean beautiful, like, pricks-you-in-the-heart, painfully beautiful. And then, at the same time, with those shoulders and that jawline and those hands that I want so badly on me, he's so tall and so broad, like, you know how sometimes you want to feel that a guy can toss you around? He could toss me around like a rag doll. And then he's got those eyes you could dive into and that mouth that always looks bitten and that strange gentleness about him that somehow never makes him seem less strong.

I fake-yawn as I walk in so it's less obvious that I've just been staring at him for the last three seconds out of view, and he looks up and smiles.

"Hey." His shoulders go square unconsciously.

I smile more than I want to, but for the love of God, I don't let myself show teeth. "Where is everyone?"

He shoves a hand through his hair as he walks over to me. "Ol went for breakfast with your aunt."

"Ah." I nod, glancing around. He's standing quite near to me. Not invasively near, but it seems like an aimless sort of closeness. Which is fine, I suppose; it's not like my heart is actually going to flatline from the thrill of it. It's just, an aimless closeness is—in my experience—quite rare but very human.

Which he is. Which we all are and tend to try to avoid embracing, but not Sam Penny. Sam Penny is human. He wears it like a badge of pride.

I glance around the empty room. "And everyone else?"

He shrugs. "Don't know." Then he pushes his hand through his hair again and tilts his head so we're eye to eye, and his look is a tiny bit hopeful. "But can I take you to breakfast?"

We're sitting outside at some place called First Watch in Bluffton. It's new since I've left, and I'll say it: they serve a fucking good waffle. Sam and I, we've been talking about nothing in particular. Flirting, mostly, and I've intentionally not asked him my hard-hitting, nosy questions up until now, but I still want to know everything about him, so I decide to dive right in once he's on his second coffee.

"What's it like being an addict?"

He drops his head as he laughs, then looks back up at me and the light from the sun makes his eyes look like little stars—or maybe the light's just coming from inside of him?

"I miss it," he tells me with a solemn nod.

I blink. "Really?"

"Fuck, yeah." He laughs, shaking his head at himself. "All the time." He swallows—he's telling the truth. He does miss it—he actually misses it a lot, I think.

I lean in toward him. "So you started drinking because of your mom?"

He stretches his head upward and strokes under his chin absent-mindedly. Unconsciously self-soothing, that little cutie.

He makes an "mmm" sound that I love, but it's a considering sound; he's not sure. "Kind of." He shrugs. "I liked drinking before Mum died, but once she died, I liked it more and more."

"Were you hurt in the accident?" I frown.

He looks over at me again, but his eyes are lost in time. He gives me a weighty smile. "I was, yeah."

My heart sinks. "Badly?"

The memory of pain flashes across him, and the way it splays on his face makes my bones sting, which I find strange because my bones never sting for other people, and I begin to wonder whether perhaps Sam Penny isn't "other people." Maybe Sam Penny isn't "people" to me at all.

"I was in a coma for a week." He juts his jaw forward. "Fractured four vertebrae, broke my femur"—he touches his right leg—"broke my fibula"—he touches his left leg—"scapula and clavicle, on my left side—"

"Sam," I sigh on his behalf, my stomach all tense for the pain he's had, but he's still going.

"Couple broken ribs—and a big shard of glass pierced my left kidney."

He lifts his shirt to show his scar and I swallow so heavily, because holy God—and then also, shit—because he catches the look on my face, and then his face twitches with a subdued delight. He definitely did that on purpose. He knows what his body looks like. I hadn't seen it yet (though I could have imagined it), and him sitting there slumped back in the restaurant chair casually lifting his shirt to show me the scar that runs down a little left of the center of him is the sexiest thing I've ever seen. So much so I might actually burst into actual flames.

He lowers his T-shirt back down, and I give him an unimpressed look that is really a very thinly veiled very impressed look. He fights off a smile.

"And then modeling and then coke," I say to him, making sure I have it all in order.

"Modeling, then coke, then other stuff, then more coke."

I nod a few times, then pause to look over at him. "Do you think you have an addictive personality?"

This is a test, obviously.

He shakes his head quickly and dismissively. "I was just sad and didn't want to stop."

"So why did you, then?"

"I overdosed when I was twenty." He squints back in time. "My sister stopped speaking to me." He's frowning as he recalls. "It fucking sucked—I woke up and she was sitting there fucking fuming and then she left." His shoulders do a little shrug, but so does his mouth. He hates this memory. "Left me alone in the hospital. She just didn't come back. I was filthy at her for weeks after... But then, without her talking to me, I guess after a while I got it. That after everything—after losing Mum, and then kind of losing our dad too because he just never came back to who he was before she was gone—" He swallows heavily. That hurts him to think about. "We only had each other, really—and I knew that, and still, I was like, this flippant little fuck, gambling with the life of the only family she had left—" He sighs, annoyed at himself, but I'm staring at him, starry-eyed.

"Just because I fucking lacked the motivation to heal properly after what happened to our mum—so I pulled my head in." He shrugs. Like it isn't the biggest deal in the world.

I need you to listen to me when I say this: I could not be more attracted to this man if I tried.

"Whoa," is all I say, and I wonder if I'm going pink just looking at him, because he tries to squash a smile. Doesn't really work though, so I'm just looking at him with big round eyes, unsure of what to say, and he's sort of smirking at me because my big round eyes aren't just big and round; they are dilated as fuck.

I clear my throat. "Are you and your sister okay now?"

He nods. "Yep." He smiles. "Best friends."

That makes me happy.

He pulls out his phone and flashes me a photo of a little girl. "That's my niece." He looks so proud of her, and it's so cute and so sexy.

I stare at her sweet face: really blond hair, but big blue eyes, a bit like his. "She's beautiful." I smile at him. "Do they live in Los Angeles?"

"Yeah, sort of." His face lights up a bit. "They're in Dana Point. So pretty close."

"You see them a lot?"

"Yeah." He nods. "Every week."

He smiles again after he says that, and I love how much he loves them. I wonder what it's like to feel that about your siblings. And it's so unlike me, but I'm not thinking about how my face is presenting; I'm thinking about him.

And then, under the table, Sam kicks me gently. "What's that big smile you've got there?"

I straighten my face right out. "No big smile. This is a regular smile. I'm happy for you."

He smirks. "Are you?"

"Mmhmm." I nod. "Because you were a wayward soul who turned his life around, and now you have a precious relationship with your niece and sister, and it's—"

He cuts me off. "Precious, is it?" He's smirking again.

I roll my eyes. "Stop."

He nods his chin toward my face. "It's a fucking big smile..."

"Nope." I shake my head, stubbornly.

"You have a big smile for me," Sam says, way too pleased with himself.

"Yeah, well." I shrug a bit aggressively, because I've gone petulant now. "You lick your bottom lip every time you look at me, and your pupils are dilated, so—"

"Yeah." He nods, interrupting me again. "They are."

I swallow heavily, because I know he knows what that means, and I'm quick-as-I-can trying to figure out whether he meant what I think he just might have implied.

And then, from behind me:

"Well hello," says my mother's voice.

"Mom—" My head pulls back, and if I were paying attention to my body better, I would have noticed I careened a little bit in Sam's direction. "—What are you doing here?"

She waves her hand somewhere behind her. "Prayer group."

Sam nods a couple of times pleasantly, and her eyes fall on him for a few seconds before she flicks them back to me.

"You two have been spending a lot of time together," she says, and how she says it, it's neither sharp nor cold—it's just a statement. But she shifts her shopping bags in front of her, creating a barrier between us.

She's uncomfortable, and I don't know whether it's me or Sam who makes her uncomfortable. Potentially both? Sam is a reformed alcoholic, and my mother could write a thesis on why Carter girls can't be with men like him, and I'd be lying if I didn't admit that that makes Sam Penny all the more dangerously sexy to me.

"I suppose we have." I give her a tiny shrug. "I'm just being a good host."

"Mmhm." She purses her lips. "How good?"

"God," I scoff. "Mom—"

"Sit," Sam tells her suddenly, interrupting us as he kicks out a chair for her.

She looks a bit alarmed but sits anyway.

Her face is so poised. It's fake. The poise, I mean. And parts of her face, but mostly how poised she is. It's always poised, but it's also always fake. Keeping up appearances is of the utmost importance for Southern women, and the women in the South talk. People live in each other's pockets, know all your secrets, all your business... You have to look together all the time, even if you aren't, because if you don't, the world may as well go to hell in a handbasket.

I don't know what it was like after they sent me away. I wasn't here to see any of the fallout or how it affected her or Dad or their social standing in this weird little place. I was already banished by the time Mom saw Oliver kissing the exchange student by the water one night, but it would have killed her.

Not out of parental empathy, but because it was a social hit.

Everyone knew about me and Beckett because Maryanne made sure everyone did, and there were whispers about Oliver all of his life that Mom not only squashed but misled to dispel.

I overheard her telling her prayer group that they needed to pray for Oliver because she found him with a girl in his room with the door closed, which was either a flat-out lie or I was the girl. Regardless, it was an intentional misdirect and my first peek into the psyche of acceptable sins according to my mother.

She'd rather Oli be a heterosexual fornicator than a gay one. I was a heterosexual fornicator and I too was banished, but that isn't wholly her fault, I've concluded over time, because society has massively different sexual standards for men and women that were imposed onto her too, not just me. She just reacted from those impositions.

"Where's Oliver?" she asks, looking around.

"He's with Vi," I tell her, and she fusses with the hem of her skirt.

Sam nods his chin at her shopping bags. "What do you have planned for the rest of the day?"

"Oh." She bats her hands. "The girls from church are taking me shopping."

"Yeah?" He smiles at her. "For anything in particular?"

He's making an effort. Holding eye contact intentionally. What's he trying with her for, I wonder?

My mom looks at him for a second longer than would be normal, probably because she's wondering the same thing, and then she shakes her head. "Browsing, probably."

"Well, I like that color on you." He motions toward her dress.

Boat neck, cream, sleeveless.

Then Sam Penny smiles at her, and her eyes soften a bit. I wonder how he's so disarming all of the time, because I'm pretty sure that if I said that exact thing to her, she would have rolled her eyes and said, "Listen Georgia, you don't have to like it, only I do."

My mother looks at me, pats my hand. "What are you wearing tomorrow, darling?"

It's not a tender pat. It's more like tapping me back to a consciousness I didn't know I'd lost.

"I don't know yet." I give her a tight smile.

"Nothing to…" She trails. "You know." She gesticulates with her hands as she gives me a look, then clearly decides that's too vague an instruction. "Why don't you borrow something of your sister's?"

I feel the contempt flash across my face.

She gives me a look. "Your sister always looks so lovely."

"And I always look…?" I leave it open-ended for her.

Her mouth twitches, but she says nothing. "And while we're talking about this, make sure Oliver doesn't wear something too…" She leaves it hanging for a second, then leans forward and whispers, "Camp."

She looks around self-consciously, checking if anyone heard her say her version of the C word.

"Oh shit," I sigh, ruefully. "I think he only packed his sparkle rainbow suit."

She rolls her eyes all impatient before she arches her brows. "Is everything a joke to you?"

I open my mouth to say something, but Sam stands up quickly.

"We're running late." He eyes me. It's intentional and communicative: *Let's go.*

I copy him. I don't know why. It's a reflex, I guess?

He stands, I stand. He tosses a fifty-dollar bill on the table.

"We'll see you this afternoon, Margaret." He gives her a gentle smile and then he does something I'm not even remotely expecting: he throws his arm around me and leads me away.

Unfortunately, by "away" I mean just back to the car, not to France or like, a cabin in woods where we have crazy around-the-clock sex, but it is away from my mother, which is something enough, I suppose.

My car's parked around the corner, and when we get to it, he takes the keys from me and then opens the passenger door, waiting for me to get in. I do, and then he does the next thing I'm not expecting: he crouches down next to me.

"Are you okay?" He watches me closely.

His concern for me is becoming less and less masked by the second. The progression of his mannerisms toward me since Monday make me feel like I've swallowed a beehive.

At the start of the week, the night he came to my room, it was the way his eyebrows creased and dipped that made his concern transparent to me, but now I don't need to read bodies to read him. Now his whole face is chiseled with concern. Brows low, head tilted, mouth parted and tongue pressed into his bottom lip, and I'm so jealous of that lucky tongue because I'd quite like to be pressed into his bottom lip too.

I give him a quick nod and drop his gaze, because I know how my eyes look right now too, and I probably look high as a fucking kite.

Sam's mouth twitches as he tries to conceal a smile, and then he closes my door. He sits in the driver's seat.

"Why'd you do that?" I ask. I nod back in the direction of the diner.

"Dodge you getting in a fight with your mom?"

I nod again.

He starts the car and shrugs as he peels out onto the street. "Two reasons." He glances at me. "Today isn't the day you'll get her to see the world the same way you do. And also, her husband just died, so you should be nice to her."

"Well, my dad just died and she's not nice to me," I tell him with tall eyebrows.

He gives me a look like, *really?* But even then, he throws me a bone. "Yeah, I know..."

I cross my arms over my chest. "But you're on her side?"

He gives me the same unimpressed look he gave me a second ago, and I know I'm being a brat, but for some reason exasperating him gives me a rush.

He doesn't bite though, which is annoying. His eyes just fall from my eyes to my mouth then back up again, and then he looks at the road and grips the wheel a little tighter before he lets his hands slip down to three and nine, and you better believe that I'm imagining those hands slipping down me.

"Where are we going?" I ask after a few minutes.

"Cemetery," he tells me as he taps the Google maps on my screen.

I crinkle my nose. "Why?"

"There's something we've got to do."

17

SAM GESTURES HIS HAND AT an empty plot in the ground.

I blink at him. "What?"

"This is your Dad's..." He trails off. "You know..."

"Grave?" I offer.

He scratches his neck. I think he's nervous. "Yeah."

"Why didn't you just say grave?" I ask, watching him for the answer.

And he scratches his ear.

I squint at him. "Why are you nervous?"

And then Sam Penny lets out an exasperated laugh and lets his head fall back toward the sky. "You're so fucking hard to be around."

I frown and he catches it, then grabs me by my arm quickly.

"Hey," he says in a quiet voice as he shakes his head, then ducks down so we're eye level and shifts some hair from my face. "I didn't mean that. I was joking."

He's never done that before, that kind of touching me... It's possessive and threadbare with its intent, and *jarring* is the wrong word because I think that has negative connotations, and trust me when I say that there was nothing negative about it, but something about him touching me startled me.

Maybe because I've wanted him to since I met him?

It's not the residue of what happened with Beckett, by the way. I've had sex a lot of times since then with other people, which involves substantially more action than arm-grabbing and hair-brushing, and I was fine. It's a different sort of startled. Startled in my heart, maybe? Because Sam should be a stranger to me, but he isn't. Like I've dreamt of him all my life and I've just woken up and it's bleeding through, and I know him…

I know I don't know him, but I know him. And I hope he knows me too.

"So why are you nervous?" I ask again, trying to regain control of the situation or, at the very least, of myself.

"Because I don't want to fuck this up."

I try not to smile and lift my eyebrows up instead. "Fuck what up?"

"Shit—I mean—" I try not to look too smug over his parapraxis. He shakes his head at me, half-amused, half-serious. "I don't want to upset you."

I arch my eyebrow. "Why would you upset me?"

He scratches his neck again, but he doesn't know he's doing it. "I want you to talk to your dad." He gestures to the square hole in the ground.

I look from the hole back to him. "There's no one in there."

He rolls his eyes. "There's no one in 'there'"—he uses air quotes—"anymore anyway. It's about closure."

"I don't need closure." I fold my hands over my chest. "I'm fine."

"You"—he ducks his head so we're eye to eye again—"haven't dealt with your dad dying at all."

"Yes, I have." I say but it comes out a bit like a sigh. A weak lie at best.

"How?" He shrugs with his eyebrows. "And when?"

"I don't know—in the—" I let out a frustrated noise. "I don't care—"

"Bullshit," he says, confident in his diagnosis.

"Don't—" I point at him as I sigh out of my nose, annoyed. "I don't like it when you do that to me."

He nods. "I know you don't."

I give him a look. "Then stop."

"I will—" he concedes. "After you talk to him."

"Penny—"

And then he does it again—he reaches for me, pushes some hair behind my ears, and I stare at him with big, wide eyes.

"Do you trust me?" he asks, head tilted with perfect sincerity.

I groan a little, and he lifts his eyebrows as if to say "Do you?"

I give him a glare and put my hands on my hips. "You're fucking this up."

He gives me a gentle push toward the plot in the ground. "No, I'm not."

No, he's not. That fucking know-it-all.

I cross my hands over my chest and then shove them through my hair. "What am I—I don't know what to say. Where am I speaking?"

He stands behind me. Like, very behind me...*behind me* behind me. Close enough that I can feel the warmth of him against the back of me. So close enough that I can feel his breathing on my neck, and it's so steady and there's something about the steadiness of Sam Penny that makes me feel sad and afraid and hopeful and lost and confused, and I find myself longing for that steadiness, which I've never really had in anyone before but wish I had in my dad.

Sam points to the hole in the ground to focus me.

I clear my throat.

Then I say nothing.

He nudges me again and I turn around to glare at him, but it's a very disempowered glare because our faces are so close, and being near him like this feels like smelling petrol—you just keep inhaling forever. I can't completely tell which way's up and which way's down anymore.

"Hi, Dad," I say uncomfortably. I clear my throat again. "Sorry about your heart attack—"

"Fuck, Georgia." Sam sighs and laughs at the same time. Then he clears his throat. "Hey, Mr. Carter," he says from over my shoulder. "We didn't get a chance to meet—I'm Sam. Penny. I'm um—" He pauses. "I'm Oliver's AA sponsor." I feel him nodding behind me. "You'd be really proud of him. He's done a lot of good, hard work. I'm here with your daughter—she's like, really fucking cool too. Kind of weird and sometimes annoying," he concedes, "but...pretty great."

I try not to smile too much.

"You'd be proud of her—I don't know how much you talked. She's pretty quiet about you. But she's super smart…I mean, Cambridge-smart. And she's a total knock-out," he adds, and I'm so glad he can't see my face, because I'm not just the cat who got the cream; I'm the cat who got the whole fucking cow. "Doesn't really know how to talk to people if she can't see their faces, though, so I think this is kind of hard for her, or something…because you're—" He lowers his voice. "Dead."

I laugh once and turn around to face him.

Our faces couldn't be more than seven inches apart.

"I don't know what to say," I tell him, frowning, feeling like I'm somehow failing both him and my dad.

"The truth, Gige." He gives me a gentle look.

And I'm aware he's never called me that before, and I've never really cared what people call me, but my nickname in his mouth makes my stomach do a backflip.

Sam nudges me. "Tell him how you feel."

I shake my head.

"Georgia, when are you coming back to South Carolina?"

I frown. "Um—never."

"Then you might never get to tell him how you feel again."

"It's a hole in the ground!" I point at it and he turns me back to face it, but leaves his hands on both my arms, and it makes me feel safe. Psychologically safe. Him holding me how he's holding me gives my brain permission to look at feelings I've otherwise thrown blankets over in the back of my mind.

I take a big breath. "I am…" I pause, and Sam squeezes my arms again. "Angry at you."

I nod once. "I'm angry at you. And I didn't like you very much. Not often, anyway." I pause. "I don't know whether you've gotten worse in my mind with the distance and over time or if you were just kind of always shitty? I really—I don't know. I hated you for how you dealt with Oliver's sexuality. I hated you for how you let others treat him because of it." I hold my breath for a second. Sam moves in closer behind me. "I wonder sometimes, if you had treated him differently, would everyone else have? You set the tone for the whole family. Tennyson loves what you loved. Mom would believe that the earth was flat and made of cardboard if you told her, so if you had just..." I trail off, shake my head, and take a breath.

Sam shifts behind me, closer again, and now he rests his chin on top of my head, and then his arms slip from my arms to around my body. I could close my eyes and cry about how supremely and surprisingly unlonely I feel as I talk to my dead dad via a hole in the ground.

"Keep going," Sam says, but it's muffled by my hair.

"You were good at providing"—I nod to myself—"for us. Fiscally, I mean. You were good at providing for us like that, but what does that count for? I don't know." I shrug. "Maybe I'm just ungrateful..." I trail off again and then find that my voice gets a little caught in my throat as I say, "I kind of just wanted a dad."

Sam shifts behind me, and I wouldn't say he kissed the back of my head, but I certainly wouldn't *not* say that either. I guess I'd say that technically he pressed his mouth against the back of my head. I think I'd maybe allow myself to call it a Freudian Kiss. Which isn't a thing; it's a thing I just invented now, but if it was a thing, that'd be the thing it would be.

I don't think Sam would say he kissed my head either. I would say he wanted to, though, and this makes me braver.

Not that the boy I think I like not-kissing me makes me brave, because I'm all for self-empowerment and being brave on my own. But there's much to be said about being believed in.

"You didn't really know me," I tell my dad. "You didn't even try. And now you're dead, so I can't know you either."

And then I feel sad and angry and I spin around so I'm face-to-face with Sam.

"Can I stop now?"

His face looks raw and his eyes look ragged as they snag on my mouth. He nods quickly, then pushes some hair behind my ears again. "Let's go."

18

THE GRAVEYARD THING MADE US different with each other.

You know how there's an invisible threshold you cross when you like someone where you go from just friends to something else? I don't know what the something else is, and even though technically Sam and I are still just friends—if that, if we're speaking on a technicality—the proxemics would imply there's been a shift.

The standard interpersonal distance for talking and interacting with friends is one and a half to four feet, but Sam and I now don't tend to be farther than one foot apart from one another whenever we can help it.

That sounds so sterile, I know, but actually it isn't. It's sort of romantic, because when someone's standing that close to you, it reduces your vision field around you, which means you have to rely on your other senses, like smell and touch.

When we get home, Oliver isn't there yet, which means Vi must have taken him shopping, or maybe he's found a cute boy. I hope he finds a cute boy, because then we both have, and Oliver can fall in love with him, and I can run away with Sam, and Dad's funeral won't be just a depression spiral waiting to happen.

I'm not even fully sure how it happens, it just sort of does—I guess we were walking down by the lake or something, but Sam and I end up in the *SS Avoidance*.

It's just sitting there, floating by the dock, and I've never even been on the boat with anyone but Oliver because it was a rule we had when we were teenagers—that we wouldn't because it was just ours, but Oliver's not here, and he's broken that rule himself a couple of times.

So me and Sam, we don't row out into the water; we just lie there next to each other, staring at the sky from the floor of the boat, which is tied to the dock so it can't go anywhere. I hope that isn't a metaphor for me and Sam.

I also wonder why he hasn't kissed me.

Our proximity is appropriate for a nonawkward kiss, and he's wanted to before, I could tell—but now he has me lying down in a boat and he's just looking at the clouds?

"Do you believe in heaven?" Sam asks the sky.

I glance over at him. "Yeah."

He looks at me, surprised. "Really?"

I nod. "Really."

He props himself up on his elbows. "So you believe in God?"

"Yeah." I copy his posture. "Don't you?"

He looks at me dubiously. "No."

I frown a little. "Why?"

"I don't know." He scratches his head, thinking. "I just—some things don't add up, you know? Like, he's supposed to be this big God of love or fucking whatever and then he sends everyone to hell if they don't believe in him?"

And his eyes look sad, and I know we're talking about his mom now.

"I think your mom's in heaven," I tell him.

He flicks his eyes, amused and maybe a little caught. "She was a Buddhist." He gives me a weak shrug. "She doesn't fit the bill."

I squint at him because it's all I can do to keep myself from touching him. If I look at him properly, I'll have to touch him, I'll just have to; he's too beautiful not to. "I think in the Bible, the point is that Jesus paid the bill."

"What about all that repenting shit? And you've got to whatever through Jesus to get into heaven."

I snort a laugh.

"What?" He frowns playfully.

"You've never been this vague or ineloquent about any topic ever."

He sniffs a laugh.

"Here's what I think." And I sit up to tell him. "People read the Bible wrong. It's a diary of normal people, like us, from thousands of years ago, trying to make sense of the God they'd heard of from their ancestors. They didn't write it for us to read it now. And I think people read it without the true social or historical context, and they bring their own instead."

Sam watches me, listening.

"That God that my mom thinks she serves—he's so much smaller than who I think the real one is. The real one—to me, he's everywhere, in everything. And sure, maybe he speaks through the Bible. But also maybe he speaks through Narnia, and Harry Potter despite J. K. Rowling lately, and the trees, and science, and the stars, and black holes and the ocean and the way the sky looks sometimes, and you can feel it in your chest."

I glance at Sam, and there's a hint of a little smile on his face.

"And I don't think they're not letting your mom into heaven because she didn't believe in the God that modern Christianity claims to represent. I think he's good." I shrug. "And I think he loves everyone, and he wants everyone to be okay, and I think almost everyone who is, like, earnestly seeking God—people aren't seeking that out of ego; they're looking for the meaning of life and they're looking beyond themselves for it—and, I mean, I don't know anything, except that I think God is the kind of guy who when someone dies, he'll sit there and sift through every heartfelt thought, every drunken prayer, every desperate plea for help, every Mumford & Sons song that you've sung to look for a hint of a confession that you believe in him."

Sam purses his mouth and nods once. "Your God sounds pretty cool, I guess."

19

THERE WAS ONE TIME WHEN we were younger—not long before they sent me away, actually—when Oliver and this boy from our school, Louis Janson, ran away for the weekend together.

Neither of them were out of the closet, but they had a weird cover story and everything in case they got caught. And here's the sort of weird world that we live in: instead of telling our parents that they needed to go away for something to do with a school project, they decided to skip town without telling anyone (except me), and if they got caught (which they would and they did), then they'd lie and say they drove to Atlanta to meet up with a couple of girls they met online.

I got home from the library that Saturday evening, and you know how sometimes you walk into a place and you can just feel it? I walked into the house and it hit me in a single second...this weird tension.

My dad was away, I don't know where—that wasn't crazy unusual—but there was a man standing in our kitchen. Louis Janson's father. He had a dark look about him.

Oliver had told me bits and pieces about how hard it was for Louis. Louis's dad was the school's football coach. Louis was on the wrestling squad for school, and rumors always swirled that there was a reason he played a sport where he rolled around with other guys. I remember

Oliver saying that however weird our dad was about Oliver, Mr. Janson was a million times worse. As though his son's (unconfirmed) sexuality threatened his own. But isn't that just always the way?

As soon as I walked in, my mom and Mr. Janson stood up from the table.

"Where are they?" my mom asked, folding her arms over her chest.

I know better now, but at the time, my mouth would have pulled down a little and tightened as I swallowed nervously. "I don't know what you're talking about."

"Where is Oliver?" my mom demanded, walking over to me.

"How would I know?" I shrugged, and Maryanne and Beckett appeared at the doorway, observing.

"You always know," my mother tells me.

"You're his mother." I pushed past her to open the fridge. "Isn't that your job?"

She slammed it shut. "Tell me, right now."

I turned to look at her slowly. "I. Do not. Know," I overenunciate.

Of course I knew. I always knew. Oliver told me everything, every single thing.

And then Mr. Janson rushed me—grabbed me by the arms and held me tight enough that I'd bruise the next day.

"Where are they?" he growled.

And here's something that would fuck me up for a real long time after this: I looked at Becks, not my mom—who, by the way, was frozen still with nerves or fear or horror, I don't know—because she was no help. So with my eyebrows low with worry, my breath quickening, feeling a little bit in danger, I found myself looking to Beckett Lane. I didn't know why at the time, but that wasn't even the part that fucked me up the most. The part that really pulled a number on me was Beckett's face, staring at Mr. Janson's hands gripping my arm.

And I didn't have to know how to read faces back then to know what Becks was feeling. Beck's eyes were so dark and angry; his jaw was tight and his brow was set. He wanted to kill that man.

"You listen to me," Mr. Janson yelled, shaking me back to his attention.

"Hey, let her go," Beckett called over to him, but Mr. Janson kept going.

"Your piece o' shit brother has taken my boy to some sinful hellhole, and I want you to tell me where, right now, or so help me God—"

I stared him square in the eyes and conjured up the most convincing face I knew how to make at the time. "I don't know!" I cried, lying. "I swear it—I have no idea! I haven't seen Oliver since yesterday morning!"

He was still gripping me, and no one was helping me, and I was worried no one would, so I remember thinking I needed to focus on the pain—think about how he was hurting my arm, and that maybe then my eyes would get teary and he'd feel bad and drop it—

And for a second, it worked. Mr. Janson's face softened, his grip loosened, and his jaw unclenched.

"She's lying." Maryanne yawned from the doorway.

Beckett's head snapped over in her direction, eyes all wide, maybe a little bit appalled, definitely a bit angry—but Maryanne didn't even clock him, just stared over at me, holding my gaze.

"She's lying, Mama." She walked all the way into the kitchen, arms folded over her chest, eyebrows cocked. "I saw her last night—she was talking to Oliver in the driveway. He had a weekend bag and she hugged him goodbye."

And then the grip was tighter again, and Mr. Janson was angrier than he was a minute ago, and he slammed me backwards into the fridge.

"Whoa—" Beckett sort of barreled toward us, but Maryanne grabbed him by the back of his T-shirt, stopping him in his tracks. I saw them exchange looks—

"Tell me where my son is, you lyin' little bitch," Mr. Janson spat.

"Go to hell," I spat right back.

"Okay," my mom says, peeling Mr. Janson's arms off of me. "It's time you leave—"

"Your"—here he said that word that starts with an *F* that bigots like him like to use sometimes—"kid's got my boy and she knows where—"

"Get out," my mom told him, pointing to the door. "Get out, right now. Or I swear to God himself, Nolan—I will light you up and make damn sure the whole town knows about it."

Mr. Janson let go of me, and my mother marched him to the door, slamming it behind him. She walked back into the kitchen, and I was flooded with an overwhelming sense of gratitude for her, which was both rare and unnerving for me.

"Mom, I—" I started, but she interrupted me.

"Go to your room."

I blinked, confused. "What?"

"Go to your room and do not even think about leaving it until your brother comes back."

"But I—"

"You don't think I know when you're lying to me?" she yelled, frantic. "I always know! You think you're so clever, Georgia, but you're not; you're just lyin'. Always lyin'! To cover your behind...to protect a boy who at the minute is probably going to hell anyway. You wanna protect him, you start praying for his soul to straighten out." She pointed up the stairs. "Now go!"

Oliver and Louis didn't come back until late Sunday night, and my mother was staunch with her threat. I wasn't allowed to leave the room. Every time I tried, I was sent straight back.

It was the longest weekend of my life. Beckett visited a lot.

By the time Oliver got home, sporting his story of an internet romance with some girl online (a lie that was readily swallowed by our desperate mother), he was presented with his consequences, and then he came and fell face down on my bed.

He glanced up at me, tired, ready to say something, but took one look at me and frowned. "What happened?"

I didn't have the words.

I couldn't tell him, none of it.

Telling him about Louis's dad was only the tip of the iceberg, and that alone would have destroyed him with guilt anyway. Telling him about Becks—it was too late and it was too far in and it had happened so many times by then. I was too confused by what it meant that I looked at him for help and why he looked angry when someone hurt me, and what it meant that he tried to stop it when someone was hurting me. Those are questions you never should have to ponder about your sexual assailant, least of all when you're fifteen, and yet there I was, marooned in a despair I felt like I was drowning in and gagged into a self-imposed silence because I was too little to know how to deal with any of it.

And then I started to cry.

"Gige." My brother's face crumbled in concern.

And his concern made me cry more, loud and ugly and anguished, and he hugged me and asked me what was wrong a thousand times, but all I did was cry until I was asleep.

When I woke up a few hours later, Oliver hadn't moved; he was just watching me, frowning, staring at me like I was a crooked picture on the wall he couldn't quite get straight.

I swore nothing happened, that it was my period and that I was fine.

He didn't believe me; he knew me too well to believe that.

If he was more like me, he would have pushed. The truth, no matter the cost. But all our lives, Oliver has loved me in a way where he'd never hurt me; even if hurting me meant loving me the most, he couldn't. You might argue that means he doesn't love me that much, but you'd be wrong.

There are a lot of kinds of love in the world, and not all of them make sense all of the time. The way love was delivered to Oliver, full of conditions and hoops to jump through and lies to abide by, being loved and being hurt were two sides of the same coin. How that translated in the way he loved me was this: He would never force me to tell him something; he'd never push me; he'd never challenge me in a serious way; he would never do anything to ostracize me or make me uncomfortable. He loved me a dysfunctional amount, and love and dysfunction are a peculiar pairing that flavor everything with a specific brand of contradiction. See, Oliver loved me so much—too much, you might even say—that he'd rather leave me hurting if it meant it hurt me less at the time.

After maybe an hour or so on the *SS Avoidance* with Sam, we head back into the house and find Oliver there, sitting on the couch, looking bored.

Sam grins at him when he spots him and grabs Oliver affectionately by the shoulders, and my brother's face lights up. His eyes go a little wider, a little smile emerges, and I wonder if I see some pink spring to his cheeks.

"Where the fuck have you two been?" my brother huffs.

Sam thumbs toward the dock and I'm already cringing before he says it. "Georgia took me on the boat."

Oliver tenses up, swallows once. He nods coolly. "Oh."

Sam flicks his eyes in my direction, confused.

I purse my lips, a little guilty.

Sam catches the vibe and drums on Oliver's shoulders, which he's still holding. "What'd you get up to today, man? Where've you been?"

Oliver shifts his body to block me completely from the conversation, so I sit down next to him to reinclude myself.

"Vi and I had such a good morning." He's only talking to Sam. "We chatted about life, and love and death, and it was so good for the soul—I can't wait for you to get to know her better; she's really the best, most authentic, loyal"—I think that was a jab at me—"person you'll ever meet—we could grab dinner with her now?" Oliver offers, hopeful.

"Yeah." Sam nods as his eyes trail over to me—that's definitely not lost on Oliver. The *yeah* is open-ended, as though Sam's asking me a question—his eyes hold mine and he swallows once. He's getting really bad at concealing his faces. "Georgia, what are y—"

"She's busy," Oliver tells him.

Sam's mouth goes a little tight, and he bangs his clenched fist on Oliver's shoulder twice. Gestural slips. Something's bothered him.

"...Yes." I nod once. "I'm...busy." It's my worst lie in about nine hundred years, but I'm shitty at Oliver for excluding me and I want to make him look stupid to Sam.

Sam Penny's mouth twitches how it does when his eyes are on me, like we're up to our necks in secrets. "I've got to run to the bathroom," he says, holding my eyes intentionally, full of concern. He wants to know whether I'm okay.

I give him a tiny, singular nod to tell him I am, and then he jogs upstairs.

Oliver turns to me immediately, eyes wild. "You took him on our boat!" he yells. "You're unbelievable!"

"Oliver," I start, but he shakes his head, angry.

"You'll do anything for a guy."

That feels like a slap. It also doesn't feel like my brother at all.

"Whoa." I blink as I take shallow breaths. "I—what?"

"We swore, Georgia!" he says loudly. "We swore we'd never bring anyone onto our boat except us!"

I let out an exasperated laugh, looking at him like he's crazy. "Yeah! I know!" I nod, emphatically. "I know what we promised! I know what we said our deal was. But don't you come at me like you're the fucking high emperor of maritime law when I know for a fact that on at least two occasions you have fucked randoms atop our innermost secrets and adolescent memories—"

Oliver freezes. "I—"

"Seriously?" I give him a look and shake my head with a shrug. "I saw you, Oliver. I saw you with the exchange student—a few times, actually! And then once with some guy I didn't recognize." I give him a *so fuck you* look. "And shut the fuck up. If I want to take Sam on the boat, I'll take him on the fucking boat."

Oliver glares over at me. "He's not here for you, Georgia; he's here for me."

And now, the way he said that—I don't know—it sounds like Oliver resents me.

Which is ironic, actually. Because I know for certain that there's at least a part of me that resents him.

I shouldn't, but I think I do. Nothing that happened was his fault. He didn't make what happened to me with Beckett happen. He didn't make our parents like my sister more than me. He didn't make me pick him over the rest of my family. He didn't ask me to give him half of my inheritance. And I'd do it again and again because it was unjust how they treated him and what they did to him. How they excluded him burns me up inside. But watching him piss away what I lost my family to give him—that stung.

And I'm sure the hypothetical life I'd have if I hadn't given him the money looks better in my imagination than what it would have actually been in reality… In no world are Maryanne and I best friends, or even friends. In no world does my mom like me more than her. But I think what I did fractured me and Oliver.

Him with the pressure of what our relationship cost me, and me with the weight of what I lost. And how, no matter what I'd do or how hard I'd try, I couldn't repair the damage our family caused my brother.

So Oliver and I might be the Adjectives, but our personal adjective is *broken*.

"Yeah, fine, Ol." I shrug, annoyed and tired. "So who's here for me?"

Oliver gives me the meanest look he's maybe ever given me. "Beckett?"

I pull my head back, mouth ajar.

What the fuck.

"Okay!" Vi says, walking into the room. "Let's you and me"—she points between her and me—"let's go, right now."

She grabs me by the hand and pulls me away.

"And you." She points at Oliver, eyeing him. She shakes her head. "Dick move."

20

ARE YOU OKAY?" VI ASKS as soon as we're in the car.

I give her a wary look. "Oliver has never ever, ever, ever in my whole life deliberately tried to hurt me. Never. I—" I shake my head, still can't really believe it. "Never has he even come close to holding what happened with Beckett against me—"

"I know, sweet pea." Her face pulls like it's hurting her too. "He's just tender right now."

I mean, no fucking shit he's tender, but what he's tender about is what worries me.

Or who, maybe.

"Has he been spending time with Maryanne?"

She sighs and rattles her head around. So that's a yes.

"He used to be just mine." I find myself frowning.

"Baby, you worked so hard to make him feel accepted in this family—"

"But Maryanne isn't accepting him; she's manipulating him."

"How do you know?" Vi frowns.

Oh gee, I don't know, Violet. I have a master's degree in psychology and behavioral science from Cambridge, and I'm a year and a half into my PhD while working for one of the foremost behavioral experts in my field.

But I just look out the window as I sigh and say, "Because she manipulates everybody."

Vi gives me a long look, both sad and curious. "You still dating that guy back in London?"

I roll my eyes. "You know I'm not."

She plays offended. "How would I know you're not?"

I eye her. "Why don't you just come out and ask what you're stepping around...?"

"All right." She nods. "You sleeping with that Sam boy?"

"What the fuck?" I bang my hands on the dash. "No! No, I'm not!"

She glances at me. "But you want to?"

I shake my head, annoyed, somehow feeling condemned over my past and judged for my future all at once. "Well, I mean—yeah!" I stutter. "Of course, yes—have you seen him?"

"I—yeah. I get it." She nods again. "He is—wow."

"Right?" I blink.

She eyes me playfully. "Well, does he want you back?"

I roll my head back, pretending I don't like the conversation. "I don't know!"

The corner of her mouth tugs in disbelief. "You don't know?" She snorts. "Yes, you do."

"Fine," I relent with a laugh. "Yes, I know."

"Well?" She blinks, expectantly.

"Is romance dead?" I yell in loud exasperation.

"No, but my brother is—" She gives me a look. "So just throw me a goddamn bone."

"Does dead brother trump dead father?"

She sniffs a laugh. "Probably not normally, but you didn't like him that much, so."

It hurts her to say that; it's plain all over her face. The way it pulls and pinches. She's never let it affect us, but it has, on many occasions, complicated things.

She loved my dad. Loves? Loves, I think is the appropriate tense. I don't think you just stop loving someone once they're suddenly gone. I think that's what makes it hard.

Violet loves him. Always has. She's never loved him in a blind way, though. She knows he was a garbage dad to Oliver and then consequently me as well. She knows, and I remember watching it shred her every time he acted like less than the man she thought he was.

That makes it tricky. It was always hard for me to figure out which was my real dad. The guy she knew or the guy we knew? She's mourning the guy she knew.

It's weird, they're not alike at all. She's fun and free and creative and brave, and he was, like—painfully straight-laced. Not passionate or interested in anything really, beyond planes. He loves planes. I never saw his nose in a book, I never saw him see something he thought was beautiful and stop to look at it… Just the most restrained man on the planet.

I know she's trying to avoid it, hiding behind me and Oliver and being there for other people, but avoiding grief is a kind of grief. It's what we do when we can't feel what we need to feel to progress. I know that's true because I do it too. I think I'm doing it right now.

"Are you okay?" I ask her, half in case no one else has and half so she can't ask me.

She gives me a smile that's trying to be brave but isn't; she just watches me for a few seconds out of the corner of her eye.

"You and me," she sighs. "We're not that different. I never fit in with my mom and dad. Philip's an asshole and a dumbass, so your dad was always the only one I liked. And now, besides Clay, Phil's the only one I got left."

"You've got me?" I offer, and she reaches over to touch my face.

"Yes, honey. I guess do."

She pulls up to the Saks OFF Fifth, just outside of Bluffton.

"Tell me," she says, as we walk inside. "How's your mom doing?"

I take a big breath. "Are you asking me the daughter or me the nearly-psychologist?"

"Both," she says as she picks up a black dress from Roberto Cavalli and holds it against herself.

"From a professional standpoint, she's experiencing what's classified as traumatic grief—"

"As opposed to what?"

"Anticipatory," I say as I inspect a pair of Attico's Grid studded sling-backs that are too bedazzled for a funeral but I think I'll buy anyway. "Can I get these in an eight, please?" I hand them to a sale assistant nearby and then I look over at Vi. "She's in what they call the 'numbing phase.' It's when everything hurts too much to fully comprehend it, so she doesn't..."

Vi gives me a long, pointed look. "It sounds familiar."

I'm self-aware enough to have already wondered whether that's the phase of grief that I'm in, and maybe I'm in an abstract part of it, but my mother's grief and my grief are incomparable because our relationships with the deceased are also incomparable.

"Mom's in a phase of adaptation." And I smirk because she'd hate the word—she thinks it's unbiblical—but it's true, she is. "She has to relearn her place in the world without Dad, and I don't think she's the sort of person who'd have thought about it much before now. So I think she's doing okay." I shrug. "Relatively." I glance up at Vi. "For who she's lost and how suddenly she's lost him, I think she's doing okay."

"And what does daughter-you think?" Vi asks, handing me the black Gramercy pleated stretch-jersey maxi dress from Staud.

"I've contemplated trying to get her drunk and make her take the Inventory of Complicated Grief so I can gauge where she's at officially."

"That sounds like psychologist-you still."

I sniff a laugh. "We're melding."

She leans in toward me and gives me a smile that's laced with a lot of pain.

"Make sure you're doing some grieving too."

21

GROWING UP, OLIVER'S ROOM AND my room were in the far wing of the house at the end of a fairly open corridor that turned into a narrow corridor with a bathroom at the end of it.

After shit started to happen with Beckett a bit repetitively, I began to drink a bit, just to blur the nights a little, but never ever like Oliver. If I could have read people then like I can now, I would have spotted the dependency beginning to develop.

On the weekends when Maryanne would most likely bring Becks over, Oli and I would sit in our bathroom and drink champagne. I'd sit in the bathtub, no water, clothes on, drinking so that I was never in less control than I already was in the rest of my life, but just enough to take the edge off the lack of it.

Oliver would drink till he was sloppy.

My parents had to know—had to—he was hungover most mornings, but like I said before with "acceptable sins"… *Selective awareness* is another way to put it.

I didn't mind how ostracizing our bedroom placements were for the most part, but I also think it made things easier for Becks. Oliver's overdrinking became a part of the pattern, actually, because eventually Becks would come looking for me, and we'd be in the bathroom, and he'd help Oliver back to bed, tuck him in, nudge his cheek, put some water by his bed, and then he'd come back for me.

Whether I stayed in the bath or moved back to my bedroom, it didn't really matter.

This fucked me up for a long time, made me wonder whether I fed into it. Whether I helped him or let him. Whether me drinking led him on.

This all of course took place during that horrible age where expressed and/or obvious consent was really emphasized, and I think what happened to me dwelled in neither the black nor the white. There wasn't language for that at the time—but I believe now "gray rape" is the umbrella term—to help us wade through nuances and conversationally facilitate the complexities of what Ashley C. Ford so aptly refers to as the "spectrum of harm."

It took me a long time to realize that something doesn't have to always feel wrong to be wrong. It doesn't even have to be violent to be wrong. But I was fourteen, and he'd kiss me and I wouldn't kiss him back, and he'd push me down on a bed and climb on top of me, and he would touch all of me, and I'd be stiff as a board, and he never stopped.

Maybe he'd say I never stopped him. I never did, I guess.

Maryanne never again came looking for him when he'd disappear. I know she knew it was happening still, in an active way. I know she knew it wasn't a once-off, because one night after Becks had finished with me and had gone home, she stood in my doorway, and I remember how her face looked: deep with concentration—like she was trying to work me out. Furrowed brows, pinched eyes—nothing super telling, no real reason I'd remember the way she was looking at me that night except for the words she said.

"Why you and not me?" she asked, head tilted. Her eyes were full of tears, which was misleading. Sociopaths don't feel empathy. These tears weren't for me. They were frustration tears.

Why me and not her? She needed to know. She'd wanted him for so long... What was she doing wrong?

"Why?" she asked again, standing over me.

I didn't say anything; I just stared up at her because I didn't really understand why then either. I hadn't even really identified the betrayal that happened when she walked in on it the first time and did nothing.

I wouldn't realize for years how heavy that weighed on me, but it did. It does still, I suppose.

I thought all that shit would mean I hate being in my bedroom here, that it would be triggering or uncomfortable, but there's something about coming back and sleeping in that room that makes me feel…stronger, I guess?

This does mean, however, that my bedroom and where Sam Penny's sleeping are directly opposite one another.

You can bet your bottom dollar I've left my bedroom door ajar when I've done quick changes, and he's never once accidentally seen me partially naked, but Oliver has, unfortunately.

"Ew," was all he said. Gay brothers are so good for your ego.

It's Thursday night, I'm home from dress shopping with Vi, and Oliver and Sam are nowhere to be seen—they've been out for hours, and I don't like being in the house without either of them here.

I heard my mom come up the stairs before—she called for me—and I actually hid in my closet. It occurred to me while I was hiding in there that if she found me, it would be fairly inexplicable, but I didn't have it in me to hear whatever it was she wanted to say to me.

So I've spent most of the night in my bed, pretending to sleep so that my mom keeps not talking to me, and it's been rolling around my brain what it'd be like to roll around with Sam Penny, and I feel a little shitty about that because Dad's funeral is tomorrow, but honestly, for all we know after what Tennyson said, maybe Dad was rolling around with someone who wasn't Mom, so I should be allowed to think about Sam, and fuck you, Dad, anyway.

There is one hitch in my Sam Penny daydream, though. One thing that my mind keeps snagging on.

What Oliver's face did when Sam touched him this afternoon—I've pored over it a hundred times, put it under the microscope in my brain… I even checked the FACS for microexpressions I might be missing, but there were a few I decided I didn't want to know he was making.

But the microexpressions I didn't want to check played on a loop in my mind, because I knew them anyway. AU1 straight off the bat with a AU6 and a AU12 in its slipstream.

In their crudest form? Surprise, then happiness.

Fuck me.

Oliver's lying on his bed in one of the guest rooms, door ajar, shirt off, and somehow he looks posed? And I wonder whether he's doing the same thing with the door that I am.

"Hey." He looks away from the TV and gives me a lazy smile. "What's up?"

Sibling relationships are weird. There's this elasticity to them that's both comforting and dangerous. Oliver said something sublimely hurtful to me earlier, and I know that he knew it hurt me, even without him knowing all the facts surrounding it. I know he knows what he said about Becks would have been like a punch in my face, and yet there is no apology.

And there doesn't really need to be. Even if there should be.

Maybe it's that "blood is thicker than water" shit that everyone misquotes, or maybe—more likely—it's attachment bonds, which are real and powerful, and I think Oliver and I are bound by at least two: familial and selective social.

Our relational pattern, until now, would have him believe that he can say or do anything he wants to me and we'll just…rubber-band back to being who we were before it happened. He is right—kind of. But elastic wears over time. It stretches more, gets thinner, loses its shape. Even when you want it to snap back to what it was, it doesn't always work like that.

I sit on the edge of his bed. "What are you watching?"

He nods toward the TV. *Outlander*, season one. I mean—who can blame him? Jamie Fraser, hello.

And then I wonder the worst possible thing: Do me and my brother have the same taste in boys?

When we were kids, we both loved Devon Sawa and JTT. We used to send each other Harry Styles photos all the time. We were equally as infatuated with both boys in *Pearl Harbor*.

There was one time in high school where I think we liked the same boy, which was already complicated to me because I liked him during the Becks Phase, and one of my coping mechanisms for the Becks Phase was wondering whether I had feelings for Beckett—I think because if I did, maybe it would have meant that what was happening to me wasn't happening against my will? Or that maybe if I liked him, it wouldn't be so bad? I didn't like him, though. I think I tried to tell myself I did, but it became apparent that I didn't actually, because I for certain did have actual feelings for Toby Lindholm. I think Toby also had feelings for me, because one time he came to a big party Oliver threw while my parents were at a conference, and Toby was in Oliver's grade, and Oliver had been talking to him for a bit of the night, but now, in retrospect, I can see Toby was talking to Oliver to talk to me, and then Toby kissed me in the kitchen, and I guess Oliver saw it, and he wasn't weird about it, but he wasn't not weird about it either?

And I didn't really understand what was wrong; maybe I was still trying to see the world in black and white. I couldn't comprehend why Oliver—who I knew liked boys—would waste his time liking a boy who didn't like boys.

Delightfully simplistic.

"You're a bitch," Maryanne told me after Toby kissed me. I don't think she was even truly incensed by what happened as much as she likes to take every opportunity she has to disparage me. I don't know how she knew. I guess there's an implication there that Oliver at least cared enough about Toby to tell Maryanne about it. He's done that before—when we're fighting, or something's off between us, he'll go to Maryanne, and she'll accept him with (conditional) open arms for as long as it's beneficial for her to do so. It used to kill me when he'd do it;

the betrayal of it would press down on me like a boot on my neck. And now that I'm older, I get it, how alone he was in our family. It would have been terrifying. He needed an ally, and he'd find an easy one in Maryanne when the common ground was hating me.

I stare over at my brother lying on the bed, fold my arms over my chest, and make sure I have prime viewing before I ask him what I'm about to.

"Do you like him?"

"What?" Oliver says quickly and blinks four times. "No."

His head doesn't move with his words. He takes a sharp breath and holds it in. Automatically I look up at the shape his eyebrows are making, and I'm about to replay in my mind the way his mouth just sagged at the edges, but then—I do something I never do. I stop myself from reading him. This is the answer he's giving me, so this is the answer I'll take.

And you can slice it any way you like; I can tell you all day till the cows come home that I'm just respecting my brother's right to privacy and that's why I'm not going to read his face, but that's a fucking lie and we all know it.

The truth is I don't want the truth, not this time.

So I just nod and flash him a smile. "Okay."

I close his door behind me on my way out and walk back toward my bedroom, down the other end of the hallway where Oliver's staying, right as Sam Penny walks out of the bathroom holding a pile of clothes, only a towel around his waist.

I take one look at him and smack the hallway lights out as I pass them, because eyes naturally dilate in the dark and it won't be as obvious that I want to jump his bones.

Sam stops outside his doorway, waiting for me. He gives me a long look for a quick second. "You okay?"

I smile up at him, suddenly feeling tired and less okay than I thought I was. "Yeah," I lie.

"Did you find something for tomorrow?"

"Mhm." I nod. "I see you haven't." I poke his bare abdomen. Rock-hard. Lust pools in my stomach. Kill me.

He presses his lips together and swallows. "I'm sorry about before," he starts. "I don't know why Ol went—"

"No." I shake my head. "I know you're not here for me. I'm sorry if I've commandeered so much of your time."

"No," he says quickly. "You haven't. Your—" And even in this darkness I've thrown us into, I can see his eyes shift from my eyes to my mouth, where they hover, and then he drags them back up to my eyes.

Our proximity in this moment is undoubtedly less than one foot, less than half a foot, and the corridor we're in allows for more space between us than that, but it's obvious we have neither want nor need for it.

"I'm what?" I ask him quietly, and my breathing has quickened.

Sam slips his hand around my waist and jerks me quickly in toward him.

Proximity report:
Chests: pressed against one another.
Feet: overlapping
Faces: four inches, at most.

This close to him now, I can make these nonverbal, nonvisual observations:

His hands aren't clammy or sweaty at all, nor are they cold. They're warm. He's not nervous.

His grip is strong, so he is sure of what he wants, and I am it.

His breathing is steady-paced and deep. He's calm.

And with my legs pressed against him, I can attest that he is definitely packing, and in this moment, very locked and loaded.

"Your—" He swallows, then clears his throat. Then he does a tiny headshake. "Your dad just died."

"Weird time to bring that up," I say.

And then he lets out a single, quiet laugh before his head falls back toward the ceiling, breathing out in exasperation.

And I'm confused. His hands are still on my waist, he's still holding me against him, but he's moved his face away from me. I look at him as close as the light will let me. "You don't...want to?"

He looks at me again quickly. "No, I want to. I do. I just—" His mouth pulls downward, sporting a hint of regret. "I don't want to fuck us—" He flinches as he says that and quickly corrects himself. "*This*. Up."

"You are," I tell him, not missing a beat. "You're fucking this up right now."

He gives me an amused and measured smile. A little cocky, eyes bright. "No, I'm not."

"Seriously?" I look up at him, exasperated.

He nods once.

I stare at him in disbelief. "We're not going to—?"

"Not now." He shakes his head, still AU17-ing, so at least he's bummed about it.

I flop my head forward onto his bare chest and I like where it lands.

My head tucks neatly under his chin like maybe we're Russian nesting dolls from the same set.

I sigh, sad and annoyed and hungry and lonely but not for anything else, just for him.

"I could kill you." My voice is muffled by him and I'm glad, because I think otherwise he'd have heard an embarrassing amount of emotion.

"Yeah." Sam sniffs out a quiet, nervous laugh. "Tell me something I don't know."

22

I DON'T SET AN ALARM FOR the next morning, which I don't do consciously, but I think the subtext is pretty clear. I don't want to get up for this day.

Where do I even begin?

On the day that's been designated to mourn a man I don't feel like I even really knew?

I don't even know how I'm supposed to feel. I mean, I know what I'm supposed to feel in a textbook kind of way. Bereavement is multifaceted and complicated when the person who's died is someone you had a simple relationship with (if there even is such a thing as a simple relationship?). But once you throw in a spanner like all the ways my dad failed to be a dad to me and my brother most of our lives while we watched him be one for our siblings—grieving him becomes more complicated. Because the desire for him to be that for us doesn't lessen in an honest way.

Contempt is funny like that. You can be resentful of something, hateful even—and still be jealous of it. I hated my dad for all the ways he wasn't there for me and Oliver, but I still wanted him to want to be my dad.

I still hoped through the first year of boarding school that my dad would pull up in a town car and swoop in, saying Maryanne confessed everything and please, please would I come home? And depending on the day, maybe I would have, maybe I wouldn't have. All I know is I wanted to be wanted and I wasn't and now he's dead, so I'll never be.

There's a knock on my door, and then it creaks open.

I prop myself up a little and Sam pokes his head in.

"Morning." He flashes me a smile. It's quick and a little shy.

I sit up a little more. "Hey."

He holds out a coffee mug and I hold out my hands for him to bring it to me. He sits down on my bed and looks at my shirt, squashing a smile.

"Does that say 'Hopeless Ramentic'?"

"Ah." I roll my eyes. "Yes. I actually—I don't even really like ramen—but my housemate loves it, and she got us matching T-shirts because she's like, abominably shit at gift giving." I nod and he stifles a laugh. "So I just wear it to bed to appease her."

"Right." Sam nods, pressing his tongue into his bottom lip, and I stare at it for too long, and it begins to feel like someone is churning butter in my stomach, and we're in a bed, and if he thought it was a bad idea to have sex the night before my dad's funeral, I feel like he probably won't go for morning of either, but I want to so bad that my cheeks catch on fire, and I can tell he can tell, so I just keep talking.

"She actually wears hers out. Which is weird." I laugh uncomfortably. "Because she's this super stylish total babe bisexual badass, who is like, real life best friends with Jeremy Scott, and yet still, sometimes she wanders around Shoreditch in Rag & Bone jeans and a 'Hopeless Ramentic' T-shirt."

I take a sip of coffee to stop myself from talking, and it is by far the best coffee I've had since I've left London. If not ever.

I peer up over the mug at him and he's watching me, brows perched a little. "You made this?"

He nods, smiling a little, and I want to pin that tiny, proud smile to his face forever. "I found a French press yesterday."

I take another sip. "This is good."

His smile stretches wider.

"What do I have to do for you to bring me one of these tomorrow morning?"

He gnaws on his bottom lip. Sunlight's pouring in through my windows and his eyes are so blue and his pupils are so big, and then he does his go-to self-hushing emblem: the closed fist banging absent-mindedly against his mouth.

"Not a fucking thing," he says as he licks away a smile.

I swallow heavily, because "fucking" is actually the very thing I'd like to do to solidify me getting the coffee in the morning. Not just the remaining mornings of this weird little trip we're on, but perhaps and ideally, all mornings henceforth forever and ever.

"How's Oliver?" I ask, because nothing sedates my hormones more than talking about my siblings.

Sam's face pulls a little. AU13 and AU56. Cheek lift and a head tilt to the left. He couldn't have said "so-so" any louder unless he yelled it.

"He's a little more on edge than you want an alcoholic to be," Sam concedes, and I know he only does so because he saw my eyes flick over his face, and he knows I know the answer anyway.

He gives me a reassuring nod. "But I'll handle it."

23

MY MOM DIDN'T SPEAK AT the funeral.

Tennyson did, Maryanne did, and Vi did. And the preacher.

I wasn't asked. Neither was Oliver. No surprises there, I suppose, just a nice, consistent continuation of the utter disregard extended to his youngest children publicly.

Cheers, Dad, you big jack-off.

It was open casket, which I wasn't expecting. Isn't that something they should tell us beforehand? I don't know. Maybe they did. Maybe I wasn't listening.

Or, equally likely, maybe they just didn't tell me.

It's a closure thing, open caskets. People tend to find an open casket expedites the feeling of closure. A visual example aligning with the thing your brain was telling you already.

Seeing him there in a navy suit, eyes closed, arms folded neatly over himself like he was about to go down a fancy waterslide—it didn't give me closure; it undid me a little.

The last time I saw my dad was when he hugged me behind the lawyer's office after I signed the documents for my inheritance from my grandfather's estate. He gave me this quick hug that, I think—if I'm not sweetening the memory in retrospect—was this bizarre mix of sad and sorry, like he knew it was going to be the last time.

I don't know why? Maybe because never in my life had my dad walked me to my car except for then. And it was right after I'd had a yelling match with Uncle Phil's twatty son, Troy, about how I thought we should all divvy up our money so all five grandkids, Oliver included, were given equal shares, and Troy bucked the idea so hard. So did Maryanne. So did Tennyson.

And I yelled at them, and I cried in front of them, and I felt this chapter of my life closing because I hate this town and I hate the way people here fear difference, and so I signed what I needed to sign and I got the hell out of there.

"What are you going to do with it?" my dad asked, leaning against my car, blocking the door so I couldn't get in without answering him first.

"I'm going to give him half of mine."

Quick as lightning, and I'll swear it till I die, though not a soul alive will believe me: a small smile flickered over my dad's face, but then it was gone.

"It's yours." He nodded. "You do with it what you want."

I didn't know it'd be the last time I'd see him, but it was, so it's funny that he hugged me like he did. He kind of just grabbed me, pulled me into him, squeezed me tight for three seconds, and then walked away.

And that was six years ago. Our last face-to-face interaction.

They sent me a Christmas present every year, and it was always really nice. Like, surprisingly nice. Cooler than you'd think they'd think to buy me. Last year it was a shoulder bag from Saint Laurent. The Loulou Puffer quilted shearling.

I loved it.

I've never used it because I hate it out of principle, but I loved it. Love it.

Hattie hates me for it. I have a closet full of bags and belts and scarves and whatever, and I never let her use them. Not because I'm a bad sharer; I let her use whatever else she wants. Just not those. Those stay frozen in time in their dust bags in the back of my closet.

Kind of the same place where my dad lives inside my heart.

I don't know how I swung it, but I ended up seated with Sam Penny next to me on one side and Clay on the other. Truthfully, I can only really take it as empirical evidence that God has favorites and today I was his.

Sam was right—Oliver was weird. To be expected though, I suppose. He didn't look at the coffin once. Also, I have a tiny suspicion that Oliver wasn't too pleased that Sam's seated in the middle of us.

On the car ride here, which was me, Tennyson, and Savannah (because Oliver all but pushed me past his car with Sam in the driver's seat, and into theirs), I began to hypothesize possible ulterior reasons for Oliver's behavior:

1) He's been spending time with Maryanne.

2) The grief is hitting him harder than he cognitively recognizes.

3) He's drinking again. Or is about to. [Oliver can become really quite mean (and controlling and manipulative) when he's drinking or on the brink of it.]

4) He resents me.

Not because of Sam—I don't think he knows about Sam—but Sam isn't the only reason I think he might resent me... Growing up, I would have done anything for Oliver, anytime. I would have gone anywhere, dropped anything...and over time, the more he drank, the more he pissed away his inheritance and kept making bad decisions despite my begging him not to, and with the distance of London between us, it was easier to say no to him. And once I began to, it became easier and easier to keep doing it.

In person, it feels a little harder again. Maybe he's just punishing me for the last few years? Maybe he's angry because the last time I was in LA with him, he was so fucking plastered drunk when he drove to my hotel that I called the police and had them arrest him for a DUI so he'd be ordered by the court to go to rehab. That was about a year ago.

He was really angry at first. Really, really angry... And then it changed, shifted to sorrow and grief and guilt and remorse. I don't know where he is right now in all that, and I probably should.

I never used to have to work to have Oliver tell me the truth, but I guess at the same time I was learning to draw lines in the sand, so was he. And so, it's different now.

I zoned out completely and intentionally with Maryanne up there. The parts of her speech that I caught seemed tailored specifically to jab me. How close she and Dad became after something "really hard" happened when she was eighteen, how wonderful those years were, how much she loved being his daughter, and how she always felt loved by him.

Oliver glanced over at me, catching my eyes, his own heavy. He blinked that he was sorry.

Violet's speech made me cry. For her, not for my dad. She lost her best friend. She lost her confidant. She lost someone who's been there for her every day of her life, no matter what. And maybe I cry a little at the great disparity of it all.

When Tennyson got up, I felt nervous. I'm not sure why. Maybe because I see threads of me liking him more than I used to, and I don't want him to be sad. And maybe I don't want my reasons for liking him to lessen again, and I was worried they were about to. Nothing drives a wedge between siblings like unbridled favoritism.

"My dad was a really good man," he opened with. "He was good at being a man. He loved fishing and hunting, and he swears up and down that he nearly played for the 49ers. He worked hard. Won hard. He knew money. He knew real estate. He knew cars. He'd tell anyone who'd listen to him that he was hung." The room polite-laughed, and there were a few tut-tutters.

"He loved my mum." He nodded. "So much. He loved his family. He was a faithful son to his parents and a staunch brother to Vi and Phil. And he wore so many hats, but the one I liked best was Dad."

He smiled at the room and his eyes were teary, which made me teary. I don't know why.

Sam Penny glanced at me, his mouth tugged in sadness. He leaned forward with a sigh, glancing over at Oliver, giving him a sorry smile, and very, very stealthily, blocking most of me from Oliver's view, Sam placed his hand on my upper thigh and rubbed it slowly with his thumb.

It only lasted about three seconds before he rubbed his nose and did a sniff like maybe he had something up there, and then he leaned back in the pew like he hadn't just set my heart on fire.

I glanced around to see if anyone saw, and I thought we were in the clear when Clay peeked at me out of the corner of his eye, smirking.

Our eyes caught—I was sprung, completely, totally, no-way-out-of-it sprung.

Then my uncle sniffed a laugh and threw his arm around me.

24

HOW YOU DOING, KIDDO?" Vi asks, tenderly, with a head tilt.

I look over her face—brows low, lip sucked in a tiny bit. Shallow, shaky breathing.

She's in pain.

I'm doing better than her, that much I'm sure of.

"How are you?" I ask her instead. "You spoke beautifully."

"Yeah?" She blinks over at me.

"Yeah." I smile.

"I was glad to see him again—is that weird?" She shakes her head, like she thinks it's a dumb thought. "I was glad to see my brother dead in a box?"

"Grief is weird." I give her a small shrug. "I don't think there are hard and fast rules for dealing with it."

She nods a few times and forces a smile. Then she clears her throat. "So is grief why you were getting felt up by some guy at your dad's funeral?" she asks as she drags me into a corner, hands on her hips.

"Some guy?" I blink, looking around the room wildly for Clay, that traitor.

Some guy? What the fuck?

We're back at my parents' for the wake now, and the room is too full of people who knew my dad better than I did.

"Who was it?" she asks. "Was it Sam, or—"

"Yes, it was Sam!" I growl, and I'm offended now. "I'm not as slutty as you think I am, Vi!" I whisper-yell, and her face softens.

"That's not what I—" she starts, but my chest is heaving a little.

"And he wasn't feeling me up." I'm not meeting her eye. "He put his hand on my leg when I was sad."

"Okay." She nods, sucking in her lip. AU28. She feels guilty, but she should, and my head keeps shaking.

"What happened happened ten years ago—a decade ago! I was a kid! And none of you, no one"—I meet her eyes now and let her see how much it's hurt me—"not even you, has ever let me forget about it."

"Sweet pea." Violet shakes her head. "I overstepped; I was joking! I—"

And then I walk away.

I've never walked away from her before, actually.

It's not that I'm all that angry; it's just that I'm tired of my narrative here, even from the people I love and who love me.

Redemption is an important part of every person's narrative, but not one I've been afforded. This is partially my fault, because I left and never came back—but why would I come back? And sure, it's hard to be redeemed from ten thousand miles away. But I crave it anyway.

It's not about being vindicated—because that's too embittered and there's a vitriolic undertone there that I'm not interested in—but redeemed... You don't need to only have a murky history to crave redemption, because I think redemption covers more than just our sins; it covers everyone else's too.

This town to me is full to its brim with regrets and wishes that things were different.

I don't even want the Beckett part of my story to be redeemed anymore. I want the part where my parents didn't give a shit to be proven wrong.

I walk through the living room and hear Debbie telling Sam about the gospel, and I wish she'd shut it. A surge of anger pulses through me as I panic she'll fuck it up and make God sound weird or judgmental... make him sound like he's the pricky God America might have you believe him to be.

I have to stop myself from interjecting, and the only reason I don't is because I feel so on edge, I can't be fully sure I wouldn't find out her deepest secrets and use them against her on the spot, just for talking to the boy I like about something I think she doesn't know shit-all about.

Debbie goes to church on Sunday. Debbie reads the Bible. She goes to Bible study and prayer group and the women's meeting, and she thinks these things qualify her to tell people—perfect strangers, like Sam—about the gospel, but I don't think that's true. I think the only thing that qualifies you to talk about the gospel is admitting you need it.

The concept of the gospel is counterintuitive and much easier to digest if you adhere to a strict regimen of shallow perfectionism, like Debbie does, or my mom. It's in this hollow I think most of the church resides, but I think the place God would like us to be is in the gutters or the libraries asking questions about why a good God would make a world so fucked up.

I've always thought like this, all my life. My Sunday school teacher used to sit with me in a corner and answer question after question that she couldn't have possibly known the answers to, but she tried because I think she saw the value in asking.

I understand now that I'm older that it takes a true and deep faith in God to feel comfortable enough to ask and be asked such questions, but I don't think many people like the depths.

The deeper you go, the darker it gets, but I once knew a guy who said there are shadows to his wisdom. Mom said he was a heretic because God is all good all the time, but I wonder where his goodness lands her today, when her husband dead.

I heard her saying before to her friend that God is in control, but I watched the way her mouth twitched in pain as she said it, like her body was physically rejecting what she was saying. She doesn't believe it.

And that's okay to me—I think he probably is all good, all the time, but I think *good* is probably just a vaster, more nuanced construct than we grew up believing it to be.

I think God is good, even on the day of my father's funeral. And I think he likes a redemption story.

Me too, actually.

I think it's why I like Sam… A once-upon-a-time bad boy and reformed alcoholic spends his life helping other people not make the same mistakes as him while, probably unbeknownst to him, dabbing the hearts of those around him with a soft, cool cloth.

I catch Sam's eye. *Are you okay?*

He gives me a slight and tiny wink. *Yes.*

And then I spot my mom in the kitchen. She's backed up against the fridge, hugging a large glass of rosé to her chest.

I approach her, feeling timid. "Are you…okay, Mom?"

She looks up at me like she's surprised to see me, and my heart breaks on the spot because she's in anguish. She's probably drunk too much; I can tell that by the softness of her face. That, or she's drinking and taking sedatives.

"Am I okay?" she eventually repeats. Then she sniffs a laugh and takes a sip.

"I'm really sorry," I tell her.

She glances at me from the side of her eye and then tugs on my dress. "This is nice. Is it your sister's?"

I press my lips together and take a breath. "Nope, I bought it yesterday."

My mother makes a *hm* sound.

I pour myself a glass of wine and stand opposite her. "Is there anything I can do for you?"

She breathes in through her nose, her eyes pinching.

"Do your thing."

"What?" I blink.

She squares her shoulders. "Read me."

I shake my head. "Mom—"

"Read me, I said!" she says, sharply. "Tell me what I'm feeling." She sniffs again—it's all full of emotion—then quickly regains composure. "Please tell me what I'm feeling."

I take a breath and look at her, pretend like I'm just noticing it for the first time, like it's not the first thing I saw on her when I walked into the house on Monday.

"You're in trauma," I say to her, and swallow heavily because who the fuck wants to say that to their mother? "You're in so much pain, you can't even feel it all. It's why you feel confused—confused is the most obvious thing you feel." I point to her upper face. "The way your eyebrows pull in, you're confused on the surface, but underneath, it's just..." I tilt my head—it's easier sometimes to spot emotions that way. "Anguish. And fear."

She brushes away a tear that's about to slip from her eye. Says nothing.

"What are you most afraid of now that Dad's gone?" I ask her. Nowhere like your father's wake to dabble in some light immersion therapy.

No one's asked her that before, I can tell that much. Which is crazy to me, because it's the most obvious thing about her the more I look at her. She's afraid.

She stares off at nothing for a long time, then glances at me. "How much my life will change."

I nod once.

"I married your father when I was nineteen. I'm fifty-three now. I don't know how to live in a world where he doesn't love me." She blinks a few times. "I'm alone now." She looks past me for a while, brows furrowed, lips pressed down.

"You've been alone before," she tells me, nodding her chin toward me. "How do you...?"

She trails off, looking at me with hopeful eyes, but I'm thrown as fuck by the question. I don't know how I'd even begin to answer that. Therapy? Trying to feel wanted by anyone who'd have me? Overachieving? Avoiding? Self-acceptance?

Instead, I find myself folding my arms over my chest, and before I do it, I know it's probably a bad idea, but it might be my only chance because my mom doesn't drink this much that often and I'll never get her to say it when she's sober.

"Why did you do it?" I ask, and I hate that my voice nearly breaks at the question before it's even all the way out.

Her gaze shifts from far off to me. She blinks thrice in quick succession, then sighs out her nose.

"Your father begged me not to..."

That makes my chest go tight, and I suck in my bottom lip. "Why?"

She sighs again and gives an indifferent shrug. "Said it'd be damaging to send away your brother's only real friend."

My face falters. Really? No concern for me? Like, none at all?

"So why did you, then?" I press, eyebrows up.

And then my mother looks at me with no one abject emotion present; instead, it's flickers of tones. Regret, guilt, sadness, fear, contempt, anger—

Then she says, clear as a bell, and I know it's the truth because I can see it all over her, plain as day:

"It was easier."

I tip my wine glass back and drain it, banging it down on the bench with a clatter.

I walk back into the living room, where most of the wake is, and up to Sam and Oliver.

"I'm going to a bar," I tell them. "I know you're alcoholics, so please don't feel any pressure to come—but I'm fucking done here." I give them a curt nod.

Sam catches my eye, brows dipping with concern, but I can't meet his eyes right now. If I do, I'll cry.

"I'll come," Tennyson says from a few meters away, inviting himself. He throws his arm around Savannah. "Let's go."

I walk toward the door and grab my keys out of the bowl, but Sam plucks them from my hand.

"I'll drive."

25

WE'RE AT A BAR CALLED Cheap Seats and it's perfect. Exactly what we needed—exactly what I needed.

At first it was just me, Sam, Oliver, Tenny, and Savannah. Then soon after came Clay, but no Violet, which makes me think he's been sent here to keep an eye on us because Clay would never voluntarily leave Violet on the day of her brother's funeral.

But it's fun. It's actually really fun.

No one's really talking about Dad. Maybe they're talking around Dad.

I think it's the most at ease I've seen Tennyson all week... Not feeling the pressure to feel what he should, I suppose, after the loss of a parent.

But you need a break. Your brain needs a break.

And it's fun.

I had some clothes in my car that I changed into so I wasn't wearing death clothes in the bar, and Sam's hovering probably a little closer than he should because Oliver's right there—but also, Tennyson's bought me two shots and I've had two regular drinks, so I don't completely care anyway.

I'm not drunk, not even a little, but the part of me that makes me live my whole life so that Oliver's world is cushioned is a bit drowned out.

Savannah and I are getting on real well, and I never thought I'd like a girl Tennyson likes, but I like her.

We're playing eight-ball, my brothers and Sam versus me, Savannah, and Clay. And here's a non–plot twist: Sam Penny is exactly as good at pool as you'd expect him to be.

I don't know if it's the bending over (great ass), or his laser-focus, or the way handles the cue, but I am a mess. I'm not normally a totally shit player, but every time I go to shoot, I catch in my periphery something Sam does. Nothing spectacular or noteworthy, either. He could take a sip of water and my heart could stroke out. He's just doing normal guy things, like shifting his weight between his legs, holding the cue stick against him, tilting his head as he waits for me to shoot—and I love all of it; I want to film it and watch it back again and again, because how can someone be as beautiful as he is without even trying?

I move toward him while Oliver takes his shot.

"Is it bad we're at a bar and you're an alcoholic?" I ask him quietly.

"Um." He laughs, then shakes his head casually. "I'm fine." He nods over at Oliver. "Probably better places for him to be, generally speaking, but he's..." He looks over at my brother and smiles with his eyes. He's proud of him. "He's doing good."

Oliver's making a loud joke to Tenny, who's doing his best not to laugh, but it's cracking all over his face.

I truly think Tennyson thought all his life he could maybe, like, "catch the gay." Like if he was nice to Oliver, it made him gay too. Or if he thought Oliver was funny, it meant he liked gay guys because testosterone, fuck yeah! Or if he shared a drink with Oli, he'd get like, dick juice in his mouth, I don't know. He was always so weird about him in so many really mundane ways, which killed Oliver.

I don't actually think Tennyson thinks like that anymore, but some habits are hard to break, like letting yourself smile at things you taught yourself not to. I can see it there, hovering under the surface of him.

"But you're okay?" I ask Sam, hands behind my back, swinging my torso side to side but keeping my tilted head, eyes fixed on him. It's blatant seduction and a tacit sign of submission, but I really just want him to kiss me.

He drops his chin a little and peers at me, pressing the tip of his tongue into his top lip.

"Yeah." He purses his mouth to hide a smile. "Yeah, I'm good."

And it's so fun, I'm having so much fun—and then my sister walks in.

Still in her obvious funeral dress. She might as well be wearing torn sackcloth. She leads the way, and following behind her are four other people. Her husband, some guy she was friends with in high school, Tinsley, and Beckett.

"So," she says coolly, tossing her bag down on a nearby table. "This is where the cool kids hang out on a Friday night?"

I roll my eyes. I don't know why. Maybe she's being nice. She could be. Maryanne has a knack for being able to make something sound equal parts warm and disparaging.

Tenny throws his hands, guilty as charged. "Apparently,"

"Do the cool kids skip out on their dead father's wake?" She gives him a pointed look.

"Do nondead fathers have wakes?" I ask, and from the other side of the table, Sam catches my eye and smirks.

Maryanne makes a sound in the back of her throat and walks over to the bar.

I glance at Oli and he rolls his eyes, and I'm glad we're on the same page with her bullshit today.

I lean over the pool table and take my shot, and as I do, Beckett's hand grazes my ass.

"Play nice," he says quietly, and I freeze.

Everything in the universe comes to a halt, and the sound all sucks dry except for the pounding in my ears as I'm transported back in time to my parents' house, and I'm fourteen being pulled into dark corners, and his hands are under my top and I'm as still as a statue then as I think I am now—and then I snap and turn on my heel.

"Did you just grab my ass?" I ask loudly.

AU2 and AU58. His left eyebrow cocks up and his head pulls back a little. He wasn't expecting a response. And why would he? I've never responded before.

"Ah." He sort of scoffs, but inhales too quickly afterward. "No," he says, but it's full of gestural slips. For one, his head comes down in a subtle, singular nod, which was paired with a mouth shrug. I think I catch the hint of an AU7 too. His eyelids go tight. He resents me.

Sam hears what I said to him, I know he does, because he walks over and hovers behind me, slinging the cue stick over his shoulders like it's a yoke.

"Everything okay over here?" Sam asks, glancing at Becks darkly before flicking his eyes over to me.

"Yeah, we're fine, man," Becks says, reaching for Sam to touch his arm to assure him. "We're good."

"Are you?" Sam asks me, brows a little up. "Good?"

Before I have a chance to answer, Maryanne pokes her head in. "What's going on?"

"Nothing." Beckett rolls his eyes. "Just a misunderstanding." He gives me a pointed look. "Right, Georgia?"

I say nothing, hold his gaze. Beckett squints again, clicks his tongue twice, and then goes and perches on the table, throwing his arm around Tinsley.

"You should be careful," my sister leans in and whispers in the same kind of friendly-threatening tone as before. "You have a reputation."

"Yeah, well, whose fault is that?" I turn away from her.

She sniffs an amused laugh and then says, just quiet enough so only I can hear: "Do you ever think that if you dressed a little bit more—you know—that then..."

I spin around. "Do not"—I point a condemning finger at her—"finish that sentence."

"Why do you dress like that?" She waves a careless hand at my outfit. "That's not what clothes are supposed to look like."

"Yes! They are! These are normal clothes! Completely unaltered." I gesticulate at myself. I'm in denim shorts and a T-shirt. Same as half the girls in here. "They're called distressed denim shorts! I'm wearing them exactly as Agolde made them! Do you know how many other people wear ripped denim shorts? Everyone. Everyone in the world, except you apparently, Maryanne! Because you dress like you just stepped off the fucking *Mayflower*."

"Screw you," she spits. Then says under her breath, "Whore."

Sam shifts closer behind me. The conversation is loud enough now that my brothers are edging in too. I think so is her husband.

"You know what?" I give her a curt smile. "If I'm a whore, then you're my pimp."

"Oh yeah?" says Jason, saddling up next to her defensively. "How do you figure?"

Maryanne lifts her eyebrows in defiance, like she's daring me, but she swallows like she's nervous.

Our eyes hold, and I tell myself I shouldn't do it, it's not worth it—it won't go how I think it'll go, it'll just fuck everything up, Sam might get weird, saying it won't make what happened any different—and I'm about to leave it, I'm completely about to walk away from this shit, and then I see the corner of my sister's mouth twitch upward, the tiniest expression dart over her. She's smug.

I cross my arms over my chest. "Because she prostituted her fourteen-year-old sister for popularity."

Maryanne freezes. AU1 and AU24. Wide eyes, tight lips, and another nervous swallow.

"What?" Tennyson asks loudly, walking toward us.

Sam's gone very still behind me. Very still. Cue stick still slung over his shoulders.

"Nothing," Maryanne says quickly, shaking her head.

Tennyson gets right up in Maryanne's face but points over to me. "What's she talking about, Mer?"

Oliver's watching from the side, head tilted in caution.

And then Beckett stands up.

Sam clocks him, and he's still not moving a muscle—I'm not even sure that he's breathing. There's something threatening in his eyes that I haven't seen before.

"Nothing." Maryanne eyes me pointedly, then shakes her head at Tennyson. "That's not true. It isn't what happened, she's just—"

I glare at her, and I can't believe it when the words tumble from my mouth to interrupt her. "I know you know—"

AU22, AU7. She squints and her mouth pulls in not quite a pout, but as though she's blowing air out of her mouth while making an O shape. She's trying to steady herself.

"All I know is that I walked in on you fucking my high school boyfriend."

"No." I shake my head once, curtly. "You walked in on fourteen-year-old me being fucked by a seventeen-year-old boy, wrists pinned down on my brother's bed—"

"WHAT?" Tennyson roars, and both Beckett and Maryanne pull back.

But I ignore him, because I've waited for so long to acknowledge the part that killed me the most. "And you did nothing." I stare over at her, eyes all threadbare. "You went back to your party."

Maryanne swallows and lets out this breath that sounds somewhere between relief and exasperation. It's an interesting thing about lying, actually. It takes such a toll on our subconscious to keep it going, I think that there's some part of us that's almost relieved when it's exposed.

Beckett is standing a few feet behind us, arms folded across his chest, brows low and eyes almost closed, tongue pressed against his top lip.

Sam walks over to him. He's calm still. Posture hasn't changed. He just watches him, head pulled back, jaw tight.

But Tennyson comes in hot, pushes past Sam to shove Beckett hard as he can. "You raped my sister?"

"No." Beckett shakes his head. "It wasn't like that." He looks over at me. "Tell them it wasn't like that."

I just stare at him, sort of in disbelief that this is a conversation that's actually unfolding outside my head.

"Oh, come on!" Beckett rolls his eyes. "You were begging for it!"

Sam squares his shoulders and takes a deep breath through his nose.

"When?" I ask loudly.

He makes a little scoffing noise and vaguely gestures at me, then whacks Sam jovially in the chest.

"You get it, man—she's just like that. She's—"

And I should have seen it. God—it's literally my job.

People get a look in their eyes when it comes to premeditated aggression. AU7/AU9—their eyes go tight, might even pinch, and their noses wrinkle or flare—but I wasn't looking for it. I've never known it to be on Sam's face once in my small duration of knowing him—but then, it happens so, so quickly.

Sam makes this little huff from his nose, like a nonlaughing laugh, and then he jerks his shoulder super fast and knocks Beckett in the face with the cue stick that was still yoked over his shoulders, and while Becks is reeling from that, Sam drops the cue and right-hooks him.

Then Tennyson rushes toward them, grabbing and slamming Beckett into a wall, and there's glass breaking and yelling and the crowd in the bar craters out around us, and I think Becks gets a punch in, but it's just one before Tenny slugs him again, twice.

Sam grabs Beckett by the collar of his shirt and drags him toward the door—he's thrashing and kicking and swinging, and Jason tries to charge at him, but Tennyson bats him out of the way how you'd swat at a vine that's in your path.

Sam Penny pulls Beckett outside, tosses him like a frisbee, and he skids across the ground. Then Tennyson lunges for him, but a security guard grabs him from behind.

My oldest brother bucks in the arm of the security man. "He raped my sister!" he yells, thrashing.

The guard looks at me, hovering by the door like a deer in headlights, Savannah holding onto my arm to steady me, but actually, it's to steady her because she's never seen my brother like this. Neither have I, truthfully.

Then the security guard looks at Beckett, whose breathing is haggard as he lies frozen on the ground, Sam Penny standing over him menacingly—then the security guard gives Tennyson a small shove toward them and then all hell breaks loose.

I really mean that.

It's like Sam and Tenny have been practicing this for weeks on end. They're flawless and ruthless. Jason runs in, trying to save his friend, and the other guy from their high school runs in and tries to pull Beckett out, and then they're getting hit and then it's three on two, but it doesn't matter because my brother and Sam aren't slowing down at all.

I don't know what exactly it is that crossed the line for her—maybe it's that Beckett is looking less and less like Beckett by the second—but Savannah stands about a meter away from the splash zone and calls out to my brother.

"Tenny!"

He doesn't hear her.

"Tennyson!" she calls again, firmer now. "That's enough!"

Tennyson glances up at his girlfriend like the spell's been broken.

Meanwhile, Oliver grabs Sam, pulling him off Beckett. He takes one look at my assailant lying there on the ground, eyes swollen shut, blood dripping everywhere, and holds his hand firm against Sam's heaving chest. "He's had enough, man."

The guy from high school gets Becks up off the ground and drags him away down the street.

I'm standing there, frozen and wide-eyed, and Sam peers over at me as he swipes his bleeding lip with the back of his hand.

I feel this pull to run to him and wrap myself up in him. I think he feels it too, because I see the beginning of him moving toward me, but then Tenny steps in front of me. One of his eyes is swelling closed and the bridge of his nose is bleeding.

"Why didn't you tell me?" he asks me, voice ragged.

I blink rapidly. It's an unconscious rejection of what was just said to me. "Why would I tell you?"

He scoffs like it's the most ridiculous thing I could ever possibly ask. "Because I'm your big brother!"

I clench my fists. "And you were a piece of shit big brother!"

He pauses, turns his chin to the right, and glares at me out of the corner of his eye. "Not to you."

I growl at the back of my throat, throwing my hands up wildly. "How many times do I have to tell you? You can't treat me good"—I thump my chest—"and him bad." I throw my hand in Oliver's direction. "It doesn't work like that! He is my family!"

"Well, so am I!" Tenny yells loud and clear.

"Since when?" I stomp my foot and I don't mean to. "Thirty seconds ago, when you defended my honor ten years too late?"

"I didn't know!" His breathing is getting fast again. "How would I have known?"

"You wouldn't have known!" I shake my head wildly. "That's the point! I would never have told you, because you were an asshole!"

Tennyson swats his hand at me as though he's dismissing me, but actually he's just angry. Not at me, at himself.

I feel alone and exposed, and so I walk toward the only person who's made me feel okay all my life.

Oliver's watching me closely as I approach him. His eyes are watery and he looks…something. AU4. Sad. I think he's sad? His mouth's not moving. It's hard to tell.

"Why didn't you tell me?" Oliver asks quietly as I stand in front of him.

I lick my lip. "Because I didn't."

"Why?" Oliver asks a little louder, and maybe firmer?

"Because I didn't!" I overenunciate.

"Well, that's bullshit!" Oliver yells suddenly. "Bull. Shit. You force me to tell you everything! All the time! And this happened to you, and you don't tell me?"

"So?" I shake my head, not understanding.

And then Oliver yells how he's never yelled at me before: "So why the fuck didn't you tell me?" He punctuates that sentence by hitting his own chest on every syllable.

Sam's fist clenches in reflex when my brother's swearing at me, but it's also a gestural emblem. He wants to hit Oliver.

I shake my head at my younger older brother. "Why are you making this about you?" I blink up at him.

"Because it is about me!" His breathing is picking up pace. "It's about us! What's it say about who I am to you and how you see me if you didn't even think you could come to me when you needed me?"

"I did come to you!" I smack tears away. "The second he touched me, I ran to your bedroom." I shake my head at the memory. "And it was empty. Window open. Curtains closed. 'Heartbeats' blasting. You were with that exchange student from Prague, and I knew that it would have killed you if you knew I came to you and you weren't there for me, so I let it kill me instead."

Oliver bats away the wetness on his face, shaking his head. "You still should have told me."

I cover my face with my hands for a second and then I shove him away from me. "Fuck yourself."

And then I turn and walk down the street.

26

GO WITH HER," I HEAR Tennyson say to someone as I thunder down the street.

I'm on kind of a weird and shitty road. A lot of trees, a lot of overhang. Which way did Beckett go? I try to remember. He went right, I think, so I go left. I should still be careful…though I suppose he did look quite incapacitated.

I'm a fast walker at the best of times, and this is the worst of times. I'm about ten yards away when I hear someone jogging after me, and I know it's him because who else could it be?

Sam grabs me by the arm and pulls me to a standstill.

He stands there for a couple of seconds, brows low and creased, and his eyes flicker over me like he's scanning me, looking for broken parts and things to fix, and then he slips his hands around the back of my head and pulls me into his chest.

He holds me like that for I don't know how long, but it's me who pulls away because a car drives past and I think about how Oliver seeing me being held by his sponsor is the last thing I need right now, so I cover my face for a second and then shove my hands through my hair and start walking down the street again. Sam keeps pace with me in silence.

It's strange, actually. I've spent years and years contemplating how it would feel for me to have someone defend my honor about all this, but now that it's happened—it was bizarrely nonrestorative. I think I began to believe that if someone had known, if someone knew and they came to my defense, that it would have felt the same as being defended at the time, but it didn't. It doesn't—it couldn't. And I really wanted it to. Like, I'm such a fucking idiot for thinking being saved by someone would undo being raped by someone.

It's not how it works.

This realization makes me feel alarmingly stupid for a few seconds, because I knew better—or, I thought I would have. I don't, evidently—but I should.

But then this floats through my head: *You survive whatever you need to, however you can.*

For many years, the idea of someone riding in on a white horse, defending and reclaiming my honor, was how I envisioned my redemption story playing out. The music would swell in the soundtrack of my mind and years of pain would fall off me like scales and I would be different because my savior made me feel clean again; but life, it seems, and hearts as well, are not that simple.

We walk a few blocks in silence and even still, all things about this night and day considered, I like the silence with Sam Penny. I like silence with most people, actually, but I like it with Sam for a different reason.

With everyone else, I like their silence because it talks to me. I trust people's silences more than their words. I can read the world in silence. But Sam is different. Silence with him is silence. Silence with him is five fifteen in the morning before the sun's up and it's still dark but the birds are singing. He's the heavy quilt you pull over your head when it's too cold and too early to wake up. He's the song no parent ever loved me enough to sing. He's the way water runs and bubbles over stones in a stream. He's a quiet mind.

I glance over at him and he stops walking.

He tilts his head, and his face looks pained. But I wonder if it's pained for me. "Are you okay?"

I touch his face without even thinking—his lip's all cut. His face is a bit bloody still. "Are you?"

Sam sighs and gives me a look, holding my hand to his face with his own. He shifts his head and kisses my palm. "Yeah."

"I'm really sorr—" I start, but he shakes his head, pushing my hand away.

"No." He shakes his head again. "Don't ever be sorry."

"But—"

"But nothing." He frowns. "I would have curb-stomped his head if Oliver let me."

I look up at him affectionately. "This is a new side of you."

He rubs his mouth absentmindedly as he stares at me. "Yeah, it is." He pushes some hair behind my ears. "Are you, though? Okay?"

I take a deep breath, then exhale it back out I as look up at him. "I thought that would feel better than it did."

He gives me a sad smile, then sniffs a laugh. "I'm glad I got to hit him. I know it's not about me…" He gives a tiny shrug. "But I'm really glad I got to fuck him up a bit."

I squash away a smile.

"What can I do?" He tilts his head so we're eye to eye. "Tell me, I'll do anything—whatever I can do to make it better, I'll do it."

And I don't know why the sincerity of his offer makes me tear up, but it does. I frown, but I'm not sad—I just don't really understand. "You don't even know me—"

"Yeah." He pushes his hand through my hair, and in case you're wondering, our interpersonal proximity is next to none. Ten inches between us? Maybe a little less? "But I'm trying to."

His eyes flicker from my eyes to my mouth, back and forth. They can't land, like bouncy balls in a tight corridor. My heart is pounding because he's kept his hand in my hair, and he swallows heavily.

"Fuck." He sighs as his head falls back. "Would it be so fucked up if I kissed you right now?"

I drop my chin a little and gnaw on my bottom lip. "No,"

Then he rushes me. Not that we were far apart to start with, but his mouth knocks me back with such force that I could be falling, and probably, definitely I am, but not in the literal way—but also maybe in the literal way? I can't tell.

His hand that's still tangled in my hair slips around to the back of my head, and his other goes around my waist. He pulls me tighter against him, and I don't think I'm on the ground anymore.

He spins us somehow; it feels too smooth to be real. And I'm not being dramatic when I say for a few seconds it feels like I'm floating—and then, you know when you're on a boat and it's docking and it bangs into the pier, and it's not bad at all, but it is a jolt that throws all your nerves?

I'm jolted.

Metaphorically, and also into a tree.

I die a little as his face bangs into mine, and I can feel him smile, his mouth on my mouth, before he goes back to kissing me, which I think for him, is quite a serious business.

I make a note to remember forever the way his face is a nice kind of scratchy, and how his mouth is moving like a curtain blows gently in the summer at magic hour, and how he tastes like Skittles and smells like Tom Ford, how it feels when his breath washes over me and makes me warm everywhere. His hands are firmly in their places, one locked on my waist and then one in my hair, which sometimes travels south to my face, but then it always journeys back.

I think because I've wanted to be kissed by him since the day I met him, I'm not initially thinking much about anything else—but eventually I realize that there are about a million places I want my hands to be right now and pinned between me and the tree isn't one of them.

I pull them out and throw them around his neck, slipping them into his hair, and stop just being kissed and start to kiss him back.

This sets off a fire-and-powder chain of events. He kisses me more, so I kiss him more, so he kisses me more, and I'm worried for when he stops kissing me. How can I go back to a life where Sam Penny isn't kissing me?

The great, deep stirring begins in the center of me, which some might call a longing, but I think of it more as an emptying. And it aches in my shoulders and my ribs because I know it won't be filled tonight, and when he stops kissing me, which he eventually will because he has to because that's how kisses work, it will tear me in two, because I think I've been waiting to know Sam Penny all my life.

And I should maybe be worried about spiders and bugs and that someone could see us, but I don't think I'll be worried about anything else ever again.

27

THE WALK HOME IS LONG, but not long enough in my opinion.

It takes extra long because Sam keeps kissing me at varying points of the journey, and time slips and blurs when he slips his hands into my hair. I could lose an age kissing that man.

He kisses me again when we reach the edge of my driveway, but this one is different to the others—all of the ones before this were this hungry, needy, thirsty, kicking-to-the-surface-to-breathe-again kisses, hands everywhere up and down, and we could have been driving through the galaxy at warp speed and I'd be none the wiser because it feels like that just being next to him, let alone being held by him.

But this kiss…he stands toe-to-toe with me, takes my face in both his hands, and his eyes don't flicker down to my mouth; they just stay on me, and his cheeks twitch as he tries not to smile, and I don't know why we're always trying not to smile? And then he kisses me, softly at first and then more, but his pace remains the same—the kiss just gets deeper, and I think I begin to feel my roots stretch.

I don't let my roots stretch very often. Barely ever and never suddenly. No deeper psychological reason other than the obvious ones. But I feel them stretching toward Sam, and even though he doesn't actually, somehow he smells earthy, like the wet soil at the base of an old, big tree.

He holds my hand all the way until we reach the front porch and then I let go, not him, because I don't want to know what it feels like to have him let go of me, in any capacity. Also, I don't know what this is between us, but whatever it is, I don't want my family fucking it up.

The living room light is on; I notice that before I swing open the door.

My sister's sitting on the sofa, hands in her lap, face teary, our mom's arms thrown around her.

"Georgia!" Mom stands.

Maryanne stands too.

I hover by the door, clock Tennyson leaning against a wall. His face is a little bruised, and for the first time in our lives, I notice he's distanced himself from them.

"Georgia," my mother says again, reaching out for me, and as she does, Sam shifts closer to me than he should be in their presence. Less than a foot.

But they won't notice it—well, they will, but not in a conscious way—their brains will take it in because our brains take in everything, whether we realize it or not. They'll make a subconscious note of it, but they won't know what it means more than a niggle that maybe he likes me a bit more than as a friend.

"Come here, darling—sit," she tells me, but I don't move.

My gaze is fixed on my sister's face.

People who have a narcissistic personality disorder are intensely skilled at impression management.

This is a make-or-break time for my sister. A lie she constructed and maintained for years and years has crashed and burned. She's calculated enough to know that after tonight's events, it won't be the same as it was before; she can't go on pretending like I'm the slut and she's the victim. Crying to our mom is the most logical line of defense my sister has, because my mother has a parental leaning toward her more so than she does toward me.

I wonder what she's told my mom. Whatever she's told her, I don't think Tennyson believes it, judging by his body language—slumped against a wall on the other side of the room, arms crossed to create a physical barrier between them. His head's turned away from them, chin and brows low, jaw set. The way his arms are folded, even. He doesn't realize it, but he's flipping them off. It's a gestural emblem. Whatever Maryanne's selling… Tennyson isn't buying it.

"I'm fine here," I tell her, planting my feet. I feel better having Sam behind me. I don't know why, and I feel annoyed at myself that I do. I don't think it's a guy thing—I think it's a not-on-my-own thing.

Sam doesn't do anything, doesn't say anything—it's not his fight, he doesn't need to—but the light casts his shadow on me and I know he's there and I'm not by myself, which is a very powerful thing to feel when you've felt by yourself most of your life.

"I'm so sorry, Gigi." Maryanne shakes her head. "I'm so sorry." She starts crying. "I didn't know what to do—I didn't know! I was so scared he'd hurt me or—worse!—hurt you, and so I didn't do anything! Which is so awful of me—and I can't believe that I—" She wipes her teary face. "But I felt so trapped, and so stuck, and I'm just so sorry, Georgia—" She goes on and on, and I tune out what she's saying because what she's saying with her words doesn't mean shit; all I need is her face.

Her tone and her words are distressed. Her face… Sometimes she throws in AU1 and AU4s—looks of fear and sadness—but when she does, it's out of sync with the correlating words.

Mostly, it's AU7. Contempt. Her mouth can barely conjure up a frown. From a glance it might look like she is, but she's not. It's an AU13.

Imagine the face you make when someone offers you a dirty tissue. That's how her face looks.

"Darling," Mom says. "She was a victim—just like you."

And I sort of laugh.

"Really?" I blink, incredulous.

My mom shakes her head and sighs. "Georgia—"

"Georgia!" Maryanne weeps. "I am so sorry." But she's shaking her head and moving her hands across her body—another gestural slip—she's not sorry.

"She's lying, Mom," I sigh, and I sound sadder than I want to.

My mom sighs too. "Sweetheart, no, she's not."

"She is!" I insist, and across Maryanne's face is a blink-and-you'll-miss-it AU10. A scowl. Clear as day if you know to be looking for it, but then it's gone in a flash.

"Why would she lie about this?" my mother asks, shaking her head impatiently.

"Because she's a narcissist! Literally. She has a personality disorder and she has to lie to keep the facade up—"

"Not this again, darling." My mom sighs. "She's said sorry—"

Sam lets out an exasperated *tsst* sound from behind me.

"Mom!" I flop my head backward and stare at the ceiling for a second. "You just found out that you sent me away as a child for absolutely no reason. You changed the trajectory of my whole life because you thought I fucked Beckett willingly. And you—all of you—" I clock Tennyson and Maryanne—"have held that over my head for ten years. And you found out—what—an hour ago that it was a lie, and you want me to forgive Maryanne—who knowingly perpetuated the lie—*now*?"

I shake my head at her.

"Mom, even if what's she's saying is true—which, I can't reiterate this enough, it's not. But even if it was true, even if she was scared of Becks or whatever the fuck her story is—" Maryanne's jaw goes tight. "She didn't have to perpetuate that I was a slut. Why didn't she tell you the night you saw? Why has she never come clean all these years later? If Beckett was such a legitimate threat to her—"

Tennyson shifts on his feet, eyes low, jaw jutted forward. I can tell he's been wondering the same things.

"Why has Maryanne still been his friend all these years?" I ask, eyebrows up.

My mom starts shaking her head. "Your sister's just gracious," she starts, and I let out a dry laugh.

"Get the fuck out of here." I swat my hand at her and turn on my heel. "I'm going to bed."

"We're not finished talking about this!" my mother yells after me.

I turn around from the steps and stare back at her. "That's fine, because we're not talking about this—we're lying about it."

I walk up the stairs and Sam's behind me. He moves quietly but stays close, and I get the distinct feeling that maybe he is the adult version of a nightlight. At least, that's what he's becoming to me.

We get to our narrow corridor, and I turn to look up at him.

"It was your sister," he says, nodding a few times, eyes pinched in realization. "She's why you studied what you study."

I flash him a tiny smile. "Yep."

I loved her so much. I always did. How little sisters esteem their big ones—that was me. That first time she walked in on what was happening with me and Beckett, it was so hard for me to comprehend that how it appeared to be was how it actually was. Because I wanted her to be fearful, I wanted her to be sad, I wanted her to be anything other than opportunistic—and at the time, I didn't know how to do any of the things I do, but once I knew I was interested in psychology, it didn't take me long. Words like sociopath, psychopath, narcissist—they're thrown around in people's everyday vernacular, and way too casually at that. But once I knew what they all were, I realized what my sister was, and what it meant in the context of what she did.

I give Sam a helpless shrug. I think it could have been easier to spot, too—Maryanne's narcissism—if my family looked different than it does. If Oliver being gay didn't automatically make him their challenging child, and me by association—if their affections were more evenly spread amongst us, maybe they would have seen it, but they didn't because they don't love us the same.

Sam Penny's brows lower. "How many times did it happen?"

I give him a tight smile and a small shrug. "I stopped counting after ten."

Sam hangs his head, fists balled, and then he peers up again. "Are you okay?" He nods back toward my family.

"Yeah." I swat my hand. "That was regular."

"Nothing about that was regular. This night was..." He trails off, shaking his head at the words he can't find. "Fucked up."

I tilt my head, curiously—cautiously, even. "All of it?"

He nods, and his mouth twitches with a smile. "So about that kiss..."

Sam takes a deep breath, and for a second my heart plummets like it's gone over the bend on a roller coaster.

I ask him the worst question ever uttered in the history of mankind: "Are you going to take it back?"

"No." He sniffs a laugh and takes me by the waist. "I'm going to do it again."

28

WE DIDN'T SLEEP TOGETHER.

Not because I didn't want to. I probably would have tried to if Sam gave me the legroom for it.

But he kissed me the same way he did on the driveway—not with this mad, unbridled teeth-knocking passion, but with this sure steadiness where I could feel his chest rising and falling against mine, and it was so magnificently consistent that my whole self became a puddle.

And then he pulled away, kissed the tip of my nose, said goodnight, and went to his room.

And I stood there—half-dismayed, half in awe, blinking for a few seconds—and then I took a shower and fell asleep quicker than I had in a week.

I wake up the next morning bright-eyed and disappointed that it's not next to Sam, or in the very least to him bringing me a coffee like I thought he would.

It's about 9:30 when I check the time. The latest I've slept in since I've been back in America.

No one annoying's come to wake me. Mind you, neither has anyone delightful. (Spoiler alert: the only delightful one here is Sam, and maybe at a push, Savannah.)

I wonder if it's an eggshells thing. That no one wanted to wake me up this morning because they all think I'm fragile now that they know something bad happened to me a long time ago.

I keep my pajamas on and throw on a robe. I make sure my face looks fresh and dewy though, because I want Sam to think I just look good all the time, but I don't put in more effort like I had the days before, because I don't want him to read into anything, though God knows there's plenty to read into.

I make my way downstairs, cautiously.

"She's up!" Maryanne says when I poke my head into the kitchen.

"Hi!" my mom sings, appearing in front of me. "Good morning, darling, we've been waiting for you!" She smiles tightly. It's uncomfortable, unnatural.

"Why?" I blink.

My mother lets out an airy laugh. She's trying to look genuine, but it's not, none of it is. It's strained. "Breakfast!" she sings.

And then the two of them carry out plate after plate of food to an empty table.

It's impression management, what they're doing. Neither of them can handle being disliked—Maryanne because of her disorder, Mom because of her dysfunction.

"Breakfast," my mom calls again, this time louder, and Sam and Oliver move in from the balcony.

Sam's eyes catch mine, and my heart thunders even though he's doing nothing but walking into the room to have breakfast. The way his hand moves at his side, the way he pushes it through his hair, the way all his blinks seem in slow motion—my mind slips on a ripple in time as I feel again the weight of him against me last night.

I sit down awkwardly and uncomfortably at the table, and I don't know how Sam does it, but he manages to sit next to me without it looking like he does it on purpose at all. Me on one side of him, Oliver on the other.

Maryanne across from me.

When Tenny and Savannah sit down at the table, Mom doesn't really notice what maybe the rest of us do: she's in the same clothes as yesterday.

Maryanne notices, and I watch it form behind her eyes—her chance to shift some heat.

"You slept here last night, Savannah." Maryanne stares over at her, but then tacks a smile onto the end, trying to be normal, I think—make it sound more like a question than a pointed observation.

Mom snaps her head up, suddenly paying attention. Deliriously in denial, obviously, because it's not like Tennyson and Savannah are subtle. From the level of physical comfort displayed between them, to the interpersonal distances they hardly share, to the hint of a love bite a bit below her clavicles…signs there for all the world to read, but my mother would rather read *Town & Country*.

Tennyson glares over at Maryanne and Savannah freezes under my mother's gaze, but I saw it all unfolding, so I'm ready.

"Yeah, but she slept in my bed," I tell them as I sip my coffee.

"Your bed?" Maryanne repeats, looking annoyed.

"Yeah." I nod coolly. "You know, the same one you prostituted me in a few years back—"

"Georgia!" my mother cries, and Maryanne throws her cutlery down dramatically so she can cover her face.

Mom waves her hand in Maryanne's direction. "You've upset your sister again!"

I concede with a sigh. "I am incorrigible."

Sam smiles at me and very, very covertly grazes his hand along my thigh and down until it's resting just north of my knee.

I don't blink, I don't swallow, I don't falter. I just keep on eating my scrambled eggs as though the lid didn't just blow right off the whole wide world and that balloons aren't spilling out all into the streets, glitter blowing through the air… Savannah's eyes catch mine, and she says nothing with her mouth but her eyes whisper, "Thank you."

Oliver's being quieter than I want him to be, so I guess he's still cross at me for not telling him about Beckett. I try to find his eyes, but he won't meet mine. He's fascinated by his plate.

I hate fighting with Oliver. It makes the universe feel tilted off its axis.

In fact, I'm pretty sure the only people present who like me are the ones who aren't related to me.

"Tea?" Savannah offers me and starts pouring without waiting for my answer.

She's uncomfortable.

"How are you?" she whispers from across the table. "Are you okay?"

"Yeah." I give her a smile. "Are you?"

She hesitates, then smiles and nods. "Yeah."

I'm sitting to Sam's right and he's blocking me out of his conversation with Oliver, leaning forward on his left hand, obscuring me from my brother's view—and his hand's still on me. Slowly going up and down, barely moving a visible muscle to do so. His conversation never lags, his focus doesn't seem to sway—and my heart is a goldfish shaken in a bag. Thumping and banging and knocking around. And I want to tell you my cheeks are a normal color—maybe they are, because no one notices them?—but how could they be when Sam Penny's hand is on me how it is?

Maryanne's still fake-crying across the table, but I want to explain what that means because unless you know someone like her, it's hard to imagine.

Throw away whatever image your mind conjures up with the crocodile tears your little sister used to cry when she'd lie about how you pinched her to get you in trouble. That's the minor leagues. Maryanne is in the majors.

These delicate tears roll down her face, and she looks so heartbroken and embarrassed that she's crying. She sniffs and wipes and almost everything about her is convincing, but there's something about her eyes that gives her away.

To me, at least.

"Say you're sorry, Gigi," Mom tells me.

Tennyson rolls his eyes. "Mom—"

"No, Mom." Maryanne shakes her head and sits up straighter. "She doesn't have to."

She sniffs bravely and looks over at me.

"Gigi." Maryanne sniffs again. "I was thinking today maybe we could do something fun together. Like, go shopping?"

"Oh!" coos our mom. "That would be lovely! Wouldn't it, sweetheart?" She looks at me expectantly.

"Um." I shake my head. "No."

Oliver's very still on the other side of Sam.

Maryanne's face falters.

"No, I'm sorry. That came out wrong. I meant, 'fuck no.'" I stare over at Maryanne, flash her a tight smile before I tack onto the end, "In no world."

My mother sighs. "Georgia—"

Maryanne tears up again. "Gige, I'm just—I'm trying to make it right."

Mom pets my arm. "Sweetheart—"

"Mom!" Tenny glares at her.

"Go on, darling," Mom says to me.

Sam's eyes are rounded and his jaw's set tight, and Oliver's watching more closely than I want him to.

"Go shopping with your sister. Let her fix th—"

"Mom! Shut up!" Tenny shakes his head.

"Tennyson." She snaps her head in his direction. "You do not speak to me like that."

"Or what?" he asks loudly. "You're pretty lax on consequences for everyone in the world but Gige and Oliver." He nods to himself. "Pretty sure I'll be fine."

He pushes back from the table and stalks out, passing Jason walking in.

My oldest brother glowers at our brother-in-law. "You've got some nerve," Tennyson says as he juts his shoulder into him.

"Where have you been?" my sister asks tightly as she stands. She nods toward the spare seat next to her, but Jason eyes her as he doesn't take it.

He sits in Tenny's seat.

Maryanne's eyes bug out, and I'd be scared if I was him, but he just rubs his chin.

"Had to take Beckett to the hospital, and then I just needed some…" Jason looks at her a bit foreignly. "Space."

He didn't know. He's hurt that he didn't know.

"I can't believe you," my sister says, and I scoff as I push back from the table and leave.

It's at a great personal cost that I do this, because Sam Penny's hand was not only still on me at that point in time, but the way he was gripping me—it was anchoring me to the earth and steadying me still. And when I stand and he's no longer holding me because gravity and circumstance won't allow for it, I feel a nervous kind of exposed.

It's different to the sort of bareness I feel if I'm with Sam alone, which is a formidable bareness, where he's bare too and he's covering me and I'm safe and he sees me like how the poets talk about. And fuck…I like him too much. I know I do. I shouldn't feel like that, not yet, but here we are.

And I think it's a bit of that realization that propels me toward the exit, motors me out of there in a kind of dazed dismay, because I am both. Dazed and dismayed. It's the sixth day I've known Sam Penny exists, and I like him so much, and—

"Georgia, wait!" Oliver calls after me as I walk down the hall.

Fuck.

"What?" I spin around, arms folded over my chest because I think we need barriers these days, and that breaks my heart.

"I'm sorry." Oliver cringes as he says it. "Last night was—I fucked up. That was so insanely shit of me. I was just…I don't know. It made me—" He breathes out his nose as he tries to articulate himself. "I don't know why I…"

I cross my arms over my chest and tuck in my chin. "You perceived my omission of the events as either a betrayal of the trust you assumed we shared or as a commentary to—"

"Turn it off." Oliver points at me. "It's so fucking annoying, just turn it off for an hour—"

"It's my head! It doesn't turn off! How am I supposed to just turn it off?"

"Just stop thinking!"

I stare at him, wide-eyed. "Oh my God! Brilliant! Now I'm all better!"

"Surely you can just stop thinkin—"

"If you're able to turn your brain off how you're making it sound like you can turn your brain off, then I think I understand your last few years a little bett—"

"You not turning your brain off is a real case for alcoholism," he says with a thoughtful conviction, and it makes me laugh in this bewildered, confused little way.

Oliver tilts his head. "Just say you forgive me?" he asks, eyebrows up earnestly. "I hate it when we fight."

"I forgive you." I nod.

"Good." He hooks his arm around my neck. "I'm taking you to lunch."

29

OLI AND I ARE AT Captain Woody's Seafood Bar, which is maybe a weird place to go at 11:30 a.m., but we love it. We always have.

Besides, I can eat lobster any time of the day; I don't need those sorts of limitations on my life.

"So." I drink a sip of my sauvignon blanc. "Who were you…you know…when I called you?"

Oliver shrugs, coy. "Just some guy."

"Tell me!"

"Sam." He shrugs, and my eyes practically fall out of my head.

"What?"

He snorts a laugh. "I wish." He sighs. "His name's Brent."

"Oh." I nod. Trying not to look too relieved. "How old is he?"

Oliver takes a slow, drawn-out sip of his lemonade. "Forty-eight."

I make very sure that my face displays this and this sentiment only: "Oh, cool."

I'm particularly mindful of not allowing my face to express: "Typical Oliver."

Which it is, by the way.

Oliver almost exclusively dates one type of man: older, white-collar, successful businessmen. I know, I know, it's very Freudian. I said as much to him once in a fight, that it's so typical of him to only like guys who are like Dad, and he got really angry and didn't talk to me until I took it back.

I told him I was lashing out and that my best defense is psychobabble, but that wasn't psychobabble. My brother is one hundred percent compensating for the lack of attention my father bestowed upon him with men of a similar age, race, and (for lack of a better term) pedigree, so I expected this much when he answered my question.

"What about you?" he asks. "Are you dating anyone?"

I shake my head.

"What happened to that boy? That super hot one that you were with for a while—what was he called again? Andy?"

"Anatole." My lips twitch with microsadness before I can make sure they don't.

"Right." He nods. "What happened there?"

What happened there, indeed…

"We broke up." I give my brother a tight smile.

"When?"

"About five months ago?"

He rests his chin in his hand and his eyes catch in the light. "Were you sad?"

I mirror him to make him like me more. "Yes."

Anatole and I met about a year and a half ago at Bianca Harrington's boyfriend's birthday party. She and I went to school together, and we're fairly close, mostly because she's Hattie's other closest friend.

I was sitting down by myself watching people—my favorite pastime—and he sat across from me. He was this big, sort of Jax Teller–looking guy—but better hair, better clothes. Blue eyes, a couple of frown lines, and a few crinkles around the left of his mouth. I'd later work out that was because he smirks a lot.

He didn't say anything at first. Just sat there sipping his whisky, watching me watch people, a hint of a curious, tiny smile sitting on the corner of his mouth.

I knew he was there, could feel that he was.

And I don't normally like it when people watch me. I find it unsettling—which I know is rich coming from me because I almost exclusively watch people, but I don't like it when people do it back. But I could feel his eyes on me and I wanted them to stay there.

You could say it's because he's this super hot guy and I liked the attention. I might say it's because I think a part of you always knows when something is more than nothing, and he could never be nothing.

"I'm Ani," he said eventually, leaning forward over the table between us.

I gave him a long look.

"I know who you are," I told him.

"And you are 'the lie girl.'" He nodded a few times, smiling.

"Georgia." I extended my hand and he took it in both of his, and that moment should have come with a flashing sign that said *WARNING, WARNING! YOU WILL LOVE THIS MAN,* because my whole being jump-started when he touched me. It was so visceral, it was almost enough to recoil from, but I didn't want to, and I suppose he didn't either because he didn't let go.

"Jo's told me about you." He smiled. "You're some kind of person-reading genius."

"I'm still learning." I shrugged. I don't know why I played it down.

He finally let go of my hand, even though I sort of wished he hadn't. Anatole had this magical thing about him where he could make anyone feel important just by the way he held your gaze. I want to say that was because he is—at his core—a very good man, but the truth is it was learned. He learned young that if you make people feel seen and valued, they're more likely to do anything for you, so he'd hold people's gaze in a conversation and they'd hold the back door open for him when he snuck into a country to break someone out of jail, but he'd never hold anything the way he'd eventually hold me.

Anatole Storm tilted his head. "You liking it?"

"I love it." My smile gave away just how much I did.

His eyes flickered down to my mouth and back up before he pressed his tongue into his bottom lip. It was subconscious, he didn't know he did it, but he was attracted to me. In the dim lighting, it was hard to see a lot, but that was hard to miss.

"What do you do, Anatole?" I asked, leaning toward him.

He squinted over at me, smiling. Waited a few seconds. "You know what I do."

I nodded my chin at him. "Tell me yourself."

He breathed out of his nose slowly and nodded again. "I dabble with private militia."

I gave him a look. "Don't be modest."

He squashed away a smile. "I am private militia in this country."

I gave him a small wink. "There it is."

He watched me for a few seconds, those Saturn eyes pinched. "Scared?"

I tilted my head inquisitively. "Should I be?"

A frown flickered across his face like static on a TV before he shook his head and did an AU17 with his mouth, like he couldn't believe I'd even ask. "No," he told me, equal parts cocky and quite serious. "Never again."

He had me at that point in the conversation, I can probably admit now in retrospect. His Disney prince hair, giant shoulders, and sparkly ink eyes already made him a little hard to not to be had, but he had me there. At the time, I would have liked to have thought otherwise, but when I think back to that night, my brain snags there. That was the moment.

We talked for an hour or so. People would approach us, chitchat for a minute, but more to me than to him because I think to nearly everyone else in the room, he was scary—but not to me.

At some point in the conversation, he moved next to me, and from there I was a goner because he was this mix of tobacco and leather and

Tom Ford and I think I would have drowned in him if he let me. And I do mean that in the hyperbolic, metaphoric, and the literal senses.

He nodded back toward the door.

"You wanna grab a drink?"

I eyed the lowball glass in his hand. "We're drinking now."

Ani leaned forward and said very clearly, "I think I'd like to be alone with you."

"I'm sure you would!" I laughed. "But I'm not having sex with you, though."

His face lit up, like, properly. "That is so cute that you think you have that much willpower—"

My mouth fell open in surprise, and then he started laughing, so I started laughing, and I liked how he sounded when he laughed. This deep, sort of jovial lightness that contradicts everything else about him and the world he's from and what he does.

"You're pretty big for your boots, ey?" He eyed me playfully. "I just wanted to take you for a chip."

I rolled my eyes.

"Let me buy you a drink," he told me, and he put his hand on top of mine, and I think his hand diffused into mine the way milk does when it spills into water. "Please."

I gave him a long look. "Maybe."

He smiled, tilting his head. "Maybe?"

"I'm going to ask you ten questions," I told him. "Your answers will determine whether or not I'll get a drink with you."

"Okay." He clapped his hands together once. "Fair."

"One," I started. "Name, age, and town of birth." Seems like a waste of a question, I know. But I needed to establish a baseline.

"Anatole Élisée Storm. Thirty-one. I was born in Seine-Maritime—my mum's from there. What about you?"

"I'll ask the questions," I told him, nose in the air, and he smiled. "Two. What's your relationship with your dad like?"

His eyes tightened as he thought about his answer. "Complicated."

"What about your relationship with your mom—what's that like?"

"Pretty one-sided." He nodded slowly. "Because she's quite dead."

"Oh shit. I'm sorry, I—"

Anatole shook his head like it was nothing. "Keep going."

"Okay. Number three. Who is the most important person in your life?"

He squinted playfully. "You mean besides you?"

"Anatole." I gave him a stern look even though I was playing. "The fate of you and I depends heavily on these questions—answer them thusly."

It flicked across his face, this funny mix of attraction and maybe a hint of contempt, being bossed around. I could have told you there and then why I liked him, and it was this: he was exquisitely transparent. To me, at least. He was gloriously present. Microexpressions galore...

He leaned back in his chair.

"I have a brother." He shrugged, but his eyes—AU6—he didn't let himself smile, but he wanted to; I knew that before he delivered the second part of his underwhelming response. "He's all right."

I rolled my eyes at him to make sure he knew I didn't care for his stupid "cool guy" answers.

"Is he younger or older?" I asked.

Anatole tilted his head. "Is that question four?"

"No. That was a sidebar."

He gave me a look, like he wasn't so sure, but then he answered anyway. "I'm older."

"Yeah." I nodded as I watched him. "You have that 'older brother' air about you."

His face pinched. "Is that a compliment?"

"I don't know." I shrugged. "I don't like my older brother."

He sniffed a laugh, didn't take his eyes off me as he said, "Families are complicated."

"Right?" I smacked my hand down on top of his without thinking. He glanced down at it and then back up at me, smiling a little cockily—I snatched it away quickly.

I cleared my throat. "That was number…"

"Three," he told me.

"Okay." I mirrored him, because I wanted him to keep being attracted to me. "Dating anyone?"

"Nope."

"Last time you had sex?"

He pursed his lips as he thought back, then reluctantly answered, "Two days ago."

"With who?" I asked, nosily.

"Is that question six?"

"No, it's a sub-question of number five."

He rolled his eyes. "No one."

I pulled a face. "So not really sex then, just a solo sesh?"

He laughed loudly and it made me feel smug. "No one special."

"Oh." I licked away a smile. "You heart breaker…"

His eyes dropped down to my mouth again before he dragged them back up my face and smiled at me. "Takes one to know one," he said, and that made my heart skip a beat because of course it did.

I sucked in my bottom lip. I was nervous to ask him what I was going to next, but to yield the best reaction from him, I needed to ask him when he wasn't expecting it.

"Have you ever sexually assaulted someone?"

Anatole's head pulled back, his brows dropped, and a microscowl blew across his face. Disgust. "Never."

He was offended I even asked.

Interesting, I thought. Actually, eventually he'd try to kill Beckett when I told him what happened, booked a flight to the Carolinas and everything.

"You think I'm lying?" he asked, frowning at me when I didn't say anything for a few seconds.

"No, actually." I tilted my head as horizontal as it could go and watched him. "You are very much so telling the truth."

"How do you know?" he asked, voice serious.

I gestured to his face. "Your brows went down and your lips parted." He blinked blankly. "You're insulted that I asked you. It's all over your face. If you had done *that*, you would have exhibited signs of fear or shame, maybe anger—but not offense."

He blinked away the scowl he was sporting and replaced it with a funny sort of awe. "I could probably rule the world if I had you in my back pocket."

"I don't know." I shrugged, holding his gaze. "I feel like you could probably rule it anyway."

That made him smile.

"Question seven—"

"Question eight," he corrects me.

"No." I shook my head. "The other ones didn't count."

He gave me an unsure look. "They were questions, so it counts."

"Question seven," I said loudly over him.

"Eight," he said under his breath.

I leaned in toward him. "Have you ever killed anyone?"

He paused, and our eyes caught. The answer was obvious, and I knew that how he answered would be pivotal.

Because to me, it was overt. I don't know whether he knew I knew it was overt, but it would have been a healthy assumption on his behalf to think that giving an honest answer there might not have been in his best interest.

He sucked in his cheeks a little; his brows got lower and he eyed me carefully. His head pulled back, chin jutted out—that's anger. He didn't like that question. And you'd think I would have been nervous. He was and is, beyond a shadow of a doubt, one of the most dangerous men in Britain, but he didn't and never has felt in any way like a threat to me.

"Yes." He didn't break eye contact with me.

I didn't flinch. "Do you regret it?"

His eyes flicked up as he thought back. "I regret some," he said carefully. "Not all."

I wanted to ask how many that meant, but that would have been my tenth question. Arguably it would be a worthwhile tenth question, but even then and especially now, the exact number didn't really feel like it mattered. I mean—it matters, but also it kind of doesn't.

Not to me. Not in the way maybe it should have, anyway.

I don't shy away from people because they've made mistakes. Mistakes make you human. The worst thing you could ever be to me is a liar. Anatole Storm was arguably a million bad things, but that wasn't one of them.

Fucking up and owning it is like catnip for me. The self-acceptance it takes to admit your flaws out loud to someone else is impressive, and I'd say downright admirable. Maybe I say that now as a means to justify how I'd love him in the end—which was madly and with a reckless abandon—but what other way is there, really?

He tilted his head, curious. "Drink's off, then?"

"I still have one more question left," I told him.

He crinkled his nose playfully. "You don't, but go on then, ask your eleventh question anyway."

I gave him a long, steady look—trying to figure out the answer before I asked the question.

"Are you going to break my heart? Fuck me up a little bit?"

"Oh, yeah," He nodded, smiling playfully. "Definitely."

I pointed at him. "And that was your first lie tonight."

"Guess you'll just have to come with me and see." He shrugged.

I bit down on my bottom lip. "I guess I will."

"Why did you, then?" Oliver asks, leaning across the table. "Break up, I mean?"

I give him a bit of a sad smile. "He ended it."

It was quite traumatic, actually. We'd been together—I don't know—ten months, maybe? Properly, too—he wasn't seeing other people, he wasn't sleeping with anyone else, and so we were together-together in an official capacity. I knew him, he knew me, and we were together all the time, almost living together, actually. "I love you's," outward confessions, PDA, all the kind of shit that Ani swore he'd never do but he did with me.

And then one day, he was gone.

Disappeared in the dead of night. I tried calling him, texting him, emailing him, DM-ing him. I went to his house. One of the guys who works for him told me he'd gone away on business, but something sat weird—he swallowed nervously as he said it. It wasn't a lie, per se. But it wasn't regular business.

The week he was gone dragged by in slow motion. Every time my phone made a sound, every time I'd hear someone in my apartment block—every time, I thought it was him, but it wasn't.

Eight days he was gone, no contact, nothing.

He just slipped away.

And then on the ninth day, there was a knock on my door.

By then I'd begun to lose hope. In Anatole's line of work, death is statistically inevitable. I kind of knew that going in, and I dove in head-first anyway. Not because I'm emotionally masochistic—at least, I hope I'm not—but because he was fascinating to know, exciting to be with, painfully human, and impetuously honest. But none of those qualities precluded him from death. If anything, they sort of invited it more. It was around day five I'd begun to process the imaginary and hypothetical death of my boyfriend, and I was four days deep in quasi-mourning when he knocked on my door.

The wave of emotions that hit me once I saw him—I don't even know where to begin. You would have thought I'd be angry... And maybe after relief, anger came in hot for a second or two, but that was before I saw his face.

Black eye. Swollen, beat-up bottom lip. Cut on the bridge of his nose. Busted eyebrow.

"What happened to you?" I asked quietly as he stepped inside.

He shook his head. "I can't—"

"Well." I looked up at him. "Where have you been?"

"Georgia, I can't tell y—"

"What happened?" I asked, louder.

"Georgia—"

"Did you kill someone?" I pressed, and our eyes caught.

He said nothing.

"Who?" I pressed again, and he turned away from me, but I ducked around him so I could see his face.

"Stop."

"Who!"

"Don't ask me," he growled.

"What happened?" I asked again, watching his face, and he swatted his hand at me.

"Don't do your fucking shit on me!" he yelled. "I told you not to ask me—if I wanted you to know, you'd fucking know!"

I grabbed his wrist to spin him around. "So tell me!"

"I can't!" he said through clenched teeth.

"That's bullshit!" I crowed at the ceiling. "You left me! You just disappeared! You didn't even leave a note! And then you come back looking like that and you can't tell me what happened?"

He shook his head again. "You know what I do."

I shook my head back. "You've never done this before."

He swallowed once and his face quite drastically and quickly changed from angry to... It was hard to pick at first, but it was scared. It was definitely scared.

"Yeah, listen." He swallowed—intense emotion or nerves, I couldn't tell. "Georgia, we've gotta call this."

I went quiet. Or maybe the world did. I can't really remember. Sound dropped off, and all I could hear was him breathing, and it walloped me in the guts when I realized how much I'd missed that sound.

"What?" I asked softly.

"We need to break up."

"Are y—are you with someone else?" I asked, my voice smaller than I wanted it to be.

His eyes locked on to mine and he shook his head again.

"Then no! No. I don't want—"

"I don't care. We have to."

"No!" I don't know when I started crying, but I realized then that my face was wet.

"I can't—"

"You can't what?" I asked loudly. "You don't get to just decide this without me!"

He pressed his hand over his mouth. It was a gestural slip. Self-hushing. There was something he wasn't telling me...something part of him wanted to but the other part wouldn't let him.

"Storm." I looked for his eyes, and when I found them, they were far more ragged than I was expecting. Glassy and heavy with a fresh pain I hadn't really seen before. And then he took my face in both of his hands, tilted his head so we were eye to eye.

"I love you," he told me. "Look at me—I'm in love with you. Am I lying?"

My bottom lip trembled.

"No," I answered softly.

"I love you, and I swore I wouldn't ever put you in danger, Gige." He held my eyes, not looking away. He wanted me to see he was telling me the truth. "And if you stay with me, then I am."

I pushed him off me. "What are you talking about?"

Anatole Storm gave me a solemn, weary look, and he almost couldn't get the words out. "They'll kill you."

I drew in a sharp breath. "Who?"

"Anyone who wants to hurt me."

"No." I shook my head, confused and reeling. "I'm safe with you—"

"No one's safe with people like me."

"What happened?" I asked again, yelling.

His jaw jutted out. "Stop fucking asking—"

"No! You're being stupid. You love me—so much. What are you doing?"

"That's the problem." He gave me a hopeless shrug. "I do love you. So much. And—"

I cut him off and overenunciate my question. "What happened?"

"Something happened with Julian's sister."

I went quiet. "Is she okay?"

He looked a bit dazed—didn't say yes or no—just breathed out a breath I didn't even realize he was holding. His eyes caught mine, and the weight of them was so heavy they sank me like a stone.

"We're done now." And as I opened my mouth, he shook his head. "It's not a conversation, Georgia. I'm changing my number tomorrow. Don't come to my house, don't call. Don't contact the boys—"

I was crying again, and his heart broke on his face. He rushed to me, his hands on my face only for a second before his mouth swallowed mine.

"I have to keep you safe," he told me as he pulled away, then pressed his mouth into my forehead.

How I felt when Anatole held me I was quite sure I'd never feel again, especially back then. At the time, Ani somehow felt like the safest place in the world. Probably because the truth—no matter what it costs—is to me, he was the only safe place to exist. He never lied to me. He would never; he knew what it meant to me, so I knew even as he was doing this—what he was saying must be true. That I would die if we stayed together.

It almost felt worth it. Proper love always does.

And then we had sex. It's almost biblical that we did. That whole "eat, drink, and be merry because tomorrow we die" kind of attitude.

It was probably stupid. Break-up sex usually is.

I didn't have any lingering hopes that I could change his mind; I knew I couldn't. Storm doesn't change his mind.

It's not the perfect way to say goodbye either, though we all make arguments that it might be. It's highly imperfect and entirely flawed and the reason we do it is science. It's just arousal transference.

Pretty believable with a guy like Ani anyway, who, arguably until this week, remained the most beautiful man I'd ever seen.

Anatole took a long time to get over. Three months. I know that doesn't sound like a long time, but it was because I didn't avoid it. Three solid months of the unrelenting everything.

You can't avoid the avalanche of emotions that come with the termination of a relationship; you can only prolong them, which I refused to do. I looked every feeling I felt square in the eye and stared it down until it rolled over. The grief would come in waves, and I'd miss him on certain days, at certain hours, but for the most part, I had closure, because it wasn't rejection and no one fucked up. We were in love and it didn't work.

There was nothing either of us could have done to make it work. He was born into that life, and I wasn't.

Wondering and questioning why things are the way they are, not accepting the present and permanent—they're all really solid ways to slow down progress.

But the truth is (and I don't think this sort of revelation requires a psychology degree), there was no way it could have gone differently without him risking me, and at the time, I was happy to be risked, but now I'm glad he loved me enough to let me go.

Do you know what Ani's parting words were to me as he was leaving?

"It's gonna feel for a minute like I went and broke your heart and fucked you up, but I swear to God, Gige—it's the other way around. You're going to fall in love in a few months with someone who's not like me at all, and I'm going to fucking loathe you for it." He chuckles. "But I need you to...to let me go, because I probably can't let go of you. I love you more than I meant to. I really did just plan on shagging you that night," he told me, and I laughed even though I was still crying. Then he pressed his mouth against mine, and he never spoke to me again.

"Sounds like Mom would have hated him..." Oli sniffs, amused.

I laugh. "Oh, Mom would have hated him!"

"I think I would have liked him," Oliver tells me with a smile, a fry dangling from his mouth.

I nod, thinking of Anatole fondly, because it's impossible for me not to even now. "I think he would have liked you too."

"That all would have been so hard." Oliver frowns and touches my hand.

"Yeah." I give him a tender smile. "It was."

His eyebrows do something. AU1. But it's not quite surprise. Hope, maybe?

"So you're not over it yet?"

I mouth shrug. "Well, no—I am."

"How?" Oliver sits back in his seat, shaking his head. "If you loved him so much? It's been, what, like six months?"

I frown a little. "Five."

"Exactly." He gestures at me. "So how could you be?"

My head pulls back and I blink a few times, surprised at what he's challenging me over, but if I read between the lines, I guess I'm not too surprised at all. "Because Oliver, I worked hard at it... I killed myself to get over him properly, but I did."

"Oh cool." He nods. "When's the self-help book coming out?"

"It's already out, and it's called *Grow the Fuck Up*." I roll my eyes. "Asshole."

He gives me a tight smile. "I'm joking."

And I don't know why he says that. I don't know why he'd willingly lie to me. "No, you're not." I peer over at him.

He rolls his eyes a little, and my heart sinks when I think of how we used to be. I can't find the pathway back to the place in time where we only rolled our eyes at everyone else.

"You want to get over someone quickly?" I stare over at him. "Feel everything. Every shred of loss, everything you're missing now that they're gone. On lonely nights, be lonely. When you're sad, look it in the eye. Every single memory I had of Storm, I ruminated on them for weeks on end and it felt like I fell into a fire, and then somehow, one day, after months of pain and months of forcing myself to feel all of it, I saw a picture of him and I didn't feel like I was going to die anymore."

My brother says nothing, just blinks.

"I was heartbroken, Ol." I nod. "Completely. But I'm not anymore, because I stared it down. That's the secret—" I give him a tight smile. "I'm not afraid of pain."

I can tell by his face that he takes that personally, though I don't consciously mean for it to be.

"And what?" Oliver says—AU7, eyes pinched. "I am?"

I sigh. "People don't develop substance dependencies by dealing with their problems; they develop them to numb them."

He sniffs a laugh. "You think you're better than me."

I shake my head, because this isn't sounding like my brother anymore.

"Never, ever, ever, ever have I ever thought I was better than you, Oliver—never. But I am in more control of myself; that's just a fact."

I'm watching him closely, trying to play out in my mind what comes next in this conversation.

His face is tight and pulled; he looks distracted and sort of sad.

I fucking hate it when Oliver's sad. There's something about the way his eyes go. The brown in them goes greener. His brows crease in the center and his bottom lip pulls in, and every time I see him like that, I remember him making the same face when I was seven and he was eight and our dad had just crucified him for playing with my Barbies. It was so tremendously fucked up, and Oliver was so deeply hurt but tried not to show it because Dad would have hated that too (which was probably worse), and that was the first time I can remember watching someone make Oliver feel less-than for being himself, and that's what I think of every time he looks sad.

My brother swallows and looks away, down and to the right. Brows furrowed, consternation written all over him. Then he glances up and gives me this long look, his mouth twitching as he does. He has something to say but he's considering whether to say it.

He leans forward for a second and then shifts back, and I can see it ticking behind his eyes, this question begging to be asked.

I watch him patiently, wondering where this is going, but I have a feeling I already know, and I'm prepping myself for the answer just in case.

If I'm right about what he's going to ask me, I'm going to have to deny something in a second, and the part where he'll catch me is in my response time. Even a millisecond or two of a delayed answer could subconsciously suggest to him that I'm not telling him the truth. I need to make sure my body language matches my words, that my tone remains steady and nondefensive… I should probably even sound a little confused? A direct answer first and then confusion, that would be organic.

Three.

Two.

One.

He cringes before he asks it: "Is there something going on with you and Sam?"

I knew it.

"No." I pull my head back, consciously, so it's as though I'm taken aback by the question. I'm not. I bend my brows in the middle to look confused. "What?"

He lets out a laugh and relaxes a little. "Good."

"Why?" I ask, making sure my blinking rate stays the same. Approximately one blink every ten to twelve seconds is the average rate a person blinks, but blinking has been known to decrease when someone's in the throes of a lie. After the lie's finished, their blinking doesn't just go back to normal; it speeds up.

"Just wondering." He shrugs like it's nothing now.

I like how the body betrays you like that, that it wants the truth to come out no matter what.

I like the truth, and I hate that I'm lying to my brother, but I don't know what the answer is.

I just know that wasn't it.

30

OLIVER AND I GET HOME in the late afternoon and when we do, Violet's sitting on the front steps. Her eyes are red from crying and all of her gets heavier when she sees me.

News travels fast in a small town. I sigh bigger than I mean to as I climb out of the car.

She stands up and walks over to me, bottom lip trying to hold it together but failing miserably. It's not her fault. How she's reacting is natural. She's guilty—it's all over every ounce of her being—she thinks she could have done something. I'm not angry at her for thinking this, I'm not angry at her for being sad, it's just—delayed grief is such a weird phenomenon if you've already grieved it.

Oliver gives my arm a squeeze as he walks away and inside.

Vi stands in front of me and I pace myself, tell myself to be gracious, that this is news to her and it would have broken her heart then if she knew, but she didn't.

She gestures toward the path. "Can we go for a walk?"

I nod once. She takes this big, staggered breath, then breathes it out—and I know I told myself to be gracious, but I swear to God if one more person asks me why I didn't tell them, I'll punch them.

"Are you okay?" she asks once we round the corner of the house. She stands still; her eyes can barely hold mine they're so weighed down with remorse.

"I'm fine."

And I mostly am; it's not a deflection. There are parts of what happened that kill me still now, flashes or memories of touches that I didn't want, but for the most part, most days, I'm okay.

"How?" She blinks.

I give her a sad smile. "It was a long time ago for me, Vi."

"But—"

I offer her a tiny shrug. "I've been in therapy since Mom and Dad shipped me away."

"They sent you away because they thought you were sleeping with Maryanne's boyfriend, but he—" She wipes away falling tears. "Your dad would—"

My dad would nothing, I'm fairly sure.

She sniffs and shakes her head and then she looks at me in this squinty confused way, and I can see it happening behind her eyes: she's combing through her memories, flicking back to her thoughts of who I used to be when I lived here, wondering whether I asked her for help in a silent kind of way, and it pains her—it's obvious it does.

"I let you down." She nods, like she's resigning to it.

"You didn't."

"I should have known."

"I—" I shake my head. "I wouldn't have told anyone back then."

"Why?" she asks, and it's so desperate.

She doesn't understand. And to be fair, it's a hard thing to explain, let alone understand, if you aren't a psychologist or a victim.

I sit down on the little step that hems the garden path and sigh. "I was fourteen when it started."

She sits down next to me, chin in hand, staring.

"And back then—even now, really—there's not a lot of discussion around the physiological effects of rape."

She frowns a little. "What do you mean?"

I press my tongue into my bottom lip and think back to the moments I try to avoid, wonder if there's a way around saying it, but there isn't, and I don't think it's the sort of thing we should talk around anymore anyway.

"Sometimes I'd come." I glance at her, and she looks taken aback. "And that really fucked me up."

"Oh," she says, and she's blinking a lot.

"And it took me forever to even say that out loud—I think I only ever said it to my therapist—because it *is* confusing, and you'd think you'd only come if you're like, a happy, willing participant, which I wasn't. But sometimes I'd come, so I began to wonder whether I was."

"Oh, Gige." Violet sighs, sadly.

"And it wasn't until she compared it to being tickled that I realized—like how you can hate being tickled and still laugh when you are—the laughing isn't a sign of enjoyment; it's a physiological response to something happening to your body. Orgasms are the same, so it turns out."

"So you didn't tell anyone." She nods, and I think she's getting it.

"I wasn't really sure what I'd be telling them?" I shrug. "Maryanne's boyfriend keeps having sex with me and...what?" I trail off. I knew Beckett could tell the times when I came, and I think it validated it in his mind or gave him tacit permission or something, because he knew about as much about female orgasms and the physiology of it all as I did. "I didn't know what any of it meant."

"Honey." She touches my face. "You weren't supposed to." She shakes her head and looks away from me. "I could kill that boy."

I grimace. "I think they nearly killed him last night."

"I heard." She glances at me. "Good, I'm glad. Clay said Sam was real mad." She's peering at me out of the corner of her eye.

"He was." I press my lips together.

"So what's happening with you two?"

"Nothing," I say reflexively.

Vi rolls her eyes.

"Something," I say instead. I laugh once. "I don't know—we haven't talked about it."

She smirks. "So what have you done?"

"Not a lot," I admit somewhat ruefully.

She smiles at me warmly, then pauses. "Does Oliver know?"

"No." I purse my mouth. "I don't want him to yet."

"Why?" she asks me even though I know she knows the answer already, and I shrug like I don't.

"I'm just figuring things out," I lie.

She stares straight ahead. "Mmhmm."

31

I WENT TO DINNER WITH VIOLET and Clay after that, and it was so good to spend time with just them because they remind me that not all grown-ups are fucked, but I didn't get home until way later than I'd hoped.

Today was the least amount of time that I've seen Sam since I met him, and I know that sounds clingy, but then I suppose I won't see him again come next week, and that's the sort of revelation that could drive a person to eat a two-pound lobster in twenty-five minutes. But it was all for nought, because then they took me for dessert and I kissed my chances of kissing Sam tonight goodbye.

The lights are off in the house when I get home; no one's awake.

I'd hoped maybe Sam would be in the chair in the living room "reading"—or even actually reading would have been fine—but he's not.

I head upstairs to my room, and that's when I see it: his bedroom is light on, and it's flooding our narrow corridor with light from his open door.

He's sitting on the bed, black jeans and a white T-shirt, knees up, book in hand, and the mundane-ness of the moment makes my heart ache for all the other mundane things I don't think I'll get to see him do: clean his teeth, pick up the morning paper, buy some milk, ask for directions—

Sam Penny doing any of those things would be poetry, but him like that on the bed with a book is Shakespeare.

"Hi." I lean against his doorframe.

He looks up, and the way his whole face lifts when he sees me makes me want to cry on the spot, because how many people just light up because you walk into the room? One in a lifetime, two maybe?

"Hey." He tosses the book to the side, then stands up and walks over to me. "How was your day?"

I smile at him, tireder than I mean to, but Sam Penny undoes all my guises and I sigh.

"Um—heavy?" That tired smile morphs now into a grimace I've not permitted to be on my face. "What about yours?"

"Yeah." He shrugs. "It was pretty good. Tenny and me went fishing."

I let out a single laugh. "Why?"

Sam's face falters for a tiny second. "He's your brother."

I swallow. "You mean Oliver's brother..."

"No." He shakes his head coolly. Shoulders square, pupils dilated. "I mean yours."

"Oh." I purse my lips and my cheeks go pink, those traitors, and he squashes a smile as he watches me, and I could catch fire under his unflinching gaze.

"At breakfast this morning, Oliver asked me if anything was going on between us," I tell him.

Sam's head pulls back, a sliver of an AU1 and an AU12. It's pretty locked up on his face, but I can still spot it: surprise and happiness.

"What'd you say?"

"No?" I say it, but there's an upward inflection, and his eyebrows flick up quickly.

Okay so, no—*now* he's surprised.

He squints at me a little and tilts his head. "It's okay if it is, but is that the truth?"

Our interpersonal distance is clocking in at about one foot, two inches at this second, and his feet are directly toward me, and I don't mean to, but I'm staring at his mouth while biting down on mine. I sniff a laugh, because—"No."

He presses his lips together and nods, smiling. "Can I take you on a date?"

"What, now?" My cheeks go pink again.

"Yeah."

I frown. "I've had dinner."

He makes a half laugh, half *pfft* sound.

"We'll have it again." He shrugs. "Or—don't? I don't care—I just wanna—what's your favorite place in South Carolina?"

"The airport," I say, deadpan.

Sam Penny rolls his eyes. "Come on."

I purse my lips and pretend like I have to think about it.

"Are you up for a bit of a drive?"

"With you?" He blinks a couple of times, then smiles. "Yeah, I'll take the long road."

"Did you and Ol have a good lunch?" Sam asks, glancing over at me from the driver's seat.

I don't know why he's driving when I'm the one from here, but there's something about boys in cars and the way they hold the clutch…

"Yeah," I nod. "It was good. We kind of just…caught up."

He looks back at the road, but his mouth does something weird. It pursed or it twitched? I don't know. Something.

"What?" I ask, staring at him.

He glances at me quickly. "Nothing."

Then he looks back at the road. He swallows.

"What's that?" I ask, tilting my head to get a better look at him.

"What's what?" His face goes tight, eyes squinting a little, cheeks pulling up.

I plant my finger on his cheekbone. "That."

He flicks his eyes over at me, a little annoyed, but it dissipates quickly. He blows air out of his mouth like it's nothing. "Oliver mentioned in passing today that you seemed pretty hung up on your ex."

I snap my head in his direction. "What?"

"Don't be angry at him." Sam shakes his head. "He was just—"

"Lying!" I blink.

Sam's face goes still. "So you're not still in love with him?"

"I *love* him, I'm not *in* love with him."

Sam glances over at me, and maybe for the first time since we met, he looks cautious. "That's not like—a fucking stellar answer, Georgia..."

I sigh. "We didn't have this fiery, death-storm breakup—"

"Yeah?" He interrupts, eyebrows up. "So what did you have?"

That could be the sharpest he's ever been with me, and I'm fuming. Not with Sam—I'm practically soaring over Sam's microexpressions. Contempt, maybe a twinge of fear, a bit of anger. That's a lot of strong emotions swirling around something that—technically, aside from me—has nothing to do with him. But Oliver? Oliver, I could murder.

Because he knows I'm not hung up on Storm... I was explicit about it. So he's just lying to Sam for his own benefit.

Sam's looking at me, waiting, those suspended eyebrows trimmed with annoyance and impatience, and I feel my ego inflating over his reaction. I sigh and I tell Sam the story—who Anatole was, what he did, the disappearing, the danger, the breakup—and the further into the story I go, the sadder he looks.

"I'm not angry at him," I tell Sam. "I'm not bitter at him—I'm grateful for him, actually. And I love him, and I want him to be safe and happy, but I'm fully aware now that if I was with him, I'd never be safe, and if I was never safe, he'd never be happy."

Sam glances at me. "Do you think he's going to kill me in my sleep?"

"Oh, no." I wave my hand dismissively. "He's much more a 'shoot you in the face while you're awake' kind of guy."

Sam rolls his eyes, and it's only then I realize we've stopped driving. It isn't a huge drive, I suppose—about a half hour from my parents' house.

"I can't believe you dated a mercenary..."

I grimace. "I really think he was more like, a private contractor with an army at his disposal."

Sam tosses me a sarcastic glance. "Oh, is that all?"

"It didn't mean anything." I shrug. "He was just my boyfriend with a weird job."

Sam climbs out of the car and opens my door.

I stand up and he stands there, toe-to-toe with me, brows furrowed. "What'd you tell Oliver?" he asks.

"I don't know." I shrug. "The same story?"

Sam purses his mouth and makes a *hm* sound.

"What?" I blink.

And his face pulls a million microexpressions, but then he shakes his head. "I—did you? Never mind."

I watch Sam's face, looking for clues. He's annoyed. There's contempt on his face; he doesn't want there to be, but there is. He's jamming his mouth shut, which I think I'm interpreting as a self-hushing emblem.

I take a shot in the dark. "I was explicit with Oliver about my position with Storm."

"Explicit?" he repeats, thinking and frowning.

I nod. "Is there a chance you misinterpreted what he meant?"

Sam gives me a long look, then shakes his head again. "No, he was pretty explicit himself."

"Oh." And suddenly I feel less bad for saying nothing was going on before.

And then Sam Penny grabs my face and kisses me. This big, deep, wave-against-a-cliff kiss that knocks me back a little, but his hand is behind me, and it catches me briefly before he presses me into the door of the car. The hand on my face slides into my hair, and I think I've never felt safer in my life, pinned between him and a car, his chest grazing mine as he breathes a bit raggedly. The more I kiss Sam (which, admittedly, is substantially less frequently than I'd like to), the more I realize something about it hurts me, but not in the bad way—in the good way?

You know how there's a good kind of hurting? Like rubbing out a cramp? Or great sex, sometimes? Being near him hurts me all over my body. I think it's because he's what all the songs are singing about. Every single fucking one of them, they're singing about him.

So maybe it's the cosmicness of it, or maybe it's the way his mouth feels against mine—like it's some sort of soul resuscitation, like Sam Penny is a heart-stretch put on the planet to reinstill faith back into mankind so we have something worthwhile to write the poems about.

He pulls back a little and smiles at me before he sighs, content.

He offers me his hand, and I stare at it for a few seconds before I take it, not because I don't want to, but because aimless closeness is still a new concept to me.

He leads me a few steps into the darkness and then he pauses, glancing back at me.

"I don't know where I'm going."

I smile at him and lead the way.

It used to be called Prince William's Parish Church, but now they call it the Old Sheldon Church Ruins. It burned down first in 1779 in the Revolutionary War, and then they rebuilt it about fifty years later, but someone burned it down again during the Civil War. I think it's so interesting that the names of things can change after something bad happens to them.

These old church ruins sit amongst giant oak trees and gravestones dating back the last three hundred years, and I've always loved it here.

Always. Violet showed me it when I was nine. It's where Clay proposed to her.

"Holy shit," he says, staring up at the stripped-back pillars in awe.

The sky is inky and starry and clear, which makes it feel ethereal and otherworldly, but the hauntedness of the droopy oaks grounds me and reminds me that it's all real.

Because it so easily could not be.

Sam Penny in that white T-shirt, in his black jeans and those old

Cons he wears, looking like that, kissing like that—it's where you hope you'll go when your head touches the pillow.

"Isn't it the most beautiful thing you've ever seen?" I stare up at the big arch, which is my favorite part, I think. "Even though it's broken?"

"Yep," he says quietly, and he's looking just at me.

32

I WAIT IN BED ON SUNDAY morning for as long as I can, hoping that Sam will bring me up a coffee, because it would be romantic and telling if he did, but he doesn't.

I actually wait so long that I eventually begin to worry that everyone will think I'm slovenly, so I get up and have a shower.

I don't know why it happens, but I feel a pang of sadness as I stand under the running water at the memory of that night and my mother shoving me all heart-and-soul-mangled in here, freezing cold, to wash away the sins I didn't commit.

The bathroom's been redone since then… It looks different, new tiles, new fixtures… The bath, shower, and vanity are all in the same places but have been replaced, which makes it stranger, because it makes it feel like I'm remembering something from a bad dream, but I'm not. It's a weird abstract reality I lived once upon a time, and my mind walks around this old house and I try to think of a room here where I have a happy memory.

I'm standing in front of the mirror, staring at myself with a towel wrapped around me, when there's a knock on the door.

I frown at it. "What?"

"It's me," Sam says through the door.

I adjust my towel and check my reflection. I'm bare-faced, but my cheeks are flushed pink from the heat, so at least my eyes look bright. "Come in."

He walks in and freezes when he sees me towel clad.

He stares at the towel two seconds longer than he probably should have according to social etiquette, and it makes me smile, though I try not to let him see.

"I, uh..." He trails, blinking a few times—his cheeks going pink too. "I just wanted to see—" He swallows and focuses very intently on my eyes. "Whether you were awake..."

"While I was showering?" I tilt my head. "You wanted to know whether I was awake when I'm upright and in a room that's not my bedroom?"

He nods, though it's reluctant as the silliness of his statement begins to settle upon him. Nevertheless, he decides to double down. "Mhm."

"Well, would you look at that!" I give him a look. "I am."

"Good." He nods a few more times, his eyes round and bright. "Okay, well—"

He turns to leave.

"Why don't you bring me coffees in the morning?" I call after him, and he stands frozen for a second before he swivels on his foot and turns around.

He lets out a single laugh.

"You did once," I say, "and then you stopped, and I thought you would—I think you said you would."

He nods, coolly. "I did."

"But you haven't since."

"I know." He's smirking now, that asshole.

"And you like coffee so much, and I thought you liked m—" I cut myself off and press my lips together, glancing up at him.

Penny's eyebrows shoot up and he smirks playfully. "What's that now?"

"You do, though, right?" I ask, shifting on my feet, crossing my arms over my chest.

He tries not to smile. "I do what?"

I know he knows what, so I give him an impatient look, but he just shrugs airily, waiting for my answer. I growl at the back of my throat. "Like me?"

He peers down the bridge of his nose, and he looks more amused than I'd like him to. "Yeah," he says.

"No, but I mean, *like-like*—"

"Like-like?" He scoffs. "What are you, eight?"

I fold my arms over my chest. "Answer the question."

He nods his chin at me. "Ask it better."

I square my shoulders and look him straight in the eye. "Sam Penny, do you have romantic feelings for me?"

He thinks for a second, and the way his mouth is pursed makes me nervous for the splittest of seconds.

"My feelings for you are...strictly romantic." Then he adds as an afterthought—"And often sexual."

I snort a laugh, and he grins. "Are you not going to ask me how I feel about you?" I blink, ready to give him my answer.

He shakes his head, unfazed. "No, I know how you feel about me."

"Oh." I swallow. I don't know why that felt like such a sexy thing to say.

"I thought about it, by the way." He ducks his head so he can see my eyes. "The coffee. I just thought it was obvious, and I didn't—I wasn't sure whether we were..." He squashes his mouth together, amused. "... being obvious?"

My eyes are a bit round now. "Oh."

"Oliver would probably notice," he tells me, which is true. "Tenny would notice," he adds, which is—somewhat oddly—definitely true.

"Right."

"They can notice?" He looks for my eyes. "If you want them to, I d—"

"No." I shake my head, my cheeks going pink at the thought of my brothers knowing that Sam Penny and I like-like each other, and I'm grinning like a big loser at the thought. "It's not a big deal—"

"Have mine," he tells me, offering me his mug, but I don't notice what's in his hands because I'm distracted (always distracted) by his face.

"Your what?"

"I meant my coffee, but..." He smiles. "You can have my—fuck—have whatever you want. Have everything." His tongue is pressed into his bottom lip, his pupils are dilated, and his gaze flickers from my eyes to my mouth to my eyes to my mouth to my eyes, and he swallows heavily.

I take a step closer to him, which means there's nothing, barely inches between us, and I glance up at him.

I didn't see it last night, but the fishing he did yesterday left some pink along the bridge of his nose and across his cheeks. It makes his eyes stick out in a way that makes my skin prickle, and his lips look bitten pink. I think that's from the sun too, but I wish it was from me.

I get a nervous swirl in my stomach as he peers down at me, waiting—the corner of his mouth is pulling up as he does his best to look serious. You know how anticipation and nervousness can feel the same? They feel the same.

I've never kissed him before. He's just kissed me. And he's going to kiss me back, I know he will—obviously—but I just can't believe I might get to have a nice memory in this bathroom.

I push my hand through his hair, which I've never done before either. There's fistfuls of it; it's thick and tousled and his head moves with my hand, but his eyes don't sway from mine and he doesn't move a muscle—he just stands there, waiting for me to kiss him.

This is the first time I notice our height difference. Until now, him being the initiator of the kisses, he has, I supposed, always tilted his head or ducked or something to facilitate it, but my tip toes aren't going to cut it. I perch up on them anyway, and he's still watching me, waiting.

I hook my arm around his neck and pull him down toward me, and a smile cracks over his face as our mouths touch. His arms fold around me and he pulls me in and holds me snug against him as he kisses me back, deeper.

He lifts me up onto the bathroom sink, but his kisses don't miss a beat, and my towel is probably in a bit of a dicey situation, but I don't mind because my hands have the top button of his jeans.

His stomach tenses as I graze it, and he smiles as I trace the top of his Calvin's.

He pulls back for a second, his eyes searching for something in mine. Permission, I think. And I wonder if we're going to…? Here and now on this sink. I don't mind; I'd take him anywhere. It'd be my absolute pleasure (pun semi-intended).

I pull him back toward my mouth, and he tugs me by the back by the hair, his mouth moving to my neck—

"Sam?" Oliver calls out from the other end of the house, but definitely on the same floor.

Sam and I jerk apart.

"Fuck," I whisper.

He shakes his head and whispers, "I'll just go out—"

"And what, you were just hanging out with me in the bathroom while I'm naked? No—that's not—"

My brain switches into overdrive. The options are finite. Suspicion is likely no matter what direction we go. If we risk Sam just walking out as though he was in here alone, we risk Oliver walking in and seeing me.

Denial would be futile. There's nothing we have to discuss that anyone knows about that's pressing enough for a towel conversation alone in a bathroom upstairs—

I grab a toothbrush and shove it into Sam's mouth, run the faucet, and put my mouth to it right as my brother walks in.

"Oh," is what Oliver says when he sees me in the towel.

I look up at him, consciously blankly, swish some water around my mouth, then spit it out. "What?"

Sam grins over at him, toothbrush hanging from his mouth, and I swallow my heart whole because he's so hot.

"We're talking about church," Oliver says.

"I'm not going," I say.

"Did Gige just say she's not going?" Tenny says from outside the door, and then he pokes his head in. "Hello—put some clothes on." He nods at me in the towel. "What's going on here?"

"You're all in my bathroom." I emphasize the *my*.

"That onion tart gave me weird breath." Sam shrugs, half telling me, half telling my brothers, and he's a better liar than I'd have thought.

Oliver's watching me closely, the corners of his mouth pulling out. Contempt. Whether it's conscious or not, I can't tell, and I'm fractionally ashamed to admit, I care increasingly less.

"So you're not going to church?" Penny says to me right as Savannah appears at the doorway also.

I shake my head.

"Me either then," Oliver says.

"Let's take the boat out!" Savannah claps her hands together once.

I roll my eyes. "Is there a better place to have this conversation than my bathroom?"

Sam looks over at me, curious. "I thought you liked God?"

"They're talking about church, not God," I clarify. "And actually, I said I like Jesus."

Tenny rolls his eyes. "They're the same thing."

"No." I shake my head again, resolute. "Jesus came down from heaven to save us from eternal damnation, but God just stayed up there. He was like…pretty hands-off in the saving of the world."

Tennyson makes a face like he disagrees. "Other than the sacrificing of his one and only son."

"Right," I concede.

"So we're going on the boat?" Oliver asks, looking only at Sam, who shrugs amicably.

"Sure—whatever you want."

Oliver smiles warmly, then glances down at himself as he walks away. "I'm getting changed—this is not a boating outfit."

Tenny stands at the doorway, eyes flicking from me to Sam. He looks at Oliver walking down the hall, then nods toward Sam's toothbrush. "You might want to put some toothpaste on that, man."

33

DO YOU EVER MISS IT?" Sam says, propping up on the sunbed of Dad's Sunseeker 86 and looking over at me. He gestures around us.

"South Carolina?" I clarify.

He nods.

"No." I toss Savannah an apologetic look. "Sorry, but no."

Sam nods again, thinks more. "Would you ever move back to America?"

Savannah glances at me, and I am conscious not to let any of the feelings I'm feeling inside myself turn up on the outside of my face—because something about the question feels loaded.

"Um." I purse my lips, trying to imagine myself back in any American city any time soon. "I don't think so."

His eyes flick up, glance toward the right—he's thinking, but he doesn't say about what.

"I really like my job," I tell him even though no one's said anything, and Savannah looks at me—eyebrows a millimeter or two higher than normal—her interest is piqued. She looks back at Sam, waiting to see what he says.

"Yeah, no." He shakes his head dismissively—thoughtlessly, actually. "I know you do."

Quick as light, I give Sam these "what the fuck?" eyes and barely tilt my head in Savannah's direction to tell him to be careful, and he does his best to pivot quickly.

"I mean. No, like—yeah—it's a pretty niche job."

Savannah sniffs a laugh and picks up her phone, starts scrolling.

Sam glances over at me, tosses me this "whoops!" face, and I stare back at him, sporting some subdued but undeniably felt mild horror.

"*Terrible*!" I mouth at him. He rolls his eyes and glares over at me playfully and my heart stops dead in its tracks. He should never wear clothes. Ever. At least, he should always have his shirt off like this.

Sam Penny looks like someone who surfs every day, which maybe he does—he is from Australia. Broad shoulders, impressive chest, and that troublesome V hot boys have pointing somewhere southern.

Our eyes hold for longer than they probably should, but it feels okay because both my brothers are on the driving deck, and although Savannah's with us, she's texting someone.

I'm wearing the bubblegum pink Xandra bikini from Hunza G and Sam's eyes fall down my body. Then he swallows as he looks away.

I think if my brothers hadn't come today, maybe we would have—you know? I want to.

The way Sam's looking at me right now clarifies for me that he wants to as well—his thumb pressing into his mouth, looking at me out of the corner of his eye with a half-cocked smile, and for all I know, someone could be actively tasering me, it feels so electric.

"I'm going to see what the boys are up to," Sam tells me, tossing his phone onto the lounge.

He holds my eyes until he passes me, chuckling as he does, I think because the tension is too much. I don't know what to do with it either.

It's easier to keep in check when my brothers are there, because brothers are real sexual coolants, but without them here to hose us down, it's getting increasingly difficult to maintain normal composure in Sam Penny's presence.

"So," Savannah says, putting her phone down. "How long have you two been hooking up for, then?"

I let out a single laugh that sounds more like an exhale, and before I can even say anything, she laughs too and rolls her eyes.

"Don't even," she tells me, eyebrows up.

I pull my sunglasses down from on top of my head so she can't see my eyes, but they don't cover my smirk.

"Firstly." She sits up straighter. "You're lying—and secondly, if you're not, he was just eye-fucking you so hard, you're about to be."

I make this weird nervous laugh that I don't mean to make, and her face lights up, and she races over to me.

"Oh my God!" she whispers. "Have you had sex?"

I shake my head. "No!"

"But you've kissed."

I pause. The pause is damning—and I'm better than that—and I can't come back from my initial reaction anyway; there's no way I can. But also, I really want to be able to talk about him to someone.

I take my sunglasses off and look over at her. "Yes."

She grins at me, but I frown at her.

"Are we being that obvious?"

"No." She shakes her head, like it's no big deal. "I just saw his hand on your leg at breakfast yesterday morning."

"Oh, shit."

"I didn't tell anyone." She holds my gaze to make sure I know she's being honest.

"Not even Tenny?"

She shakes her head again. "But just so you know..." She gives me a bit of a grimace. "I think he already suspects something."

I frown as though that's not already apparent to me (which it is), but I'd like to know why she thinks that in case other people might think that too. "Why?"

"The other night, he asked me if I saw the way Sam looks at you, and I said yes, and he asked if I thought he was a good guy, and I said yes, and then he just kind of nodded and changed the subject."

"Oh." I purse my lips.

Savannah glances up at Sam, who's laughing in the sunlight with my brothers, and if I could freeze-frame this moment, take out all the context and the subtext, it would nearly be perfect—but context and subtext is everything.

"He's so hot." She eyes me. "What are you doing? Why are you hiding it?"

I swallow and my brows bend in the middle. "I think Oliver has feelings for him."

"Shut up!" She blinks. "No—really? Tenny said that too, but I just thought he was being an ass."

I say nothing.

"Have you asked him about it?" she suggests.

"Oliver?" I clarify, and she nods. "Yeah. He said no."

Her eyes pinch as she waits for the rest.

"He was lying," I concede, and I cover my face with my hand. "Oh, shit! I'm a terrible person!"

"Sam's not gay!" Savannah shrugs, helplessly.

"Yeah, but—"

She gives me a look. "If you liked a guy that was gay and Oliver liked him too, do you think Oliver wouldn't be with him?"

Once upon a time, maybe. "Well, that's different."

"Why?"

"Because I'm not a masochist." I roll my eyes.

"Who's a masochist?" Oliver asks from behind us, then sits down.

Sam and Tenny join us too, and I eye Savannah, silently begging for her silence.

"Maryanne?" Oliver offers.

I shake my head, firmly. "Definitely not."

Tenny snorts. "She's more of a sadist."

"No, she's not." I try not to be annoyed by him throwing around a term he clearly doesn't understand.

My oldest brother rolls his eyes because he thinks I'm just being a smartass.

"Seriously," I press. "She isn't."

Savannah cringes. "She's pretty awful, Gige..."

She's never called me that before, but I like her and I'll allow it.

"Yeah, but—" I shake my head. "Sadists derive sexual pleasure from watching people in pain. They're often, like, killers or rapists." And every single one of them looks at me wide-eyed and horrified at the mention of the R word. I widen my eyes back at all of them for how silly they're being.

"...Beckett isn't one either," I clarify.

Tennyson asks, "How do you know that?"

"Well for one"—I glance over at my brother—"when you confronted him, the first thing he said out of the gate was that *I* enjoyed it. He was justifying what he did."

I stare at them, waiting for them to all go "ahh," but they don't, so I keep going.

"Beckett needed me to like it for him to like it. Which is untrue of a sadist. If he was a sadist, he'd have needed me not to like it." I pause, watching them to see if they're following along. "That's how I know Maryanne isn't a sadist."

Sam frowns. "How?"

I give him a long look. "Because if she was, she would have watched."

Tennyson makes a sound at the back of his throat, and everyone looks a bit traumatized except for me, because I dealt with it a while ago.

Savannah thinks about it. "But she didn't stop it."

"Right." I nod. "Because she's a narcissist with sociopathic tendencies."

Oliver lifts his eyebrows, waiting for more information.

"The day after the first time it happened and Maryanne walked in, she came home from school and they were...together. I don't know what the parameters around that were—I don't know if they ever discussed it, if there were rules or an official decision was made—but Maryanne, in a spilt second, had an opportunity to advance socially and get what she'd always wanted. It didn't matter that it was at my expense." I flash them a quick smile. "Typical narcissist."

"Fuck." Tennyson sighs as his eyes glance upward and left. "You know, I remember when you were like, one, and first learning to walk—it was at Grandma and Grandpa's—and you took your first steps, and everyone was clapping and cheering, and Maryanne was like, four—and she just came and shoved you over."

That actually makes me laugh—like, properly makes me laugh. Because for one, a nonnarcissist kid could do something like that, but in context of Maryanne, it really is very funny. Oliver lets out a dry laugh too, and Tennyson gives me a long look with ragged eyes, trying not to smile—but not Sam.

Sam is solemn. Very much so. I get the distinct feeling that making light of anything that's caused me pain will never roll over well with him. But laughing at things that hurt you, almost no matter how you slice it from a psychological standpoint, is usually positive. It's often considered a coping mechanism, or in my case, a sign of psychological recovery.

"Do you think there are going to be any surprises in the will?" Oliver asks.

And Tenny clocks me, I see it from the corner of my eye, but I don't look at him because that would tell everyone there was something to consider, so I just say a bored and toneless, "No."

No mouth shrug, no nose crinkle, no eyebrows lifting, just a straight "no" and a slight shake of the head.

"Dad was so straight-laced," I add. "What could be in there? He has a secret kid?" I scoff.

Tennyson's jaw juts forward subconsciously, but Oliver sniffs a laugh. "Yeah, right."

34

I CAN'T HELP BUT FEEL LIKE maybe it was on purpose that we spent the day on the boat—and I do mean the day. The boys caught us redfish off the side of the boat and grilled it for lunch and then again for dinner. By the time we docked back in at home, it was well past nine and our mother was internally livid but externally trying to be gracious.

Maryanne had gone home after dinner, and so it was just Mom and Debbie at the breakfast bar, drinking wine. Mom asked us about the boat, and Debbie told us about the sermon at church this morning but told me I probably wouldn't have liked it, and when I asked why, she said, "You just wouldn't have," which I think means she thinks I'm a disagreeable person, which isn't true. I just don't like her.

I hadn't gotten much alone time with Sam today, and I wasn't sure how I even would at this point, so I make a quiet but intentional announcement that I'm going to bed.

Sam's eyes lock on mine and he rubs his mouth absentmindedly.

"Night!" Oliver sings.

"I'm kinda tired t—" Sam starts, but Oli interrupts.

"No! I have an idea, let's—"

I begin to hear my brother launch into a plan, but I don't catch the finer details.

I lie awake in my bed for hours. I leave my door cracked open so I can see him when he comes, but the time drips into the early hours of the morning, and I begin to wonder whether maybe we've got our wires crossed? Was today not leading to where I thought it was?

I'm barely ever wrong, but sometimes I am.

I eventually give up and go and have another shower, washing off all my expectations of how I thought this night would go.

After this shower, I don't apply mascara and I don't put on any of the tinted lip balm from By Terry that makes my mouth look perfect; I just apply the normal balm.

Before, I was wearing a black camisole from Cami NYC, but now I change into some jersey pajamas from Eberjey—which is what I actually sleep in, because they're so comfortable, it's a joke.

I do my best not to feel stroppy about it, even though I do a little. It's not like Sam and I made plans out loud… It was a conversation we may or may not have had with our eyes, and I could have imagined it all, and it's probably really actually Savannah's fault—completely!—because she said we were about to have sex and so my expectations shifted.

When I walk out of the bathroom, his bedroom door is open now and his lights are on, and I walk past without looking inside because I feel a little dejected.

"Hey," he calls after me quietly.

He gets off his bed and walks toward me.

"Hey." I give him a tired smile.

He takes me by the wrist and pulls me inside his room. "I'm sorry—Oliver kept talking and talking, and I—"

"No, it's fine." I shake my head. "You're here for him."

"Yeah, I know," he concedes, looking at the floor, and then he peers back up at me. "I wanna be here for you now too, though."

I feel like a flower blooms right there on my face, right in front of him. I nod my chin back toward downstairs. "How did you get away?"

He shrugs. "We were just talking on his bed. He fell asleep."

I smirk. "You fell asleep in bed with my brother?"

Sam gives me a playful look. "No, your brother fell asleep in bed with me."

I cringe. "Well, that doesn't bode very well..."

He laughs. "I guess not."

"What?" I kick him playfully in the ankle. "You're not going to defend your honor?"

He nods coolly. "My honor's fine."

"Well." I bat my eyes. "I wouldn't know."

He gives me a crooked smile. "Do you wanna know?"

And that line hits me like a stone sinking in my stomach.

"Maybe I do." I shrug airily. "Maybe I don't."

I don't know why I'm playing hard to get. Maybe because it would be so fun to be gotten by him.

"Okay." He licks away a smile. "Goodnight, then." He talks a step away from me.

That asshole's playing hard to get with me too.

"Wait," I pout.

He raises his eyebrows. I gnaw on my bottom lip, frowning up at him.

I huff. "Do you want to have sex?"

"Uh." He smirks, like the control he has right now way too much. "Do you mean in general? Or with you?"

"With me." I frown again.

"And now, or...?

"Like now." I interrupt him.

He swallows heavily. "Yep." He's pink and flustered and I get an adrenaline rush of lusty power. Sam clears his throat. "Uh—do you—should we—here?"

"Yes." I nod.

He nods back. "Okay."

"Okay." I nod again.

He sniffs an amused laugh as he takes a step toward me. He presses his mouth together and then slips one hand around my waist, tugging me in toward him. His other hand is on my face, his thumb on my cheek as his eyes flicker over me.

And you know that moment right before kissing, where your noses are grazing and your breaths are tangling? It hangs there like Christmas Eve when you're a kid, all excited, merry joy, and his mouth is getting closer to mine, and it feels like he's hanging the last stocking on the fireplace before we light it—our mouths brush lightly for a second before he throws a packet of fire starters on the logs and we roar to life.

I hope this is how we'll always kiss, like it will always feel like a surprise. Even when I'm expecting it. Even with my eyes open, as soon as our lips touch. It's like the universe springs into Technicolor.

And he's very good with his hands. I mean, *very*.

He has me pressed against the doorframe in his room; his mouth moves from mine and down my neck and his breath on me feels like when you climb into a hot shower after you've been rained on.

"Wait." I pull back, looking up at him.

His mouth hovers above mine. "Are you okay?"

I grimace a little. "Weird question."

"Oh, good." He gives me a look. "I love weird questions before sex."

He smirks and I laugh, and then he nudges my head with his.

"What?"

I take a deep breath and squint up at him. "Can we do it in my room?"

A grin cracks over his face. "Yeah, for sure."

He moves ahead of me and casually walks inside, standing in the center of my room. He's in black loose-fitting jeans, a gray T-shirt tonight, still—like always—no shoes. Hands dangling at his sides, watching me with a slight tilt to his head. I quietly close the door behind me and just stand there, suddenly feeling a bit nervous.

The good kind. The feeling you get right before you're about to do something brave, or something confronting, or something that might change your life.

It's a funny distance between us. Too much space. I can see all of him. His stance, feet shoulder-width apart, head squared but still tilted, arms folded over his chest.

"You okay?" he asks kindly.

"Yeah!" I nod quickly. "I just..." I wave my hand like it's nothing. "I've had sex in this room before, but it's just—um—never been on my terms?"

His face softens.

"Okay." He glances around uneasily. "Whatever you want—we don't have to—"

"No." I shake my head. "I want to. In here."

"Okay."

"I've just never—"

He nods. "Yeah, I get it." He points to my bed. "I'm going to lie down over there." And he does. He glances back at me as he stretches out, hands behind his head, mouth twitching with a smile he's trying not to show. "And whenever you're—whenever—"

I purse my lips and walk over to him, feeling shyer than I want to. Not because I'm not sure of what I want, but because I know exactly what I do.

He squints up at me. "Are you sure you want to—?"

I nod solemnly. "Yes."

"I wouldn't be mad—"

"You're not about to be the first person I've slept with since Beck."

He exhales and lets out a tiny laugh. "Fuck! Thank God—that was a sentence I didn't know I wanted to hear, but—"

My head pulls back, surprised by his relief. "Do you not want to do this?"

He sits up and swings his legs around the edge of my bed, frowning.

"Don't misinterpret this as me not wanting to sleep with you. I've wanted to"—balled fist, absentmindedly hammering into his mouth, his go-to self-hush that I think is exclusively for me, or in the very least, for his less virginal thoughts—"since you felt me up on the day we met."

I laugh.

"I just..." He trails off and squashes his mouth together, and then he looks at me quite seriously. "I don't want to fuck us up."

My eyes go round and my heart goes mushy and I move toward him, sitting on his lap.

I look from his eyes to his mouth to his eyes, and my cheeks go pink as something somewhere deeper than my belly goes hungry.

"You're going to have to make the first move," I tell him quietly, but Sam shakes his head.

"Please?" I press.

He nudges my cheek with his nose, then kisses my cheek. "You can do this." He pulls back a little so our eyes meet. "You're in control."

I swallow nervously and then I reach for the hem of his T-shirt, tugging it up and off of him and my eyes fall to the scar from his accident. Without my permission, my brows bend and my bottom lip juts to a tiny pout—despair that he was once-upon-a-time hurt.

Sam sees it, our eyes catch and hold for a couple of seconds before he rests back on his arms, smiling at me patiently.

I undo the buttons of my pajama top and it falls open.

His eyes falter from mine just for a second, but his cheeks flush and his breathing quickens.

My heart is thudding like the Macy's Thanksgiving Day Parade marching band as I lean in toward him.

He doesn't close his eyes; he just watches me getting nearer and nearer to him, a tiny smile tucked into the corner of his mouth.

And then I kiss him.

Barely at first, but then my hands slip from his face to his hair, and once I do that, he tugs me in by the waist and he kisses me like the world will end if he doesn't.

I fumble for the button on his jeans and Sam lies down, bringing me with him. I kick his pants off and his hands slide down my body, under my shorts, and then he pulls me out of them. There's nothing but Calvins between us now.

Kissing Sam Penny on this bed is the greatest thing I've ever done with my life up until now. Forget Cambridge, forget my internship, forget loving Storm, forget getting to confront my sister—

This is it.

This is what music exists for. This is why the birds sing. This why the tide pulls and the water falls. It's why the sun rises and it's why the moon hangs there all ghosty white.

I shift a little bit so I'm under him, and it could crush me, the amount of happy I feel in this moment. He's kissing me everywhere; up and down his mouth drags, and my breath gets caught in my throat, making little gasps. He peers up at me, grinning as he shushes me.

I pull him back up toward me, because kissing him is the best silencer, but I'm dying for him now, and I think he is for me too, because he chokes out, "Now?"

And I nod and he pushes into me.

He drops his forehead on top of mine and takes a ragged breath as he hooks his arm around my neck, pulling me in closer and tighter, as though we weren't already the closest two humans can be in this lifetime.

I pause and look up at perfect him.

"Are you okay?" He frowns a little, and I nod again, brushing my lips against his.

"Yes," I say quietly.

I take a photo in my mind, let history rewrite itself for a second. It doesn't erase it, but it scribbles over it a bit in a louder color.

35

WHEN I ARRIVED AT BOARDING school in England, I had a decent amount of sex.

In retrospect, it was both a reaction and an outworking. It was an act of self-discovery and the commencement of my decompressing of the last year, as well as the start of a long road to processing the complexities of what happened with Becks.

It was also me stepping into the role my parents had set the stage for me to play.

The first couple of times I did it were weird and traumatic for both parties because I obviously didn't tell them the situation around how I'd had sex before, just that I'd had it—and that didn't end well for anyone. Neither me nor them. I'd cry and flinch and freeze, but I'd never tell them to stop.

Three boys. I slept with three boys in my first year of boarding school. One of them's gay now.

And then after that, I dated a boy from school whom I did love, and our sexual relationship was littered with good and bad. I never told him what happened, but I think he eventually guessed because I was pretty up and down.

After he and I broke up, I went off it for a bit. Midway into my second year at university, I began to see a therapist because my lecturer said she saw in me repressive behavior and watched me avoid normal things my peers liked as a means of self-preservation, and she confronted me about it.

If today I could be classified as a functional person, she and my therapist, Lucy, were and are the reasons that I am.

Then there was a guy called Henry. We had a few mutual friends—he knows Hattie and Bianca. I slept with him mainly just because he was super-duper hot and very good at it. But even then, very early on in the developmental stages of my particular and niche-market skill set, I could tell he was spotted with issues himself. He and his best friend had fallen in love with the same girl. I was the distraction, which was kind of sad, but the sex was good, and I wasn't a whole enough person at the time to care that he was only with me because he couldn't be with someone else. I think I was just grateful to be having sex on my own terms.

Not long after Henry came Anatole (with a few spatterings of one-night stands in between), and I can't stress this enough: he was so beautiful, and beautiful really can cover a multitude of sins. Literal and figurative. And I think once upon a time I thought Storm was my endgame, but he wasn't. If he was, we'd still be together.

A romantic endgame is something I've spent much of my adult(ish) life considering. It sounds ominous, and I guess it is in some ways, but so is love if you're doing it properly. Ominous and hopeful in one fell swoop.

And this is the feeling I have as I wake the next morning in the exact position I fell asleep in after Sam and I had finished.

The sun's barely up. Light's cracking the horizon and the birds aren't out yet. Sam hasn't moved an inch, his arm thrown over me the same way it has been this whole time, and his chest is rising and falling in the same rhythm it has been all night, and I'm hit with this surge of dread and wonder.

There's a chemical your body releases after you have sex. Oxytocin. It's a neurotransmitter and a hormone. Its base evolutionary function is to bond you to another person, so mothers don't leave babies even when they cry all the time and they're annoying, so cavemen don't leave vulnerable cave women for hotter cave women.

It tricks you into thinking you're in love.

And as I lie here, sneaking glances at Sam Penny, I tell myself what I'm feeling is the remnants of the oxytocin, but if I was reading myself, I'd know it was a lie. I couldn't say it with a straight face.

It's been seven days today since I first met Sam Penny and I can confirm with absolute certainty that I am completely in love with him.

Ridiculous, I know. It's fucking insane, actually.

I've flown off the handle and it isn't like me at all. And if I wanted to pull it apart, I could say I'm in distress; it's a trauma response and I'm latching on to him because of that. There are a lot of emotions swirling around me at the minute—that's true. Sam Penny is a safe harbor—also true. But what else is true is this: Sam Penny is undoubtedly the greatest man I've ever met.

Besides the obvious—that he is without a doubt the most flawless-looking man on the planet, and I could write a sonnet about what it's like to be wrapped up in him, and I'd need a full day just to graze the surface of describing the shape of his mouth—there is, maybe more significantly, the invisible.

How he thinks, how he feels, how he processes, how he wonders, how he breathes... He does all those things better than the rest of us, and not because he's perfect—he's not, I know he's not—but that's just why he *is*.

He is fully aware of and thusly alive in his weaknesses; it's where his humanity thrives.

He's the most human person I've ever met, but not in the same way I could say about Anatole. That would be true too, but it's different.

Storm is a slave to his impulses. He acts on a whim, he's trigger-happy (and -sad), his emotions exist on the most accessible plane of who he is, and he responds to all of life from that place—which is, large in part, incredibly human.

But Sam, he's like the embodiment of Friedrich Nietzsche's

Übermensch—that elusive archetype—and frankly, a daydream of someone who is persevering and strong-willed enough to master the entire spectrum of what it means to be a human. Ugly, beautiful. Happy, sad. Terrifying, wonderful.

Sam sees the world through this peculiar and raw lens of knowing there's bad out there. He knows it, can see it, recognizes it—he might even acknowledge it, but it doesn't seem to affect him. He just breathes deep and constant until the good he knows is coming comes.

And I don't know if that's innate or learned. I don't know whether nearly dying a couple of times gave him perspective or turned him into the Dalai fucking Lama, or if that hike he took in the Himalayas really spoke to him or whatever, but—

He never seems to react; he only responds. Except for that night he hit Beckett in the face with the pool cue, but I feel like that's a free pass.

He'd tell you, if you asked him, every weakness he has, every flaw in his character... But then you'll watch him be bigger than them, and you'll watch me turn into a puddle of goo.

So I love him. I know I do, and I know that that's insane, but nothing is more insane than the part where I think he might love me back.

And there are things I could do that would bring absolute clarity to the question mark that hovers over that statement, but the older I grow and the better I get at seeing people the way I see them, the more I understand that all truths aren't just apples hanging off a tree waiting for me pick them.

Some things people have to tell you themselves.

And I could be wrong anyway. I mean, I'm not—the way he hovers, the way he watches me, the way his breathing shifts when I walk into the room, the way the edges of his face soften when he talks to me—I'm not wrong.

This is the hopeful part.

And here is the ominous one: I don't know what happens next, because today is the day of the will.

And then what? Then he goes back to California with my brother and I go back to Blighty? Oliver won't stay here longer than he has to, and neither would I, but maybe for Penny I would (which is another reason that I know I love him). But I don't know what I'll do.

When I was twenty, I started using La Mer's Crème de la Mer. Before then, my skin was fine, good even...but once I started using that, it became great. And now I can't unknow how great my skin can be. And this is how I feel about Sam.

I can't unknow him.

I think I'm probably different now because I've known him.

But I don't know what that m—

He stirs. His eyes flutter a few times before they open slowly, and as soon as he sees me, he smiles, and my heart's in my stomach.

"Hey," he croaks.

"Hi." My cheeks go pink.

He rolls on his side and smiles more. "Hi."

I drop my head and stifle a laugh, face on fire, mouth watering.

He ducks his head so he can find my eyes. "You going shy on me?"

I peer up. "Your unflinching gaze is pretty intense for zero o'clock in the morning."

He gives me a little shrug. "Yeah, well, get used to it."

He brushes his mouth against mine.

I roll on my back and look up at the ceiling, twiddling my fingers, and I feel him watching me—eyes pinched a little, waiting.

"Can I ask you something?" I ask the ceiling with big, round eyes.

"Yeah, for sure." I can hear the smile in Penny's voice. "I've been waiting since last night for you to ask me something weird and possibly invasive."

I flick my eyes over at him and throw him a dark look.

He licks away a smile.

I clear my throat so I come off nonchalant. "How often do you have casual sex?"

Pause.

"Was that casual sex?" he asks. I can't totally pick out his tone.

I purse my lips and keep staring at the ceiling. "Was…n't it?"

He shifts so he's in my line of sight, looking down at me. "Was it?" He lifts his eyebrows. "Casual sex I have sometimes. That…wasn't it."

I squint over at him. "What was it, then?"

He cocks a smile, then drags his lips over mine again. "You're cute."

No doubt an intentional sidestep of my question.

I can see a hint of trepidation in his eyes. He thinks we're on the same page, but because I've asked it, he isn't irrevocably certain, so he doesn't want to say. His mouth's twitching with all the things he isn't saying.

I'm not cute, he's cute. Cute as a fucking button, and I find myself chewing on a nail and grinning at him, and I'd feel like a loser if he wasn't smiling back how he is.

He pushes some hair behind my ears. "You feeling okay?"

"About?"

"Us." I like that his cheeks go instantly pink, and he shakes his head quickly once but laughs at himself anyway. "This," he clarifies, gesturing casually between us.

I give him a look. "You really need to get that slip of your tongue under control…"

He gives me a look back. "That's not what you said last night…"

I pinch my eyes at him, and he does it back but a smile cracks over his face. He glances at my window, then back at me. AU14. His mouth pulls at the sides a tiny bit.

"I should probably go grab a shower before Oli wakes up and gets fucked off." Contempt. Minor and subdued, but there.

"Okay." I nod, flashing him a quick smile.

He gives me a long look, then kisses me again. It's not rushy or urgent. It's not a bookend kiss, he's not signing off, he doesn't say goodbye—he just kisses me, hands in my hair, soft and melty, and then he slips out of my room.

His kisses are commas.

36

THERE'S A FUNNY FLURRY IN the air around us all that morning. Maybe for me it's two flurries. The flurry of Sam, but probably more predominantly, a weird feeling like we're on our way to talk to a dead man.

My mom is quiet in a way that seems subdued, and I wonder whether maybe she's on something? Debbie is with her again, and while I don't like her, I can appreciate how supportive she and her husband have been to my mom. She's made everyone breakfast, she's helped my mom pick out an outfit, and she's driving Mom over.

Maryanne's dressed for mourning again, and I stare at her black dress from J. Crew and wonder whether her neck is perpetually itchy from all those high collars.

She gives me a dark look when she sees me, but she's not even aware she's doing it, I don't think. It's as though her aggression toward me is deep-seated and barely conscious. Her eyes flick up and down the little black Stern mini dress from Staud I'm wearing (it has sleeves, so everyone calm down!) and she rolls her eyes. I'm appropriately dressed, I just want to say.

It's not quite summer yet, but we're in the Carolinas. It's hot here. I look fine to sit uncomfortably in a room with people I don't really like and probably get left a disproportionately low amount of inheritance compared to the two favored siblings.

It's Tennyson who corrals us out the door, pointing. "Mom, you go with Debbie—Oliver, you ride with Georgia. Maryanne and Jase, do you want to come with me, or will you take your own car?"

Maryanne doesn't like being told what to do ever, so she rolls her eyes and fishes for her own keys in silence, muttering about how this is a hard day for her and Tennyson should be nicer, and I wonder if it's actually possible that she can block out that he was Tenny's dad too.

And mine and Oliver's, but he was a different dad to us, so I think it's incomparable.

But Maryanne and Tens, they had the same dad.

This day might legitimately be difficult for Maryanne, but because of who she is and what her personality disorder means, she'll pit her grief against everyone else's and hers will be worse and harder, even if it isn't. She will take center stage in this meeting with our father's lawyer.

She might let Mom have a minute in the spotlight, not because it was Mom's husband who died, but because it's what a narcissist would do to gain the upper hand. Letting the grieving widow grieve is the right thing to do, and because we've all spent so much of our lives accommodating Maryanne—it's innate to our mother at this point—it'll dupe Mom again, like it has a thousand times before.

It's like Maryanne knows how and when to preload people with tokens, and she does it with such foresight that when it's time for them to regurgitate the loyalty or the yielding she so requires, they just do it. My sister can pull strings in people they don't even know they have.

Sam comes down the stairs, pushing Oliver in front of him, both hands on his shoulders, and my heart stops in its tracks, because I guess it just does that around Sam now.

He's making him walk down the stairs, I can tell that much. There's trepidation all over my brother.

Oliver's wearing tight black jeans, a white T-shirt with the sleeves cuffed up, and Gucci loafers, and Maryanne's husband eyes him like he's weird, but actually Oliver just looks handsome. He looks perfectly handsome.

And how his face looks right now is breaking my heart. His jaw is tight and his brows are lowered; his eyes can't settle. It's how he looked every Sunday we'd go to church and he knew everyone in this stupid town was whispering about him before he had even come out. Mom and Dad would drag him there for his sexuality to be bound and his spirit to be trampled, and this is how he looks now, like he's walking into the lion's den. Maybe he is.

Sam keeps his hand on my brother, steadying him because Oliver needs it, but he looks over at me, his eyes more intentional and raw than they probably should be. His eyes flick down me the way eyes do once you've seen a person naked. I grab my keys from the key bowl and say, "Let's go," and walk out the door because something in my chest catches with how Penny's staring at me.

Like my whole life has been a corset done up too tightly, and slowly he's unlacing me.

He opens the passenger door for Oliver and then wordlessly climbs into the backseat of my car, which I didn't want him to do, but he had to, because why would he sit in the front instead of Oliver?

It's maybe a forty-minute drive to Beaufort, and I look over at my littlest big brother in the passenger seat. Oliver's got his head leaning back against the headrest, staring out the window, and the soundtrack to this moment is "(No One Knows Me) Like the Piano" by Sampha, which is bitter in its irony because nothing in our mother's home knows either of us.

"You look nervous," I tell him.

"I'm not." He frowns at me more than he already is, accidentally accentuating my point.

I sigh and roll my eyes. "Can you like, just do me a solid this morning and not make me work for the truth?"

Oliver gives me a long look, a bit resentful but mostly just afraid. "What if it's like last time?"

"Then it'll be like last time." All I can do is shrug. "And I'll give you half and we'll never talk to these people again."

He nods absentmindedly, but I know his question isn't about the money, and I've wondered about it myself. Not just about him, even though definitely about him—but me too. What if they reject us—again?

Like they have a thousand times before, in a million different ways. What if our father's Last Will and Testament is a document immortalizing his rejection of us?

I don't have an answer. I don't have a way to soften the horrors that may lie before us. I have nothing comforting to say to my brother beyond the trifling "we don't need them" shit I've thrown him too many times before, which is both true and irrelevant all at once.

We don't need them. But we would like them.

We get there last because my sister drives like the rules of the road don't apply to her, and I'm also still used to driving in England, so I'm being extra careful.

I'm disappointed everyone's already inside when we get there, because Dad's lawyer is a vibe.

It's hard to tell whether Desmond Clarke is an older gay man or just, like, very into purple? For someone of his generation, in a town like this, even if he was, I don't know whether he'd feel like he actually could be, so I've never asked and he's never told and it doesn't actually matter, anyway. All you need to know is that he's eccentric and flamboyant and so wonderful and charming and warm. He makes my mum and Maryanne megauncomfortable, so naturally I've always really liked him.

I was hoping to get to see them dodge his attempts to hug them, but when we arrive, they're all already seated.

"Darling." Desmond grips both my arms. "Always a vision." He gives me the dead-dad smile.

I shift my hair backward and over my shoulders because I don't feel like being a vision today.

"And I've not met this one before." He looks past me. "Which one are you with?"

"Me." Oliver smiles brightly, and how happy he looks to say that pangs me with a guilt I probably should feel all the time at this point. Dull, like a butter knife in the stomach.

Instinctively, in that moment, Sam and I would want to look at each other; that's just what this particular circumstance asks for. We'd be glancing at each other in an attempt to self-affirm that what Oliver just declared was, in fact, false. Sam is not Oliver's. Bodies always give us away.

But not mine. I know where my eyes will want to look, and I know the little things other people pick up on without meaning to that give them "just a feeling" that something's going on, so even though Sam looks at me when Oliver says that, I just look at Oliver with a disinterested but somewhat apparent smile.

Oliver sits down, Sam following, and Desmond whispers to me, "That boy's not gay."

I sniff a laugh. "I know," I whisper back.

More than you realize, old man.

Violet moves through our family to get to me, and she gives me a big squeeze, then brings my hair back forward over my shoulders, and I know she does this on purpose. It's not to belittle me but to affirm me. I have hot-girl hair. I know I do. Boys love it; girls hate it.

Maryanne despises it.

Violet used to say you could tell what mood Maryanne was in by how I wore my hair. Out, pleasant. Ponytail, cloudy. Bun, look out.

My aunt boops me on the nose. "You look good, baby. You feeling good?"

I give her a tight smile and a shrug because I don't know how to answer that. "Are you?"

She breathes in and sighs. "Not really."

I squeeze her hand.

"Thank you everyone for coming here today," Dessie starts, sitting behind his desk. "And can I first off just express my deepest and most heartfelt condolences to each of you, but particularly you, Peggy." He reaches for my mother's hand.

Maryanne sniffs loudly, and I roll my eyes before I can get a hold of them.

She glares over at me and I discreetly flip her off, which I think I've done a million times in my head but never outside of it, and her eyes widen and her nostrils flare: AU9.

Contempt. So, nothing new then.

I stare her down for a second longer and then shift away, thoroughly enjoying not being under her thumb. As I shift my gaze back to Des, I see Sam in my periphery, looking straight ahead but trying not to laugh.

Des clears his throat. "Shall we get started then?"

There's a murmur of agreement, and we all nod or something of the sort, and I find myself crossing my arms over my chest because I'm more afraid than I want to be.

It's not about the money. I don't care about the money. It's about it being written down for all the world to see that my dad loves me and my brother less than the other two.

And it occurs to me just then, that my dad died thinking I slept with Maryanne's boyfriend. He'll never know I didn't. I'll always be a slut to him.

Dessie flips through some papers then peers around the room and flashes us a mass apologetic smile, "I, William Marcus Carter, resident in the City of Okatie, County of Beaufort, State of South Carolina, being of sound mind and body, not acting under duress or undue influence, and fully understanding the nature and extent of all my property and of this disposition thereof, do hereby inscribe, publish, and declare this document to be my Last Will and Testament, and hereby revoke any and all other wills and codicils heretofore made by me." Des glances back up at us again before proceeding.

"I devise and bequeath my property, both real and personal and wherever situated, as follows: To my wife and the mother of my children,

Margaret Elizabeth Carter, I leave our family home in Okatie, Beaufort, SC. 207 Callawassie Drive, as well as a 10% share of my company, W. Carter Air, and the deed to our vacation home in the Florida Keys—"

Mom shifts in her seat and I think she looks uncomfortable, or in the very least, underwhelmed.

Admittedly, I don't know a lot about their estate. I don't know what they own, I don't know what they have in the bank, I don't know where they've invested. I know that dad has an airplane parts company that makes bank, the boat, a little jet, the Keys house, and more cars than it's sensible for one man to own.

Des continues, shifting his gaze to Vi. "To my sister Violet Carter-Reed, I gift Panfilo Nuvolone's *Still Life with Grapes, Peaches, and Pears.*"

Clay gives her a knee a squeeze and a kind smile.

Des turns now to Tennyson, who swallows—his eyes that have become increasingly sweet to me are all big and nervous. "To my eldest son, I leave the remaining ninety percent of W. Carter Air and my 1963 Shelby Cobra. To my youngest daughter"—Desmond's eyes fall on me—"Georgia Carter, I leave Lot 42 of Adams Shore Drive in Moultonborough, New Hampshire." Oliver's face scrunches up as he mouths "what?" to me, and I just shrug because like fuck do I know. I quickly glance at Tennyson—even he looks confused.

Des keeps going. "My first-edition copy of *The Love Affairs of Lord Byron* by Francis Gribble"—Sam snaps his head in my direction at that, and our eyes catch even though they shouldn't, and his face tells me that he believes this is incontrovertible proof that his theory was right, and maybe it is, but what the fuck does that even mean?—"and my Adirondack cedar guide boat, *The Saint Emilion.*"

At that, my mother breathes out her nose probably a bit louder than she means to and flicks her eyes upward, which I believe was her absolute best effort at not rolling them all the way.

Desmond clears his throat. "To Alexis Beauchêne, I bequeath my lake house—"

The room goes still.

"What lake house?" Oliver asks first, and for a second it makes me sad, because he's so removed from the rest of our family that he hasn't noticed the most integral bit of information we were all just delivered.

Dessie rattles off an address I clock in my memory (I also clock Adams Shore Drive, Moultonborough), but I'm not looking at him anymore. I'm looking at Maryanne, whose face has contorted into the most extreme version of annoyed a person could be, and then proceeds to loudly ask the question the rest of us are all thinking:

"Um, who?"

Des clears his throat. "Alexis Beauchêne," he says again, and then, upon realizing none of us know who that is, he shifts uncomfortably in his chair.

Tennyson's gone stiff as a board. I can see it all over his face. Who else could it be? It's the girl. It's that girl he told me about. It has to be.

"Hold on." Maryanne shakes her head. "Who is that?" She looks around at everyone. "I've never heard of her, who is she?"

"I—" Desmond starts, and his eyes are darting around to each of us.

My mom's very still.

Tennyson's going to give himself away if he doesn't pull his face together in a hot minute. He's like a rabbit caught in a fence, but he's lucky because no one's focusing on him at all; the rest of our family is staring at Desmond Clarke like he just announced he has a third nipple.

My mom cranes her neck at the papers. "Who is that? Can you—tell me? Who is—who is it?" She swallows.

"Uh." Desmond blinks, and I wonder whether attorney-client privilege is coming into play. "Ms. Carter—"

"Mrs.," she clarifies sharply.

"Mrs." Des nods. "Mrs. Carter—I...I'm so sorry, I can't. But I can assure you that this will was drafted up only a little over nine months ago, and the preceding wills for the duration of the time I've been your husband's lawyer have always included Alexis Beauchêne."

"Okay." My mom shakes her head—so, not okay. "So this lake house, it's what? A small house on a swamp in Florida or something?"

"Er." Desmond clears his throat again, but I'm already typing the address into Zillow.

"It's estimated value is four-point-seven million dollars," I say.

"WHAT?" Maryanne yells.

"What?" Oliver blinks.

Tennyson pales more. Violet's blinking a lot, and Mom looks nauseous.

I glance over at Sam because I want a split second of a reprieve. His brows are low and he swallows heavily once, and my heart slows a little, probably in sync to his blinking.

I look back at my bug-eyed family.

"Who cares?" I swat my hand. "It's fine."

"Speak for yourself." Jase rolls his eyes.

"Son." Des gives him a look. "You're not even in the will."

I give Jase a smug smile. "Who cares if Dad wanted to leave someone a lake house? It's not our money, anyway—it's up to him what he does with his stuff."

"Shut up!" Maryanne bursts. "You didn't even know him."

In my periphery, I see Sam arc up a bit, and I want to look at him to tell him it's fine—and also just to look at him—but both actions would give us away.

"Yeah, well whose fault is that?" I spit.

"Why are we having this conversation again?" my sister growls. "I said I was sorry; I told you that I didn't—"

"Yeah, but you're a fucking liar," I interrupt.

"Guys." Tenny touches my arm, but I shrug him off.

"You just need to let it go," Maryanne tells me. "I can't keep going around in circles with you—"

"It's been three days!" I yell.

"Four-point-seven million dollars?" Oliver says loudly.

"Wait"—Jase—"I'm not in the will?"

"You guys—" Tenny.

"You're incorrigible." Maryanne.

"And you're a fucking asshole." Me.

"Who's Alexis?" Clay.

"Why aren't I in the will?" Jase.

"You're filthy," Maryanne spits at me.

"And yet, my hands are cl—"

And then there's a loud whistle.

"ENOUGH." Tennyson stands up. "We're done here." He shakes his head, looking at Des. "I'm sorry, we're going to have to come back—we can't—we've gotta have a talk."

Desmond nods quickly, probably quite relieved by the out just extended to him. "Of course." He shuffles the papers away.

My mom's sitting there, still in her chair, hands in her lap, staring off into space. Violet touches her arm gently, helping her up, but my mom moves her arm away. It's not a jerk; it's not reactionary or even necessarily conscious—she looks so dazed and out of it.

Maryanne flies through the office door, storming ahead, and Debbie walks toward my mom—

"What happened?" She blinks, looking around. "I heard yelling."

But I don't stay to take the blame for the downfall of that meeting. I'm jogging to my car.

Oliver runs after me. "Gige?" He calls out, worried.

Sam jogs behind him, and in my periphery it looks like slow motion because that's just how attractive he is. "Are you okay?" he calls, also worried—those cuties.

I look back at him and throw him a quick smile. Absolutely I am—I'm great. This, right here—this is my sweet spot.

"Four-point-seven million dollars!" Oliver calls out to no one in particular, and I don't respond. "Why are you running?" He yells again.

I reach my car. "Because someone here knows something and they're lying about it, and I need to get to them before they work out how to make it look like the truth."

"What?" My brother blinks as he climbs into the car.

I start the engine and look over at him, bright-eyed. "The game is afoot, Oliver!"

37

I DON'T HAVE A DOG IN this fight. Let's start there.

Financially, I'm pretty comfortable. We all had college trust funds separate from what money our grandfather left us. The money from him, I put in a high-interest account until I dated someone who was good at stocks (Storm), and then I made a decent amount of money, and so I don't particularly care if Dad gives a lake house that I didn't know existed to his secret girlfriend.

I'm a little intrigued by the secret girlfriend though, only because I wonder if I'd have picked up on it if I knew him better.

On the way home in the car, I concoct a plan with Sam and Oliver and reiterate it to them on the front porch before we walk inside.

"So, Oliver." I eye him. "About fifteen seconds after we've walked into the kitchen, I want you to say, 'So who is Alexis Beauchêne anyway?'"

"Got it." Oliver nods once.

The fifteen seconds is to allow me to position myself optimally to see as many reactions as possible.

"And you—" I dip my chin toward Sam, trying to keep as casual and innocuous as possible.

"I'm watching for head movements and changes in eye shapes," he tells me obediently, and I will kiss him a lot for remembering that later.

I nod at him approvingly, and our eyes catch and my heart sparks, and it feels conflicted with this swirly mix of excitement and frustration to be in love with him but then to have to pretend I'm not.

Rooftops were invented so I could shout off of them about Sam Penny, and here I am barely able to look at him in the eye.

We walk inside and everyone's already gathered in the kitchen, bickering and talking loudly, and this is going to be hard.

At work we'd have cameras set up so we could catch their reactions, slow them down, and I could go over their faces with a fine-toothed comb, but we don't have that luxury. Standing in the corner, Sam acting as an extra pair of eyes is going to have to do.

Savannah's here now, but she won't know anything unless Tennyson knows something, and I think I already know what he knows, but I'll put a mental tab on him just in case.

Mom, I'm sure knows jack shit.

Oliver knows less than her.

Maryanne, Jase, Violet, and Clay—they're who I'm watching closest.

As soon as I walk into the kitchen, Maryanne shifts so she's standing directly opposite me. I don't know whether it's to pit herself against me on purpose or by accident, whether it's innate or conscious.

"What took you so long?" She glares over at me.

"Nothing." I shrug innocently. "I drove as fast as I could; I couldn't wait to be reunited with you."

"Gige." Tens rolls his eyes.

"Daddy's dead! And you're just..." Maryanne says in her teary voice that's very convincing if you don't understand the wind-up emotions like the one she's displaying. You don't go from zero to one hundred. Not authentically, anyway. "You're just"—sniffle—"making everything so much worse, Georgia."

"What's Lot 42?" Tennyson says, folding his arms over his chest. Best I can tell from the looks of him, it's a genuine question. He doesn't actually know either.

I shake my head at him and offer him a shrug. Oliver and I looked it up on the way home. It's nothing. It's an empty plot. Unlike the mystery lake house he bequeathed to some random woman. I tell the room as much.

At that, Maryanne presses her mouth together to disguise the fact that that pleases her. She's pleased he left me, essentially, nothing.

I toss Oliver a look, not in the mood to give Maryanne the space to gloat, nor am I able to afford the brain space to pull at the thread of what it means that my father left me that. He catches my eye.

"So who the fuck is Alexis Beauchêne anyway?" he asks loudly.

Tenny: AU1. Brows flicker up and down quick as a flash of light. Fear. (Expected.)

Maryanne: AU14. The right corner of her lip pulls down and her eyes twitch, and for a second they're slits: contempt. (Classic.)

Mom: Also AU1, but it means something different with her. Her eyebrows raise the tiniest bit in this tender, hopeless way: sadness. (Expected.)

Jase: AU5. His eyes tighten and so does his jaw: anger. (Possibly expected, but fucking entitled.)

Clay: Nothing. (Boring.)

Violet: AU20. Her mouth pulls a little.

Sam clocks me and swipes his mouth, discreetly pointing at Violet, and I nod once.

"Seriously?" Oliver says, and he's being so helpful. He crosses his arms and harrumphs. "No one knows who she is?" He raises his eyebrows in expectation.

Mom glances around—she knows nothing. Nothing at all. She's just finding out about Alexis Beauchêne along with the rest of us.

But Violet—her mouth is pulling to the side. Her arm is crossed over her body, forming a barrier between the rest of us, and her other hand drums mindlessly against her mouth—self-hushing.

"Nope," I sing out. "No one knows anything."

"Seriously?" Maryanne blinks. "Aren't you some sort of detective?"

I give her a long look. "You think I'm a fucking detective?"

Oliver starts laughing.

"You think I went to London and what, just toddled off to Scotland Yard?"

"You went to Cambridge, Georgia! We get it!"

"Yeah," I shoot back. "Where'd you go again?"

She didn't finish. She got married instead.

She glares at me, and I know it's mean to do it to her, but it's also kind of fun. Narcissists need to feel like the smartest people in the room. They have such obvious and easily pushable buttons, especially for someone who's studied psychology. And I know it's petty, but I have twenty-four years (plus interest) of sibling frustrations pent up, and they're all bubbling ugly to the surface.

"Four-point-seven million dollars is a lot of money," Jase says.

My mom sits down.

"Are you in debt or something?" I frown over at him.

"No." And he's not lying.

So he's just greedy. Nice.

Violet's still unmoving though.

Debbie is cleaning dishes that I'm pretty sure were already clean with a furious and deliberate fever, because the room is tense but I don't think she feels like she can leave it.

"Mom," Maryanne sniffs. "What are we going to do?" Sniff. "This person we don't even know is stealing nearly five million dollars from us!"

"It's Dad's money, not yours!" I say. "And he obviously knew them—"

"Georgia." Tenny eyes me and nods toward Mom, who's staring at me with glazed-over eyes.

"Mom?" I tilt my head, watching her.

"I don't know who she is," she says, looking directly at me but definitely through me.

She's not lying. She's just defeated.

And suddenly, I have a dog in the fight. It's small and stupid, like a Chihuahua or something that'll probably die two minutes in, and it's probably stemming from that fucking deep-rooted desire to be accepted by my mother, but I want to figure out who the fuck Alexis Beauchêne is.

"Mom?" I say again.

"What, Georgia?" she sighs, looking over at me tiredly.

"I can find her."

She stares at me for a long moment, and then all she does is nod once and walk out of the room.

And then I'm up and out of there, walking to my dad's office, taking Oliver with me.

And I know that anyone I want there will follow me, Sam included, but I want him there for a different reason.

Maryanne won't come; she'll have to do something that proves she's smart and not in debt—impression management.

"Where are you going?" Violet calls after me as I walk across the courtyard.

I ignore her and keep walking because her tone is speaking volumes to me.

Her heels click-clack urgently across the pathway. "Gige!" she calls again.

Tennyson's close behind her as I walk into Dad's office, sit down behind his desk.

I stare across at the opposite wall—there's a small watercolor painting by Wayne Ensrud. Couldn't be bigger than thirty inches across. It's a nice painting, actually; I like it. I don't know why it's in here though. Their house is so un-arty. He—William Carter—is inherently so un-arty that if you were to imagine the kind of art he'd hang in his house, the only thing I can imagine him maybe being okay with would be something like one of Piet Mondrian's *Composition* pieces. Not that they're simple, but my father would perceive them as such. Or, at least he would have, I think. But that painting on his wall... I don't know. I squint over at it. *Blue Skies Over...* where again? I always forget. Somewhere near Bordeaux. I asked my dad about it once, he said it was a gift. I asked from who and then he blinked twice, and his brow went sort of heavy and he said, "A friend."

I shake my head to clear my mind (but do dog-ear that thought for later) and then I get to work, rummaging through his desk.

"What are you looking for?" Tennyson asks as he walks into the office.

I look up at him. "You tell me."

"You know what I know!" He gesticulates, frustrated.

Truth.

"What do you know?" Oliver looks over at him and so does Violet, but her eyes flicker wide with surprise. AU1.

When Tens doesn't explain, Oliver looks over to me. "What does he know?"

But I ignore him too, and start riffling through papers that I don't give a shit about. Papers can't tell me anything. You can write anything down, delete a word that changes the entire context of a document. Documents can be hidden and shredded. Documents are flawed extensions of our lies, and I don't need these papers; I need what me riffling through the papers does to the rest of the people in the room: it puts them on edge.

"What are you doing?" Violet steps toward me, frowning. "There's nothing there! You're just—"

I sit down at the desk and start typing. "Password?" I call out.

"I don't know it." Tenny scowls at me like it's a stupid question.

"Really?" I blink. "You're the vice president, so what was the big plan for if something happened to Dad?"

"Georgia." Tenny eyes me.

"What do you know?" Oliver asks him again.

Violet moves behind the desk. She's protecting something. "You're never going to—"

"How long have you known about Alexis Beauchêne?" I ask her quite suddenly.

In a split second, she bites down on her bottom lip—self-hushing—but then she shakes her head. "Just now. This morning."

I ignore her lie. "Where does she live?"

"I don't know!" Violet growls and shrugs, defensively.

"New York?" I ask.

Nothing.

"Atlanta?"

Nothing.

Sam shifts in the corner, uncomfortable at the awkward family drama he's once again been thrust into the middle of.

I rack my brain for places I know my dad goes.

"Vermont."

Nothing.

And then I wonder…

"New Orleans?"

Her mouth twitches, and Penny notices too. He's getting good.

I tilt my head. "What aren't you telling us?"

"Nothing!" She crosses her arms over her chest.

Barrier. She's distancing herself from me.

"Does she live there?"

Violet shakes her head, her eyes getting smaller. "Stop."

"So she lives there."

The boys are just staring at me, waiting for me to pull the bunny out of the hat. Sam doesn't, but my brothers think it's magic—we all know it's just deduction and paying attention to details. Squeezing people in ways that make them uncomfortable until they leak the truth.

I stand up and go toe-to-toe with my aunt. "Tell me everything you know."

She presses her lips together in tacit defiance, silencing herself.

I don't like lies. The truth is the most powerful thing in the world to me, and I take it personally whenever someone stands in the way of it being known.

"Tell me now, Violet, or I swear to God I will turn over every single stone in his life until I know it all."

"Why?" she demands.

"Because he was our dad!" Oliver yells.

"Oliver," she sighs. "There are some things you just aren't privy to as children—"

"Yeah, but," Tenny butts in, "you don't get to decide that."

"He decided that!" Violet stomps her foot. "When the information was excluded from you, your father decided that! Please, leave it alone."

And now I'm intrigued. Because she's really trying to deter us. Like, really, really.

Her eyes are begging me, and maybe a week ago I could have let it slide—I had different rules for South Carolina and the truths we all kept in the dark. Everywhere else in the universe, I'd light fires under people to make the truth come out, but here, I think I was probably afraid of it.

Not even afraid of what the truth said about me, necessarily—more so, what it said about my parents once the lies fell away.

My parents' previous perception of me afforded me an acceptable explanation for why they loved me less than the other two, but without it now, they love me less for me. Not because they think I did something slutty, not because they disapprove of the person they think I am—they love me less for the innate and the unchangeable, and that is a truth I've hidden from for the last ten years. I can feel it stinging me on the edges of my soul, but I'm like a dog after a bone with the truth, and now that one's out, I want all of it.

"I can't," I tell her, resolute.

"Gige, I love your dad the same way that you love your brother." She gestures to Oliver. "To death and for free. For me." She sighs deep and heavy. "Please—please, let it be?"

I give her a long look before I step around her.

"I'm going to Louisiana."

38

NEW ORLEANS?" MOM BLINKS. "WE don't have any business down in New Orleans. How on earth would he have met anyone?"

I shake my head, interrupting. "Don't jump to conclusions." I catch Tennyson's eye. Neither of us think this is a conclusion she's prematurely jumped to. "I'm just going to go down, sniff around—I'll figure it out. It'll be okay."

Tens gives me a long look and Savannah catches it, looking between us in confusion.

Mom nods a bit vacantly.

"Well," Oliver sighs. "You know I love a road trip." He sidles up next to me and I smile a bit. I'm happy he's coming. Some of my favorite memories are driving away from this house with Oliver next to me. I rest my head snug against his shoulder, and I have a surge of affection for my brother—and then pangs of guilt prick through me as I wonder how he'd feel if he knew I slept with Sam. How he'd feel if he knew I'd like to do it again.

I stomp on those prickly feelings because they're getting ahead of themselves anyway, and I throw Oliver's arm around my own shoulder to smother the ones my feet just missed.

"I'm going too," Tennyson announces, chest puffing up.

"Unnecessary." I swat my hand. "We'll be fine without you, Eagle Scout."

"I'm coming." He shrugs. "You drive like an old lady with an eyepatch."

I frown at Oliver. "I'm a good driver."

He wobbles his head, uncertain. "You're bizarrely strict about the ten and the two..."

"That's good driving!"

Oliver sniffs a smile, and I look over my shoulder at Sam, whose eyes are locked on me. And I'm going to have to tell him he has to get better at looking like he hasn't seen me naked, because I can tell in his eyes—his gaze hovers too much. Not for my liking, it's perfect for my liking, but for hiding our secret whatever from my brother(s)—it's no good.

"I'm coming too then!" Maryanne announces.

"Absolutely not," I say.

Maryanne's nostrils flare and her jaw goes tight. "You're not in control."

I wave my hand in her direction. "If you're going, I'm not going."

"Great." She shrugs, smug. "We don't need you."

"Of course we fucking need her." Oliver rolls his eyes. "What skill set do you have?"

Maryanne looks at him sharply and I want to punch her for it. Death stares, that's one skill she has in spades.

"You need to stop being dramatic," Maryanne tells me, and I see Sam arc up in my peripheral vision, and so does Savannah, for that matter—but I'm not worried about anyone thinking I'm sleeping with her, so I throw him a glance: "Cool it."

"Maryanne—" I shake my head. "I've spent half of my life playing the character in the narrative you wrote out for me. I'm done—I'm not getting in a car with you" I shrug. "If you want to go to Louisiana, go to Louisiana. I'm sure that MRS you got from that year you did at Shaw will come in real handy."

Tennyson flicks me in the arm. "Easy. Mer, you don't need to come."

He steps toward her. "You just stay here—relax, look after Mom—"

"You're siding with her?" Maryanne blinks, incredulous. "I can't—what the fuck! Her, Tennyson?"

Tens rubs his face, all tired and angry. "So what if I am! You fucked up, Mer. All this time, you've trashed her and let me trash her, and for what? Why?" He's asking genuinely. Tennyson's guilt-ridden from head to toe.

Maryanne's weeping begins on cue. "It was a mistake!" She looks over at me. "Let me make it right," she says in her crying voice, carefully crafted to sound remorseful and hopeful and brave, but the lack of movement in her eye area gives her away. It's neutral. There's no genuine emotion at all.

"No," our mother says suddenly. She looks at Maryanne in a way I don't think she's ever looked at her before. "You'll stay."

"But, Mom—"

"No," she yells louder.

Maryanne makes a gurgling sob and flees the room, Jase running after her, which has got to be a full-time job in and of itself, so no wonder they're nosy about the will.

"I'm going to have a shower," I tell no one and everyone. Wash them all off and away.

Showers are a hard reset for my brain. I use them as a signal to myself to start up and power on again. If I'm going to find the girl my dad's been shagging in Louisiana, I'm going to need a shower.

I'm only in there for five minutes when there's a knock at the door.

I growl internally and out loud. "What?"

Pause.

"It's me," says Sam, muffled through the door.

"Oh," I say. That's all I say.

"Can I come in?" he asks, quieter.

"Um." I glance down at myself, naked in the shower. "I guess? It's open."

He walks in and closes it quietly behind him, grinning over at me.

"Why do you leave it unlocked?"

I shrug. "The only person who'd ever come in here while I'm showering is Oliver, and he knows how to jimmy the lock anyway, so—"

Then I realize I'm naked and fold my arms over my chest, shifting behind a tiled area where the shampoos live that comes up to my waist.

He snorts a laugh and waves a hand at me. "What are you doing?"

"I'm naked!" My cheeks go pink.

"I saw you naked this morning," he laugh-sighs.

"That was different!"

"How?"

"We had sex!" I whisper-yell.

Penny's face softens a little. "I remember." He waves his hand nondescriptly in my general direction. "Are you really hiding yourself from me?"

"You know it's a common nightmare people have, about being naked in front of clothed people."

He rolls his eyes. "You're not standing here doing a naked presentation."

"That's easy for you to say." I gesture to his dressed self.

He rolls his eyes again, and then reaches back for the scruff of his shirt and pulls it off, discarding it on the floor.

"There." He shrugs, and I swallow heavily. "Now we're even."

I get a hold of myself and shake my head, then point to his pants.

He scoffs a laugh. "Nice try."

He walks over to me, and through the fog, his eyes are bright and dilated. AU6. Cheeks pulling up. He's happy.

His eyes flick down my body then back up again before he calmly says, "I just wanted to check you were good with me coming to New Orleans?"

I chew my bottom lip how I wish I was chewing on his. "I'm counting on it."

"Okay." He smiles coolly and nods. "Are you okay?"

"About what?" I blink up at him, water falling from my eyelashes.

He pushes some wet hair behind my ears and searches my face.. "All of it. Your Dad, Violet, Maryanne… You and me?"

He saves his most important question for last.

"So my dad's having an affair, like every other man in America." I scrunch my nose up.

Sam gives me an intentional look. "Not every man."

Something about what he says makes me feel shy, so I talk past it. "Even so, it's not like I had this perfect image of him that's now suddenly been shattered. I knew he was an asshole to me and Oliver—I guess it turns out he was sort of an asshole to all of us…" I shrug like none of it matters to me, but I think all of it matters to me a lot, just in a way that's too high up on the shelf of my subconscious for me to reach.

Penny's eyes go tender. "And Violet?"

"She's doing what she thinks is right. She's just—protecting him the only way she has left."

"Maryanne?" he asks softly, but as he does, he subconsciously thrusts his chin forward. Sam Penny does not like my sister, and that makes me smile a little.

"Zero fucks." I nod, resolute. This is mostly true.

He tilts his head. "And what about you and me?"

So many fucks. More fucks than I know what to do with.

So I just mirror him, tilting my head too and lifting my eyebrows. "What about you and me?"

He tilts his head the other way, squinting at me playfully. "I asked first."

I lean in closer. "I asked second."

He does his best to lasso in his smile, and he's going to kiss me, I know he is—I can tell now because I know his tells—and I don't know how much kissing we'll get to do once we get to Louisiana, so—

"Georgia?" Oliver calls to me somewhere distantly.

Fuck. Shit—fuck!

Sam's eyes go wide. Oliver couldn't be farther than sixty feet away; if he was, I don't think we'd have heard him.

The average male stride is two-point-five feet...counting for that, we have approximately twenty-six seconds to figure out what to do, but let's bring the clock forward to twenty to play it safe.

I look around my bathroom frantically.

"I'll lock the door!" Sam whispers urgently.

"He'll just pick it!"

"Fuck!" Sam says, eyes wide.

Fifteen seconds.

There's only one way in and out of my bathroom. Sam could get in the bathtub, but Oliver might perch on it.

Twelve seconds.

There's no linen closet... He could hide behind the door, but that's risky, Oliver might see.

Nine seconds.

"Shit," I squeal and grab Sam by the wrist, pulling him into the shower.

Four seconds.

Three seconds.

"What are you—?" he starts, but I yank him in and push him down behind the shampoo wall.

Two seconds.

Sam looks up at me from the shower floor, squashing away his biggest smile yet, and I am aware that I am fully naked in front of the person I love in secret.

One.

The bathroom door swings open.

"Gige—"

"Oliver!" I scowl, like I would even if I had nothing to hide.

"What?" My brother blinks at me, innocuous.

"Oliver, I'm having a shower!"

"Oh!" Oliver nod, inconspicuously and uses air quotes. "A 'special' shower?"

"No!" I squawk. "Just a regular shower, where I don't want to be naked in front of my brother."

"Oh, calm the fuck down." He swats his hand. "It's disgusting and no one's looking."

And I could actually die on the spot—my brother doesn't notice though, thank God—he's looking at himself in the mirror. Runs his middle fingers under his eyes that look a little more sunken than I'd prefer them to. "Have you seen Sam?"

I'm conscious of the muscles in and around my eyes not moving in any way I don't want them to, and the only way I want them to move is for me to look annoyed.

"Yeah." I toss my brother a wry look. "He's in here with me."

That's a tactic to throw him off. Hiding the truth in plain sight.

Oliver rolls his eyes. "I don't know where he's gone—hey." He looks over at me, and it's right then I notice Sam's shirt on the floor.

Oh my God. My heart is pounding because I think we're about to be sprung.

I'd notice. That's the sort of thing I'd notice.

Shit.

Oliver frowns a little and tilts his head. "You're cool with Sam coming with us, hey?"

I can't help but sigh with relief, but I mask it by sticking my face under the showerhead and letting the water run over me.

"Yeah, sure." I spit some water out of my mouth as I look over at my brother, shrugging indifferently. "Whatever."

Oliver purses his lips. "Where do you think he's gone?"

"I don't know! Maybe to a bathroom where people don't just bust in on you all the time? Get out!"

Oliver rolls his eyes again. "You need a 'special' shower."

"Out!" I squeak.

He harrumphs and slams the door shut.

I look down at Sam, soaking wet and shirtless at my feet, and he stares up at me, laughing silently, and I do my best to not smile—and we're both frozen in this weird, hilarious, frenetic, urgent terror, not wanting to moving in case Oliver marches right back in.

About thirty seconds pass, and slowly, Sam stands.

And the way he rises feels like watching a tree grow in fast forward. When he's standing at full mast, I feel the same way I did when I stood at the bottom of the Empire State Building and looked up when I was nine.

He slips one hand around my bare waist and pulls me in toward him, and with the other he holds my face, and he just stares at my mouth for the longest few seconds in the history of time, and then his mouth crashes into mine and he pushes me up against the shower door.

That old lusty ache radiates through my bones and I want him in ways I know I can't have right now, but that doesn't stop me from pulling him closer toward me.

Sam's hands start going all the places I want them to go, and I pull back a little, looking for his eyes, mine all heavy with "sorry's" and tacit "I love you's."

"It's probably not the time..." I tell him, and he flops his forehead down on mine, crestfallen.

He sighs big out of his nose and kisses me again, but softly this time. "Yeah."

After the shower, I pack a bag and make my way downstairs.

Sam's already down there, in a different pair of nonsaturated black jeans and a different white T-shirt, and it's getting harder and harder for me to pretend he's nothing to me.

"Where've you been?" Oliver asks Sam brightly, appearing at the bottom of the stairs with a Balmain weekend bag.

"Ah." Sam swats his hand dismissively. "Just went for a walk."

"Oh." Oli smiles, thinking nothing of it, and walks out toward the car.

Tennyson's watching Sam and his eyes flick to me and then back to Oliver. He nods his chin at Penny. "Was it raining out?"

Sam's face falters, confused. "No?"

Tens cocks an eyebrow at Sam's damp hair and then looks over at me and mine. "Good shower, then?" he asks me, eyebrows tall.

I keep my face very still, as neutral as possible. "Weird and pervy question coming from my oldest brother, but yeah, thanks—it was great."

Tenny glances between Sam and me and bites back a smile. "I bet it was," he says as he walks toward the car.

I cast Sam a "fuck" look and he reaches for my overnight bag.

I do quick emotional and social IQ math in my head and conclude it'd be more overt to thwart his attempt to carry my bag, because maybe he's just being a nice guy and he'd do that for anyone, and it'd be weirder and draw more attention to us if I didn't let him, so I let him. My heart sparks a bit, because even though it's nothing, it's the first something he's gotten to do for me that isn't in hiding.

My mom's standing out on the front steps watching us, and I walk over to her, but she doesn't look at me as I do.

"It's going to be okay," I tell her.

She watches the horizon of nothing for a few seconds longer before she looks down at me.

"You'll tell me what you find?"

I nod.

Then she moves past me to hug Tennyson, and for a split second it hurts me, but then she sort of collapses into his arms, and even though it often is, the distance between us today is not about me at all.

Violet stands at the top of the steps looking down on me.

"You sure you don't want to come?" I call up to her.

She shakes her head solemnly.

I take a few steps up toward her. "What am I going to find out there?"

Violet gives me a long look. "You get why it is I can't tell you, right?"

I nod once. "To death and for free."

"To death and for free." She nods back. "I love you though."

She wraps her arms around me.

"I love you too," I tell her as she pets my hair.

I trot downstairs toward the car.

"Y'all drive safe, okay?" she calls out to the boys, waving at them.

Tenny's driving, apparently. He's at the driver's side, kissing Savannah.

"I'll miss you, baby," he tells her.

"Get a room," I groan at him.

"Maybe I'll just get a shower." My brother gives me a pointed look and Savannah hits him in the arm.

She smiles at me. "Bye."

I give her a small wave as Tens climbs into the front seat.

He looks back at Oli and Sam. "Let's go find this bitch."

39

TENNY'S KNEE-DEEP IN THE STORY of how he met Savannah, and it's cuter than I expected from my brother, but if I'm honest, Tennyson is starting to surprise me in general.

Tens saved her from a weird blind date at a bar in college. Pretended that he knew her from high school and intervened and began to walk her home. He took her to a movie instead, and then they were together.

"What happened with you and Maryanne?" I ask him.

"Nothing." Tennyson says, staring straight ahead. So, something.

"It had to do with Savannah?" I ask, mostly giving him the chance to tell me himself—which he doesn't; he just gives me an unimpressed look.

"Oh, come on." I roll my eyes. "You were so close before and it's different now."

"Yeah—" He does this big "so what" shrug, and gestures toward me. "She—you know—"

I shake my head at him. "Your dynamic had changed before you found out about me."

His jaw juts forward and I know I've hit a nerve, but he doesn't say anymore.

"I like Savannah," I tell him. I half tell him because it's true but also because I wonder if it'll get the truth out of him.

He peers out the corner of his eye, exasperated. "She told Mom that Sav and I were sleeping together."

"So?" Oliver says from behind us.

Tennyson looks back over his shoulder, annoyed that more people than just me are hearing this.

"It's sex," Oliver tells him. "Everyone has it."

"Yeah, well—" Tens cracks his neck. "Mer told Mom, and all the girls from church too, and you know them—" He tosses me a sorry look. "They love someone to talk about."

Sam blows some air out of his mouth. "Sorry, mate. That's pretty shit."

And Ten's brow tells me how much our stupid sister being mean to her weighs on him—even though they've been together four years now, he said, and he loves her in a way where it's still fresh on his face. It takes all that is strong within me not to glance back at Sam.

I pull down my passenger side mirror so I can see if he's looking at me. I can't tell whether he was before, but our eyes catch in the reflection and his mouth twitches with a hint of a smile as he looks out the window.

"So check it, Tens." Oliver drums on the back of Tennyson's chair. "Do you know who our baby sister was dating right before she left London?"

"Who?" Tennyson looks at me, not at Oliver.

I roll my eyes. "No one."

"A mercenary," Oliver announces dramatically.

Sam looks at me through the mirror. I flick him a look that tells him I'm sorry for this.

"That was like, five months ago."

"A mercenary?" Tenny blinks. "How the fuck did you meet a mercenary?"

"Through a mutual friend." I shrug. "And he wasn't a mercenary."

Tennyson looks at me out of the corner of his eye. "What was he then?"

"A private contractor."

"Of…?" my brother asks.

My mouth shrugs without my express permission. "…militias."

"OH! MY! GOD!" Tennyson yells, staring at me in fascination.

"They were together for ages too!" Oliver tells him brightly. "Super in love."

Through the reflection I see Sam look back out the window, pressing his tongue into his top lip.

"Oliver!" I snap my head in his direction, feeling cross.

"What?" He blinks.

"Shut up!"

"Why? You were!"

Tennyson glances over at me. "Were you scared of him?"

I give him a look like he's being silly. "Of course not."

"It didn't bother you?" Tenny presses.

"I don't know…" I trail off. "I didn't care, really. I don't care what people have done before they met me." I catch Sam's eye in the mirror and he suppresses a smile. "Or what they do, really—as long as they don't lie. Storm has a weird job; that's all it was to me. As long as he didn't lie to me, we were good…" I trail off again.

Sam doesn't know he does it, but he gives a tired sigh, and I want to climb over these seats and into his lap and tell him about how none of it matters anymore and all I can see is him.

"So." I look at Tenny, trying to shift the conversation away from me and Storm. "Are you going to propose soon, or what?"

Ten's face shifts to shy.

"You are!"

He rolls his eyes.

"She's really cool," I tell him.

"You think?"

I nod. "I thought she was maybe a bit dumb at first, but I was wrong. She's really clever and super hot. Like, pretty out of your league."

He gestures to himself. "I'm a catch."

I roll my eyes exaggeratedly.

"I don't believe in marriage," Oliver announces.

I scoff, turning around to face him. "Since when?"

Ol's been dreaming of a big white wedding all his life. He's desperately wanted someone to be committed to him for as long as I can remember.

"It's a sham." He shrugs. "It's just another way for society to control us—"

I blink at him a few times, tilt my head at his words, trying to find the root of them. There's no conviction to his conviction. "Who are you regurgitating right now?"

"No one." Oliver scowls. "I just don't believe in marriage anymore."

"Well," I sigh, turning back around to face the road. "I guess that's good, because a big chunk of America doesn't believe in marriage for you either."

He kicks my seat.

"No, it's good. Saves me a lot of yelling and picketing."

There's a longish pause…long enough that it's loaded.

"Sam doesn't believe in marriage either," Oliver says in a tone that I don't think I should pick at.

I stare straight out the windshield, a frown breezing across my face, and I feel Tens glance at me.

Sam shifts uncomfortably in his seat and throws a look at Oliver.

"You're taking what I said out of context." He sounds annoyed, which makes me turn around. Sam barely ever sounds annoyed.

"Put it in context, then," I tell him.

Sam glances cautiously out of the corner of his eye at my two brothers—a bit like, "Really? This, now?"—but I cock an eyebrow up as I wait for his answer.

He purses his mouth for a second, pausing before he speaks. "I said, I don't believe in marriage as a form of validating commitment—like, if you're going to cheat on someone, you're going to cheat on them. A fucking piece of metal on your finger won't stop you. If you're going to leave, you'll leave. Rings and paper, they don't mean shit."

"Charming." I turn back around, grumpy.

"Vows, though..." he keeps going. "I'm okay with some vows."

"You said you thought the institution of marriage is a sham," Oliver announces.

"Fuck, dude." Sam sigh-laughs, and it makes both me and Tenny turn around. "I said the religious institution of marriage is a sham." Sam shakes his head. "In the context of people like you and other queer people. Because they don't want you to get married, and then they're up in arms about fucking outside of marriage. They're just setting you up for a loss, and I don't like it."

Sam gives Oliver a full-stop look, and Oliver looks like a scolded puppy.

I look at Sam; my eyes flick over his face that I've searched so many times, who I felt like I knew in a way I've never known anyone, but who, actually, I still have so very much to learn about—And for the briefest second, it makes me feel like I mustn't really be in love with him, because how could I be? How could I be in love with someone and not even know that they don't believe in marriage? I decide to flick that though away, though, because it would be foolish to think you need to stop learning about the things you love.

Sam and I hold eyes for a second, and the tacit tension surrounding the subtext in the conversation we're having flickers between us in the unspoken way people who've been intimate can communicate in ways other people can't hear.

I think he looks nervous. I think he knows what I'm about to ask.

I tilt my head. "When was the last time you were in a long-term relationship?"

Sam presses his lips together and holds my gaze for a split second longer than what's normal. "A while."

I nod coolly and face the front.

"It's not a commitment thing," he tells the car but really it's me.

"That's what guys who are afraid of commitment say," I tell him, not looking back.

"I'm not afraid of commitment," he says, but his mouth shrugs and he doesn't realize that what he's doing says something else.

"That's the other thing they say."

He sniffs a laugh, and nods once clearly. "I'm not."

I don't even think he knows his body's giving him away.

"Whatever you say." I give the road I'm glaring at a small shrug and turn Avicii up louder.

I don't know why I feel annoyed, but I do. Stepped on, or something. I fell in love with Sam without asking his permission—without asking him anything, really. He doesn't need to believe in marriage, that's fine—unideal, but fine. I don't want to love someone who's afraid of commitment, though. Trying to make someone commit to you who's afraid of commitment is like trying to tie down a tarpaulin once a hurricane's already started. I'm not doing that.

Tenny's watching me closely, and I find it weird, having been ignored by him most of my life, to have him paying attention to me at all, let alone this much.

I snap my head in my oldest brother's direction, giving him a look, pointing at my eyes and then the road. "Hello?" I growl. "I'd like to live to see the light of day once again!"

My big brother rolls his eyes.

"I swear to God, Tennyson, if you get us killed before I get to solve the mystery about the Homewrecker From New Orleans, I will torment you for eternity."

"Can't imagine it'd be all that different from the conversation we're having right now." He gives me a dickhead smile.

We pull in for gas about an hour and a half later, and while Oliver goes to the bathroom, I browse the aisles for snacks.

Sam follows me. He picks up a Hershey's bar and inspects it. "Do we need to talk?"

"Nope," I say, walking into the next aisle.

"Georgia." He sounds tired.

"What?" I look up at him, bright-eyed.

"What are you doing?"

"What are *you* doing?" I emphasize the *you*.

He rolls his eyes. "Is there something you're not s—fuck, spit it out." He shrugs, frustrated. "Do you want to ask me something?"

Yep. "Nope."

He makes a *pfft* sound and walks away.

40

I THINK PROBABLY IF I COULD write it all out on a giant timeline and look out over it all, I could pick out the exact day that Oliver's drinking really started. Not the first time he drank, but the first time he drank how he'd continue to drink. Gun to my head—I can't say I blame him.

That day, I came home from school a little later than normal, and as soon as I walked in the house, I could hear yelling. And it was real yelling too—this nasty, persistent, wear-you-down hollering.

My mom mostly, but sometimes my dad…and holy shit, I hated it when my dad yelled. My mom was the yeller in our house, but when my dad yelled, the earth shook.

He didn't not yell to be kind; I think he just didn't yell because he didn't care. I'd hear him raise his voice to Tens sometimes, about trying harder, focusing more, being better—never to Maryanne. Never to me either, but his nevers regarding me stretched far wider than yelling.

I remember knowing that whatever they were yelling, they were yelling it at Oliver. They'd never speak to Maryanne or Tennyson like that.

I walked into the kitchen, and I knew what was happening straight away. They'd found Oliver's magazines that he hid behind the pipes under the bathroom sink. They were laid out on the bench.

Mom was horrified. Dad was pale the way you'd imagine a homophobic man would be when he finds out his kid is gay.

And Oliver was heartbroken. That's all I could see; the rest melted away.

His eyes were brimming with tears he wouldn't let himself cry now, but I'd hear him cry them later, chastised for being curious about his sexuality that no one in the world would talk to him about here, and punished for feeding his curiosity on his own accord.

He wasn't ready to come out. He wasn't ready for them to officially know what we'd all known all along. He wasn't ready for them to reject him once and for all.

"They're mine," I blurted out. My parents' heads snapped in my direction—it just flew out of me; I didn't even really think about it.

I was fourteen at the time. Sexually active, unbeknownst to them (and primarily against my own will), but sexually active nonetheless. I didn't need them to think I was a virginal, white, flower child anymore; I didn't feel like that on the inside anyway.

Being the sort of fifteen-year-old who hid porn under her bathroom sink, that was more aligned to how I felt in those days.

"I beg your pardon?" my mother said, eyebrow cocked, hand on her hips.

Oliver's face was frozen, eyes wide.

"They're mine." I nodded, swallowing heavily.

My mother's face contorted in horror. "What are you talking about? Where in tarnation did you get magazines like those?"

"A girl from school," I lied.

My father looked over at me curiously, tongue pressed against the inside of his cheek, and his eyed pinched a little. I don't know whether he believed me.

My mother walked toward me, shaking her head slightly, peering down her nose at me.

And then she slapped me. She never slapped me before then, and she hasn't slapped me since.

My head swung in the direction she hit me and I let it stay there, facing away from her, blinking, trying my best not to cry.

"You sicken me." And then she walked away, my dad after her.

Oliver waited a few seconds before rushing over to me. He threw his arms around me and pulled me into his chest.

"Why did you do that?" he asked as I began to cry.

Except, even then, I don't think I was crying for me.

Maybe it was a bit out of shock—no one had ever hit me before—but mostly, I think I was crying for him. Because I felt for a tiny, falsified second what my brother must have felt living in a small town in the South every single day. Fucked up and rejected for no acceptable reason at all.

41

WE'VE DRIVEN FOR ABOUT SEVEN hours and it's getting late, close to midnight when Tenny pulls off the interstate to a shitty inn. We're just a little outside of Pensacola, and he kills the engine, yawning.

"Let's call it a night," Tenny tells everyone, but mostly me.

"I can drive," I say.

He shakes his head. "You've been yawning since Georgiana."

"I'm fine," Sam offers. "I can drive."

Tennyson shakes his head again. "We keep driving and we'll get to New Orleans at three a.m., and what'll we do then anyway? May as well stop now." He shrugs. "Have a proper rest."

He doesn't wait for the rest of us to have any thoughts; he just climbs out of the car—which is an annoying thing to do, but I sort of respect it, though I'll never tell him that. It's so decisive even if it is a bit pricky. Tennyson gets both his bag and mine from the trunk, then walks into the motel lobby.

Instinctively I want to glance back at Sam, but I don't let myself, because I feel sad and wretched and, also, Oliver's too close—which maybe doesn't even matter anyway now.

"We'll get two rooms, please," Tenny tells the man behind the desk.

The guy's not George Clooney, I'll tell you that much. He's balding weirdly and unevenly. He's in a stained tank top and Terry Richardson glasses, but in an unironic way. He takes a swig of Mountain Dew Liberty Brew.

"Two?" I blink. "I'm not sharing."

"Yeah, you are," Tennyson tells me without looking back.

I frown. "I don't want to share."

"I don't mind sharing!" Oliver says brightly.

"Fine." I shrug. "I'll share with Oliver."

Oliver scrunches his face. "I'm going to share with Sam," he announces.

I glance between Oliver and Sam, exasperated. "Why?"

Sam's just watching me, brows low. I think he's annoyed at me too. We haven't really spoken since the gas station, which was about three hours ago.

"Because he's my coach," Oliver says.

"And I'm your sister."

"Share with Tens."

"I don't want to share with Tennyson." I fold my arms.

"Fine! Fuck," Tennyson growls, shaking his head. "We'll get a third room." He turns back to the guy. "We'll take a third room."

The guy puffs out his mouth and shakes his head. "Don't got a third room."

I push in front of my brother. "You don't have one extra room? In this whole complex?"

"Lady, this ain't Taj Mahal."

"Yeah," I scoff as I glance around the room I'm standing in. Bug zapper in the corner. Ripped-up sofa. Flickering light. "No fucking shit."

Objectively and honestly, the flickering lights and the blue-light bug traps and the linoleum floors are all, like, very on-brand for a murder aesthetic, so I'm glad that I haven't backed myself entirely into a corner I'd probably die in and instead am sharing with my six-foot-two brother who never skips arm day.

Not–George Clooney holds up two sets of keys. "I got one with two doubles and one with one king—"

"Doubles!" I yell, lunging for the keys. "Give me those." I snatch them grumpily from the weird desk man.

Oliver looks a bit pleased, and eight hours ago I would have been fuming, but now I don't know. I don't know whether I have the right to be fuming.

The man points us to our rooms, which are a few doors apart on the second level.

Tennyson carries my bag up the stairs, and I follow, and Sam watches me the whole way up. His gaze weighs on me heavily, like a coat I never want to take off, and my brain is swirly with thoughts and feelings.

"See you boys in the morning." Tennyson nods at Oliver and Penny. "We'll text you when we wake up."

I don't say anything as I walk into our room, and Tenny follows behind me, tossing my bag on the floor.

Overly patterned bedspreads, bright yellow walls with a weird blue carpet.

It's technically clean, but it doesn't feel clean, and I'm frowning so much my face starts to hurt.

"What happened?" Tennyson asks.

I blink over at him like I'm confused, but I know exactly what he means. "What are you talking about?"

He gives me a look.

"Nothing." I shrug.

"Why are you suddenly a bitch then?"

"I'm not." I glare over at him.

He scoffs, pulling off his shirt. "I'm taking a shower. Take whatever bed you want."

I perch on the bed farthest away from the door and switch on the TV. *SVU* reruns. Maybe this night is turning around after all.

I grump there on my bed, thinking about Oliver lying next to Sam, and I feel a pang of jealousy.

About five minutes later, Tennyson reemerges in just a pair of gray sweats and falls onto his bed, blowing air out of his mouth.

"What?" I look over at him.

"It's her, right?" He glances at me, nervous. "It has to be."

I purse my mouth. "I mean, it makes sense."

Tenny nods, thinking to himself. "Yeah. Fuck. What are we going to—I mean—Mom'll be—"

I shake my head. "She already is." I shrug. "So we just give her what closure we can."

Tennyson nods again, distracted—jaw tight, eyes pained.

My phone buzzes, and I glance down at it.

UNKNOWN:

Outside

It's from a contactless number in my phone, but I know it's Sam's because Oliver put us in a group chat at the start of the week to streamline his complaining about Mom, and I accidentally learned the number by heart.

"Um." I blink a few times, trying to think through the lie I'm about to tell my brother so it's believable. "I've got to get something from the car." I stand up, walking toward the door.

Tens stands up. "I'll get it for you."

"Er." I pause. "No." My voice goes squeaky. "I'll do it—I'm fine."

"Oh." He snorts a laugh and plonks back down on the bed. "Yeah, I can't get that for you."

I roll my eyes at him like he's so immature. "Whatever you think you know, you don't."

"Right." He gives me a disbelieving look.

"You don't!"

"Right!" He grins, annoyingly.

I start to walk away.

"Hey," Tens calls.

I glare back at him. "What?"

"Forgetting something?" He holds up the car keys, licking away a smile.

I growl under my breath as I walk out of the room.

Smug bastard.

I look around the poorly lit balcony.

There's a vending machine casting a vague light on a shadow I could never mistake.

He looks over at me, his white T-shirt a little blue from the glowing Pepsi sign. His eyes go extra bright under the light and his mouth is pouting a little, and I stare at it for a few seconds because it's begging for it, and then Sam grabs me and kisses me, urgent, desperate, arms wrapped around me, pulling me into him.

I sink into him, kissing him more, and we fall against the vending machine.

He pulls back and peers down at me, smiling a little. "Did we just have our first fight?"

I pull back my head in false surprise. "Hold on, sorry, do you believe in 'we's'?"

He sniffs a laugh. "Oh, so we're about to have our second..."

I give him a tight smile, eyebrows up. "There you go again with that 'we.'"

He shakes his head at me. "You got something to ask me, just ask."

I straighten up. "When exactly was the last time you were in a long-term relationship?"

Sam takes a big breath in and sighs it out. "Nine years ago."

Fuck me. That's longer than I was expecting. I try to keep my face cool and steady, but I think my heart's about to break.

"Why?" I try to ask lightly, but the connotations are heavy and we both know it.

He sniffs again, tired. "You tell me."

I roll my eyes at him. "I can't."

He gives me a dubious look. "Sure you can."

"That's a very broad request."

"Is it?" Sam tilts his head before he shrugs. "You read people for a living, Gige. Read me."

I throw my hands into the air. "I have no information. I don't know any of the defining details of your past relationships, none of the dynamics, how you met, when you met, what state either of you were in when you met—"

He shrugs again. "Ask away."

I tilt my head and give him an unsure look.

He nods his chin toward the car. "Let's talk in there."

He takes my hand in his—no talking—and walks me over to the car. I love my hand in his. My whole hand gets enveloped.

He opens the car door and we climb into the back seat of my brother's car, where I turn to face him.

"So." I watch Sam's face closely. "Do you know why?"

"Why I haven't been in a relationship in a while?"

I nod.

"I think so."

I shrug. "Then what am I doing?"

"Practice?" he offers, smiling a bit, but there's something about it that feels reserved.

I purse my lips. "Are you sure?"

He nods once. I look at his face for a long second and try to brace myself to hear a lot of answers I don't think I'll want to hear but probably really need to.

"Name?" Me.

"Nicola." Him.

"How old were you when you met?" Me.

"Eighteen." Him.

"Her?" Me.

"Nineteen." Him.

"Where?" Me.

"LA." Him.

"Together for how long?"

He waves his hand. "Two years? Two and a bit."

"How'd you meet?"

His eyes flick up and left. "Party."

"What kind of party?" I watch his face. "Like—birthday party, Chuck E. Cheese, Tupperware?"

Sam rolls his eyes as he leans in closer toward me. "A party-party."

"Was she a user?"

His eyes drop from mine. He nods.

"Recreational or addict?" I ask.

Sam cocks a small smile and leans over, brushing his mouth against mine.

"What are you doing?" I ask, his mouth still against mine.

"Kissing you." He kisses me softly again.

"Why?"

He sniffs a laugh. "Because you don't fucking pull any punches and it's..." He wipes his mouth absentmindedly. "Hot."

I feel my chest swell and I pull back a bit because I want him to keep being proud of me.

"Answer the question," I tell him.

"I mean, it all starts off recreational."

"So, addict." I nod to myself, and in my periphery, I see him smile a tiny bit as he watches me. "You overdosed when...?" I trail. "Twenty?"

Sam nods again.

I look for his eyes. "Where is she now?"

He takes a big breath in and shrugs out a sigh with his whole body. "I don't know." He looks away, mouth twitching with AU10. Contempt.

"You don't know?"

He shakes his head.

"Why?"

Sam shrugs again, and it's like he thinks he's being dismissive, and it's the least emotionally aware I think I've ever seen him. "Just don't."

"Oh." I'm starting to get it, I think.

"What?" He gives me a curious look.

"Did you get high together a lot?"

His face pulls tight. "Yeah."

I swallow, then nod again. "Okay."

He watches me, and it strikes me that he might be nervous…the shape his eyes have taken, the chin angled down toward his chest—

This is it. This is what he couldn't put words around. He knows it about himself; he just doesn't know how to tell me.

"You don't have problem with committing to something," I tell him. "You're an addict—you're as committed as they come. It's not a marriage thing; it's not even a love thing. You're…" I tilt my head, looking at him only a few inches away from me, watching me watch him, letting me unfold him in the backseat of my big brother's car. I frown at him, sadly. "You don't know whether you were addicted to her or the drugs."

His eyes drop down and to the right: he's recalling an emotional memory or a bodily sensation.

Our bodies tell all our secrets.

"We were always together, always high—I don't think we ever hooked up sober—so I was high from the drugs, but I could have been high from the sex. I don't know. I can't tell."

I'm frowning because I hate the thought of him having sex with someone else. His hands on their body, his mouth on theirs—it makes me feel like something's clawing at my stomach.

Sam's face scrunches up in thought. "Loving someone's an obsession—and being in love, even fucking—you get that high."

"Oxytocin." I nod.

"They say it's as addictive as coke."

I nod again. "They do."

Sam presses his lips together tightly—he's self-hushing. "I don't have a good lid on myself with pacing things that make me feel good."

I give him a dubious look. "Yeah, you do..."

"Yeah, right." He scoffs. "That's why I've taken it so fucking slow with you."

I shrug, then offer, "I don't have an addiction problem and I haven't taken things slowly with you."

He breathes out his nose and looks away. "It's not the same."

"How do you know?"

Then he glares over at me. "Because you don't look at me how I look at you."

Interesting. A hint of resentment.

"You don't know how I look at you—"

Sam cuts me off. "I can see."

I give him an unimpressed look. "You're not in my head; you don't know what you mean to me."

Sam's face is completely littered with emotions—there's contempt, there's sadness, there's fear—

"I haven't felt anything for anyone for nine years." Sam swallows. "I was clean...of everything I was addicted to. I was clean—and then I met you."

Sam stares at me for a few seconds and then his eyes drop.

And then I understand what he's saying.

"You're afraid of transferring your tendency toward dependence," I say. "You don't want to be addicted to anything—not even me."

He holds my eyes.

I touch his cheek. "You think I'd let you be addicted to me?"

He gives me a sore smile. "I don't think you'd have a say."

Then he turns his face in my hand and kisses my palm.

"So what are you saying, Sam?" I duck to meet his eyes. "Is this over?"

He shakes his head solemnly. "No."

"Do you want..." I pause. Reword my sentence. "Do you need this to be over?"

He shakes his head again, pressing his tongue into his bottom lip.

"Penny." I hold his face in my hands. "You've had relationships with other people in these last nine years. You've been committed to them. You love your sister and your niece. Your dedication to the well-being of my brother is unparalleled."

Sam rolls his eyes, but I keep going.

"You're capable of having affections for people and being committed to them in an appropriate measure." I poke him in the chest. "You can do this."

Sam's face softens. "You asking me to fall in love with you?"

I smile coyly. "Maybe."

"Maybe I will." He shrugs. And then he looks serious. "You'll watch me?"

I nod. I'd swear to forever if he asked me to, here and now.

Sam Penny purses his mouth, twitching it as he thinks. "Are we okay?" he asks cautiously.

I flick my eyes over to him. "Are we a 'we'?"

Sam Penny raises his eyebrows up in a nervous hopefulness, his cheeks pink even in the dark. "Yep."

"Oh." I swallow heavily, heart beating like the drum in "Hot For Teacher."

He looks for my eyes. "Is that okay?"

"Yeah."

He presses his hand into his mouth, wiping away a smile. "Okay."

"Okay."

We stare at each other, about six inches apart, and my eyes can't land on him. Eyes—mouth—eyes—mouth—

But Sam's zoned in on my lips, and have you ever been to Typhoon Lagoon in Florida? The Disney theme park? There's a big wave pool, and every fifteen minutes this whistle blows a few times as a warning that something big is coming, that you should get out of the water if you're afraid or not a good swimmer. Then there's this deep woof of a boom, and then this gigantic wave comes and you ride it into shore, if it doesn't knock you over.

The way Sam's watching my mouth, I'm telling you, I can hear the whistle—I notice his breathing getting faster, which makes mine get faster, and I feel the grown-up equivalent of how I felt when I was a kid at the wave pool and I knew it was going to knock me clean over. It's that nervous-scary-exciting feeling you get when you're a kid doing something semi-dangerous but mostly good and definitely fun—you want it to knock you over, that's the best part. I suck in my bottom lip because that's what I do when I feel exposed, and I swear to God, I can hear the woof-boom, and then he kisses the shit out of me.

I pull him down on top of me, and the way he's kissing me, I'm a puddle on the floor.

I pull his shirt off.

He doesn't stop kissing me as he unbuttons my striped vintage Ralph Lauren shirt, and when his hand touches my bare skin, I catch on fire, but it's okay because Sam Penny is the fire blanket the universe throws to me.

My body arcs up into his and I clamber for him, but his hands are firm and steady, and it's quicker than last night—more rushed and urgent, desperate in our longing. I guess fights do that to lovers.

He doesn't let go of me after, holds on to me for dear life as he sits up and pulls me onto his lap, holding my face in his hands.

He's panting quick and heavy, eyes dragging with tired blinks and a spent smile on the surface of his mouth.

I tilt my head, looking at him. "Can I ask you something?"

He cocks a half smile. "There she is." He kisses me again and nudges his face with mine, then nods with his chin, waiting for me.

I purse my lips as I square my shoulders. "What's our sex like compared to…drug-addled, high sex?"

He smiles, squashing it as best he can. "Incomparable."

I feel a frown flicker across my face. "Why?"

Sam Penny pushes some hair behind my ear. "Because I can remember ours."

42

DID YOU FIND WHAT YOU were looking for?" Tennyson asks first thing when he wakes up the next morning.

"Shut up." I slam the bathroom door. And yes I did, thank you very much.

Sam and I stood outside my motel door for as long as possible, his arms wrapped around me, his chin on my head, me playing on a loop the part where he said "maybe I will." about loving me—and then he kissed me for the thousandth time and my heart sank as he walked away to sleep in a bed with my brother.

"I love you," I called after him in my head.

We all pile into the car the next morning after collectively deciding to blow off breakfast until we saw something we recognized, like a Denny's.

Tenny takes the front again, and I hope for a second that Oliver's in one of his Tennyson-obsessed moods, but he's not.

"You take the front," he tells me brightly, opening the door for me.

I smile at him, but only on the outside, because I'd really like to sit with Sam back there in the quiet and think about all the ways and places he touched me last night in that seat.

I climb into the front seat and glance back at Sam, who winks at me quickly before Oliver gets into the car.

Tenny peels out blasting AC/DC, which has been his go-to for as long as I can remember.

"What the fuck!" Oliver says loudly and suddenly.

I turn around and am face-to-face with something gold and metallic. My eyes take a second to focus, and then…

Shit.

Condom wrapper.

Shit, shit, shit.

"What?" Tennyson looks back and sees it and looks straight back to the road.

All these thoughts happen at warp speed, flying through my brain.

Okay, now, my basest instincts would have me look at Sam. That's what I naturally want to do for more reasons than just because I love him now. Loving him now is peripheral. You look at the things you want to protect, and you look at the person you're caught in a lie with, and these things would give me away.

Sam doesn't have the same control with his face as I do in a situation like this. He's looking at me, eyes wider than they should be—in fact, his eyes are looking so fucking sprung that if Oliver was looking at him, he would have picked it up in a second.

I need to react, I know I need to react…

If the condom was mine, if I recognized it how I actually do, my natural response would be a mouth shrug, a jaw drop, a nervous swallow, something like that.

If it wasn't mine, if I had no idea about it, probably I'd look disgusted or at the very least, show some contempt.

Gut instinct tells me to go with disgust.

I scrunch up my nose and blink at it, consciously keeping my breath in rhythm.

"Oh, fuck." Tennyson sighs. "That's—shit. It's mine."

"What?" Oliver blinks.

I look over at my biggest brother.

"It's mine," he repeats.

Oliver says, "It wasn't here yesterday."

"No, I know." Tenny shrugs. "I couldn't sleep last night, so I went to this bar—I probably drank too much. There was a girl—I don't know, it was stupid."

Oliver stares at him, wide-eyed. "You cheated on Savannah?"

"Yeah." Tenny shakes his head, but won't realize he's doing it. It's a deception leakage, but it doesn't matter as long as Oliver doesn't notice it either.

"Why!" Oliver asks, leaning forward.

"I didn't plan on it. It was—st—I was...stupid."

Oliver sits back in his seat, shocked.

"Don't tell her!" Tennyson glances back, looking nervous.

"Of course we won't tell her." I look at Tennyson and then pointedly at Oliver. "We'd never."

I give Oliver a look, who then nods. "We'd never."

Tennyson blows air out of his mouth and shoves his hand through his hair, gripping the steering wheel tighter.

"Wait, gross." Oliver leans forward again. "Am I sitting in your sex seat?"

Tenny glances back at him. "Hate to break it to you, man, but I've had sex in that exact spot more times than you'd care to know."

Ew. I cringe in real life and internally.

Oliver thinking Tennyson's cheated on Savannah is interesting, because it takes Tennyson down from the pedestal on which Oliver keeps him, and it's also afforded Oliver a (fake) secret to share between them.

As we drive, I talk about the very normal things I very normally talk about, and Tens asks Sam about being an alcoholic, and Sam tells us about a place in New Orleans called the Old Absinthe House, which is like, two hundred years old and allegedly has the world's best gin and tonic.

About an hour later, we find a gas station with a coffee shop nearby. Penny and Oliver run across the road to get us coffees, Tenny pumps the gas, and I sit in the car for a minute or so thinking about the weird turn of events and the way Tennyson lied to protect me.

I get out of the car and shove my hands in my pockets.

Tenny glances over at me, face riddled with amusement, and he scoffs back a laugh. He looks away and looks back, eyebrows cocked like he already knows the answer. "You're sleeping with him?"

I nod once. "Yeah."

He shrugs and gives me a look. "How long's that been going on for?"

"What are you doing?" I glare over at my oldest brother. "You and I aren't close!"

"So what?" Hurt and guilt flashes across his face. "That means we can't ever be?"

"Why do you want to be?" I blink, wide-eyed.

"Because I fucked up, okay?" he yells. "I fucked up, Gige. I was a piece of shit brother, and you got..." He trails off. He can't even say it.

I give him a long look and then eventually shake my head. "Tennyson, nothing that happened to me was your fault."

Tens's face pulls tight with shame and guilt that isn't his to bear. "He was my friend."

I shake my head again. "Still not your fault."

"I'd bring him to the house—I'd get him to drive you places so I didn't have to—"

I keep shaking my head. "Still not your fault."

He juts his jaw and looks away. "I should have been someone that you could have told," he says, and he's angry at himself.

"Tennyson." I say his name gently. "Even if you were that person to me back then, I wasn't okay enough with myself to have been able to say—out loud—what was happening to me. None of this is on you."

Tennyson nods, but I don't think he necessarily believes what I'm saying.

I fold my arms uncomfortably over my chest. "You didn't need to cover for me this morning."

He looks at the numbers clicking over on the gas pump and just shrugs.

I purse my lips and kick the ground with one foot. "Thank you, though."

He shrugs again. "That's okay."

The years of hurt and pain and silence begin their undoing as a different kind of silence hazes between us.

"I think I'm in love with him," I offer.

Tens looks over, eyes wide, head pulled back. "What?"

I press my hands into my eyes, feeling stupid. "It's probably a trauma bond—or oxytocin? I might just be latching onto him, forming an inappropriate attachment because of—"

"Or," my big brother interrupts, "it might just be because he's a good guy."

I glance up at him, my eyes embarrassingly hopeful. "Yeah?"

Tens presses his tongue down into his bottom lip and nods, smiling a little. "Yeah."

I try not to smile too much because it makes me feel see-through, but Tennyson smiles back, and the way he does it makes me realize that at twenty-five and thirty respectively, he and I have just now had our first tenderhearted sibling moment.

Better late than never, I suppose.

43

WE PULL INTO THE VALET at the Ritz over on Canal Street in the French Quarter, and it's just about as gorgeous as you can imagine.

Everything in this town, the Ritz Carlton included, seems to sport a droopy loveliness, like the whole city is a Southern belle fainting in the hot Louisiana sun. The city smells of a time we'd all rather be from, ripe with some sort of old magic, thick with a formidable lust and heavy with a fog of dreams both realized and lived but also lost—and I can see how you might fall in love with a person here, have a secret affair with a woman your family's never heard of, give her a lake house no one else knew existed.

This is undoubtedly and somewhat unfortunately the most beautiful, romantic hotel I've ever been to in my life, and I'm here with the boy of my dreams, and we're saddled with my buzzkill brothers.

We're standing in the hotel lobby waiting to be served—we don't have a reservation, but they were still showing rooms online—and Sam is fucking up so much right now. I feel like he's smarter than he's being; we've *been* smarter than he's being—

But I'm standing in front of him, and he's hovering. Hardcore hovering.

Interpersonal distance matters so much on a subconscious level, and luckily Oliver is in front of me talking to Tennyson so he can't see it, but Sam's practically a helicopter right now, and I can feel my brain and my heart beginning to have an argument because I love Sam hovering, I want him to hover forever, but I can feel his breath on the back of my neck, which means he's likely less than half a foot, he has to be—and anyone, anyone at all could sense that there is something more than nothing going on between us.

The concierge calls us forward and Tenny does the talking, but I take the opportunity to shift, moving myself next to Sam instead of in front of him and leaving about a foot and a half between us, which seems acceptable for two nonintimate, non–in love, quasi-friends who have been in a car together for the last twelve hours and attended one funeral together.

But then he shifts toward me—whether it's conscious or not, I can't really tell, but the subtext is clear and my heart is that wilting Southern belle—he just wants to be near me. He definitely loves me; his whole body is leaking it—but I wonder if he knows he loves me yet?

I glance over my shoulder at the door and whisper to him, "Back it up," as I do.

His face falters for a second, confused: "What?"

And I go to move when Oliver swings around, glancing at the space that isn't between us, and frowns at me.

"Geez, Gige, give him some room." My brother pushes between us. "I gotta pee," he tells us all without looking back.

"Well." Tennyson turns around, grinning big. "You guys don't look like you're fucking or anything!"

"I told you!" I shove Sam Penny away from me, but the shove is really softened by the fact that I'm grinning at him. "You're being so obvious right now!"

Sam blinks, looking between me and Tennyson. "He knows?"

"Fucking everyone here knows!" I whisper-yell, glancing haplessly around the foyer of the hotel.

Sam frowns. "How?"

I gesticulate with frustrated abandoned. "Proxemics!"

"What?" my brother and my Sam both say in unison.

"When did he—?" Sam looks at me, then turns to Tenny instead. "How did you—?"

"When could he have possibly hooked up with some random girl in his car last night? That was our condom wrapper."

"Oh—yeah, hey—" Penny gives my brother a grateful look. "Thanks for that."

I eye Sam. "You need to pull it together."

He frowns, equal parts amused and offended. "I am together!"

"Standard interpersonal distance for nonintimate humans in our social dynamic would be at a minimum, one and a half feet—"

My brother interrupts, rolling his eyes, "That's not a thing normal people notice, Gige."

"Untrue." I point at him. "You notice all of it, everyone. You all compute it; you just don't know how to read the data."

"Yeah," Sam sighs. "I don't think he's going to notice that..."

"Of course he'd notice that." I gesture to Tennyson. "You noticed."

Tens shakes his head. "No, I didn't."

"You were giving me stupid knowing looks and annoying faces in the car the day after Sam and I had just met—which, by the way, was well before we even came close to hooking up." I raise my eyebrows at him, smug in my own rightness. "And whatever you were picking up on—that was all based purely on nonverbal cues you unwittingly picked up, so." Tennyson squints, and it's a tacit concession. He knows I'm right. He wasn't just being randomly annoying; the clues are in the body if you're looking for them. "As will our brother, who's jonesing megahard for Sam."

Sam breathes out of his nose loudly.

Tennyson scrunches his face up. "Don't use hard in that sentence."

"Really?" I give him a look. "Does the homophobia have to come out right now?"

"I'm not being homophobic, Gige." He rolls his eyes again and gives me a small shrug. "It's just pretty on the nose."

Stage left: "Oh my Lord!" Oliver sings loudly, walking over to us, and Sam takes a conscious step away from me, making an "are you happy?" face as he does. "The marble in that bathroom is to die for."

"Yeah?" I smile.

"All I'm saying is, once we wrestle that lake house off of this bitch, I'm redoing my en suite." He gives us a merry shrug. "What are y'all talking about?"

Both Tennyson and Sam seem to freeze up—idiots—idiots! Who am I working with? If I could shake my head at them, I would, but I can't.

As we all (should) know, a half-truth is always the best way to lie—

"Proxemics." I smile, bored.

Oliver frowns. "What's that?"

Sam catches on—*finally*—and thank God. "She thinks you can tell if people are hooking up by how close they're standing next to each other."

"I can."

"Ugh." Oliver swats. "Boring! Gige, I'm so proud of you, you're so smart, but for real, no one gives a shit about how the way you cook your eggs implies something about mother issues." Both Sam and Tennyson snort back laughs, and Oliver is delighted. "Anyway, is our room ready yet?"

I'm grateful for the depth of his disinterest in my career. Oliver's never cared; he's never wanted to know how to peer inside the minds of other people. I think he's afraid of what he'll find.

How our parents treated him, how our whole town did—I think he thinks knowing more just means more pain. It's a fair assumption, though likely incorrect, because pain begets pain, shame begets shaming, and not being tolerated begets intolerance. Oliver not caring about what I can do always felt like a small gift to me, because he was the one I care about using it on almost more than anyone else. Keeping him safe, keeping him clean, keeping him alive—I used every trick in my books on him.

Oliver throws an arm around my shoulders and pulls me away. "Can you believe it about Tennyson? Holy shit!" His mouth rounds in surprise.

"Yeah!" I blink big and surprised, warp-speed trying to mentally navigate how to approach this. I shouldn't encourage it, shouldn't be too invested, nor should I be uninvested. "It's pretty crazy."

"Savannah is awesome," he tells me with firm conviction.

I smile and nod. "I agree."

He purses his lips, thinking. "She'd probably break up with him if she knew."

I nod again, frowning this time. "So we should make sure she never finds out."

"Right," Oliver says, a bit absentmindedly. "You'd want to know though, right? If someone cheated on you?" He looks at me, frowning as he waits for my answer.

Fuck. He's got me. I can't say no; we both know that'd be a lie. Maybe until a day and a half ago, the thing I cared about more than anything in the whole world was the truth—anything less than it would never be enough.

"I guess." I shrug, and my face pulls back into a frown. "It's not really our business though."

"Right." I think he agrees.

I see his eyes flickering in the world of hypotheticals, but I know never in a million years would he do anything to hurt Tennyson.

"You think Dad's cheating?" he says after a minute.

"Well." I give him a wry look. "Not anymore."

My brother rolls his eyes. "Do you miss him?"

"No." I give him a confused look. "Do you?"

His mouth shrugs as he shakes his head, so yes.

"You know he thought about you," I tell him.

Oliver gives me a worn-out look.

"Mom told me that when everything happened with Beckett that night, he begged her not to send me away."

Oliver's face falters, confused. "What's that got to do with me?"

"She said he didn't want you to be alone."

A tender sadness bleeds through my brother's face, and his sharp edges burn away like a piece of paper dissolves in fire.

The nicest thing you can ever do for another human being is see them, and really see them, at that. To be understood is one of most base desires we as people have, and it was one that Oliver wasn't only deprived of, but often quite deliberately denied. All our lives he wanted our dad to see him and to care what he saw, and I think just now my brother got a glimpse that our dad did.

44

MUCH TO MY SILENT DISMAY, the room division isn't much better than the motel.

Sam and Oliver each have their own rooms, and Tennyson and I are sharing one.

And it's not like I thought me and Sam were going to get a room together, but maybe if Tenny and Sam were sharing, I could feasibly and arguably inconspicuously sit on a bed with Penny for five minutes and it wouldn't have to be a secret.

The assumed ticking clock that's hanging over whatever the fuck me and Sam Penny are weighs heavy on my mind as I wade through all the things I'll likely never get to do with him before we have to go our separate ways. Not dirty things either, just normal ones…

Staying up all night talking.

Getting hooked on a Netflix show together.

Going to the grocery store.

Getting into bed and having a fight about who should get up to turn off the lights.

Getting caught in the rain.

Watching him fill up the gas tank.

Reading a book next to him—

And maybe daydreaming about doing those things is wasteful with him because he's the Übermensch, but also he's just the boy I love now, and I'd love to get the opportunity to text him one day to bring home some milk, but I don't think I'll get to.

It's the knock on me and Tennyson's hotel room door that jerks me out of my grief over a life I'll never live.

I try not to make eye contact with Sam Penny as he walks in with Oliver, for two reasons.

One, I think he sees through me, and I know my eyes would look raw because my heart is; and two, indifference should keep Oliver off our tracks.

Oliver tosses himself down onto the couch. "How's the recon going?"

I drum my fingers on my Macbook impatiently, tipping my head back and forth, unsure.

Sam leans back against a table, looking around the room. Holy days, the things I'd have him do to me in this room were I afforded the opportunity, but alas—parental infidelity awaits.

"Do you remember the address?" I ask Tennyson.

"What address?" Oliver asks.

Tennyson and I both look up and over to him, staring for a few seconds before looking at each other.

"I could find it." Tens turns, grabbing his own laptop, sitting down next to Sam Penny—who I'm a *we* with, by the way, in case you've forgotten.

"What address?" Oliver repeats.

"Just—another address." I shrug, but it's weak sauce, even for me. It's why you should never multitask when you lie; it's where you'll slip up.

My focus is on research at the minute, so I'm not focused on the delivery of the lie, and it comes out like garbage. I'm mouth-shrugging and AU14-ing all of the place. My face pulls, my mouth dimples; I'm lying and even a toddler could spot it.

Oliver squints at me. "Bullshit."

I glance over at him.

Nothing makes Oliver happier than catching me in a lie. It makes him feel like Superman.

He's eyeballing me hard, brows up, waiting impatiently, and I can feel Sam watching me too, but I can't look at him—it would be telling if I did—so I just look at Tens.

Tennyson grimaces and Oliver's frown deepens.

"What?" Oliver looks over at me. "You two have secrets now?"

Tennyson shrugs, not sensing the tenderness. "You guys have had secrets for years."

I can't steal Sam and win over Tennyson in one week. "Just tell him." I shrug.

"Why didn't you tell me?" Oliver asks, pointedly.

Oliver's eyes hold mine and they're asking a lot of questions, and not one of them has to do with the girl I didn't tell him about. I think he's... betrayed? It's splaying out on his face as an AU7. Eyelids tightening to a squint—it could be anger, and maybe he thinks that's what he's feeling, but it's unlikely.

Betrayal is likely.

And I get it. We were, for so long, each other's only people.

And that's not normal, I know that's not normal, or even vaguely functional, but we were all we had. And that really only changed a few years ago after Grandpa died. The weight of our lives up until then became too heavy for just the two of us anymore, so it crushed us, but in a silent way neither of us knew how to put words around.

"Whose address is it?" Sam asks, watching me how he shouldn't. Even though he's moving the conversation along to help me, his feelings are too raw in his eyes.

If Oliver wasn't having a mini-crisis in his mind about the state of our relationship, Sam's eyes at this second might have been enough to tell Oliver all the secrets I'm hiding from him.

"Dad was wiring some money to an account down here for a while," Tennyson says. "I thought it was weird—asked him about it—he said it was for an office space and to ignore it."

"But it wasn't—" I shook my head. "When Tennyson looked into it, it was a residential space."

"For who?" Oliver frowns.

And I shrug. "We're guessing, probably Alexis Beauchêne..."

Both Oliver's and Sam's eyebrows lift in surprise.

"I called the real estate agency asking for a name, but they said they could only speak to Dad." Tens scratches the back of his neck. "The address has got to be somewhere. I would have written it down." He's tapping away at his computer.

Oliver gets off my bed and walks into the bathroom, and I follow him.

"I'm sorry," I say as I close the door behind us.

"What else aren't you telling me?" He sounds a little hopeless.

Fuck.

He already looks hurt and sad; if I tell him now, it'll crush him.

I widen my eyes a little and tilt my head. "Oli, you're overreacting." I can't believe I'm lying to him again. Three days ago, I loved the truth more than anything, and Sam Penny's waltzed in and usurped its crown.

I don't want to lie. I hate lying.

But the only thing I hate more than lying is hurting Oliver.

What am I doing? I get a wave of nausea.

"What happened to us?" he asks, folding his arms over his chest.

He doesn't really want the answer. He's scared of what the answer might be, but he's found himself in the peculiar emotional dilemma where the pain of not knowing outweighs the security of ignorance.

"You and me—" He wiggles a finger between us as though I didn't know who he meant. "We used to be everything to each other—what happened?"

I pull my head back and give him a small shrug. "You became a flaky drug addict who pissed away a million dollars on powder and cars and boys."

My brother scoffs, but his mouth does an AU25. His bottom lip drops open just a fraction—he's hurt. "So it's all my fault?"

"I didn't say that—"

"And you just fucking disappeared!" Oliver thumps his hand down on the bathroom sink. "You got me arrested, put me in rehab, and then fucking vanished!"

"Who the fuck do you think paid for Betty Ford, you dumbass?"

"So who asked you to?"

"No one!" I growl. "And no one had to. And I would do it again a hundred times over if it helped you."

"I didn't need your help!"

"Of course you needed my help! You always need my help!" I yell, but the last part's an accident. His head pulls back in surprise and hurt, again. Why am I hurting him so much right now when I've spent my whole life trying my best not to? "Shit—that's not what I meant."

"Well, what did you mean?" He juts his chin forward a little. Contempt.

I press my lips together and think before I speak this time. "You got to a place where you couldn't help yourself anymore. And you were the only family I had, so..." I trail.

He leans back against the vanity. "So you had me arrested." He sighs.

I look up at him tiredly. "Do you know what the last thing you said to me before you got sober was?"

Oliver eyes me suspiciously but shakes his head.

"'I'm just gay, you're the slut. Why's my sex worse than yours?'"

"Fuck." His head drops into his hands. He looks up at me, eyes all heavy with sorry's. "I was—"

"I know. I know who you are, Oliver. So I knew when you said that, you weren't you in that moment."

He nods quickly, but that's not an answer and it's not a resolve. What he said isn't what happened to us though, and we both know it.

I take a big breath. "I can't tell you properly—or in a way with words that give it the gravitas it deserves—what it's like to watch someone you love more than anyone else kill themself. And that's what you were doing. Just...slowly. And I didn't know how to be there for you in that, when you were drunk or high, and every time I was with you when you were those things, there'd be this tipping point where it became obvious that you resented me for something"—he opens his mouth to say something, and I cut him off—"and that's okay if you do! You're entitled to feel whatever you feel—I'm not mad at you for it, it's just…I really felt like I spent so much of my life pouring myself out for you, and I couldn't stomach the idea of me failing you too."

"Oh, Gige." He frowns in a different kind of way. "You and—" He blows air out of his mouth. "Maybe now Sam? Are the only people in the world who haven't, so…"

And I could cry. Honestly, I could weep on the spot.

What am I doing? And what the fuck am I going to do?

My brother steps toward me and wraps his arms around me tight. "I'm sorry."

I take a deep breath, steady my racing heart. "Me too."

"For what?" I hear the frown in his voice.

And I'm so glad he can't see my face. "For everything."

45

AFTER WE'RE ALL SETTLED INTO our hotel, we head out to dinner.

Napoleon House on Chartres Street. Tatty, scribbled-on walls, dimly lit, old wooden chairs and tables—old wooden everything, actually—it's like going back in time.

We sit by a window with a lace curtain that's drooping a little in the center, and I have the best Pimm's cocktail of my life, so England should be ashamed of itself. Sam manages to sit across from me at the dinner table, and plays footsie with me the whole fucking time, even with Oliver next to him.

Sam and I being a *we* has really numbed any former convictions he had around us being covert about our feelings for one another. He holds my eyes too long, he's almost always smiling every time he looks at me, he clocks me in the middle of conversations he's having with anyone else—just checking I'm still there—and it worried me at first, but the more Pimm's Cups I have, the less I care.

I don't get drunk. I just get buzzy enough to dull the edges of my concerns.

My brain doesn't switch off naturally… I don't ever just see a face for a face, a human as a human. They're always a closed book I want to open and riffle through the pages of. I don't think I was always like this; it's learned, but once you've learned what I've learned, it's almost impossible to unlearn—though alcohol does help. It suppresses the release of a chemical in our brains called glutamate, which is a neurotransmitter that would normally increase brain activity and energy levels, help you stay alert, notice things. With alcohol cockblocking glutamate, all the while increasing my brain's production of GBA (which is another neurotransmitter, except this one has a sedating effect), it's the perfect recipe for a busy-bee brain like mine to catch some z's.

We wind up in a bar on Bourbon Street. Bit of a dickhead move considering half of us are alcoholics, but Tennyson's apparently wanted to go to Arnaud's French 75 all his life, so here we are.

"*Esquire* says it's one of the top five bars in the country," Tennyson says, looking around in awe. Old and woody, the way you'd imagine a former gentlemen's club would look.

"They're alcoholics!" I blink widely, but Sam tosses me a little wink.

"I got this," he tells me, brushing his hand against my waist as he walks past me and over to the bar, leaning across it.

"Two cokes." He looks back at Tennyson, questioningly.

"Washington Cobbler," Tenny says over the crowd, and the bartender nods.

Sam points at me.

"French 75."

"And a French 75," Sam says, passing the bartender his card. "You can keep it running."

He turns back around, and our eyes catch like they just seem to now, and it's getting worse.

The white mosaic floor is dotted with tiny black hearts and trim, and I wonder in my mind-numby haze what it'd be like to decorate a house with Sam Penny, but I only wonder that for a second before I pull a face at myself and demand internally that I get a grip.

"So," Tenny says as we sit around a table with our drinks. He elbows Oliver. "You dating anyone?"

That question is a big deal coming from Tennyson—I've never seen him ask Oliver a question about his personal life—and I see it sort of startle Oli at first. He blinks a few times before he shakes his head. "No."

"What?" Tennyson rolls his eyes, and as he does, Sam slips his hand under the table and rests it on my knee. I swallow, stare straight at my younger older brother, and lift my eyes up like I'm waiting for the answer like everyone else.

"I don't know." Tennyson keeps going. "I don't know what men find—like, what guys like in other guys, what's attractive as a man if you like—"

"We get it, bud," I cut in, giving Tennyson a playful nod. "You're not gay."

Tennyson gives me a long-suffering look before he looks back at Oliver. "I feel like you'd do well," he says with a shrug.

Oliver looks so pleased—his shoulders square up a little, and I wonder how long he's waited for Tennyson to ask him something like this, to give a shit. Maybe his whole life.

"Yeah." Oliver smiles, chuffed. "Yeah, I do okay."

"But there's no one?" Sam asks, giving him an encouraging smile, and I feel myself swallow, and if I were watching me, I'd have seen how my jaw went tense, and I'd have known I was nervous about something, but I'm not watching me, I'm watching Oliver. How his eyes tightened at the speed of light at the question. His eyes also flicker fractionally to the left—he's thinking of someone—and then he swallows and shrugs dismissively. All of that happens in about one-point-five seconds, but I see it and my stomach drops to the floor of the bar, and I feel my control on my face slipping, so I just stare at my cocktail.

"Uh." Oliver smiles at Sam, and to me, it's the most obvious confession of feelings I've ever seen in my life, but people are good at sidestepping the things they don't want to acknowledge. "I have a bit of a thing for someone, but I've—Georgia will tell you—" He gives me a smile and a nod, and I brush Sam's hand off my knee because what the fuck am I doing? "I've not historically had the best taste in men."

Sam retracts his hand, doing the worst job in the history of ever covering the tracks of his hurt all over his face, but I can't look at him. For one, because without context, why would I? And two, if I do, I will cry.

"No." I shake my head at Oliver, trying to sound how I always would with him—trying my best not to sound like I'm about to set my own happiness on fire. "That Wall Street dad-turned-DJ was…nice."

Oliver snorts a laugh and Tennyson glances over, interested.

"What are you looking for in a—" Tennyson stumbles at the word, but he's trying. I can tell he's trying. "Partner?"

"I don't know." Oliver shrugs as though the person he's talking about isn't sitting right there in front of him. "Just someone…healthy, and, like—emotionally in tune." My younger older brother's eyes land on Sam—hover for a second longer than they would have if Sam meant nothing to him—and then he flashes a smile at Tennyson. "Why? Do you know anyone worth my time?"

Tennyson laughs. "I'll keep my eyes peeled."

I'm consciously not quiet for the rest of the evening. I do my best to hold all conversations and all eye contact as I normally would, but I'm desperate to get out of there.

I keep suggesting we call it a night, but Oliver's waited his whole life for Tenny to give a shit about him, and so he doesn't want to leave. Sam offers to take me home, but I say no, and Oliver tells him pretty quickly that I'm fine. ("She can be tired, who cares. She's grumpy all the time anyway.")

Sam spends the rest of the night trying to find my eyes, and I spend the rest of the night trying to avoid his. We get back to the hotel, and it's less bad than I thought—we each have separate rooms this time, sort of: Tennyson and I have a two-bedroom suite, and Sam and Oli each have their own rooms on different floors. I gave Sam the most indifferent and vague closed-mouth smile and wave that I could muster when he got out on his floor. He gave me these eyes as the elevator door was closing that felt like something tearing through the flesh in my stomach, pain shooting down my fingers, like I wasn't just betraying him but also myself by denying him.

And I knew it wouldn't take him long—I could see it swallowing him whole, how confused he was... So thrown, so—kill me—heartbroken, I knew as soon as we got back to our respective rooms that I'd hear from him.

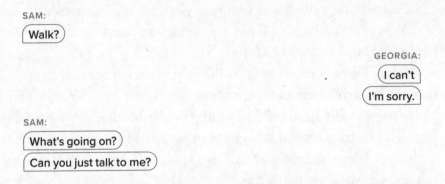

SAM:

Walk?

GEORGIA:

I can't

I'm sorry.

SAM:

What's going on?

Can you just talk to me?

I don't reply. Not because I don't want to. Of course I want to. Not replying is harder for me than it is for him. I'm the one having to show restraint when I want nothing to do with the word.

Tennyson's in the living room watching *Top Gear* on the television, so I try to distract myself with it.

After Sam's text goes unanswered for about fifteen minutes, there's a knock on our door. I glance over at it, but I don't move.

Tennyson frowns. "What's going on with you?"

I crinkle my nose at him, annoyed by his newfound awareness of me. "Nothing."

(Something.)

He rolls his eyes and gets off the couch to open the door.

"Hey." Sam steps around Tennyson immediately, walking toward me.

Tenny just stands there, brows knitted together in fresh confusion.

"Can we talk?" Sam stands over me.

I look up at him, and my eyes well up just at the sight of his face.

His cheekbones get extra dug out when he's sad. I know that now. I didn't want to know that, and I certainly never wanted to be the thing that made him sad. His eyes go bluer too. Which makes his mouth look pinker. He gets more beautiful when he's sad, how is that fair? That's some fucking bullshit, that's what that is.

I try to stand firm in my wilting resolve. "No."

"Just walk with me," he pleads. He's blinking a lot. "Please?"

"Um," Tennyson says, still by the door. "I'm gonna..." He thumbs toward the hallway, then he points his finger a me. "Are you...?"

I shake my head. "I'm fine."

So I'm not fine, actually—but not in the way where I can't be left alone, which is really what he was asking. Tennyson nods, and the door closes with a hotel thud.

It hangs there for a second, all the tension, all the feelings, and then, like a burst dam—

"What the fuck are you doing?" Sam's eyes are wide, heart broken inside of them.

I press my tongue into my bottom lip, trying not to cry. "We can't do this."

Sam stares at me, confused. "What?"

I gesture at him wildly. "You're the guy!"

His head pulls back—surprise. "What?"

I roll my eyes. "Oliver likes you."

"No." Sam starts shaking his head.

"Yes!" I yell. "And I knew that, and I still let this—shit! I'm a terrible person—I'm—"

Sam keeps shaking his head. He doesn't believe it—I'm not sure which part exactly.

"No—"

"Yes!"

Sam takes a big breath, and I see it all processing behind his eyes. "Are you sure?"

I look at him like "fucking seriously?" and then he lets out this heavy sigh.

"I'm not—I mean—nothing's ever going to happen between him and me."

"I know."

Sam gives me a look. "And something's already happened with us—"

"But it shouldn't have!" I tell him, feeling the shame of it all up to my neck. "I shouldn't have let it—that was so selfish—"

"So be selfish!" he yells as he shakes his head again, wildly now. AU1—he's nervous, or afraid. "Please! Please, be selfish. For me."

"Sam..." I cover my face with my hands. I don't want him to see my resolve weakening, but it takes less than two seconds for him to peel them off.

"Georgia—you and me together—" He gives me a look. "This is—it's not normal. I'm not going to find this again."

"I know," I concede. "But—"

"So, fuck it. It's okay to be selfish sometimes!"

I pull a face. "I don't think that's true. I don't even think you think that's true!"

"I do now." Sam nods, decidedly. "For you, I don't care."

"You should care," I tell him. "It's not like you not to care."

Sam swallows and then sighs. "I do care—it's just..." He trails. "My priorities have shifted."

"Yeah." I flick him a look. "I can see that."

Sam gives me a pointed look. "They've shifted by necessity."

I lift an eyebrow. "How's that now?"

Then he shrugs like it's simple. "You're the priority now."

I cross my arms over my chest, immediately uncomfortable. This is new, and the newness is unsettling. I don't even clock it in myself that I'm placing a barrier between us with my arms—but Sam does, he stares at them, his face lightening in amusement.

"And I don't know whether you've been someone's priority before," he says as he reaches over and gently uncrosses my arms. "Maybe the mercenary's, but then, maybe not—I don't know. Doesn't matter though. You're mine now."

I tuck my chin, unsure. "I think Oliver should be your priority."

"Nope." Sam shakes his head. "He can be yours—he should be yours, and I want that for him, but you're mine now, okay?"

I swallow heavily, stare at him with round, nervous, all in-love eyes, because fuck! That was romantic. "Okay."

Sam Penny gives me a small smile, then kisses the tip of my nose, then over my face and down my neck, and his facial hair tickles and I squirm and I'm instantly so mindlessly happy with his nose poking into my neck that I manage to forget for a second that my happiness is terribly and intricately linked with my own brother's unhappiness.

46

I DON'T KNOW WHAT IT SAYS about me that one conversation with Sam undoes my resolve regarding Oliver. Sorry, that's a lie—I know exactly what it means. Sam's usurped Oliver's position of importance in my life, and I can't tell whether that's a good or a bad thing. Maybe both, but it's definitely and absolutely terrifying, all the while being a commentary on the irrelevance of time in love.

I think Oliver's been usurped before. I probably would have put Storm before him, but they never met so I never had to. It wasn't even something I ever consciously considered, and definitely never in the ways it might practically roll out in my life. Now it's one of my primary considerations.

Have you ever felt like maybe your life was about to change? I have a few times.

The time Beckett walked into my room.

The time I was dragged out of that room by my mom.

The time Storm knocked on my front door.

The morning I woke up next to Sam Penny.

You get this foreboding sense, somewhere deep inside of you…it's guttural. Deeper than subconscious, more tangible than the speculative "universe" guiding you—maybe it's a slip in time, or maybe it's just pure instinct.

And you just know…after this thing…everything's going to be different.

536 Esplanade Ave, Apartment B. That's the address of the woman. The whole house is painted a light, sea-foamy green, white trimmings and dark green shutters. It's pretty. I like it. My mom would hate it.

Both Oliver and I look at Tennyson, who's just staring at the door, trepidation all over his face. He knows. He can feel it too, that everything is about to change.

Sam's a few feet behind us, farther away than I'd like him to be—but what can we do here? I glance back at him to steady myself. The left side of his perfect mouth tugs upward and he gives me a quick wink, which was bad of him to do, but it was admittedly weak of me to look at him in the first place. I know doing it was incredibly revealing, but I'm relying on my brothers being too absorbed in their own concerns to pick up on anything, and I needed the assurance.

"You do it." I elbow Tennyson.

He breaths in and out through his nose once, jaw clenched, lips pressed tight together—and then he knocks.

I was sort of expecting a quiet, warm-up knock, but it's loud. That knock means business; there's no pussyfooting around with the knock.

There's movement behind the door, and I feel myself straighten up.

It opens, and I pull my head back in surprise.

She's young. My age, maybe a tiny bit older. Dark brown hair, brown skin, big brown eyes. Probably biracial. Undeniably gorgeous.

She raises her big, bold eyebrows inquisitively. "Can I help you?"

No one says anything for a good four seconds.

"Are you Alexis Beauchêne?" Tennyson finally asks.

AU4. Her brows lower in confusion, but not utter. She knows the name; I can tell that much.

"No," she says, looking at us suspiciously.

"Well, does she live here?" Oliver asks, shrugging.

AU4 again. "Look, who are you?"

I suspect then, Alexis Beauchêne does in fact live here. I step forward. "Do you know William Carter?" I ask.

AU1 and AU24. An inner brow lift and a nervous pressing of the lips together—so that's a hard yes. "Um—"

"Are you having an affair with him?" I ask before she has time to answer.

Immediately her brows go low and her mouth pulls open—disgust. AU9. AU16.

"No." She eyes me, annoyed.

"Look." Tennyson steps forward. "Where can we find Alexis? We need to talk to her."

"Why?" She folds her arms over her chest. It's both defensive and creating a boundary.

Oliver frowns. "We just do!"

Her body language tells me we're not going to get anywhere with her like this. Her feet are firm and planted apart on the ground, her arms are still folded over her chest, and she's blocking the doorway. She knows something, or she's protecting someone.

I nod my chin behind her. "Is she in there?"

She shakes her head, annoyed, and gestures to the street. "You need to leave."

I watch her for a few seconds. "He's dead," I announce rather unceremoniously, as is my way, apparently—but this time, I do it on purpose, so I can watch the way her face moves with the news. It all goes slack, except her eyebrows, which lift in shock. She blinks a lot.

"What?" she whispers. "I—"

She steadies herself against the doorframe. She has an emotional connection with our dad, that's for sure. You don't react like that to a stranger's death.

"He's our father, by the way," I say, and our eyes lock in this funny way.

She mutters something in French under her breath, then looks between me and my brothers with these sort of glazed-over eyes. "When?"

"Two Fridays ago."

"Oh, mon dieu." She shakes her head again—breathing quickened. This girl really knew our dad. Though nothing about her behavior makes me think their relationship is sexual, and thank God because, again, she looks about our age.

"Funeral was on Monday," Tennyson tells her.

She lifts her hand to her face in quiet shock. "Oh, seigneur."

We all wait in silence for a few moments, watching this stranger grieve our father. It's so peculiar and so detached that I fight all my impulses to turn around and find Sam's eyes to ground me like I know they would if I'd let them.

"Where is she?" I ask again, trying to stay focused.

The girl stares at me for a few long seconds, before she finally says, "Out of town."

"Till when?"

She opens her mouth and nothing comes out.

"Can you contact her?" I ask, getting impatient. "Get her to come back?"

"Yes." She nods, barely. "Um—tomorrow. If you give me your number, I'll—"

Tennyson hands her his business card before she can even get her sentence all the way out. He would have business cards, wouldn't he?

She glances down at the card and then back at my brother.

"I'll text you later after I—" the girl's voice trails off again.

Tennyson nods anyway. "Okay."

I'm the first to turn away from her.

Walking down the steps, my arm brushes against Sam's, and it burns me with this confusing want and sadness.

"I'm sorry," she calls after us. "I'm so sorry. Your father was such a good man…"

I look back up at her. "What's your name?"

"Maya."

I press my tongue into my bottom lip. "Maya, I think we knew very different men."

47

AFTER WE LEFT MAYA, WE all went to dinner then wound up back in Tennyson's and my suite because it's the biggest—just watching TV, not really saying anything, because everything that's going on around us is exhausting, and sometimes talking is taxing. It's kind of amazing though—I've never really had this before. Sitting on a couch with my brothers in a communal space. Oliver and I mostly hung out in our rooms, or on the *SS Avoidance*, or on one of the docks around the property, away from the house and all the people in it. I don't think I have a single memory of voluntarily sitting in a common area, watching television in a fairly comfortable silence, sandwiched between my two older brothers and not feeling remotely compelled to shift away from Tennyson when my arm brushes up against him.

At one point, Tennyson looked over at me and says, "Gige, would you be okay if Ol and I go play golf tomorrow?"

"What?" Oliver says, looking over at Tens—first he's heard of it.

"There's a Peter Dye golf course here," Tennyson tells him. "I've always wanted to play—thought you'd maybe play it with me?"

I look between them. "Why are you asking my permission?"

"I'm not asking your permission." Tennyson rolls his eyes. "I mean, you can come if you want."

Oliver elbows me, which is a swift and mildly painful way of telling me I actually can't come, regardless of want.

Then Tennyson catches my eyes for the quickest sliver of a second before his eyes flicker toward Sam. Is he...giving us time together?

"Yeah." I shrug. "Whatever, I don't—I have no interest in golf."

Oliver looks over at Sam, eyebrows up and hopeful. "Do you mind if Tennyson and I do that tomorrow?"

Sam goes to speak, and at the same time, his eyes go to mine—inappropriate and overt, but I suspect from Oliver's vantage point it could have looked like Sam was gauging the room as a whole.

"No, man, of course not!" Sam smiles over at him.

"Great." Tennyson claps his hands together. "Well, tee time is seven o'clock."

"PM?" Oliver clarifies.

"No." Tennyson gives him a pinched look. "AM. And it's about a thirty-minute drive."

"Oh, shit." Oli frowns now, sporting his first bit of disappointment. He sighs, standing up. "I guess we should go to bed, then." He looks at Sam, who stands up on cue.

Oliver swoops down and kisses the top of my head then heads to the door, turning back.

"See you in the morning!" he tells Tennyson brightly.

Tenny nods. "I'll meet you in the lobby at six thirty?"

Oliver pulls a face before he nods back. "Night!" he calls cheerily.

Sam pauses in the doorway, mouths quickly that he'll call me. I nod back and then he leaves.

I glance over at my brother, and he gives me a dumb smile. "You're welcome," he says.

"What?"

"Figured you two could use a day." Tennyson shrugs. "And that I owed Oliver some one-on-one time."

I stare over at him, and I don't really know what to say, how to speak to this new, thoughtful part of my brother that's emerged and I'm rapidly growing increasingly fond of.

He just gives me another small smile. It's a nothing-y smile, and something about it stings me in the heart a bit, like—around my brain rattles the thought of how my life might have felt and how it could have been different if he was the kind of person back then that he seems to be now. He looks back at the TV and keeps watching it, and then my phone flashes with a text from Sam.

SAM:
Should I come back down?

GEORGIA:
Yes.

SAM:
I'll give it 15...

GEORGIA:
Ok

SAM:
Should I stay?

GEORGIA:
Yes.

About fifteen minutes later, there's a knock on our door. Tennyson stands up to get it without a question—even though we both know it's probably for me—because he's from the South and the men here are pretty well mannered.

Sam walks in a second later, holding his toothbrush, which for some reason is the cutest, sexiest thing I've ever seen. And the sight of the two of them—man I love, brother I once basically hated and now reluctantly adore—standing by the door of the hotel room I'm sharing with aforementioned brother on a trip we're on together to find our father's mistress. It's all so absurd, I let out a quiet laugh.

"What?" Sam asks, tilting his head.

"I don't know." I shrug before I gesture at Tennyson. "I believe Tennyson cleared the coast for us tomorrow."

Sam looks at him, eyebrows raised with a gratefulness that I'm learning he often sports on his face. That's sort of his default disposition—grateful. "Thanks, man."

Tenny nods, moving toward his bedroom, then flicks Sam and I a look. "Try to clean up after yourselves this time…"

With one hand, I cover my face; with the other, I flip Tennyson off. He laughs and goes to his room.

"Hey," Sam says, smiling at me from the door.

"You brought your toothbrush."

A little flicker of confusion breezes over his face. "You said I was staying."

"Yeah, you are—but you don't have anything else, just your toothbrush."

"I have a couple of other small things. Circular. In my pocket."

I squash a smile. "But no spare clothes."

His eyes fall down my body. "I didn't think I'd be needing them…"

I shake my head, quite sure. "You won't."

We have sex in the shower, because we didn't get to the other time and I've thought about it nonstop ever since, and fuck—he's magnificent, everything about him. How he breathes, how he moves around a room, him washing his hair after—art.

"What?" he asks, toothbrush hanging out of his mouth.

"I don't know—you, with your brushing your teeth in just a towel—" I swallow.

He lifts his eyebrows, waiting for more. "Yeah?"

I shrug. "It's like we're actually together…"

He lets out a single laugh, as though it's a funny thing to think. He puts down his toothbrush, spits out his toothpaste, wipes his mouth, then takes a step toward me. "Georgia." He puts a hand on my waist. "We are actually together."

I tilt my head because I want to see if he's leaking any signs of nervousness, but he isn't.

"Are we?" I ask as I walk out of the bathroom and into the bedroom, pulling some pajamas out of my duffle bag.

He follows after me, a little smile flickering over his mouth. "Yeah…"

"*Together*-together?" I clarify as I look over at him.

He nods once. "Yep."

And I make sure I'm watching him closely before I ask this next one: "Like, exclusively?"

His chin tucks, brows furrow—surprised, maybe even a bit offended. "I mean, I fucking hope so…"

I hold my pajama top against myself, and it's a shield for a person I don't need one with. "Well, I don't know what you have going back on in California."

He pulls a face and gestures to me. "Do you have shit going back on in England?"

I raise my eyebrows at him. "I do not."

"Okay." He shrugs defensively, and I mirror him and say "okay" back too.

Sam presses his hand into his mouth—something to say, trying to figure out how to say it—and he breathes in through his nose. "Listen." His eyes find mine. "There are girls I've hooked up with before, right—and then there's you."

"Who you've also hooked up with," I tell him playfully, but he's not playing. His eyes are serious.

"Don't say that. We're not hooking up."

"We literally are." I roll my eyes. "We just did. Twice."

"No." Sam gives me a stern look, which is a sexy thing to do to someone, and I don't know why, but it probably has roots in paternal issues. "We just had sex twice. We don't hook up. We've never hooked up—it's not the same with you as it was with them."

I give him a long-suffering look. "Why?"

"Because." He shrugs as he reaches for the pajamas I've still got clutched to my body. He takes them from my hands. "I've met you, and I'm different now."

I scoff, roll my eyes, hope that it's enough to distract from the fact that my fucking traitor face is blushing without my permission. I want the scoff to be enough for him to think that I think it's silly and embarrassing, not endearing and somehow incredibly sexy. But it doesn't work; he just watches me—stares, really—as he bunches up my tank top before he slips it over my head.

Is he—he's…dressing me?

He gets my pajama shorts, bunches them up too, then kneels down, nudging my ankle so I raise my foot. He pulls my shorts up, then stays there knelt down as he smiles up at me, face all perfect and pleasant.

"Am I lying?" he asks calmly.

I reach for his hand, pull him back up to his feet. I pretend like I'm trying to figure it out—like I don't already know—as if Sam Penny isn't just a giant, open book of a man, waiting for me to read him and pore all over his pages.

I slip my arms around his waist.

"No," I tell him.

He pushes some hair from my face, nodding a little bit. "So, yeah—we're together."

I swallow once. "Okay."

He pokes me in the ribs. "*Together*-together."

48

THAT WAS OUR FIRST SLEEPOVER," I tell Sam the next morning. He's playing Wordscapes on his phone, but he glances over at me.

"I stayed in your bed that night after the first time we slept together."

"No." I roll my eyes. "You had to sneak out so no one would find out. It doesn't count."

He rolls his eyes back, and I can tell he doesn't entirely agree. "Okay, sure. Our first 'real' sleepover then." He glances at me again. "How'd you find it?"

I roll onto my stomach so I can stare at him more easily. I wonder how much of my life moving forward will be about how to angle myself so I can stare at Sam.

"You're a quiet sleeper," I tell him.

He nods. "I am. So are you. Kind of hog the bed though..."

I prop myself up, surprised. "Do I?"

"Yeah." He eyeballs me. "For a pretty small person sharing a pretty big bed with a pretty big guy, our ratio was way off."

I rest my chin in my hand. "How off?"

He takes a breath, exits Wordscapes, and tosses the phone down on the bed beside him, then blows the air out of his mouth. "I think you took three-quarters of it. Or thereabouts?"

"How is that possible?"

He gives me a steep look. "I literally have no idea. But I feel like, moving forward, you should really only have a third of the bed..."

My mouth falls open and I balk at him. "How is that fair?"

He pulls a face. "We have really different-sized bodies, Gige."

I ignore the fact that my heart flutters when he calls me that, because it's so familiar and I want him to be familiar with me so badly. "It should be fifty-fifty."

"And here I thought you'd be a believer in equity over equality."

I give him a look, fold my hands over my chest. He laughs, then pulls me up on top of him, like it's nothing.

"You ready to do some real couple shit today?" he asks as he pushes some hair behind my ears.

I bat my eyes. "Like what?"

"Like... I'm going to hold your hand in the street," he says.

"Whoa!" I beam up at him. "Slow down."

"And I'm gonna walk with my arm around you..."

I let out a low whistle. He keeps going.

"And I'm going to take you on a proper date—in public—and I'm going to kiss you in the restaurant."

I shake my head at him playfully. "I think that's illegal."

He swallows before he says very simply, "I think I've waited my whole life for this day."

And just so you know...as far as days go...top tier. We go to breakfast at a café nearby, and when I go to sit down next to him, he pulls me onto his lap instead. I've never sat on his lap in public before and, oh my God, it's a thrill.

We sit like that the whole time. Me in his lap, him drinking his black coffee, and me drinking my iced latte, because now that we are together-together, it feels like he should know that I think black coffee tastes like sad, dirty water. The whole time we're in the café, his hands keep finding themselves in places I could just die over—my lower back, my knee, my waist—and I've obviously been touched in much more interesting and salacious places in my time, but none hold even half a candle to the weight of his hands resting on me in ways that would make no one else blink an eye.

After that, we just walk around Magazine Street. Do a bit of shopping. When I go to pay for my things, Sam has already bought them. I tell him that he didn't have to do that and he says, "Get used to it."

We kiss in public, we hold hands, he holds doors open for me, he carries my bags, slings his arm around me—we, in conclusion, do the most generic, regular shit that couples do together, and it is, in a nonhyperbolic way, probably the greatest day of my life.

That afternoon, a little after two, I get a text from Tennyson telling me they're probably thirty minutes away, so we make our way back to the hotel. I make a joke about us having to "consciously uncouple" now that the boys are on their way back, but Sam doesn't like that—I can tell by the way his body goes.

I'm in an armchair in the lobby of our hotel, and Sam's sitting on the coffee table opposite me because I think he thinks the other chair is too far away. And it is; it's positioned so that if two strangers were—by necessity or random chance—each sitting in one, neither would be uncomfortable, but not so far that if you were sitting in the chairs with someone you know, you wouldn't not hear them. It's just too far for Sam's liking.

"We need to talk about this," he tells me.

"Talk about what?" I ask, though I know exactly what.

"He's going to find out eventually, Gige..."

My eyes drop to my hands, but he doesn't look away from me.

"We can't keep it a secret forever—"

"No, I know," I tell my hands.

"Do you want to keep us a secret?" Sam asks, poking my knee.

"No." I shake my head quickly. "Of course not."

"Right, then when are we going to tell him?"

"Gee, I don't know." I roll my eyes. "Maybe when we've figured out ourselves what we're doing..."

He stares at me, unflinching. "I know what I'm doing."

I lift an eyebrow. "Any plans to let me in on it?"

Sam shrugs playfully. "I like to keep you on your toes."

"You've never kept me on my toes. Your perfect, dumb face isn't even an open book, it's a billboard on a highway with a spotlight shining on it—"

He starts laughing.

"Speaking of..." I give him a tall look. "We need to get our story straight."

"For what?"

"For when Oliver inevitably asks us what we did today. Remember—the best lie is a half-truth."

"Wait. Remind me what a half-tr—"

"Hey!" says my oldest brother loudly, I think to give us a not-very-subtle heads-up.

I give him a grateful smile anyway. "Hey."

Oliver skips over and throws himself down onto my lap. Sam catches my eye, even though he shouldn't.

"Who won?" I ask them.

Tennyson points at Oliver, who flicks me a proud look. I beam up at him.

"Oh my gosh!" I whack him, impressed. "Look at you! A golfer!"

Tenny, being a good sport, shakes his head as he smiles at our brother. "He's pretty good..."

That's a lie—he's lying. The shaking of his head and what he's saying are in direct disagreement. Oliver, apparently, is not a very good golf player, but this is a lie I'm happy to let slide.

Oliver looks over at Sam. "What'd you get up to?"

I look at Tennyson so Sam doesn't even have a chance to catch my eye before I answer on his behalf.

"We went to breakfast," I tell the group. "Did some shopping."

"Yeah." Sam nods, catching on. "Magazine Street."

Oliver looks back at me disparagingly. "You made him go shopping with you?"

"I didn't make him." I roll my eyes as Sam says, "I was happy to..."

Oliver focuses on Sam, gives him a sorry look. "You must have been so bored."

AU4 and a quick flash of AU7 from Sam—he did not care for Oliver's insinuation that I'm boring, and he really needs to get a handle on his feelings for me.

"Yeah, he must have been *so* bored," I say, trying to distract from the microanger Sam just sported for all the world to see. "I'm *so* boring. Men never want to hang out with me."

Oliver flicks me. "Stop."

Tennyson catches my eye. "How are you feeling about this afternoon?"

"Good." I shrug, though not really all that good. "You?"

He nods but presses his lips together tightly. AU24. He does not feel good about this afternoon, but I don't tell him that either.

"I've been thinking about it, actually." I look at all the boys. "I want to ambush her with strategic questions. Rapid fire. It'll help me get the truth faster."

"Okay." Tennyson nods. "Are we doing the asking?"

"Oliver, I want you to say first to her, 'Are you having an affair with our dad?' Sam"—I clock him—"then you ask, 'When did it start?' And then Tens, you hit her with, 'Did the two of you have a child?'"

"Gige," Tennyson sighs. "There's no way that he—"

"There's actually literally a very obvious and overt way," I tell him rather firmly.

"Yeah, but—" My brother rolls his eyes. "But he wouldn't have."

I shrug. "I guess we'll see."

49

THE ADDRESS THAT MAYA GIRL gave Tennyson is in the Garden District. I don't know much about Louisiana real estate, but I know that's a really nice place to live.

Tens tried to call her, but she didn't answer. That made me immediately suspicious. Not in a way where I feel like we're going to this address and we're going to be mugged or trafficked or anything, but something's amiss...

An entirely different address than the one we found? Maya's address was the one in Dad's office—does this mean he's been paying for this house too?

When we get there, the four of us just stand in front of it and stare up. It's not huge from the outside, but there are plenty of stairs up to the porch that wraps around the front of the house.

"Well, it doesn't look like the house of a whore," Oliver declares to no one in particular.

I glance at him. "What does a whore's house look like?"

"I don't know." he shrugs. "A second-floor condo on the corner of Ocean and Alta?"

Sam pauses. "That's where you live."

Oliver gives him a wink.

"Well, come on then." Tennyson leads the way up the stairs to the porch, and we all trail after him.

"Are you nervous?" I ask him, quiet enough that Sam and Oliver can't hear him.

"No," he says automatically.

"Liar," I whisper.

Tennyson looks back at me. "Can you"—he gives me a long-suffering look—"not?"

I nod quickly. "Sorry," I say, and I mean it.

My big brother shakes his head. "I just have this feeling like Dad's about to get tackled off of the pedestal I've had him up on for years."

I nod again, and I have nothing to say because I suspect he's probably right, but saying as much will bring my brother no comfort at all.

We're both just standing on the doorstep of this random woman's house now, Sam and Oliver in tow, none of us moving.

I glance at him out of the corner of my eye. "Me knock, or you?"

Tenny blinks twice, then takes a deep breath. "Me," he says, and then he knock-knock-knocks on the door.

And then the door opens. Too quickly, I'll recall in retrospect. But I'm not paying my best attention even though I am trying to. If I was, I'd have noted that the door opened too quickly. Almost as though while we were watching the house, the house was watching us.

Per the plan, the boys were meant to immediately barrage the woman with questions. But now that the door's been opened... Well, all our practicing in the car ride over—poof!—out the window. And in their defense, I get it. I mean, it wouldn't have happened if I'd been the one tasked with asking the questions, but to be fair to them, we're face-to-face right now with a massive curveball.

It is, in fact, a man standing in front of us.

"Hello," says the man. An accent? What is that? Hard to tell from only one word. *God, this poor man.* I can't help but think his day is about to become considerably worse.

Tennyson's mouth falls open as though he's going to say something, but he doesn't; he says nothing. Actually, no one says anything.

"Where's Alexis?" I ask.

The man swallows. Now, swallowing is interesting because it's something we do naturally all the time. It's a mechanical function of the body that happens mindlessly, constantly, without our consent or awareness. Its biomechanical function is to aid digestion and oral hygiene... you know, wash away bacteria and gross mouth stuff. However, when we're nervous, the autonomic nervous system tightens the muscles in our throat, and then, in this hyperaware state, we become overly sensitive to the automatic bodily functions that are normally controlled by the autonomic nervous system. How do we know whether he's nervous-swallowing or regular-swallowing? Frequency, mostly.

He gives me a tight smile. "Why do you ask?" he says in that accent again—European, definitely—and then he swallows again.

"Are you her husband?" I ask.

"Brother," he says, and something's off. Lots of things, actually... It all feels off and weird, and I don't know why, nor am I personally saddled with the patience to find out, which is why I bust out of the gate with: "We suspect she may have been having an affair with our father."

He blinks three times. Blink, blink—blink.

"Who is your father?" he asks, and I don't know why, because I know he must know. That Maya person gave us his address; he must know who we're here about.

"Will Carter," I say anyway.

He swallows again, then nods once—definitely not surprised to hear our father's name—and I'm about to ask where Alexis is when he sort of vaguely gestures for us to come inside. It's not even an all-the-way invitation—more like he steps out of the doorway and says, "Won't you?"—but it's not really authoritative either... He doesn't want us here—that's fine, I can't fault him for that. He's uncomfortable with our presence, but judging by the way he tilts his head as we trail in one-by-one, he is in the very least, perhaps, a bit fascinated by us?

His eyes do snag on Sam, I notice—and it's just for a second and frankly, nearly barely there—but I do notice it. AU44 and AU20—an eye squint and a lip stretch. He's confused Sam's here.

But why would the presence of Sam be confusing to him at all?

We sit down in the living room, and it's—I've got to say—exquisitely decorated. Whoever's house this is—and I'm not entirely sure whose house it is—has impeccable taste.

Crazy high ceilings, like fourteen feet high. Restored crown moldings, cool-toned dark, reclaimed hardwood floors, giant windows that flood the room with light, and eggshell blue accents scattered about, like that nineteenth-century French giltwood wingback armchair in the corner. Some art too, in those ornate gold baroque frames—mostly landscapes, a portrait too. I wonder whether the kitchen has one of those "still life" vegetable paintings that Europeans seem to love for some reason.

This man is handsome though, I'll give him that. He couldn't be Alexis's husband; no way would you pick Dad over him. Our dad's fine, not unattractive at all. But it'd be like, Colin Firth and Brad Pitt—both attractive, sure, but one is more overtly attractive, right?

Not that this man looks like Brad Pitt at all. Like, yeah, he's gorgeous, but for one, he's Black. He's really tall, broad shoulders, in good shape, with these warm eyes that I'd on another day quite like—but on this day, I suspect he's covering for that sister of his when he asks, "Why do you think they're having an affair?"

"Because they're having an affair," I say to him, my voice unwavering.

He says nothing, just holds my gaze.

"So how did they meet?" Tennyson asks, puncturing my strange little reverie.

"Who?" the man says, and that strikes me as odd.

"Alexis and our dad..." Oliver says, giving the brother a funny look.

"Oh." The man laughs. It's a funny laugh though—forced, maybe?—no genuine emotion attached to it, no genuine movement on his face either. I squint at him, and I can feel Sam watching me, because he's always watching me nowadays even though it's completely inappropriate in this present moment. I can't think about him watching me, even though it makes me so embarrassingly happy, and every time Sam looks at me, it's an undeniable feather in my cap, and I don't have time to put a feather in my cap right now; I'm trying to work out if Alexis's brother has had Botox or not. Could be why his face isn't moving like a face otherwise should.

"Through me, actually," he says, and it's on that *actually* that I finally hear it. He's French.

"How did you meet?" I ask.

"Work." He gives me a closed-mouth smile, and that combined with the one-word answer raises a red flag for me. He doesn't want to talk about how they met. It's uncomfortable for him.

My eyes pinch. "You work in civilian aircrafts?"

"Oui," he says, swallows again.

"Doing what?" Tennyson asks, leaning forward.

The man breathes in through his nose. "I fly them."

I stare at him for a few seconds, let the silence thicken between us enough for him to feel a little uneasy.

"You're a pilot, you mean?" I eventually say.

"Mon dieu!" He sort of exhales a funny laugh, then shakes his head. "Thirty years I've been in America and I still forget the words! Yes. A pilot."

I nod along as though I believe him, which I definitely don't. "When did you get your pilot's license?" I ask breezily.

"What?" The man's face pulls at that one. All the boys look confused at that one, actually.

"When?" I repeat, shrugging lightly like it's just a question.

"Uh—" He swallows, blinks twice in quick succession, and his eyes flicker ever so slightly toward the left before he says, "1993."

And that, ladies and gentlemen, was a lie. Why would he lie about that? Even if he forgot, you'd just say you forgot—and besides, I don't think a pilot would forget. They're like Horse Girls, but men. They don't fucking shut up about their planes and their flight times and their craziest landings. Flying is like a bug people catch; it gets under their skin, melds into their essence—they don't forget things like when they got their pilot's license. Most of them have waited their whole lives up until that moment to get it.

I glance around his house, and my eye snags on the art again. One in particular, one of the landscapes… There are some people, a camel, some Grecian pillars back in the distance, some guy in front of a rock, and something tugs on my brain—*God, it's familiar*. I squint at it, but I can't place it, and I get this annoying buzzy feeling under my skin that I get sometimes where there's something in front of me waiting to be realized, but my consciousness hasn't figured it out yet, and my subconscious doesn't know how to communicate it to me either.

This French guy's still banging on about how he met my dad, and the boys are all nodding along, but I'm not. I should be paying attention, I know I should—but God, there's a loose thread in my mind and I need to tie it off. And this room—there's something about this room that's throwing me.

There's another room through a doorway—lots of books—that's all I can see of it from here. I wish I was closer, but I'm not, so I give this room another glance—tilt my head, because that helps sometimes. And upon second glance, nothing about his home suggests that what he's saying—admittedly, he's not said all that much—is actually true. Now, in the spirit of full disclosure, there's also nothing in his home that implicitly implies he's beyond-a-shadow-of-a-doubt lying either, but the truth is we leave the clues of us everywhere, in ways we know and in ways we don't.

Take my home, for example. My fridge doesn't sport birthday cards from my family or photos from vacations we shared together. It does, however, have the menu for the Greek restaurant a block away, a Lisa Frank poster that has a kitten with rainbow angel wings, and a photo of me vomiting in the bathroom of Buckingham Palace with Hattie kneeling beside me, both thumbs up. Bianca took the photo. It makes me laugh every time I see it. And it could just be a menu, posters, and a photo, but it isn't. It's the place we order from when we've had hard days, our emergency safe-food restaurant. It's the poster that Hattie hung in her room for years as a child when she knew she was bi before she was ready to tell anyone. It's a photo of Hattie in a four-thousand-pound dress on a bathroom floor with me as I throw up because Hattie is more my family than my family. So yeah, it's just a fridge, but actually, my fridge, my home, spread throughout it, there are the clues of me everywhere. We're always leaving clues.

And then—my brain reaches up and grabs one of those threads that's flailing in the wind of all this.

"You're French," I say a bit suddenly.

"I am." The man nods.

I put my chin in my hand. "From where?"

Oliver flicks me in the arm and tosses me a look like I'm an idiot. "France?" he says.

I roll my eyes at him, then look back at the man. "Which part of France?"

"Oh—" He waves his hand dismissively. "A small town outside of Bordeaux."

"I love Bordeaux," I say, but I don't think I necessarily say it with the proper emotions that should accompany a declaration of love—there's no tenderness on my face, no joy, no longing—my brain's too busy now. I do love Bordeaux—that wasn't a lie—but I think the first domino has fallen.

He swallows again, then flashes me a quick smile. "The wine or the place?" he asks, trying to keep it light.

"Both," I tell him with a curt smile and a nod. I turn to my brothers. "Have you been?"

Tennyson shakes his head. "No..."

I glance at Oliver and Sam. They both shake their heads too.

"Oh—you really should." I give them a bit of a rueful look, then pause, glancing between Ol and Penny. "Maybe you two shouldn't. Alcoholics," I tell the man, and he doesn't react beyond his eyes flicking between the two briefly, and that's weird—it should probably surprise him, two young men under thirty, already alcoholics. But not even an inner brow raise.

"Well, technically, he's an alcoholic"—I gesture to Oliver, before motioning to Sam—"and he's an addict."

Sam's eyes tighten—he's not sure what I'm doing, but he knows I'm doing something.

"So, a small town near Bordeaux?" I stare over at the French man, nodding gently, trying my best to smile and not look like an interrogator.

He nods, but swallows as he does, before he smiles back at me. It's strained now though.

"East?" I flick my eyebrows up.

His face falters. "Quoi?"

I rephrase the question. "An hour east of Bordeaux?"

He nods again, cautious now. "Oui."

Saint-Émilion! It drops into my head like a present down a chimney, and I feel my brain sigh because this whole time my mind's been on a side-quest, trying to remember the name of the place in Dad's office painting. And that's it. Saint-Émilion.

"Sorry," Tennyson jumps in. "What is your name?"

And it's the strangest thing…The man stares at me for two full seconds before he turns to my brother and answers him.

"Henri," he replies.

"Henri, that girl we met yesterday—" I try not to squint at him even though my brain is definitely squinting at him.

"That was my daughter," he tells us with a proud smile. The first genuine emotion I've seen from this man. "Maya."

"Maya. That's…" My voice trails because that loose thread is ringing like a motherfucking bell in my mind. I shake my head at myself. Tell myself to pull it together. "That's…not a French name…"

He nods, thinking to himself. "No, I believe it's Sanskrit."

"So." Tennyson adjusts himself in the armchair he's sitting in, and I can tell by the way his body's squaring up that he's going to try to take this over. He thinks I'm doing a bad job, that I'm not learning anything. "Where *is* your sister, Henri?"

"Cancún," he replies, and Oliver says, "God, I love Mexico," and then Oli asks him a few pleasant questions—like, a totally normal-person questions—like where's she staying, how long she's there for—boring shit like that.

And the whole time, Sam's watching me—admittedly more than he should, but it's good, I think. It centers me, grounds me or something. His eyebrows dip, and even though he says nothing aloud, he asks if I'm okay, and I give him a barely perceptible nod, except I know he can perceive it because our connection is intimate and we're acutely attuned to each other at this point, so he knows it's a lie. He knows I'm not okay; he can tell there's something amiss because he can feel it in me, which, on a separate note, is completely incredible, and fuck, I really need to tell Oliver, don't I? It's just—

I snap my head suddenly in the direction of that painting on the wall. The landscape with the man in front of the rocks.

Wait.

I interrupt—I don't even know who I interrupt—someone was talking who isn't me, and it doesn't matter who, because I talk over them anyway. "That painting"—I point at it—"is by who?"

Henri's face lights up a little, pleased to talk about it. "Charles Lock Eastlake. It's—"

I stare over at him, and if I was watching me, I'd say I wasn't concealing a single thing. I'm AU1 and AU26 (inner brow raise and a little jaw drop)—that's surprise, and arguably, maybe fear—plain as day all over my face.

I shake my head slowly as I watch Henri. "No, I know what it is." I glance over at my oldest brother. "I need the room."

Tennyson pulls a face. "What?"

I'm louder now, bossier. "Give me the room."

"Gige, shut up." Oliver rolls his eyes. "You're so dramatic, just—"

"Tennyson." I stare at my biggest brother, ignoring the other one. "I need the room."

Tennyson is starting to look annoyed now. "Not yet."

And then I turn to Penny and give him a look.

"Sam," is all I say—and I've never done that before, and I shouldn't have done it now either, invoking that "intimate" trump card. I haven't used it till now, even though I've wanted to a million times, and there were a hundred moments before this one that would have benefited me more to invoke it then, but I really need the fucking room.

And in truth, the fact that I've not invoked it till this moment—Sam's surprised, but now he's on a mission.

He looks at my brothers, nods toward the front door. "Let's give her a min—"

"Oh, come on—" Now Tennyson rolls his eyes.

"Why are we listening to her?" Oliver shakes his head. "She's—"

"The only reason we're here," Sam cuts in as he gives my brothers a look, standing to his feet. "Let's just give her a minute."

Tennyson grumbles as he walks out, and Oliver looks irritated that Sam's doing my bidding, but he doesn't look clued in, which is good—that's not what I wanted—I just need to get this man alone for a few minutes.

Sam's the last one out, and our eyes catch.

"If you need anything," he says, even though he shouldn't, because Oliver could have heard him, and the data about Sam and me that Oli's subconscious is compiling might find these compounding occurrences overt enough to finally offer the knowledge to his consciousness—but I can't focus on that right now.

I nod at Sam, flash him a quick, grateful smile, and then he closes the door.

Henri gives me a smile. I think it might be forced. "You run a tight ship."

I give him a little shrug. "Someone has to."

He sniffs a laugh, like he finds me pleasant. Like, genuinely, almost. "You never told me your name."

I wonder if he already knows it. "Georgia," I tell him anyway as I offer him my hand.

"It's a great pleasure to meet you, Georgia."

"You too." I flash him a smile, try to make it look sincere, but I'm not committed to placating him enough to do my "thinking of puppies" trick. "How long have you been getting Botox for?" I ask.

Henri laughs again, incredulous this time. "I like how straight you are, it's very European…"

And that's not an answer, by the way, it's a deflection—so I say nothing and wait for him to answer my question.

After a few seconds, he clears his throat. "A man my age? For the last fifteen years." He gives me a suspicious look. "Is it that obvious?"

I nod, and he laughs again.

"To me," I clarify. "I study faces for a living."

"Do you?" he says, but he says it without any surprise in his voice. I don't think I've ever told someone what my job is before without it raising some questions or fascination from their end, but he's exhibiting none of that.

"Yeah, I do. So I notice the way faces move—or don't move, in your case. Otherwise the work is very well done."

He laughs again. "Would you like a drink, Georgia?"

"I'd love an iced tea," I tell him. I wouldn't, actually. I just want him to leave me alone for a second.

"Sure."

"Is that a sitting room?" I peer past him into the room I want to get into. "Can I—?"

"Oh." He nods emphatically. "Please."

And you know, I'll preface all this: I have a feeling. And I suspect that I'm going to find what I think I'm going to find, but I want to be sure before I draw any definitive conclusions, so I make my way in there, and I can hear him clattering around in the kitchen, putting ice in glasses; I can hear the pouring of the tea—all of that, it's just white noise to the sitting room though, because now that I'm in there, God, it's immaculate. Floor-to-ceiling white, ornate bookshelves, taller than even the tallest man could reach, so there's one of those sliding ladders like Belle has in *Beauty and the Beast*. And all the books, they're bound so they look the same...and all of them...they are what I think they'll be. A million copies, volumes, and editions of names we all know. Robert Frost, Walt Whitman, Edgar Allen Poe, Sylvia Plath, Pablo Neruda, e. e. cummings, T.S. Eliot, William Blake, Elizabeth Barrett Browning. You know, really famous names, like Rudyard Kipling and Oscar Wilde and Ralph Waldo Emerson and Maya Angelou…

Then there's Alfred Tennyson, Marianne Moore, Mary Oliver, and George Gordon Byron.

My eyes fall on a framed degree. Poetry. Cornell.

He walks back into the room, and it's like he realizes in that moment what me staring at his degree means, and his face is immediately drenched with concern—AU2 and AU20—

"Georgia—"

"Oh my God."

"Georgia…"

I shake my head. "You…"

"Mon cœur, please, if you'll just—"

He moves toward me, but I push past him, barreling through his house, through the living room where there are no clues of him flying planes because he doesn't fly planes. I bust through the front door and sort of tumble down the stairs, and it's bad—it's all bad, because the urgency on my face, how distraught I look, it's enough to send Sam into a rightful state of concern—concerned enough that he forgets that I'm only his in private, not in public. He's forgotten that I am, in the eyes of the only person on the whole fucking planet who matters right now, nothing more than that person's sister, who he—Sam—technically, barely knows and has little-to-no connection with.

But as I barely make it down the stairs and into the front yard of my father's lover, where I sort of willfully fall into a little bush of common purslanes that I then throw up in, it's Sam who gets to me the fastest. He basically throws himself at me, falling to my side—his hands on my body in ways they shouldn't be, like the small of my back, my waist—

"What happened?" he asks.

I throw up again, and Sam keeps his hand on my back. He shouldn't have his hand on my back.

Tennyson looks from me vomiting in the garden and back up to the man on the porch, who's staring at me all horrified and mortified and heartbroken, but fuck him, and same.

Sam touches my face—my face!—so stupid in the scheme of things, but I think there's such a violence to the act of vomiting, and I think both my brothers are in such an intense and confused spiral of emotions that as Oliver runs to my other side, I don't think he barely even registers it as the overt display of Sam's feelings for me that it is.

"Are you okay?" he asks.

I shake my head as I stare into the garden I just threw up in.

"Georgia," Sam says loudly, clearly, trying to gain control of the situation, still holding my face in his hand. "What happened?"

I look past Sam back up at the man—our eyes lock.

"Gige, what the fuck is going on?" Tennyson looks scared now—flashes of AU1 and AU25—but he's masking that fear with anger, because it's easier to be angry than it is to be afraid. Anger is ours to wield against our attackers; fear is the lack of control we feel when we're under siege, and believe me—Tennyson's reality is now under siege.

I stare at the man one more time—AU1 from him also—he's afraid as well. I suppose he should be, all things considered.

Tennyson lifts an impatient eyebrow, waiting for my answer, and then I look over at Oliver, who's very quiet now. He looks afraid too. I cover my face with my hands for a second, try to compose myself as best I can. I take a breath.

"He's gay," I tell them.

Oliver looks confused. "Who's gay?"

"He is." I point to the man, then gesture vaguely to the universe around us. "They are."

Tennyson takes a measured breath—holds it. "Who's they?"

I glance at him briefly, and I know he knows before I even say it.

"We were right," I tell Tennyson. "Alexis Beauchêne and Dad were having an affair." I look back at Oliver as I point to our father's lover on the porch. "And that man is Alexis Beauchêne."

50

IT DOESN'T EVEN MAKE SENSE," Tennyson says, staring at the strawberry shake in front of him.

We're at some hot dog place on Magazine Street. I don't know why. Oliver said he wanted fries, though now that they're sitting in front of him, he's not eaten a single one.

"It's actually more common than you'd think," I say, but no one says anything back.

"Maybe they hooked up once, and he's blackmailing him with the house," Tennyson says, sounding hopeful, and yes, that's a weird thing to hope for, but I let it slide this time.

"He isn't," I say, positive of at least that much.

"How do you know?" Tennyson asks loudly.

I catch eyes with Sam for a few seconds before I look back at Tenny. "We're all named after poets."

"What?" Tennyson blinks before he says, "And so?"

I'll explain it later, I guess. Our father's lover's college major isn't my primary concern right now.

Sam's just staring at Oli with a worried bend in his brow, and Tennyson isn't worried about Oliver, but I think that's fair enough. I think his world is caving in on itself for the second time in a fortnight.

And that younger older brother of mine, who my heart is so aching for—I reach for his arm and touch it gently.

"Are you okay?" I ask him, and he's staring directly at me but isn't all at once, so I say his name. "Oliver?"

"What?" He blinks a few times, as though he's coming to.

"Are you okay?" I ask again.

"I—" He shakes his head. "I don't know. Am I validated or devastated?"

"You can be both," Sam tells him.

"Or neither," I offer. "There are no prerequisites or parameters to how or what you should be feeling right now."

Oliver nods. He doesn't hear what I'm saying though, and something about how he looks makes me feel so nervous and so on edge, and so I sort of just keep talking to try to make him feel better.

"Angry, relieved, betrayed, happy, vindicated—whatever it is, all of it would be fine, and all of it could be true, and still nothing about anything that's happened in our family's treatment of you up until this moment will ever be permissible."

Oliver stares at me; his eyes look glazed over.

"Which is all to say"—I try to give him a reassuring look, and God, have you ever tried to give someone a reassuring look when you're not sure of anything?—"as has always been the case, their treatment of you has nothing to do with you."

And the way Oliver's eyes move, I feel like he heard that part. At least, I hope he did. Sam catches my eye, gives me a small, subtle smile that makes me think he's maybe proud of me, or something—which is sweet, but also, it's not as subtle as no smile.

"Do you think Mom knows?" Oliver asks the table.

"No." Tennyson shakes his head, not a doubt in his mind. "There's no way—"

"Well," I cut in, giving him an apologetic look. "At least not consciously."

"Stop." My oldest brother rolls his eyes, exasperated. "Gige, not everyone can read—"

"No, Tennyson," I interrupt again, because of this I'm sure. "Everyone can. And not just can, they do."

Sam puts his arms on the table, leans in, interested. And what I'm saying is interesting, and they should all probably lean in, but just Sam does, which is strike a million against him at this point.

"It's why everyone's always banging on about vibes," I go on. "That's not some hippy-dippy new whatever we've just discovered—it's people picking up on the tiny inexplicable things that they see without knowing they see it."

Tennyson's eyes pinch, suspiciously.

"So no, I don't think Mom consciously knows Dad was having a decades-long affair with another man," I say, eyebrows up. "But I do suspect she will have wondered over the course of their relationship whether he could possibly be attracted to men."

Tennyson drops his head in his hands and exhales. He sounds grieved.

And that's fair, don't you think?

It doesn't feel homophobically charged; it feels like he just found out his father isn't who he thought he was. I mean, fuck, I get it—our father isn't who I thought he was either. Even if the version of him we just uncovered is one I'm slightly more interested in knowing than the one I thought he was, he's still a stranger now. But then, I suppose he was always a stranger to me and to Oliver. He made himself that way to us. Kept his paternal distance. I wonder if he did that because he saw flecks of his true self in us and found it confronting or painful?

I wonder if he's just an absolute fucking prick?

I guess either way, he's the latter. I don't think you can slice him in a way right now where that isn't at least the smallest bit true. Or the biggest.

What kind of person lets his children be treated how Oliver was treated—how I was treated—when he too was gay and he too was an adulterer? I'm not even a fucking adulterer, really.

And he died thinking I was.

I don't know why that thought suddenly makes my heart feel like its knees have been capped, but it does, and I take this big breath that I think will just be a breath, but when I do, it's all staggered and full of feelings I wouldn't ever usually show at a table of people, because as it happens, all of those people at said table stare at me.

Across Sam's face flickers that dangerous concern for me again, and I try to placate him indirectly with a smile before I climb over Tennyson to get out of the booth.

"Are you good?" my brother calls after me.

I nod back. "Just gotta pee."

I don't though; I just need a minute. I go into the stall, shut the door, and lean back against it. I let myself feel for a minute the grotesque weight of it all. The years of lies that have pressed down on our whole family, squashing and contorting our lives and selves. Who might we all have been if truth was allowed to live under our roof?

"Gige?" calls this perfect, Australian voice, and I squeeze my eyes tight shut.

"You okay?" He taps on the door gently. I sigh quietly—not because I don't want him in here, checking on me—I do, of course I do—but because of course I'm not.

"You shouldn't be in here," is what I say back.

"I don't care," he says without a second thought.

I don't care either; that's the bad part.

I open the stall door, and he's standing at there, waiting for me. Our eyes lock, and it's with a wonderful kind of in-sync-ness that what happens next is suddenly happening.

There are a lot of theories as to why people like to have sex when they're under immense stress or, say, like, about to die (as per every disaster movie ever). Whether it's an exertion of control, self-soothing with the oxytocin our system floods us with, good, old-fashioned post-disaster sex, or just the shameful cliche of not wanting to feel alone.

God, what does it say about who I am, that my father—knowing who he himself was—still found me unpalatable enough to spend a great deal of his life avoiding me?

It's almost like a sore relief to have Sam's hands on my body after today. My mind has been in a constant state of aching, but him touching me feels like a cool compress. And it escalates quickly, from us kissing in the bathroom to Sam boosting me up around his waist and the fly of his jeans undone and me pressed up against the bathroom stall and—

"I fucking knew it."

And I just freeze. My eyes are closed still, and I keep them closed for a second longer because when I open them next, I'll see my brother's face, and it'll be all marred with hurt and betrayal, and so it should be. Everything will be fucked once I open them, so I just leave them for a second.

Sam speaks first—which is good of him, bad of me.

"Ol," Sam starts.

My eyes are open now, in time to see my brother backing out the door, shaking his head at me in painful disbelief.

"How could you?" he says just to me. He's not talking to Sam, it's me. I'm the problem. I think I might always be the problem?

"Oliver—" I reach for him, but he jerks away from me.

"No!" he spits, then his voice trails. "Don't you..." He looks me up and down. He doesn't even glance at Sam. "Fuck you."

And then he spins on his heel and darts away.

51

HE TOOK THE KEYS. WHEN he fled the bathroom, Oliver grabbed the keys from our table and bolted to the car, taking off.

It wouldn't have taken a rocket scientist to figure out what just happened, I don't think.

When Sam and I emerge, Tennyson is standing by the door of the restaurant, watching our car drive away. He looks back over at Sam and me, jaw tight—he looks fucking pissed. I don't think he's looked at me like that this whole entire trip—maybe not even ever. The glare shifts to some kind of judgment, shaking his head as he pulls out his wallet. He fishes out too much money for the food we ordered and bangs it on the counter.

"Come on," he tells Sam and me, then waits for neither of us before he leaves.

"Gige," Sam says, grabbing my wrist. He's worried about me. Worried about us, maybe. He should be.

I move my wrist away from him, even though it hurts me to do so. "Not now," is all I say. Because what else can I say? Loving him how I love him has fucked everything up.

I chase after my oldest brother.

"Where's he going?" Tennyson asks without looking at me, waving a cab down.

At that, I glance at Sam, and his face bends in a way that terrifies me and floods me with guilt.

Tennyson catches what neither of us are saying. "I thought he was sober."

"You're only sober until you aren't anymore." And my voice gives away how worried I am.

Tennyson rubs his hand over his brow—beyond stressed now—and says "fuck" under his breath.

A cab finally pulls over. Tennyson gets in the front seat. When the driver asks where to, Tennyson looks back at me. Just me; he seems to be ignoring Sam. "Well, fucking come on, Sherlock."

"He's at a bar."

"Great," he says, turning back around. "That narrows it down."

Sam gives my brother a dark look for that exchange, but Tennyson doesn't see it. I glance out the window, try to focus my brain as best I can. I know the answers, I always do. Wherever he is, there will have been clues. People are never unpredictable, even if they think they are.

So where is he hiding? And is he really hiding, or does he want to be found?

There are different ways pain can play out, a million different ways, but in my experience with Oliver, there are two.

There's the version of pain where something hurts you so badly, you don't even realize the full extent of the injury until later. Like that time with the magazines—I think that hurt him so much in an unspeakable way that he barely reacted at all at the time, but like I said, as best I can tell, I believe that's when the secret drinking started. That's one kind of route for pain, the quiet one.

And then there's the loud one, which demands to be felt. Me in the bar with Becks.

Oliver feels entitled to this pain—he is entitled to it. I fucked up, I betrayed him, Sam betrayed him. He knows he's done nothing wrong, just that he's been wronged. And when you've been wronged as many times as he has, you want so desperately for someone to make it right.

The question is less "where do we find him?" and more "who does he want to find him?"

I glance at Sam. "What was the name of that bar you said you went to before?"

I was right, that's where we find him.

And I do want to clarify, I don't believe Oliver came here for attention. He is an addict, and when an addict loses control, they have the impulse to turn to the thing that makes them feel better. Do I think he subconsciously picked a place that Sam could find him in? Yeah, probably. The same way I think I probably subconsciously allowed myself to hook up with Sam in a public bathroom because of the burden it's been to keep him a secret. We weren't discovered in the secret bathrooms no one knows about; we were in the restroom of a busy restaurant with my brothers a few meters away. And in no way did I consciously want Oliver to find us or see what he saw, but our subconscious is the real boss. Our conscious actions might be the ship we're sailing, but our subconscious is the rudder that steers it.

I stand there for a few seconds, watching him—Sam does too—both of us surveying our damage.

A half-drunk what I'm assuming is a vodka soda (Oliver's former go-to) sits in front of him, and I know it's not his first by how his eyelids drag when he blinks.

My heart sinks, because it's my fault.

Then he spots us. Oliver's face turns to a scowl before he stands and goes to move away.

We all rush toward him, but I'm the fastest.

I reach for him. "Oliver—"

"No." He snatches his hand away from me in a way that makes me feel like he thinks I'm disgusting now.

"Oli—" I reach for him again, but he smacks my hand away.

"Get away from me, you slut."

I catch Sam's eye—I can feel the anger on him for that—but I beg him not to react without saying a word. I try to tell him with my eyes that I don't need him to save me, I need him to save my brother.

I nod at Oliver. "I'll get away from you," I tell him gently, trying my best to placate him. "If that's what you want."

He glowers at me. "I don't want anything to do with you."

"Okay." I nod, pretending my heart isn't breaking. I don't try to get closer to him. I just stay put, but that's not going to work for Ol either, because he's mad. He's got things he wants to say; he's ready to fight and he doesn't want all the anger he's harbored for so long inside his body anymore.

"I can't believe you." He shakes his head. "I can't believe you'd do that to me—after everything, you're going to take Sam from me?" His eyes fall down me. "Fuck you."

"I'm not taking S—" I start, but he cuts me off.

"—I said fuck you." That was a bit louder than before, and some people stare.

Tennyson shifts uncomfortably.

"I hate you," Oliver says, quieter now. Actually, he says that like he means it, and a weird panic ripples through me as I wonder whether he does.

"Oliver," Tens says. "You don't mean that."

"Yes, I do," he says, staunch, only he's not looking at Tennyson, just me. "So fuck off."

"Okay." I begin to retreat, and Sam looks from me to Oliver, torn about what to do—like there's a choice. Like I'd even want him to come with me.

"Should I—?" Sam glances at Oliver, then to me—asking the question.

Oliver looks over at Sam, panicked, almost—more hurt creeping onto his face too.

"No." I shake my head quickly, nipping the thought in the bud. "You stay. I'll go."

"You can't go by yourself," Sam says.

"Yes, I can. I'll be fine," I say, continuing to back away toward the exit.

Sam is properly annoyed now. "Stop. No." He looks at Tennyson. "Can you go with her?"

Tennyson looks at Oliver and then over to me before he nods.

Oliver scoffs, rolling his eyes.

"Please just stay," I say quietly to Tennyson.

He shakes his head, then looks at Oliver. "I'll be back soon. I'm just going to drop her off, okay?"

Oliver's jaw is tight, eyes all resenting. He nods, then sort of throws himself back down in the chair he was in before.

"Keys?" Tenny holds out his hand.

Oliver pulls them from his pocket and drops them into Tens's palm.

We walk to the car, me trailing behind him. Oliver didn't remember exactly where he parked it, so we're sort of aimlessly walking, just looking for it, and for the first few minutes it's silent.

It feels how it used to now. This tension between us that meant we'd never be close. Two people related by blood who'd never willingly spend time together, let alone be in this close a proximity to each other unless they were forced to.

And no one forced him, but I suspect Tennyson knew what I did—if he hadn't agreed to take me home, Sam would have left Oliver to do it himself, and that's terrible, and I want that not to be true, but I think that it is. I'm in my head, worrying about what that means, spiraling so much, so fast, I sort of forget Tennyson's even there until he says—

"Did you need to fuck him in the bathroom?"

I turn to him, blink twice.

"I—" I go to say something, but nothing comes out. I don't know why. Truthfully, it's a valid question. Truthfully, it still felt like a slap.

He keeps going. "In a restaurant, Gige? On the night you find out Dad's gay?" He shakes his head, disappointed in me. "I mean, Oliver was right there—"

"I know!" I yell back, sort of suddenly. "Okay? I get it! I fucked up. I'm a fuck-up, I'm a slut! I'm a total disaster."

Tennyson sighs. "That's not what I'm saying."

I look away. "Maybe not with your mouth. But it is the subtext."

Tennyson breathes out his nose. I've got him there.

It goes quiet between us for almost a minute before he shakes his head again, looking at me. "I just don't know why you'd even want to—"

"Because, Tennyson, I don't have any other fucking frame of reference," I say loudly and clearly.

His brows bend, he looks confused. "What?"

"Besides Oliver, I don't have a reference for intimacy or closeness or sense of security with a man that isn't sexual. How the fuck would I?"

"Dad never—"

"No." I scowl. "Of course he never—but we didn't have the same dad, Tennyson. You had one who loved you and wanted you and spent time with you and delighted in you, and I had one who sent me away because he caught me being raped by my sister's boyfriend, and as is the status quo in our household, he chose to believe the worst in me—"

Tennyson sighs again. "Gige." He looks at me, head a bit tilted now, but I don't want his head tilts.

"And that's fine, whatever—believe whatever the fuck you want. I am the disaster. I am the slut, and I am the fuck-up who slept with Sam even though I knew Oliver liked him. I am all the things that Maryanne's said I am." My eyes fill with tears. "It wasn't the truth back then, but it is the truth now."

"Georgia—"

I stick my hand out and hail a cab. Mercifully, one pulls in.

"Georgia," he says again.

"Please leave me alone," I say, my voice breaking. "Don't follow me."

"Just let me take you back to the hotel, we don't need to talk—"

"I don't need you to take me back to the hotel. I've been on my own before—I am fine on my own, okay?"

And I am, actually. Fine on my own. Better, even. I always have been.

It's how I know how to be. Everything that's happening, all of this shit is because I started trying to—whatever.

Because it's true. I *am* all the things Maryanne said I was. It was a prophecy, not a declaration of truth. We just didn't know it back then.

And actually, it's worse—I'm worse than she even said, because Maryanne is Maryanne and fuck her, right? But Oliver? That I'd do this to Oliver?

I'm not a slut, I'm a monster.

But I'm done now. It's done now.

I'll fly back to South Carolina tomorrow morning and leave for London tomorrow night, and I can be done with all of it.

Sam and I, we're done.

We have to be.

52

TENNYSON ACTUALLY FOLLOWED ME TO the hotel, which was sort of (objectively) sweet of him. All the way into the hotel, even.

He kept his distance, didn't speak to me in the elevator—watched me go into our room, then left and went back to Oliver, I guess.

And good. He needs him, I don't.

Being alone right now though, it's not a good feeling. But I feel quite sure I deserve it, so I sit in it as though it's some sort of self-prescribed penance for my sins. And listen, we're all sinful, but I think it's a lie that all sins are equal. Not all of them are. Not all of them could be.

I think sins are weighed by their intent and their destruction. Jean Valjean stealing a loaf of bread for his starving family isn't the same as Scar killing Mufasa and letting Simba think he did it.

So while my intentions weren't ill, I didn't try to pull back, I didn't try to not love Sam. And I didn't just fall into loving him; I leaned, willfully, over the barrier. Some might even say I pole-vaulted over the barrier. That, and my destruction radius? I'm fucked. And I can pretend sitting in my bad feelings all alone is enough, but the truth is, I know what I need to do.

It's a little past 3:00 a.m. when I hear the hotel door open.

"I'm just going to shower down here, and then I'll go back upstairs to him," I hear my oldest brother say.

I hear the man I love breathe out, tired. "Thanks, man."

And then my bedroom door opens, and Sam Penny fills the doorframe.

I'm sitting in the center of my bed in my pajamas, legs balled up under me. His face sort of lights up when he sees me, and it makes me want to cry.

"Hey." He gives me a tired smile.

I swallow, because I'm nervous. "Can we talk?"

And he knows immediately. The smile disappears and he gives me a steep look. "Don't—"

"Sam—"

He starts shaking his head. "Georgia, don't—"

"Penny, this has to end!"

"No," he says loudly as he rushes toward me.

"Yes," I say louder back.

"No! We're not doing anything wrong." He says that slow and steady, but also annoyed.

He's pissed off. Not at me though—I can tell it's not at me, and I think that makes it all worse.

My shoulders drop. "Are you insane? Did you not see my brother tonight? What seeing us together did to him?"

"It's just a fucking weird situation." Sam covers his eyes with his hand, then wipes it down his face, tired and exasperated. "And yeah, it's shit. I'm not saying it's not shit, but we're not doing anything wrong—"

"Sam, there is no way you could believe that that's true."

"But it is true, Gige." He holds my arms. "It's a shitty situation, but it doesn't mean that—"

I stare at him with round, heavy eyes that want so desperately to be vindicated in my poor decision-making.

Sam swallows before he pivots tactics. "What is it that we're doing that's so wrong?"

"Hurting him!"

He shakes his head quickly. "We're not hurting him on purpose."

"That doesn't make it okay! We're still hurting him! Didn't you see his face?"

And Sam looks crushed at that, like he knows it's true. "Georgia." He breathes out my name, and it feels heavy this time.

"We can't keep doing this, Sam—it'll kill him…"

"This'll kill me!" he snaps accidentally, and his eyes go wide after he's said it. He presses his hand into his mouth and steadies his breathing. Four breaths in and out of his nose. "Georgia—fuck." He swallows heavily. "Please don't do this. Please."

His eyes go glassy, which is some strange signal fire to my body to let a traitor-tear slip out of my eye. I smack it off my face before he can reach for it.

"Sam…"

"No, don't 'Sam' me—just don't—" He licks his top lip, presses a finger into his mouth—self-hushing. Then he shakes his head at himself and swallows again, then squares his shoulders as he stands tall.

"I love you," he tells me, resolute. "I'm in love with you."

It hangs there for a second, bold and awkward and shiny, like a disco ball with the lights on full.

My lips pinch and I give him a reluctant look. "…I know."

He lets out a single dry laugh. "Fuck," he says as he shoves his hands through his hair while simultaneously shoving away the tension that was there between us just a second ago. He sits down on the edge of my bed, then leans back. "How long you been sitting on that for?"

I twist my mouth as I sit down next to him. "I've suspected it since Saturday but was definitively sure by Monday night." I swallow. "When did you know?"

"That I love you?" he clarifies.

I nod.

"Last Tuesday," he tells me, gaze unflinching.

I roll my eyes. "We met last Monday."

"Yep." He flicks his eyebrows up, daring me to question him. "So don't pull this shit with me, Gige—there's no failsafe for loving you. Once you're in, you're in, and I'm in."

I tuck my chin, suspicious. "You're sounding like an addict."

"I am an addict," he tells me, sure.

"You're not meant to be addicted to me."

"I'm not addicted to you, I'm in love with you," he says matter-of-factly. "I don't need you, I want you. And I want you because I know you." He searches for my eyes. "I know you, Georgia, and I know you've spent your whole life shouldering other people's pain and their secrets, usually at a massive cost to yourself, and now I'm here, and I'll help you shoulder some of it, but because I love you, I'm also going to help you draw some lines, because for a psychology major you have some real fucking shit boundaries with your brother."

I toss him a look because I didn't love being called out like that, but I wonder if it stings because it's true? "Sam, we—"

"Georgia—no," he says, firm now, then he gives me a cautious look. "Unless it's what you want. If this is about you, if you don't want to be together anymore, then it's a different conversation..." He lifts a cautious eyebrow. "Is that the conversation? Is it what you want?"

I give him another scowl. "Of course it's not what I want, but—"

"Then no," he says, then sort of scoops me up, pulling me on top of him. "This—stop with your martyr shit, okay?"

My bottom lip wobbles as he rests his forehead on mine. "Did you hear him?" I barely say.

Sam wipes under my eyes with his thumbs. "He's not himself right now."

"No, I know." I sniffle. "Some of it's true though."

"None of it's true," Sam says very assuredly.

And I think to myself, wouldn't it be so lovely if we viewed ourselves through the same lens as the people who love us?

"I don't know what to do," I tell him, my eyes all desperate. "He's so angry, I don't know what happens next—"

"I can talk to him," he offers.

"And then what?" I shrug. "For him, then what? Then we're just two more people who've fucked him over."

"Gige." Sam gives me a look. "We haven't fucked him over—we're just in lov—" He stops in his tracks, then gives me a frowny-cautious look. "Wait, you didn't say it back."

I smirk, enjoying the feeling of being a bit in control. "Do I need to?"

"Well, yeah." He tilts his perfect head, raising an eyebrow that his hair flops forward over anyway. "That is how the typical exchange tends to go..."

I shake my head, amused and drunk with power. "So needy..."

He squints at me, looking more sure of himself.

"You love me," he tells me.

"Do I just?"

"Yeah, look at you, how you're looking at me—those pupils are dilated as fuck, and you're swallowing a lot, and"—he presses his fingers into my neck—"your pulse is elevated, and—"

"Well—so?" I pout. "You love me too!"

"Yeah." He grabs me by the waist and tugs me in closer to him. "Too fucking right."

I smile as I rest my chin on his chest, and he squints at me again.

"Georgia..."

"Mmm?"

"Say it back. Properly." He cocks a small grin. "Out loud."

I shrug and roll my eyes like it's boring and mundane, and as though the words haven't been trying to jump out of my throat since Monday morning. "I love you."

He tries not to smile too much, squashes it right down, but it squishes out the edges anyway. Then he rolls on top of me, looking down. "Good girl."

I nearly die on the spot.

"Hey..." He pushes some hair behind my ears. "Can you not...do that again?" He swallows once, nervous. "Talk to me next time—talk to me anytime—but you can't just—treat me like that. It's not fair." Mouth shrug. "I won't let you."

"Okay." I nod, solemnly.

I say sorry, and he kisses the top of my head, and then we lie there for a bit, me on top of him, his arms tossed over me with a casual possessiveness that I could weep over.

"So—" I shift positions and wriggle into his chest. "We're in love."

Sam nods back decisively. "We are in love."

I lift my eyebrows. "Now what?"

53

PROMISE ME YOU WON'T BE aggressively protective?" I say to Sam as I tug on my jeans the morning after everything happened.

"Only if I need to," he calls back to me from the bathroom. I hear the sound of teeth brushing.

"If it's Oliver." I poke my head through the bathroom door. "Not even then."

Sam wipes his mouth with his hand. "Gige—"

"Sam." I shake my head. "He can say whatever he wants, whenever he wants—"

"He can't," Sam says as he checks his perfect reflection in the mirror. "There are limits. But sure, I see your point." He moves toward me. "Do you feel okay?"

I shrug, ask the question I've wondered all night but have been too afraid to ask. "Did he say anything last night? About me—? Or us?"

"I—" Sam starts, then swallows. Uh oh. "He was really drunk."

I flash him an uneasy smile. "That bad?"

"I didn't say—"

"You didn't have to."

I've experienced my brother in a relapse; I know how he can be. It's not Oliver-specific, it's addicts. Oliver would never say a majority of the things he's said to me mid-relapse were he sober, and he'd fight anyone else himself for saying them to me. Addicts aren't themselves when the monster takes over, I know that, and still, I feel so many different kinds of nerves as Sam and I walk into the hotel restaurant the next morning.

Oliver and Tennyson are sitting at the table already, same side as each other. Oliver lowers his sunglasses as we approach them, eyes me like a bug.

"Morning," Sam says, on both our behalf.

"Hey." Tennyson gives us a tired smile, and I get the sense that he's had *a night*.

I give Ol a gentle smile. "How are you feeling?"

He takes a long sip of his drink that looks like a Bloody Mary, and I wonder whether it's virgin or not.

"Fuck off." Oliver flashes me a curt smile.

"Hey." Tennyson elbows him, but I shake my head at our big brother, ask him to leave it with just my eyes.

Oliver gives Tennyson a tall look. "Am I supposed to be good with whatever the fuck's going on over on that side of the table?"

"We can talk about it?" I offer.

Oliver's eyes go to slits. "I don't have anything to say to you."

I tilt my head. "I think you have a lot to say to me."

Oliver shakes his head, stubborn. "Nothing you want to hear."

"I'll hear anything," I tell him, and it's earnest and I mean it, but when Oliver—eyebrow all cocked up and ready to fight—replies, "Will you?" Sam winces.

I nod anyway.

"Okay." He nods back. "Fuck you."

Tennyson breathes out his nose. "Dude—"

"No, I mean it," Oliver doubles down. "Fuck you, Georgia. Because this is what you do. You fuck around and steal people."

My head pulls back, sort of shocked—but I guess not really. Maybe his criticism's fair, and he keeps going anyway, even if it isn't.

"It's not like he's the first. You did it with Toby, you did it with Beck—"

Penny cuts in at the sound of a B. "Don't say it, man. You're angry, I get it—that's fine for now, but one day you're not going to be angry, and you won't be able to take that back."

Oliver's jaw goes tight before he flicks his eyes between the two of us. "So what is this? You're fucking?"

I take a breath, and I have the plan and intention to say something, but then nothing comes out. I think it's because it's such a grotesque simplification of what Penny and I are.

"Uh—" Sam clears his throat. "We have had sex, yeah."

Oliver crosses his arms. "How many times?"

Tennyson grimaces. "What's that got to do with anything?"

"How many times?" Oliver asks louder.

"Seven," I say, and under his breath, Oliver mutters, "Slut." And then Sam's whole body goes rigid with a defensive anger that he wants to spew all over my brother, and I squeeze his knee to tell him I'm fine. I've been called worse.

"We're sleeping together." I nod. "But we're also just, like, actually together..."

Oliver blinks twice. "What?"

I wave vaguely. "Together-together."

"Like, boyfriend-girlfriend?" he clarifies.

"Well." I shrug. "Like, we haven't put a label on it or—"

"Oh!" Oliver cuts in as he gives me a snarky look. "How fluid and modern of you."

Which for some reason is the thing that tips Sam over the edge.

"Yeah, okay, listen, I'll label it for you right now." Penny gives my brother a curt look. "Oliver, this is my girlfriend, Georgia. And you can't speak to her how you keep trying to."

Oliver scoffs, and under his breath he grumbles, "Unbelievable."

Sam flicks up his eyebrow, looking more impatient than he should. "What is?"

"That you've fallen under her spell..."

I stare at Oliver, incredulous. "My spell?"

He ignores me though, keeps going. "I know she makes you feel like she knows you like no one else does, but it's not real. It's just that thing she does, and it gets old real fast."

"Okay." Sam nods, patience well waned now. "Let me worry about that spell of your sister's—that I'm very willfully under, by the way." He says that last part with a point. "And you worry about how you're doing right now."

"How I'm doing?" Oliver repeats back as he pretends to think about it. "My sister and former best friend is fucking the one person on the planet who's kept me sane these last nine months, and it turns out my father is a complete and total fucking stranger who was an emotional terrorist to me for reasons that I think we can all just assume could be categorized as 'for shits and giggles.' How do you think I'm doing?"

He tacks on a faux-smile at the end for good and dramatic measure, and under any other circumstance, I'd really appreciate this flair my brother has, but right now, after that, we all stare at him because no one knows what to say. His anger at everyone—but especially me and especially, especially our dad—feels deeply justified.

I turn to Tennyson. "We need to go back and see him, right?"

"No," Oliver says immediately.

"Probably." Tens nods. "Yeah."

"Do you wanna just go by yourself?" I offer my oldest brother.

Oliver's shaking his head now. "I don't want to go at all."

"No, not really," Tennyson replies to me, and Oliver's head is bouncing back and forth as he looks from me to Tennyson and back again.

"Sorry." Ol blinks. "Do I not get a say in this?"

"No," I tell him very directly. "Not how you feel entitled to one, anyway."

Oliver's whole face pulls with indignation. "What the fuck does that mean?"

I stare at him for a second, compose myself, try not to be frustrated at his reaction right now. "It means, I understand that this is painful and hard for you—possibly even more painful and harder for you than the rest of us—but there still is a rest of us. He was still Tennyson's dad, and Mom's husband, and they deserve answers even if you don't want to hear them."

"Well, I don't want to hear them," Oliver says, obstinate.

Tennyson grabs his arm and gives him a big-brother-y look. "Then maybe you should stay in the car."

54

WE DECIDE THAT, ACTUALLY, THE best thing for everyone—for Oliver, really—would be for him and Sam to head back to Okatie, and Tennyson and I will stay here and learn as much as we can. Oliver's agreed not to say anything to anyone, not Mom, not Maryanne, not Vi (though I suspect she already knows something), at least not until Tennyson and I get back and we all have more information to go off.

Oliver's taking it all how I thought he would—which is poorly, to say the least.

If it's not a snide comment, it's a death stare, and if it's not a death stare, it's a blank, lost stare out the window, and I think that's the worst of them all.

I don't want Sam to go with my brother, even though I do. I have this strange anxiety hanging over me like an overgrown tree branch that's casting unwanted shade in my otherwise sunny garden—what if Oliver says something to Sam that makes him change his mind about me? I don't think Sam's that kind of person, but Addict-Oliver is. Addict-Oliver is spiteful and vindictive, and I am the target. Justifiably so, I suppose.

There's obviously nothing direct to Okatie because it's Okatie, but there's not even anything direct to Savannah, so they're flying New Orleans to Atlanta, Atlanta to Savannah. We're standing out front of the

Delta drop-off at MYS, and Tennyson is in hyper-fix-it mode, prebooking an Uber Black for the boys from Savannah to drive them home when they land.

I've always had a fondness for airports. I like that they sort of represent something exciting. But today, as I stare up at Sam, his arms draped around my waist, I get this weird, horrible feeling: Sam and I are going to have to do this again in a few days when I go back to the UK and he goes back to LA. It feels bad saying goodbye to him right now, and I'm going to see him again in like twenty-four hours. How's it going to feel saying goodbye to him and not knowing when we'll meet again?

It's on my face, I suppose, because Sam catches it. "What's wrong?"

I shake my head, force a smile as I glance at my brothers—I don't want to be overheard.

"Nothing," I lie. He gives me a look with a raised eyebrow—calls out my lie without saying a word.

I sigh. "Sam, what are we doing—like, how is this ever going to work?"

"We work. This is us actively working..."

"Okay, so we're going to do long distance then, or—?"

"Fuck no," he says with some conviction. "Fuck long distance."

I breathe out, mildly exasperated. "What then?"

"Well, I'm going to come to London. Obviously."

I pull back, surprised. "Why?"

"Well"—Sam squashes a smile—"Uh, primarily because you're there. But also, it's a great city. Good restaurants. A lot of history. I like those cobbled streets—"

"Sam."

"What?" He smiles.

I roll my eyes. "Be serious."

"I'm so serious." He nods once.

I flick him a disbelieving look. "You're just going to move to London?"

"Do you not want me to?" he says, and it sounds almost comically Australian, I don't know why.

I toss him a disparaging look. "Of course I want you to, it's just—"

Sam pokes me and gives me a knowing look. "Priority."

"You've known me nineteen days," I remind him.

"Yeah, so?" he shrugs.

"That's a lot of change for less than three weeks."

"Yeah..." He nods, then he shrugs again. "Still. I'm in, Carter. I'm not changing my mind. Are you changing your mind?"

I shake my head.

"Right, so—" Sam pulls out his phone and opens the Notes app. "What flight are you on? I should probably try to book the same one back..."

I hook my arm around his neck and kiss him a lot, because I love him and he's perfect, and then Oliver walks toward us, his face like a stone.

Instinctively, I pull away from Sam, flashing my brother an apologetic smile. "Sorry," I say, and it's met with an eye roll as he shoves his sunglasses on his beautiful, grumpy little face.

"See you in a couple of days?" Sam says, trying to make it less awkward.

I force a smile, but actually, I just feel like crying. I don't want to be without him. I don't want to figure this out without him. But Oliver needs him, and I don't think I can figure this out with Oliver here and hating me, so—here we are.

"Look after him," I tell Sam.

Oliver makes a nose at the back of his throat before he spins around and walks into the airport.

Sam nods at me before he catches Tennyson's eye. "Look after her."

Tennyson nods back once. "Will do."

Sam brushes his mouth over mine. "I love you," he says quietly so Oliver can't hear.

"I love you too," I whisper back.

Then Sam walks away.

I count to five in my mind, but I don't even make it to four before Tennyson says, "Y'all love each other?"

I scoff a laugh and walk back toward the passenger seat. He climbs into the driver's side, waiting for me to give him an answer. I ask, "So what if we do?"

Tennyson shrugs innocently. "So nothing, then!"

I look out the window, huffing a bit, and he peels out, driving back toward the hotel.

"I'm happy for you, Gige."

I look over at him, search all over his face for a reason that would allow me to say "No you're not" with any validity, but I can't find one. He is happy for me, that's the truth.

I'm still mad at him though, so I just say nothing.

"Are we fighting?" Tennyson asks, glancing over at me.

"No," I tell the window.

"I don't have a PhD in whatever, and even I know that was a lie."

I give him a look.

He chuckles, then stares at the road for a bit, goes quiet. Then he breathes out a breath I didn't realize he was even holding. "I don't think any of that shit about you, Gige. What you said the other day? None of it's true. You're not the fuck-up—"

I roll my eyes exaggeratively. "Really, golden boy? Self-identifying as a fuck-up?"

"Yes," he says loudly and firmly. "I was a fucking shit brother to you, and to Oliver, and look at what happened." He stares at me with guilty eyes. "We are a family of fuck-ups, Georgia—no doubt about it. You're not one of those fuck-ups though. You're the only one who isn't."

I stare at my brother for four long seconds, and I don't know what to say. "Thank you?" with an upward inflection is what I go with, because what the hell else was I going to say?

He sort of snorts a laugh again, then looks at me. "You're welcome?"

Our eyes catch, and there's that strange new warmth again that's so unfamiliar and so welcome, all at once. It's to not feel alone in the world, I think—the world can feel so lonely sometimes. Most of the time, I suppose.

"You think Oliver's going to keep quiet about it all?" Tennyson asks, grimacing like he's scared of the answer.

"Yeah." I nod. "As long as he keeps a handle on his drinking."

Tens gives me an uncertain look. "That doesn't bode too well, all things considered."

"He wouldn't do that," I say, fairly sure. "Even if just out of self-preservation."

"What do you mean?"

"I mean, whoever tells Margaret Carter that her husband was a closeted homosexual is staring down the barrel end of a wrath that even someone suicidal would avoid."

Then Tennyson's phone dings. He glances at it briefly before his eyes bug out and he tosses it to me. His hands grip the steering wheel. He's nervous.

"What?" I ask, before I look down at his phone.

There's a text from an unsaved number in his phone.

UNKNOWN:

Hi Tennyson,

This is Alexis. I got your number from Maya. I know you must have a lot of questions. I'm sorry. Please reach out if you want to talk.

Warmly,

Alexis

"Well." I stare at my brother as I drop the phone in his lap. "Reach out!"

He flings the phone back. "You reach out!" he says in a way that I can literally only describe as "like a brother would sound."

"You're the big man of the house now." I throw the phone at him.

"I'm driving! And you"—he plops the phone in my lap—"are the Oxford genius."

I give him a look. "Cambridge."

"Yeah." He shrugs as he gives me a big, apologetic smile. "I can't even get your school right. Definitely should be you who writes back."

SAM:

hey

GEORGIA:

hi

how are you? Did you get home okay?

SAM:

yeah we're back, everything's fine.

GEORGIA:

is Oliver okay?

SAM:

I don't know.

are you okay?

GEORGIA:

I don't know too.

SAM:

Sorry I'm not there.

GEORGIA:

I'm glad you're with him.

55

IT'S SUNDAY WHEN TENNYSON AND I find ourselves—once again—on that admittedly magnificent porch on Seventh Street, and we don't even have to knock this time because Alexis Beauchêne is sitting on the porch swing, holding a cup of coffee to his chest when we arrive.

He gives us a strained, tender smile—but I think that's okay. What more could I ask this man to give us?

"We have some questions," Tennyson says to him.

"I hope for you that I have some answers." Alexis stands and motions toward the door. "Please, come in."

I walk in first, my brother after me, and for the first time in our lives, my brother feels timid to me. It's funny how people present themselves in your mind's eye. Tennyson in my mind is always tall, always sure, always proud, always confident, and he's just…none of those things right now. Right now he looks lost.

He follows me wordlessly into Alexis's sitting room—it's the room where I became sure of what we now know to be true—and objectively, it is a really nice room. His collection of books, both poetry and fiction, would be worth hundreds of thousands of dollars (if not more)—so many first editions.

Alexis gestures for us to sit, so we do, Tennyson and I each taking an armchair and him taking a small chaise opposite us—and I find myself wondering, how many times has my father been in this room?

If you asked me two days ago if my father was a stranger to me, for all intents and purposes, I'd have said yes—but then, what does that make him now?

"So." Alexis gives me a tight, uncomfortable smile. "When did you figure it out?"

"The painting—*Lord Byron's Dream*—was my first warning sign..." Then I reconsider. "Actually, the first warning sign, really, if I had my best foot forward at the time—which I didn't—was that you showed confusion when you first saw Sam."

I glance between them, but Tennyson looks confused, so I keep going.

"Sam specifically," I say to my brother. "As though the rest of us weren't total strangers to him."

I think I see the smallest smile dance around the man's mouth.

"Is he your boyfriend?" he asks, and it's asked in this way that no one else has asked about Sam and me. For everyone else around us, Sam and I came preloaded, but to this man, it's just a simple question. It feels different. It feels nice...

I nod. "But he wasn't yesterday in a public way."

Alexis considers this. "He watches you."

I give him an exasperated look. "I know, right!"

"Gige—" Tennyson elbows me.

"Sorry." I shake my head, then look at Alexis again, more focused now. "It was the names, really. Our names. And Maya's." Then I roll my eyes at myself. "So really, Maya should have been the very first-first clue."

I huff a frustrated breath at myself—how the fuck did I miss that? I really am off my game.

Alexis presses his index finger into his mouth, almost as though he's forbidding a smile to arrive on his face.

Tennyson looks between us, confused. "So...it wasn't just a one-time thing then?" Tennyson asks, almost grimacing, like that's what he was hoping for. Like that might have made it better.

"I'm sorry, no," Alexis says in a way that sounds like he means it, and I wonder what it might cost a person to spend their whole lives apologizing for loving who they love.

"They were in love," I tell my brother while watching Alexis's face—he doesn't look away.

"How do you know?" Tennyson asks me. Me, not the man.

The man and I are still staring at one another.

"Because," I say carefully. "They were as much as a family as they could be, without being one."

"What are you talking about?" Tennyson sounds impatient now, so I turn to look at him.

"Our names, dumbass. No one else in our family has our names—"

"So?"

"We were all named after poets," I tell him a second time.

Tens's eyes flick between Alexis and me. "So?" he asks again.

"So—" I point to the doctorate on the wall. "He was a poetry major."

"Oh," my brother says quietly, and his shoulders slump—I don't know why they slump, but there's something so sad about it. I trust him enough at this point to truly believe that it's not a homophobic shoulder-slump as much as it is a his-life-is-crumbling slump.

"So, wait." Tennyson shakes his head, processing. "You met in college?"

Alexis nods, and my brother's face falls to a frown. "Before or after he was with our mom?"

And it's maybe now—at this specific question—I see a tiny bit of discomfort flicker over Alexis's face.

Which, actually—that makes sense to me.

I think if you've had to resort to having an affair for decades to just (barely) be with the person you love, then a huge part of your rationalization process has to be compartmentalization. Alexis has probably lived his day-to-day adulterer life having placed the mere idea of my mother inside a very airtight, very far away box.

"Does she know anything?" I ask.

Alexis shakes his head. "Nothing."

I purse my lips, because I'm not sure that could be true—how could it be?

"And this started at Cornell?"

"Oui." He nods. "We met at a—how do you say?" His face strains, thinking of the word.

"Mixer?" Tennyson offers.

"Yes!" Alexis nods, grateful. "Mixer. And for me, it was love at first sight. For him, it was..." He trails, choosing his words. "More confusing."

"How?" Tennyson asks, unceremoniously.

"Well," he starts. "We connected over art... Your father loved beautiful things, sculptures, paintings, architecture—"

Tennyson and I catch each other's eye, and our faces mirror one another's. Who he's describing does not remotely sound like the man we knew. He loved art? The only art in their house is that painting of the Boeing in the dining room, which is a fine painting—good even!—but it doesn't exactly scream "I love art." That's all there is. And the one in his office.

And then it clicks.

"You're from Saint-Émilion," I tell Alexis.

He nods. "How did you know?"

"Our dad came home one day with this really pretty white rowboat that Oliver and I called the *SS Avoidance*. Whenever we wanted to get away from...whatever—" I shrug. "We were the only ones who ever used it, we thought... But then, there were a couple of mornings I woke up early when I'd see Dad out on the water, sitting by himself."

"Doing what?" Tennyson asks.

"Nothing." I shake my head. "One time I got binoculars—" I glance at Alexis.

"I'm nosy," I tell him at the same time Tennyson says, "She's nosy."

Alexis quietly chuckles.

I shake my head again. "He wasn't doing anything. But—" I look back at Alexis. "The name on the side of it is *Saint-Émilion*."

Tennyson's head pulls back, like some pieces are falling into place.

"The painting in his office," Tens says, looking at me, eyes wide.

"Ça alors." Alexis gives both of us an impressed look.

"So you moved from Saint-Émilion to... Ithaca?" I ask him, eyebrows up.

"Oui." He laughs then stands up and moves over to one of those magnificent shelves he has. He opens up a book and pulls something out of, then walks back over to us.

He hands Tennyson a photograph.

It's of our father. He's young—like twenty-three, maybe?—next to an also-young Alexis. They're standing in front of Michelangelo's *Bacchus*.

I look up at him, surprised. "You went to Florence together."

He smiles, and the edges of it feel tender. "William wanted to be an art major, not an econ major."

That's the first time he's called him by his name, and it's strange—there's something in him calling him that, referring to him by his name and not "your father" like he has up until now, that makes their relationship come a bit more into focus for me. There's a gentle possessiveness to it, I think? Like, no one calls him William. Dad never liked it if someone did—I wonder if this is why. It was his name to one person and one person alone.

Tennyson looks confused again. "But he loved his econ professor."

"He did," Alexis concedes. "But really, he wanted to transfer to art history, but his father—your grandfather—forbade it."

"Why?" Tennyson asks, even though I don't feel like that's a necessary question. A mere twenty-five-second conversation with Brick Carter would have surely filled in any and all blanks.

Alexis presses his lips together. AU24—he's restraining himself regarding my grandfather. I can tell you this much: he has lots to say.

"I believe he was quoted to have said to William, 'that's'"—and then he proceeds to spells out the F word that isn't *fuck*—"'learning.'"

He flashes us a tight, uncomfortable smile, and I grimace, "That sounds about right…"

Alexis flicks me a look, and I feel like we'd have so many things to talk about, if we had the time and the space (which we definitely don't).

We ask him a few more questions about our dad in college, trying to piece together when it actually began, but he says that to him, to our father, they consider the night they met to be the night it began. Alexis says his life took on a different trajectory when he met our dad at that mixer. That he saw our parents fighting at this party on a balcony, and she said to him something how she was tired of waiting for him to marry her—they were already engaged at that point—but apparently, he kept pushing the wedding further and further back. Apparently she was crying, like really, truly hysterical, asking what was wrong with her, and apparently Dad just kept saying to her, "There's nothing wrong with you," over and over, but it didn't placate her. ("She was very drunk." Alexis gives us a small smile, and it's wild to me to imagine them all in the same place.) After that, she left in a huff with some girlfriends of hers. Alexis said he watched the whole thing at a distance, but there was something about how our dad's face looked every time he said, "There's nothing wrong with you," that there was almost an invisible and unintentional emphasis on the "you," because she wasn't the problem, he was.

Alexis walked over to him, kind of just to see if he was okay, and then they spent the whole night talking—until sunup, he said.

Apparently Mom heard from Dad's dorm roommate he hadn't come home that night and completely flipped out. He made up some lie about getting drunk and falling asleep at a friend's house, but Alexis said they went to a dock and started talking, and then they just never stopped.

"Hold on." I pause, thinking. "So when did it end between you?"

"Seventeen days ago." And I watch how this man's face twitches and twinges, completely full of pain, wanting to crumble but trying his hardest to not—I think on our account.

Tennyson looks from me to Alexis, then back to me.

"Fuck," Tens says, under his breath, and finally a tear slips from Alexis's eye.

My hands are on my face now, and for some reason, my heart is surging in agony for this near-perfect stranger.

"Oh my God." I stare at the broken man across from me. "Did you not know until—"

And then it cracks over his face, like a dam of grief. These huge, unconsolable sobs, not just his shoulders shaking, but his whole body.

Neither Tennyson or I know what to do, but him less so than me, I suppose. I get up and move next to the man, place my hand on his shoulder, because what else am I going to do? I don't know what to do other than try to comfort him.

It goes on for a couple of minutes, this unbridled grief that he's been holding in since he found out.

Eventually, he goes quiet. He gives me a tired, almost-apologetic, somewhat-grateful, barely-there smile.

I stare at him a few moments, trying to figure it out myself so I don't have to ask, but fuck it, I'm going to ask anyway: Sorry if this is insensitive to ask—but like, did you have a plan for this? How were you going to know if something happened to the other?"

Alexis says nothing.

"You'd just check the obituaries sporadically, hoping for the best?" I ask, eyebrows up.

Alexis gives me a look. "Mon fille, we are not that old." His faces pulls, and he corrects himself. "I thought."

"I am..." I grab Alexis's eye and say this sincerely and mean it truly. "So sorry for your loss."

He flashes me another weak smile.

"How did you spend time together?" I ask.

Tennyson sighs. "Dad takes a lot of trips."

I look between Tenny and Alexis. "Like, how many?"

Tennyson shrugs. "Two a month? Maybe three?"

I look at Alexis for confirmation. "Were any of them real?"

"Most, actually." He nods. "Sometimes I would meet him places, sometimes he'd come here, but really, all we would plan for is one week together once a year."

I stare at him, feel my heart break for some reason, feel my whole body slump with the news—there's something specifically crushing about that revelation, not for me or for us, but for them…

One week a year when they allowed themselves to be themselves, in love and free?

"Where?" I ask, but I wonder if I know the answer already. I wonder if we all do.

"Your father's lake house in—"

"—Center Harbor," I cut in.

He looks from me to Tennyson, brows knitted together. "How did you—?"

"Your lake house, actually," Tennyson says, face a bit strained. "He left it to you."

Alexis's head pulls back. He looks surprised. "Quoi?"

"That's how we found you," I tell him. "You were in the will."

He sits there quietly, wrestling with thoughts I can't even comprehend.

And then a thought pops into my mind, and I wonder if Alexis might know the answer. "What is at 42 Adams Shore Drive, do you know?"

Alexis's brown bends in confusion. "It was an empty plot."

I sigh, accidentally. I don't like sighing out loud. It gives away too much.

"But William always talked about buying it maybe, one day," he offers. "When we would imagine a different version of how life could be."

"He bought it," I tell him.

"Why?" His confusion deepens, and I mirror it.

"I don't know."

We keep asking him a billion questions, wading further into the tallgrass marshes that we can't see over the top of and that maybe we're all sinking in; that's how our father feels now. And I don't know how long we stay with Alexis for—for hours, for sure, and I don't know if anything we're asking makes anything better or worse, but once the sun starts to go down, Tennyson says we need to leave to make it halfway home before it's too late.

"Will you tell your mother?" Alexis asks as we're walking out toward our car. His brow is low, but his face doesn't look distraught.

Tennyson's face strains, and Alexis keeps going. "This information is yours now. I'm not ashamed of who I am—I will not ask you to do one thing or the other. I'd just like be prepared if—"

"We don't—" Tennyson shakes his head. "I don't—"

My brother is completely rattled at the thought, so I jump in. "We're not sure yet," I say, firmly.

Alexis nods as though he gets it.

"Who does know?" I ask out of genuine curiosity.

"Maya, my—"

"—daughter." I nod.

"She knows. She knew your father quite well, actually. She was very fond of him, and he her." He gives us a sad smile.

"We figured," I say, and Alexis looks confused.

"He was paying her rent," Tennyson tells him.

"Ah." Alexis nods again, understanding. "When she fell on hard times, yes, and she didn't tell me because I am her father and children hide things from their parents..." His eyes look faraway and tender, like he's recalling something and has forgotten we're right here—then he remembers, flashing us a quick smile.

"He didn't tell me he was doing that—how did you—?"

"We found the papers." Tennyson says.

He sniffs, amused flicking his eyes between us. "You are...thorough."

"Does Violet know?"

He nods once. "I know she knows of me, but we've not met."

That feels strange to me. "Why not?"

Alexis shrugs. "Your father desperately tried not to complicate things—"

And then I get the giggles. And I shouldn't, and I'm probably coming off so rude—but, really?

Tennyson tries to suppress a laugh himself; he does so by whacking me in the arm.

I shake my head, apologize without words as I put my smile away.

Alexis does a terrible job at concealing the small smile that appears on his own lips. "I said he tried, not that he succeeded."

Then his face, I don't know, it does something funny—his head tilts, almost as though he's fond of me, but adults are never fond of me.

"He was very proud of you," he tells me. He's trying to be kind, but I don't need platitudes of kindness.

I restrain the sigh that's trying to escape me, and instead, replace it with the most patient smile I can muster. "I know you love him, and you just lost him, so I'm trying to be respectful, but you don't know what you're talking about."

"No, I do," he says, very sure. "He was very proud but afraid of you."

I pull a face. "Why afraid?"

Alexis gives me an amused, almost paternal look. "You spot lies for a living, and he was living a big one. At least much of the time."

And then this horrible question bubbles up inside of me, one that's haunted me for years and years, and I've never asked it out loud, but I wonder inside all the time, and I don't like that I do—I think it's weak of me—but wounds are persistent with the pain they bring us until they're healed, and this wound isn't.

"Do you know why he let Mom send me away?" I ask quietly.

Alexis goes quiet, pausing on the bottom of his front steps as he thinks.

"I think he was afraid you were like him—like us. Affairs are a painful business, even if you love the—"

"She wasn't cheating with Maryanne's boyfriend," Tennyson says quickly, protectively. "He was raping her." . . . Perhaps oversharingly.

At that, I hear a quick inhale of breath—shock. Discomfort, maybe? People don't like the R word. "Your father didn't kn—"

Tennyson shakes his head. "None of us knew."

Alexis goes quiet again and thinks—truly thinks, actually—searching for an answer, almost like he's trying to channel our dad. It's the most conscious form of parenting I've ever seen pointed in my general direction.

"I always felt he allowed you to be sent away because he wanted more for you than what was on offer for you here," he says eventually, but I glance away because that feels like a cop-out. "He thought you were cheating, remember," he continues, as though I could forget. "I think that was a constant reminder for him of our own pain that he didn't want to see."

I go to speak and Alexis cuts me off.

"He struggled with this. We had many discussions over it. But you thrived in England, no? You became—" He gestures to me. "Had you stayed, you would not have been—and then, the older you grew and the more you actualized into this force you are now, you became a different kind of threat."

I feel my brows bend as I blink a couple of times. A threat?

"Before, you were a mirror where he saw something painful in and of himself, and then eventually, you became someone who could see him in a way he did not want to be seen."

I purse my lips. "That is a lot of no-win scenarios for me, isn't it?"

"For you both," he says.

I shrug, trying to look indifferent about one of my deepest agonies. "If you say so."

"I recognize your pain," Alexis says, putting his hand on my shoulder kindly, and I flick through the pages in my mind's memory, trying to remember when either of my parents have ever done this to me. "And I do not pretend to understand it, and you are entitled to it, Georgia." He says my name to make sure I'm listening, but I already am, because truthfully he's quite compelling. "But for whatever it is worth to you, and I hope it's worth something—I know he wanted more for you. He just didn't know how to give it or be it."

I don't know how to respond to that, so I resort to my go-to: mildly petulant.

"Lucky me," I say, and Tennyson—I don't know why—apologizes on my behalf, says I can be like that sometimes. Alexis dismisses it, saying he has a daughter too.

As he walks us back to the car, Alexis gives me—both of us, I guess, but perhaps arguably me specifically—his number and his email.

"Call, anytime," he says, looking at Tennyson. "If you have more questions." Then he looks at me. "Or you just want to talk—I would be very happy to hear from you. And Oliver." He pauses, briefly. "Is he okay?"

I purse my lips. "I'm not sure."

He nods, looking solemn again. "If I can be of any help..."

Neither Tennyson nor I know what to say, so I just nod and get into the car. Tennyson shakes his hand because he's good like that.

And then we drive away.

56

YOU LIKE HIM," TENNYSON SAYS around twenty-five seconds after we drive away.

"I mean—" I shrug. "He was nicer to me than either of our parents ever were, so—"

His face pulls uncomfortably. "Don't say that."

"Am I lying?"

"Maybe to yourself. Didn't you hear him? Dad was proud of you."

"And what the fuck does that matter if he could never tell me or show me himself?" I scowl over at him. "That his proudness of me had to be spelled out for me by some random French guy in Louisiana? Like, what does that say about his proudness?"

Which I guess Tennyson considers to be a fair point, because he mashes his lips together and drops it.

It's quiet for a couple of minutes, but it's not bad. I don't mind quiet with Tennyson. I never thought I'd say that, but it's true.

Eventually, he breathes out his nose and grips the wheel tighter—he could be frustrated, could be grasping for control—at this point, there are so many possible and understandable emotions swirling around.

"I wish I didn't like him,"Tennysons says, his brow straining. "I wish he was an asshole, so it was easier."

I glance at him out of the corner of my eye. "So what was easier?"

"Telling Mom…"

I look at him like he's mad. "We can't tell Mom."

Now he looks at me like *I'm* crazy. "What?"

"Of course, we can't tell her." I overenunciate my words.

"Are you joking?" He stares at me, incredulous, and I stare right back.

"Are you?"

"We have to!" Tennyson says loudly.

"Tens, tell her that her whole life is a lie? Are you crazy?"

"Yes!" he yells (probably louder than he means to) as he whacks the steering wheel, frustrated. "Fuck! Maybe I am, I don't know—" He starts shaking his head a lot. "I don't know anything. At all."

I watch him for a second, feeling sad and nervous about how sad and nervous he looks. "Tennyson…"

"No, Georgia, listen." He shakes his head more now, frantic, almost. I think his eyes are glassy. "I don't know who I am if I'm not his son—"

"Tenny, you're still his son—"

"Am I?"

"Of course," I tell him emphatically.

He shakes his head again, shrugging this time too. "But it's all a lie."

"No it's not—"

"Yes it is!" he yells. "You just said it is! That my whole life is a lie…"

"I said *Mom's* whole life is a lie."

Tennyson swats his hand through the air. "It's the same thing."

"No it's not. Listen to me—" I grab him by the arm and shake him a little so he hears me. "Our father's gayness does not impede his capacity to be a father, but it does impede his capacity to be a husband to his heterosexual, monogamous wife."

I lift my eyebrows, hope that it makes him hear my point better before I keep going.

"Everything he's ever said to you about being your dad and loving you still holds true, regardless of his sexuality, okay? He can love you and believe in you and champion you as your father, who happens to be a gay man, but that's not the case for Mom." I pause again to make sure he's following me, and I think he is. "Dad can't be the devoted, doting, adoring, faithful husband Mom's always painted him to be *and* be a secretly gay man with an active lover on the side. And I understand why you feel betrayed by this revelation, Tens, I do—but it's not the same, and we can't tell her."

"She deserves to know the truth," he says firmly to the road in front of us.

"Why?" I shake my head a million times. "For what? To what end?"

Tennyson glances over at me, face contorted in confusion. "You love the truth! Your entire existence is wrapped around the pursuit of truth. The truth at all costs, isn't that what you say?"

"It. Would. Crush her," I say slowly and clearly. "And I don't mean like, an anvil falling on her—I mean it would obliterate her. Evisceration. She'd lose everything. And she already feels like she has!" My voice breaks and my eyes fill with tears, and I don't even really know why. I guess all of it's sad. I wipe my eyes because I don't want those things in there. "The life she had would become vapor."

Tennyson glances from me to the road then back to me. "So what are you saying? We just—lie to her?"

"Yeah," I say, quietly, more and more sure that I'm right.

He glances at me. "Forever?"

"Yes."

He swallows. "I don't know that I can do that."

"But you can strip her of everything she's ever known and the identity she's built around it all?"

My brother gives me an unimpressed look before his mind starts ticking over things. "We'd have to make sure Oliver doesn't say anything..."

I nod in agreement.

"To anyone..." Tennyson gives me a look, eyebrows up.

"Yeah." I shrug. "Who's he going to tell?"

SAM:
how was today?

GEORGIA:
Informative.

SAM:
Good informative?

GEORGIA:
I really don't know.

SAM:
can't wait to see you.

GEORGIA:
same XX

57

TENNYSON BOOKED US TWO ROOMS at the Auburn Marriott Opelika Resort and Spa in Opelika, and we arrived just a little before midnight. We slept there and did the rest of the drive late the next morning.

It's maybe just after 3:00 p.m. on Monday when we pull into our family home, and my stomach lurches at the sight I see.

Sitting on the front porch swing are Oliver and Maryanne, each with a glass of rosé in their hands, and my stomach drops. Not just because Oliver's so casually drinking, and doing it publicly, but actually that he's with Maryanne at all.

Tennyson clocks it too, takes a deep breath, and sort of mutters under his breath. He's better at being composed; he has more patience than I do, always has—but then, none of these people have been the ones dealing with my brother's alcoholism.

I barrel out of the car and stare over at them. "What are you doing?"

Oliver rolls his eyes. "Like you care."

I'm confused. "What?"

Oliver turns his head in the other direction. "Go away, Georgia."

I walk up the porch steps toward them, this horrible pit in my stomach. "Why are you doing this?"

He turns back toward me just to give me a glare. "Because my best friend in the whole world has been boning the guy I'm into since the fucking second she was able to."

"Oliver." Tennyson sighs, and at that, at someone defending me, Maryanne jumps in.

She lifts that perfectly manicured brow. "Did he lie?"

Tennyson shakes his head at her. "Don't you start—"

"Or what?" Maryanne shrugs spitefully. "You're not going to let me come on your next little adventure?"

Now Tennyson rolls his eyes, and I home in on Oliver. "Can we talk?"

"No," he says, taking a sip of his rosé. He doesn't even like rosé. I mean, I personally do as long as it's not sweet, but he's always said it tastes like something poor people drink when they're trying to sound fancy.

"Oliver, please." I search for his eyes. "I just want to make sure you're—"

And then he jumps to his feet, a big scowl all over his face. "I don't need a savior, okay? I get it." He looks me up and down. "You were a fuck-up and now you're super therapy put-together girl. I don't want your fucking help."

As quietly and as gently as I can, I say to him, "But you need help."

"Not from you."

"That's fine, I don't care, as long as you're—"

"As long as I'm okay?" he cuts me off. "That's what you care about?"

I nod once decisively. "Yes."

He sniffs. "Really?"

"Yes," I say again.

"So where was that care when you were fucking the guy I brought here?" he fires.

I sigh at all of it. "Tragically present, Oliver, and haunting my mind, if you must know."

Oliver crosses his arms over his chest, and that sort of signal-fires for me what's coming next, because arm-crossing? That's a physical barrier he's placing between us. A shield, almost, and you don't need a shield unless you're going to battle.

So I'm not surprised when the next thing out of Oliver's mouth is: "You know you're a flash in the pan for him, right? He doesn't do commitment."

I say nothing back, just trade looks with Tennyson.

That annoys Oliver, who's absolutely looking for a fight.

"He's going to get tired of you," Oliver tells me, and even though they are the words of a drunk and rambling alcoholic, they are also the words of someone I love more than almost anyone, so I swallow them and keep doing my best not to react.

"You're right," Maryanne says to Oliver before glancing over at me. "He knows what you're good for. Everyone in this town does."

Tennyson moves toward her, a dark look on his face. "And whose fucking fault is that, Maryanne?" She rolls her eyes, and then Tennyson plucks Oliver's wine from his hands. "And why are you letting him drink?"

Maryanne groans, exasperated. "It's a glass of wine!"

I stare at her in disbelief. "He's an alcoholic!"

"And you're a whore!" She gives me a pleasant smile.

I don't even react, but Tennyson shakes his head. "It's getting real old, Mer."

"Just leave it," I tell him.

"No. She can't have done what she did to you for so long and then—"

"Oh my God!" Maryanne groans. "How many times can I say s—"

"Hey," Sam suddenly says, appearing at my side, hand on my waist. I hadn't even noticed him coming out of the house.

I smile at him, relieved immediately by his presence, but only for a second, because Oliver grabs him by the arm.

"Sam!" He sighs—and you know what, he has every right to sigh; I'm not saying he shouldn't be sighing, but I am saying it was a strategic emotional pivot.

Sam does his best to look attentive and caring, not impatient and frustrated, which is what I can tell he really is by the way his nose flares the tiniest bit before he turns to Oliver.

"It's too much. All their fighting is—" Oliver shakes his head a lot. "Can we go for a walk or something? I need to clear my head."

Sam looks back at me, silently asking if I want him to stay—he wants to stay—but I flash him a quick smile, barely nod but enough for him to know that's what I want him to do.

"Yeah, man," Sam says on an inhale. His reluctance is palpable. To me, at least. "Of course. Let's go."

Sam forces a smile for Oliver, then looks at me, his hand still on my waist.

"Are you good?"

"Yeah." I smile, but it's evidently unconvincing because he doesn't believe me.

"Yeah?"

I change my face, try to lighten it up. "Yeah, go."

"Okay." He brushes his mouth over my cheeks, and in my periphery, I see Oliver scowl. "I'll see you in a bit."

I walk inside, sticking close to Tennyson with a foreboding feeling that Maryanne's hot on our heels. She won't like the Tennyson-and-me development; she'll take his bonding with me as a loss of control, and a loss of control to Maryanne is a threat.

We walk into the kitchen, and—

"You're back!" our mother says as she looks up from whatever vegetable she's chopping on the bench. I don't know why that makes me jump with fright, but it does.

Her eyes round with nervous curiosity. "Did you—?"

I shake my head. "We still have some things to figure out."

"Wait," Maryanne says, going and standing with Mom. "So you went all the way to Louisiana and you didn't even figure it out?" She pulls a face. "What kind of detective are you?"

"...Not a detective." I shrug, which makes Tennyson laugh and

Maryanne roll her eyes, but not before she flashes the tiniest hints of AU9 and AU10—she's angry.

Mom puts down the knife and walks around the kitchen island toward Tennyson and I. "You didn't learn anything?"

"No, we did." I nod. "I just want to make sure what we think we found out is the truth before we report back."

"Oh," she says, and I can see her thinking about it—I can see her decide that makes sense. Then she looks back at me, flicking my way either an unimpressed or a maternal look (in my experience, they're often interchangeable) before she says, "I heard about you and the alcoholic…"

"He's not an alco—he's an—never mind." I shake my head again to correct her. "Yeah."

"So it's true?" she asks, eyebrows up. "You've stolen your brother's boyfriend?"

"No," I say at the same time as Maryanne says, "Kind of."

"Maryanne," Tennyson groans.

She shrugs innocently. "I said *kind of*!"

"So you're *kind of* lying," Tennyson fires back.

"Please!" Our mother covers her eyes. "Please don't fight—I can't take it right now."

The three of us go silent, and then I let out a measured breath as I turn to my mother.

"Sam and I are together now, if that's what you're asking."

She stares at me, and it's almost blank. I'm not sure whether she heard me or if she's just having trouble digesting what she heard—then she blinks twice and turns to my brother.

"Tennyson, sweetheart, I missed you." She reaches for him, and Tenny puts his arm around her with a sweet sort of ease I've never felt with either of our parents. "You look tired. How was the drive home?"

Tenny moves her into a different room, so then it's just me and Maryanne in the kitchen. She stares over at me, eyes pinched. "You're hiding something."

Which is astute of her, though not all that surprising. Narcissists are clever. They have to be in order to maintain everything they do. I can't tell what it was I did just now to give away that I am, in fact, hiding something, but I decide my best foot forward is to be nonchalant.

"Uh, yeah." I give her a baffled look "I literally just said we found some stuff, and I want to make sure it's true before we pass it on..."

She crosses her arms. "I'll figure it out."

"Okay?" I shrug as I stay the indifferent path and give her a puzzled look. "Or you could just wait and then I'll tell you, but whatever you want..."

At that, her eyes pinch and she slithers away.

Sam and Oliver are on their walk for hours—no surprises there—Oliver would try to keep Sam away from me for as long as possible under these circumstances. All these different people trying to exert control in all these different ways. It's enough to drive a person to drink. Which I do.

I climb into bed, have some wine, and watch *Arrested Development* on my laptop until Sam gets back from the world's longest walk.

When he walks into my room, he sighs when he sees me. But it's the best kind of sigh, like a "deep relief" sigh. Like, a "he can breathe again" sigh. He pushes my Macbook off my lap before he throws himself down on top of me.

"Fuck, I missed you." He grins before he kisses me. "I want to hear everything. What happened? How'd you go with Alexis?"

I update him on all of it, all the things we learned and what those things imply and mean, and sort of where we landed.

I tell him that apparently my dad was proud of me, and Sam replies, "Of course he was."

I roll my eyes at him. "You love me blindly."

"No." He shakes his head. "I love you very much with my eyes open. You're an absolute fucking know it all, but you're brilliant." He shrugs. "No way he wasn't proud."

I still don't know how to even process the idea of my father being proud of me, so I change the subject. "How was your walk?"

Sam sniffs a laugh and rubs his tired eyes. "Long."

"I think that was the point."

Penny chuckles. "I think so too. Hey, how was he when you got back?"

I open my mouth to say something, then close it and smile instead.

Sam gives me an uneasy look. "What?"

"Nothing."

"Say it."

"No. You'll just get cross, because you're irrational when it comes to me—"

And at that I'm proven right—without even knowing what was said, he straightens up defensively, jaw going tight. "What the fuck did he say?"

I sigh. "Sam—"

But he's not playing. "Georgia. Now."

I roll my eyes, like I think it was a silly thing, not a hurtful thing, that my brother said to me. "Just that you'll get tired of me, because everyone does. And then Maryanne tacked on a little slutty comment too, so—"

"Righteo," he says, pushing off my bed and standing to his feet. "Where is he?"

"Sam." I jump up after him. "No."

"Yes," he says firmly.

"No—" I shake my head, then pause. "Wait, did you say 'righteo'?"

"Yeah?" He shrugs. "So?"

"Just, um—" I squint at him, amused. "Is that an expression in Australia?"

He squints back. "Yes."

"Is it the common tongue amongst the other six-four men over there?"

He puts his arms around my waist, then mimics my tone as he replies, "Yes, actually."

We stare at each other, and his reactionary frustration has dissipated now, I can tell.

"Please don't say anything," I tell him. "It won't help."

"Gige." He sighs. "I'm getting fucking tired of their shit."

"Me too." I nod. "But Oliver couldn't handle you being cross at him right now."

"I don't care—"

"Yes, you do," I tell him, and his head falls back as he breathes out a tired laugh.

"Yes I do, fuck."

He looks back down at me, touches my face. "They can't talk to you like that."

"It doesn't matter," I tell him.

"It does matter," he says back.

"Please—" I give him a look. "I'm asking you, please just leave it."

Penny's lips sort of pucker—AU23—he's angry, but then he nods anyway. "All right."

58

WELL, IF IT ISN'T ALL my favorites." Vi beams at Tennyson, Oliver, and me as we stand on her porch.

She throws her arms around us collectively, forcing me and Oliver to touch in a way we haven't for a few days now. It's weird, and how weird it is makes me sad.

She lets go of us all, and the boys walk inside.

She puts her hands on my cheeks and searches my face. "You okay?"

I try to give her a smile. "Later," I tell her, and she nods, a bit intrigued as she walks in after me to her living room.

"So, how'd your little trip go?" She flashes us a smile, the edges of which are nervous.

"Interesting," Tennyson says, eyeballing her.

Vi's smile pulls tighter. "How so?" She throws herself down on her big Albany Park pit couch.

"Well." I sit down across from her. "We met dad's tri-decade lover, so that was a fun surprise for us all."

Her eyes widen and she inhales, sharp and quick—shock. "Oh my God," she says quietly, looking between us all as she sits up straight now.

"Did you know?" Tennyson asks.

Vi considers the question. "I knew he existed."

Oliver shakes his head, can't quite believe it. "You knew Dad was gay?"

She folds her hands in her lap, trying to look composed. She swallows. "I knew he had liked men in the past."

Oliver glares at her now. "And you never said anything?"

"Baby." She sighs. "It wasn't mine to say..." She gives him—all of us, I suppose—an apologetic smile. "Are y'all okay though?" She glances from Tennyson to me, then reaches for Oliver. "You, darlin', specifically?"

Oliver shrugs. "I've been better."

She nods empathically. "I'll bet."

"But that might be in large part because while we were there, I found out that Georgia and Sam have been having sex behind my back." Oliver gives our aunt a curt smile, and she glances at me, gives me an uneasy look.

"Where is Sam?" she asks the group in general, neither Oliver nor me specifically.

"At a coffee shop," I say. "Around the corner."

"They're inseparable now," Oliver tells her in a voice I don't like, and I roll my eyes.

"That feels categorically untrue seeing as we are actively...separated."

"Oh, do you want a medal for that?" Oliver blinks.

"No," I fire back. "Just a break from your yapping would be—"

"Gige." Tennyson cuts me off.

Vi sits back, looking between us all.

"So what are you going to do?" she asks.

I glance between my brothers before I carefully say, "I don't think we should do anything."

"What?" Oliver stares at me in disbelief. "So we just let him get away with it?"

I shake my head at him. "Away with what, Oliver?"

"That he was cheating on Mom all this time! That he was a fucking fake, living a double life, that him and his high horse are full of shit—" He gestures at me. "After everything he did to us...you're going to let him get away with it?"

I swallow, then nod. "Yeah."

Oliver scoffs, shaking his head in true disbelief. "No way."

"You know…" I look for Oliver's eyes, which he very reluctantly allows me to have in this moment. "I have thought so much about why he was the way he was with you, trying to make sense of it—I think he was jealous of you."

Oliver doesn't buy it, that much is all over his face, but I persist.

"You have been unapologetically yourself since the moment you jazzed-hands out of our mother's womb." Oliver rolls his eyes at that, but I can tell he semi-liked it. "You've always been who you are, even if it cost you everything, and it has, many times. Can you imagine feeling something, loving someone for decades, but not feeling able to do so out loud? And then you have this kid, and in him you see the freedom you've always wanted for yourself but weren't brave enough to pursue. A better man would have encouraged you, cheered for you down the path they wished they were walking, but"—I turn to Vi specifically—"no offense, he wasn't a better man. He was a burdened one. Burdened with loving someone he could never fully have, and forced to watch his son be brave in ways he couldn't be." I offer Oliver a small shrug. "That could drive a person to cruelty."

Vi frowns defensively at that part. "*Cruelty* is a bit of a harsh word."

"But an appropriate one," I tell her, unflinching.

"Right." Oliver nods. "So, why aren't we saying anything?"

"Because." I sigh, half because I've already had to have this conversation with Tennyson, and half because I need him to not just hear what I'm saying, but to properly understand it. "As jarring and radical as this news is for us, for all the horrifying, clarifying context it provides for us… for Mom, it just…takes."

Oliver shakes his head again, frustrated. "Takes what?"

"Everything," Tennyson says, eyes all heavy.

Oliver looks between Tennyson and me. "So we're just going to let her think she was happily married for thirty years when she wasn't?"

"What would telling her do?" I shrug. "Other than tear her whole life apart?"

Oliver stares over at me, brows low, but hearing me.

"It's already torn," I tell him. "We don't need to turn it into tatters."

Oliver breathes loudly out his nose before he reluctantly asks, "What will we say?"

"That Dad and Alexis were old friends from college. We have to acknowledge his existence," I tell them all. "To diminish him would discredit our lie entirely. Dad left him a multi-million dollar property. There's an unavoidable bond between the two men that can't be entirely ignored, even just for the sake of plausibility."

"So what's the story then?" Tennyson asks as Vi puts an arm around Oliver.

"I don't know. Maybe something about how Dad owed Alexis something—maybe Alexis saved his life? Something that would make Dad feel indebted to him. Leaving someone a property like that is a big deal, so the bond has to be equitable to that."

"Yeah." Tennyson nods along, and I think we'll make a decent liar out of him yet. "Maybe a story about how Dad nearly drowned on a lake or something? If he saved him—then Dad said one day he'd buy him a lake house?"

"Wouldn't Mom know if Dad nearly drowned in college? They were together," Oliver points out.

"Maybe that's the secret part?" I offer. "Dad was proud. Maybe he didn't want Mom to see him as weak, or something else down that vein of toxic masculinity."

I look at Tennyson, eyebrows up, asking without asking, and he sort of shrugs. "Yeah—I don't know, I think that checks out."

I look between my two brothers and Vi. "We have to swear it though, okay? Never to say anything..."

"Not to anyone," Tennyson chimes in, "because it could find its way back to Mom."

Vi zips her mouth shut. "My lips are sealed."

"Not even to Maryanne," Tennyson says to Oliver, who rolls his eyes.

Vi throws me a confused look—she's clearly not been by the house over the last few days. In normal life, in no fathomable world would Oliver voluntarily share anything with Maryanne, but this isn't normal life anymore.

There's nothing I can say to give her context, so our eyes just hold as Oliver gives Tennyson a stubborn little shrug.

"He's her dad too," he says.

Then Tennyson's tone changes, and while I would have—until this moment—said his face was serious this entire time, the way it goes now tells me that that wasn't entirely the case.

"Not even Maryanne," Tennyson says again, louder and clearer.

"Fine," Oliver sighs. "Whatever."

59

MOM PLANS THIS BIG DINNER for all of us—just trying to keep busy, I think.

As soon as we were back from Vi's, Oliver was by Maryanne's side, right up until dinnertime, like they were glued.

Interestingly, Jase hasn't been around much lately—not at dinner again tonight. Maryanne says he's working, but I don't think he has a real job, so my best guess is that he stopped feeling like the best thing Maryanne had to wield. Before, when I was romantically unattached, my sister saw that as a weakness, but now that I'm with someone (and not just your average, run-of-the-mill, Okatie redneck man like hers—I'm with the best man, and literally everyone, even she, knows it), she needs a different weapon.

Dinner, for the most part, is largely uneventful. Clay cooks us all his famous fourteen-hour pulled pork, and I'm surprised that a little part of me is genuinely happy to see Savannah when she walks in the front door.

Sam and I sit next to each other, but we're not overly physical or laser-focused on each other—we're consciously respectful of how this is an uncomfortable situation for Oliver. But he's following Maryanne's lead now, and they're on the hunt. They sit across from us and glare at me (me, not Sam) the whole time, still drinking rosé as they whisper to one another and laugh. They roll their eyes at everything I say and shoot down my words like they're clay pigeons I loaded up the sky with just for them. And I can pretend like it's fine and that it doesn't hurt my feelings to see, but for what? It does. I hate it; it makes me angry. Angry at her, but also at him, because I know he knows what he's doing, even if he's not totally himself in this moment.

Sam squeezes my knee under the table, and I get lost in my thoughts, wondering how I would have even survived these last few weeks without him.

I suppose, if he wasn't here, I wouldn't have fallen in love with him, so then this particular mess I've found myself in presently wouldn't have existed, but there would be other messes, and I wouldn't like to be in them without him anyway—that's what I'm thinking about as Oliver drains his wine, then reaches across the table to pour himself another.

"Oliver, sweetheart." My mother forces a smile, but her forehead is impossibly tense. "Don't you think you've maybe had enough?"

"Nope," Oliver says, continuing his pour all the same.

"But you've worked so hard on your sobriety," she tells him, and she's trying to be nice, I think—but Oliver flicks his eyes toward her and they're pinched.

"How would you know?" he says, tone sharp, and her head pulls back, affronted.

Honestly, objectively, it's a fair question. Our mother has been overtly absent throughout Oliver's wrestle with alcoholism, and I think overarchingly in the scheme of life, he has every right to be angry at her about it, but now's not the time. And were he sober, he'd know that.

"Ol—" Tennyson shoots him a look across the table.

"How would she know?" Oliver says again as he shrugs with faux-indifference, but he's not actually indifferent at all, just completely heart-broken on mute.

Oliver glances at Maryanne for backup, expecting it, but he's wrong. He doesn't realize that the length of Maryanne's camaraderie with him is only as long as it takes her to get to me. She doesn't meet his gaze; instead she reaches over toward Mom and touches her hand.

"Pay no mind to him, Mom, he's under a lot of stress right now."

"You have been different since you got back." Mom nods at Oliver. "What happened while you were away?"

"Oh." Oliver straightens up. "You mean besides Georgia showing her true colors?"

Maryanne barely fights off a smile, and I roll my eyes. Sam tenses up next to me, says nothing, which is good, but Tennyson doesn't like it.

"Oliver..." And there's something about how Tennyson says his name—it's too loaded or something, and Mom hears that, whether she realizes or not.

"What?" She looks between her two sons. "What happened?"

Tennyson says, trying to cover his tracks now, "Nothing happened, Mom." But he accidentally rounds his sentence out with an AU28—self-hushing 101.

Mom looks at Tennyson suspiciously. "You're not saying something."

And she's right, it's true. He's not saying something and it's painfully obvious. His self-hushing aside, his swallowing has increased in the last minute, and he's even scratching his nose...it's nonverbal cues of deception galore with Tenny right now, and she's right to be picking up on them. I'm sort of proud that she is. Nevertheless, once someone's picked up on cues, it only serves to hurt the credibility of the story we're trying to peddle if we dismiss them, so on the spot, I decide to go a different route.

"Okay, fine," I sigh as though I'm annoyed.

Tennyson and Oliver stare over at me with wide, panicked eyes. Even Sam squeezes my knee under the table. It's like they've forgotten everything I've been trying to teach them about half-truths.

"Mom." I look at her. "We didn't want to say anything because we didn't want you to get upset because we know how it might look—but there was an apartment in Louisiana that belonged to a girl that Dad was paying for."

Mom blinks a lot. "What?"

"What!" says Maryanne louder, like, borderline on a yell.

"I know." I look between Mom and Maryanne. "We were worried at first too, but—" I sigh again, and throw a glance to Tennyson, hoping he'll catch on, but he doesn't.

"Mom," I start again, my voice measured. "Something happened in college to Dad."

Mom puts her cutlery down. Her face looks a bit white, actually. I feel bad making her feel sick how I think I must be doing in this moment, but I remind myself it's kinder than the truth.

"What are you talking about?" she asks.

I breathe out my nose, try to sound reluctant. "It's kind of a long story..."

"He drowned," Tennyson says. Thank God.

"What?" Mom says, looking between us all.

"Nearly," Sam jumps in, clarifying.

I nod. "He nearly did."

Mom shakes her head. "Why didn't he t—"

"I mean," Tennyson starts. "You know Dad? He'd never want you to worry..."

"Or," I add, "an alternate headline: you know Dad, he'd never want anyone to think he was weak." Tennyson rolls his eyes at that, but I think he does it for plausibility. And it works. Us disagreeing over why none of us knew our father apparently drowned in college is very believable. Tennyson believing the best in him, me believing the worst? Very believable.

Oliver's real quiet though; that's the part that I feel like is maybe our weak link here.

"What do you mean?" Mom keeps looking between us all. "What happened?"

"Apparently"—I just dive on in because I trust me the most—"Dad and some friends were at some lake near the campus, and he had been drinking, and then he slipped off a pier and hit his head?" I say that intentionally with an upward inflection, infer that I don't really know myself—and that whatever I do know, I know barely. My uncertainty, in this case, should help sell it.

"And then this guy—" Tennyson jumps in.

"Alexis," Oliver says, finally! And I fight all my natural instincts not to throw him a grateful look.

"Alexis"—Tennyson nods at Oliver—"saved him. I think Dad's always felt indebted to him or something."

"The lake house—it was a thank-you," I tell her, to round it off.

Mom stares at all of us for a few seconds, then glances at Violet. "Did you know about this?"

Vi shakes her head. It's convincing. I'm impressed.

"So, wait," Maryanne interjects. "Who's this girl with an apartment Dad's paying for?"

"Alexis's daughter," Sam says.

Maryanne's eyes flick from Sam to Tennyson. "Why is Dad paying for this Alexis's daughter's rent?"

"I guess they kept in touch over the years?" I say again, intentionally sounding unsure. "And then they fell on hard times during the pandemic or something?"

"Dad didn't want her to lose her home," Tennyson says with more authority—believable! My heart swells with pride—and Mom buys it, I think.

She sniffs as Maryanne clutches her arm. "That sounds like Daddy."

Tennyson and I catch eyes—which we shouldn't have, since it was risky to do, but it's a natural relief response—and it's fine because no one caught it.

"It does, doesn't it?" Mom says, but her eyes look faraway. "Can I—would it be rude if I went to lie down for a while?" she says, asking the room for permission.

There's a choral response from everyone, telling her "of course" and "absolutely" and "whatever she needs," and then Maryanne escorts her upstairs.

I wonder if she's okay? It's a lot, everything—and she's probably not actually really okay. But there's something in her eyes…

Once they're out of earshot, Tennyson turns to look at me.

"You are terrifying," he whispers as Sam gives me a proud little nod.

"I'm deeply impressed with all of you," I tell the boys and Vi.

"Well." Oli rolls his eyes. "Lucky us."

I don't breathe out the sigh I'd organically like to, and instead decide to keep trying. "No, I know that would have been hard for you—"

"Yeah, well." Oliver shrugs. "This isn't about you and me, it's about Mom, so—"

"What's about Mom?" Maryanne asks, walking back into the room.

"Nothing," Tennyson says a sliver too quickly.

Maryanne turns to Oliver. She doesn't quite bat her eyes, but she honestly might as well as she says in her most syrupy voice, "Oli, what's he talking about?"

Oliver looks sort of trapped, and it makes my heart sink. He thinks he needs Maryanne because we're fighting. I don't know how to tell him we're not fighting, and yeah, he's been a fucking prick to me the last few days, but I guess, same? And no matter how much we're fighting, it's not worth selling your soul to Maryanne—but I think he thinks he's backed himself into a corner and Maryanne's his only way out.

He flashes her a quick half smile. "I'll tell you later," he says, but I don't think he means it. If he would tell her, we're fucked, but even in his current state of having fallen off the wagon, I don't think he would. Tennyson can't read him how I can though, so he takes Oliver's response at face value, interprets it as a threat to a burden he's already carrying with great reluctance and frustration, and he reacts accordingly.

"The fuck you will!" he says, coming out of the gate way too loud and hot with an unnecessary tonal escalation.

I see Sam's face shift, trying to predict the outcome here.

"Are you gonna stop me?" Oliver says, straightening up, and under any other circumstance, I'd be impressed, but for now, that little burst of confidence is mostly just inconvenient.

"Maybe," Tennyson fires back, and Savannah touches his arm, trying to curtail what seems to be happening. It's worth noting that this whole time, the left corner of Maryanne's mouth is the slightest bit turned up in a smile. She's not overtly smiling; no one else would notice it (except maybe Sam nowadays), but it's there and its message is clear: this pleases her.

Oliver tilts his head. "Do not press me."

Sam takes a measured breath, and I think he's about to step in when Tennyson throws his hands in the air. "Or what?"

"Or!" Oliver says loudly, making sure everyone is listening. "I'm going to tell Savannah what happened while we were away."

And Savannah's face shifts immediately, mostly confused but a bit laced with a nervousness that I hate seeing her wear.

"What happened while you were away?" she says softly to Tennyson specifically, but the entire room's gone quiet now, so literally everyone hears.

"Nothing." Tenny shakes his head.

Oliver gives her a steep look. "Something."

Savannah looks from Oliver back to Tennyson, moves her hand that was still resting on his arm, still trying to keep him steady, and then she glances over at me for verification.

I roll my eyes, and I'm angry now. "Literally nothing."

"Liar!" Oliver says, pointing his finger at me before flicking it to Tennyson. "The both of them."

"Well, go on..." Maryanne says, eyes wired now, ready to feed the drama more.

Tennyson gives Oliver a daring look, and I think that maybe if he hadn't done that, Oliver wouldn't have continued. I think it's an unfortunate collision of multiple factors. One: Oliver's not his best self when he's drinking. Two: Oliver has years and years of pent-up anger toward Tennyson for what he perceived as Tens's rejection of him. Three: Oliver, in one way or another, for the majority of his life, has felt disempowered. Sam and I trigger in him a sense of powerlessness. You can't help who you fall for, and you can't make them fall back. Four: Oliver, I think, has waited his whole life to have the upper hand with Tennyson, and here, he believes he finally has it.

Oliver flashes Tens a stubborn, petulant smile. "Tennyson hooked up with some random girl while we were away."

"What?" Savannah says so, so quietly, in disbelief.

"Oliver," I groan.

"Mate, what the fuck?" Sam shakes his head at Oli, and at the same time, Tennyson's eyes are bulging. He can't believe it.

"Are you serious right now?" Tens says loudly.

"You swore!" I say to Oliver.

Savannah's face turns to mystified horror. "It's true?"

I yell, "No!" at the same time Tennyson just says her name, trying to placate her while trying not to throw me under the bus.

"What are you doing?" I look at Tennyson, shaking my head, and he shakes his back.

"You don't have to—"

I cut him off. "It doesn't matter anymore."

Oliver's got his hands on his hips now, pissed off. "What are you talking about?"

I spin on my heel to face him, my eyes all wide with exasperation. "Tennyson didn't have sex with anyone!" I yell, and all the tension in sweet Savannah's brow dissipates into relief. I motion toward Penny. "The wrapper was ours, Oliver! Sam and I had sex in the car. Tennyson was covering for us, he—"

"Ever the picture of class," Maryanne cuts in, and now it's my turn to escalate things, evidently.

I point right in her face. "You can shut your goddamn mouth, Maryanne."

It flashes over her face—absolute fury. It's just for a second, and God, I love microexpressions. If you know to look for them, they speak so loudly. She's incensed that I would speak to her like that, but offense is a difficult emotional reaction to garner external support and camaraderie around, and she knows that, so she hides it, quick smart, and then she upcycles that offense into the much more emotionally accessible hurt.

She contorts her face into an emotion that resembles pain. "God, Georgia, all I've ever wanted is to—" But it doesn't quite hit because it's hollow underneath, so Tennyson cuts her off.

"Mer, shut up."

Once you've been exposed to the tricks up the sleeves of a narcissist, they're hard to ignore.

But then comes the voice of real hurt.

"You had sex that night at the hotel?" Oliver looks from me to Sam, then back to me. "I was right there."

"Ol," Sam says, brows heavy.

I offer him the weakest shrug in the world. "You said you didn't like him."

And I don't know why I say that, honestly. It doesn't matter what he said to me—it never matters what anyone says to me, and everyone in this room knows that. It just felt like it was maybe worth throwing out there, to remind him I had inquired before. Or maybe it was just plain old guilt that had me say it.

Oliver gives me a disbelieving look. "And you didn't know that was a lie?"

"No," I say quietly. "I did."

Maryanne sniffs this smug, quiet laugh. "And yet, you did it anyway."

I don't respond to her, don't even look her way; I'm just locked on Oliver now.

"How could you do this to me?" he asks, and his voice is so sad, and that's okay.

I stare up at my brother, hope he sees the sincerity in my eyes. "I need you to understand—I did not fall for Sam of my own volition."

Maryanne sidles up next to Oliver. "Did you not fall into bed with Sam of your own volition too?"

"No, Maryanne." Sam pulls a face. "That's called sexual assault..."

He pauses, then says quieter to her, "I think you're familiar with the concept."

Her eyes go to slits, and God, he's my favorite person—but now's not the time, so I stay focused on my brother. "I'd never do anything to intentionally or consciously hurt you—"

Oliver shakes his head. "Bullshit…"

"Oliver." I sigh. I shouldn't have sighed, probably. I didn't mean to sigh. But it slipped out because it's the truth of how I feel. "I've spent my whole life trying to protect you—"

And I don't know whether it was the sigh that did it, but my brother's face goes cloudy with defense.

"Yeah, and who the fuck asked you to?" Oli growls, and it's as though he thinks I'm throwing that in his face, he's so ready and willing to fling it on back.

"No one. No one needed to—I was glad to—"

"Well, I don't need you," he spits, and that stings me. Of all the things my brother has hurled at me over the last few days, I don't know why that one hurts me how it does. Maybe because for such a long time, he was all I really had.

"Why?" I flick an eyebrow up. "Because you've got Maryanne now?"

Maryanne rolls her eyes. "You can go ahead and keep my name out of your mouth."

"And you can go ahead and fuck yourself," I fire back.

"Oh, lovely," Maryanne cries dramatically at the same time Oliver tosses his hands in the air at the madness of me.

"And you wonder why she doesn't like you!" he says.

"Seriously?" I stare at him, my eyes a bit wild now. Oliver gives me a half-hearted shrug, as if to say "what?" except he knows exactly what. "What are you doing—she tortured us!"

"Unlike some people"—Maryanne eyeballs me—"Oliver's embraced forgiveness and has moved on."

I wave my hand toward my brother as though I'm presenting him. "Oliver's drunk."

"Yeah." Maryanne shrugs. "And whose fault is that?"

"His," I say without missing a beat. "Absolutely. And arguably possibly yours," I tack on at the end just for her.

Oliver steps toward me. "I'm not drinking because of Maryanne, Georgia. I'm drinking because my little sister, my former best friend on the planet, has been hooking up with the guy I'm into behind my back, who I brought to our dad's funeral to support me when I needed it. That's why I'm drinking."

"No, Oliver." I shake my head at him, apparently at my wit's end now. "You're drinking because you have poor impulse control and a predilection for numbing the uncomfortable."

"Shut up! Georgia—fuck!" Oliver yells louder than he's ever yelled at me, *ever*. It makes me jump a little, and if I was paying attention to Sam—and admittedly, I'm not, due to the fright of being yelled at—I would have noticed how his body went stiff, but I don't notice because Oliver's still yelling at me and releasing what might be a lifetime's worth of anger and steam. "No one gives a shit, okay? No one fucking cares that you went to Cambridge and you count blinks and you're a human lie detector—no one cares, literally not a single person. It's not a personality trait! It doesn't make you interesting or cool. Actually, it makes you annoying and unlikable and—"

"No," Sam cuts in as he steps in front of me.

"What?" Oliver says quietly, a bit like he forgot Sam was there.

"No," Sam says again. "You don't talk to her like that."

Oliver lets out a shallow laugh. "Oh, so you're officially taking her side now?"

"From here on out?" Sam blinks, unfazed. He nods. "Unequivocally, yes, man."

Oliver's nostrils flare, but it's not anger, I don't think. Indignation, maybe?

"This is such a fucking joke." Oliver glances away.

"Nope." Sam is totally straight-faced. "I'm just in love with her."

Both Oliver and Maryanne scoff in their respective ways—Oliver's now laced with fear, Maryanne's all saturated in disbelief, because on what planet am I loveable, according to her?

Oliver gives Sam a look. "You just met."

"I know, man." Sam nods. "We did, you're right, and I'm so sorry. If I swung your way, Ol, in a heartbeat it'd be you and me—but fuck. I love her." Sam lets out a strange breath that's all heavy with emotion. He shakes his head as he stares at my brother with absolute sincerity. "I'm in love with her, Oliver—I've been into her since the second I first saw her when she felt me up because she thought I was your boyfriend, and I've been in love with her since the morning after when we went to the beach and she wouldn't take my jumper." Sam catches my eye, throws me an inch of a smile, and I turn into a puddle of goo. "And I love you as well, Ol—I do—but I love her more, and differently, and you can't talk to her like that," Sam tells him firmly but also somehow kindly, then shakes his head again. "I won't let you. She didn't do anything wrong."

"She took you from me," Oliver tells him, and there's a stubbornness to his voice, but I don't think, if he were his actual self in this moment, he would believe that to be true. He's just reeling.

Sam's head tilts to the side. "I wasn't ever yours, dude. I know you know that. Not in that way. Not how I'm hers now." Sam shrugs helplessly. "And I know you're upset, and I know this is hard for you and you're not doing good right now, and I want you to be good and healthy and okay, but if you talk to her like that again, Oliver—mate, we're going to have a problem."

Oliver says nothing; he's gone totally quiet, and I can't tell whether he's feeling put in his place or just total despair. Or both.

"Yeah?" Maryanne smirks. "What are you going to do? Beat him half to death like you did Beckett?"

Sam looks at her, unfazed. "I hope not, but if it comes to it—"

Maryanne turns to me now.

"A violent cokehead," she sneers, and she has this smug little smile, but whatever, fuck her smile, because what I care about is the way Sam's face falls as he stares over at Oliver, who's obviously been telling

Maryanne secrets that aren't his to tell. Sam's perfect face—it looks a bit squashed, and I hate it.

"Wow, Georgia." Maryanne shrugs as her eyes fall down Sam, all full of judgment that is not hers to pass. "You sure know how to pick 'em."

And then it happens before I even consciously know I'm doing it—I lunge for her. I don't know where I'm aiming, really.

I've been Maryanne's punching bag for as long as I've been alive in one way or another, and I've never lunged for her before, but for Sam I will.

If I'm honest, I was probably lunging for her throat, but I don't quite make it there. But I do get to her—grab her by the hair and yank—and Maryanne screams like she's being murdered. I blindly claw at her, and I'm about to hit her properly, my fists all balled up and everything—when I'm picked up off the floor from behind and dragged away from her, before I'm tossed over Sam's shoulder and carried outside.

When I'm at what I suppose he considers to be a safe distance, Sam places me down on the porch.

He gives me a steep look. "Yeah, you're not getting into fistfights with a sociopath on my account."

"Narcissist," I correct him.

"Oh," He tosses me a sarcastic look and thumbs back inside. "In that case, go on back in."

"For the record," I start. "You are better off fighting a narcissist than a sociopath because they'll likely care about their face because they're vain, so they'll be preoccupied trying to—"

He cuts me off, shaking his head. "Not the time, Gige..." He takes a step away from me, looking me over. "Are you okay?"

I take his hand. "I'm fine. Are you okay? You looked sad."

Sam's eyes widen with exasperation. "You don't hit a dangerous person because I looked sad, okay—that's stupid."

"Not stupid," I say, resolute. "Worth it."

"Well, that was a long time coming," Violet says, emerging from inside.

Clay tosses an arm around me and whispers, "You could have taken her."

Tennyson and Savannah appear next.

Tens nods his chin at me. "Are you good?"

I glance up at Sam, who tosses his arm around me, speaking on both our behalves. "Yeah, we're fine."

Vi catches my eye. "Why don't y'all come back and stay at our house?"

"Oh, why?" I feign confusion. "I was so looking forward to being stabbed in my sleep tonight…"

"That's not funny," Tennyson says at the same time Sam says, "Don't joke about that."

"Guys." I laugh. "She has never displayed violent tendencies." I pause to reconsider, supposing that there are difference kinds of violence and I have suffered at her hands some of its variants. "Well, not physically, anyway"

No one laughs yet again, and I let out an awkward, low whistle. "Tough crowd."

"Come on," Violet says, opening the door to her Range Rover. "Get in the car. And you can leave your gentle comedy here."

60

SAM WALKS OUT OF MY aunt and uncle's guest room bathroom, towel around his waist after his shower the morning of the reading of the will, part two.

I'm midway through getting dressed, but my brain has powered down as I stand there in my jeans, staring at the small pile of T-shirts in front of me. I'm not an indecisive person either. I think I dressed nicer for the reading of the will before, but this time I don't feel like it.

"You look nervous," Sam says, coming up behind me. He pulls out an off-white T-shirt from my pile and hands it to me. "This one," he says.

He's magic, isn't he? I think I'm beginning to like being read. Just sometimes though.

"I am nervous," I tell him.

Sam puts his hand on my waist. "For which part?"

"All of it?" I shrug. "I don't want to see Oliver, and I don't want to see Maryanne."

"They won't say anything to you."

I give him a look. "Yes, they will."

He tugs a gray T-shirt over his head. "Then I'll say something to them."

"Sam," I sigh, and he shrugs. Just shrugs. As though he's being reasonable.

Then he looks at me out of the corner of his eye. "You reckon there's going to be any other surprises in there?"

"What?" I scoff. "Like, a surprise second lover who he's bequeathed a ski chalet? I mean, I hope not, but what a curveball."

Sam chuckles as he sits on the bed to put on his shoes.

"Hey, have you spoken to Oliver this morning?" I ask.

He nods. "Yeah."

"How's he doing?"

Sam's face pulls. "I think he's pretty anxious about it."

I frown. "That he'll be left out again?"

"Yeah, but—" Sam shakes his head. "I mean, all things considered... Why would your dad do that, Gige? He's not your grandfather."

I'm not so sure. "He is my grandfather's son though."

Sam thinks about it for a few quiet seconds, still not convinced.

"I don't think that's the sort of thing you do in death. People tend to try to right their wrongs in their wills and on their deathbeds, you know? I don't think that's how he'd want to leave the world—"

"You didn't even know him," I remind him.

"Don't need to." Sam shrugs again. "People, for the most part, they're all the same. No one's trying to be shit, everyone's trying their best—"

"Then why didn't he just confess in his will?" I ask, eyebrows up.

And then Sam gives me a look like I should know better.

"Who would that be best for?" He waits for me to answer, but I don't say anything, so he shakes his head again. "Literally no one, except maybe him."

It gives me pause, and I don't know what I think, whether that's true or not. Would the truth really be better for no one except my father (and arguably Alexis)? Or is it more that the truth would just be so heinously damaging for Mom that it outweighs it either way?

Vi knocks on the door, yells through it that we're leaving in five minutes.

There's a big lunch that's been organized for after, I learn on the way. I try to convince everyone in the car with me that we should blow it off and have a lunch with "just the good ones who we actually like"—Vi turns around from the front passenger seat and flicks me in the leg for that.

She says it would mean a lot to my mother if I was there, and I remind her that she doesn't even like my mom that much, and then she gives me a look and turns back around, acting like I'm hard work, but I see Clay smirking about it all in the rearview mirror.

We pull up to the lawyer's offices around the same time as Oliver and Maryanne arrive in the car with Mom and Jason.

Sam and I are mindlessly holding hands as Oliver walks toward the entrance to the building where we wait for him.

"How are you feeling?" I ask him quietly.

Oliver clocks my hand in Sam's. "Like you care."

Then Oliver walks on ahead and Sam's mouth tightens, defensive on my behalf.

"Go check on him?" I tell Sam.

Sam flicks me a look, but I flick him one back.

"Be patient," I tell him, and Sam nods once, though he doesn't look all the way sure before he walks quickly after my brother.

"You okay?" Tennyson asks, coming up behind me with Savannah.

"Yeah," I say by reflex as the four of us walk in together. Savannah gives me an uncertain look and I give her a third of a smile. "I just can't tell anymore whether Oliver's this upset because I'm shit and I hurt him, or if it's all amplified because he's drinking again."

"Both, probably," Tennyson says with a shrug. "I mean, it's always shit when you like someone and they don't like you back. Even worse when you like someone and they like someone else instead of you, and when it's your sister? That's got to"—he grimaces—"you know? But… the alcohol can't be helping him think any clearer."

"Yeah," I say, because what else can I say?

"Maryanne is also stoking the fire though," Savannah interjects.

I purse my lips. "I figured."

Tennyson's face twists, all riddled with frustration. "We were chatting about everything the other day with him, and I reminded him that Sam is not and has never been gay—and Mer blew on into the conversation and said something like, 'Doesn't mean he couldn't have been one day. Maybe he was on his way to falling in love with Oliver. I bet he would have, too, if it wasn't for Georgia.'"

My blood feels a bit like it's boiling. Maryanne has been not just disparaging of my brother's sexuality all his life, but cruelly dismissive. So seeing her embrace it now as weapon…? God.

"He wants to be angry at you," Tennyson says as we reach Desmond's door. "He's found someone who loves to feed that anger."

We're the last to arrive; everyone else is seated. Sam and Oliver are sitting on a three-person couch, and there's a space open next to Sam, so I go sit in it, but as soon as I do, Oliver gets up and moves to a chair beside Maryanne.

It feels precise. Like it was a calculated decision to reject me in front of everyone, because that seat was there the whole time, and he could have moved there before.

Sam glances at me, and he has a look in his eye, and I try to hose it down with the look in mine. *Leave it.*

"And we're back." Desmond smiles at us collectively, then zeroes in on me. "I understand we all have a little bit more clarity around the revelations from last time."

I wonder if he knew?

Maryanne makes a bit of a spiel about how it's so like our dad to gift someone a lake house for an act of kindness from over thirty years ago. "Most people would forget," she sniffles, and Jason puts his arm around her because that's what he's supposed to do, I guess. "But not Daddy." She shakes her head. "Not Daddy."

And then she cries a little bit. These really delicate, believable tears, and I have to hand it to her—there is some artistry here. Like, don't get me wrong—is that very same skill set terrifying and unsettling? Absolutely, yes. But it's also objectively impressive.

Once Maryanne feels adequately placated and the center of

attention, Desmond does the intro again—you know, the "I, William Marcus Carter, being of sound mind and body, not acting under duress, fully understand," blah blah… Everything is how it was the first time.

Mom gets their family home here, the Florida Keys holiday house, and ten percent of Dad's company.

Violet gets that painting.

Tennyson is left the other ninety percent and Dad's old car he loved a lot.

Me, I'm given that piece of land, that book, and the *SS Avoidance* (both of which make a lot more sense now than before). Alexis is of course bequeathed the lake house in Moultonborough that is an actual house and not just a plot of nothing, and then Desmond turns to Maryanne. Both she and Jase are watching him with eager, almost hungry eyes.

"To my daughter, Maryanne, I leave my Sunseeker 86 yacht. To my—"

"Wait," Maryanne butts in. "Is that all?"

Desmond glances down at the papers in front of him, either uneasy with the question or just Maryanne generally—it's hard to tell.

"Just a boat?" Maryanne asks again. "That's all he left me?"

No one says anything for a few seconds.

"I mean—" Savannah grimaces. "Isn't it, like, a four-point-five-million-dollar boat?"

"Who asked you?" says Jase pretty suddenly at the same time as Maryanne's whole face scrunches up.

"Shut up, Savannah!" she says. "Like, what are you even here for?"

"Don't tell her to shut up!" Tennyson scowls.

Maryanne lifts an eyebrow. "Then why don't you tell her to shut up?"

"Why should he?" I nod my chin toward Jason. "Your deadweight partner's always running his dumb mouth and we have to listen. At least she's cool."

Maryanne's eyes widen ever so slightly—that was affronting and insulting to her, completely unacceptable.

She leans in toward her husband and whispers, "Do something."

Obediently, he stands, which obviously then has Sam immediately on his feet, and before my sister's stupid husband has a chance to say a word to me, Sam points at him. "Sit the fuck down."

Jase does, quick smart, and I do a terrible job at hiding my delight, but frankly, so do Vi and Clay.

Desmond clears his throat—this poor, poor man just trying to get through the reading of this will sometime before the century's over—and gives Maryanne a ginger look. "Yes, that is all."

Maryanne puts her head in her hands, forlorn, and our mother pats her back.

Desmond catches both my eye and Tennyson's, takes a measured breath, and keeps going. "Lastly," he reads. "All funds in my personal account, totaling to the sum of sixteen million, seven-hundred thousand, I bequeath to my son, to whom I owe much to, Oliver Carter—"

And all the air in the room gets sucked out.

No one moves a muscle—no one even blinks—as he keeps talking.

"—with the condition that he must be sober for five hundred and forty-eight days to access the funds."

I stare over at Oliver, eyes wide—but not as wide as his.

"Oh my God," Maryanne says under her breath, staring at him. Mom says nothing.

"I—" Oliver starts, but then stops talking—he looks scared. He stares over at me out of habit before he drags his eyes away and over to Maryanne, then back to Des. "There has to be a mistake."

"I assure you, Mr. Carter..." Desmond gives him a gentle smile. "There isn't." Then he glances around to the rest of us. "I'll give you all a moment."

He excuses himself (probably to get a stiff drink), and everyone sits there in...it would be underselling it to say "stunned silence." It would be more appropriate to say we're sitting in like, practically electrocuted silence. Every single one of us.

And me? I am...I don't know what I am. Relieved for Oliver? So unspeakably relieved for Oliver. But also a bit…I don't know—what's the word? Crushed?

And I don't want it to be apparent on my face; I don't want anyone to see anything on my face that I'm feeling, because I don't even know myself what I'm feeling, so I make an excuse and say I'm going to the bathroom, but instead I go to the fire escape to take big gulping breaths of air.

And please don't misunderstand me, I'm so glad Oliver got it all. He needs it. Not the money, but the validation. After how poorly Oliver was treated for so long, for how much he was punished for just being himself, a final olive branch from our father from beyond the grave is so completely what he deserves, but what about me? After everything, do I not deserve some kind of kindness too?

I press the tips of my fingers into my closed eyes and try to tell those hot tears to stay where they are, and they would have too if it wasn't for that perfect, meddling boyfriend of mine, who appears in the doorway of the fire escape.

"You okay?"

"Nothing?" I swallow—a tell-tale sign of a big, powerful emotion—then I shake my head. "I get nothing except a book and a random empty plot of land—like, how fitting. How fitting that he'd cast off his empty plot of land, next to the home he bequeathed to his adulterer, to his adulteress cast-off child. Like, what the fuck—how much did he hate me? Why give me anything at all?"

Sam comes and stands behind me, wrapping his arms around my waist. "I think he was giving you way more than you realize, Gige."

I say nothing, just stare straight ahead at literally nothing. The view of the fire escape is the back of another building, but I'm staring at it right now like it's *Madonna on the Rocks*.

"He knew about your job," Sam says quietly. "Alexis said he was proud of you, remember? He knew you were good at finding out the truth… He didn't leave that land to anyone else, he left it to you. If it meant nothing to him, why not just fold it into the lake house lot?" Sam pauses to make his point. "It was intentional."

I turn around now to face him. "What was?"

"Georgia, I don't think he was leaving you the empty plot." He gives me a cautious look. "I think he was leaving you Alexis."

My head pulls back and my heart skips this strange, hopeful beat. "What?"

"I think he knew you'd figure it out." Sam shrugs. "And maybe—I don't know, maybe I'm reaching or hoping or loving you has turned me to fucking mush or something, but I think maybe he knew Alexis could be something to you that your dad could never figure out how to be for you himself."

I shake my head a little bit, because it's too thoughtful. "Nothing that I know or have experienced with my father up until this moment would imply that that's even vaguely a possibility."

"Gige—" Sam holds my face with his hand and looks at me so tenderly. "I say this with all due respect: I love you, but I don't think you knew your dad all that well."

I don't know why that undoes me how it does, but suddenly I'm crying, and there's a new kind of stinging in my heart than the old one I was used to.

Could that be true? If that's true, it would maybe mean not that he didn't love me at all, just that he loved me in different language to my native tongue, and he never knew how to say it—which, admittedly, is still tragically sad, but is arguably less candidly cruel. Could my father actually have cared about me enough to orchestrate that? Is that even possible?

61

CLAY GAVE SAM THE KEYS to his car so that we could have a minute. He and Violet rode with Tennyson and Savannah to the lunch instead. By the time we got back to the car after the reading, I must have looked—well, I probably just looked how I felt.

Sam and I went for a slow drive. We didn't say much—Sam just drove. There's not all that much to be said anymore anyway, I don't think. By happenstance, he drove to the beach that we went to on that first day—Palmetto Dunes.

Our time in South Carolina is finally drawing to a close—we fly out tomorrow, and it doesn't really feel real yet that Sam's getting on the plane with me and we're flying back to England together.

Kind of crazy to think how much has changed between the first time Sam and I were on this beach and now. How my whole life flipped, how so many lives flipped in that short span of time. I don't like it here that much, but finding Sam in Okatie has given me a tenderness for my home city that I've never had before.

After we've been there for a half an hour, Sam gently tells me we should probably head to the lunch—and he's right, we're already well late at this point.

We walk into Skull Creek Boathouse twenty minutes later, and this time Sam and I are holding hands and it's conscious and on purpose. He told me before we walked inside to not even think about letting go, that it's his job to support me and my job to let him.

Strange how doing so feels like I'm inviting drama and chaos to lunch, and when Maryanne leans over to Oliver next to her and whispers something to him, and he whispers something back, Sam just squeezes my hand tighter.

Oliver gives us (me) a loaded smile. "Having some car sex again?"

Maryanne laughs quietly and Mom gives Oliver a bit of a look.

I don't say anything, just sit in the chair that Sam pulls out for me, but Sam gives Oliver the glare of a lifetime, which shuts him up, at least for the time being.

I can tell how much it's all wearing Sam's patience thin. He's usually the image of calm and grace—"cool as a cucumber." That expression was invented to describe Sam in nearly every single scenario imaginable, except any scenario that pertains to me.

His frustration toward Oliver is mounting, no matter how much I tell him I don't mind, no matter how much I insist that Oliver will come around. I can see it. Every jab grates him, and him rolling over on them hurts him, and I hate hurting him, but I don't know what else to do.

Everyone's ordered already, so we put in ours quickly, and while the waiter's there, Maryanne asks for another two glasses of rosé.

I stare over at the glass in front of Oliver. There's maybe half an ounce left in it? I wonder how many he's had. Hopefully just the one, but then, that's not really how addiction works.

"So," Jase says, nudging Oliver in a way he—to the best of my knowledge—has never done before. "What are you going to do with all that money, man?"

Oliver laughs nervously as he shakes his head. "I don't know."

"If you need any advice..." Jase offers, eyebrows up.

"Yeah, I'm sure I will—I don't know anything about money. I'm not that good at it," Oliver says, and I wonder if I should just paint a big target sign on his back.

"You probably just want to invest it," Clay says to him, quite wisely.

Maryanne leans in close to Oliver and playfully whispers, "Boring!" but it's loud enough for all of us to hear.

And as I stare over at the absolute shitstorm combination that is Oliver and our older sister, I can't help but think Maryanne must feel like she's struck gold right now. She had coincidentally already aligned herself with Oliver before she knew he was the one Dad left all his money to.

"It was so good of Daddy, don't y'all think?" Maryanne glances around the table, eyes rounded with a faux-sorriness. "After Grandpa didn't leave Oli anything... That was so fucked up, by the way." She says that last part to Oliver specifically before she whips her head around to Mom and flashes her an apologetic smile. "Sorry."

Oliver stares over at me across the table, and I maybe spot a glint of tenderness in his eyes at the mention of that whole mess. I briefly wonder whether he knows our siblings and our cousins all declined to redivide the money our grandfather left us so that we all, Oliver included, received the same amount. I'd never tell him, and I doubt the others would either—it hardly paints them well. I wonder if he knows anyway.

"Dad left him a lot of money," Maryanne tells technically the table, but really she's just speaking to Oliver. "He should have some fun with it too."

Oliver nods emphatically, eyes lighting up at the thought and the possibilities. That's the magic word to someone who has ADHD. They're absolute suckers for fun.

"Is there a car you've always wanted, or like, a holiday house somewhere?" Maryanne suggests in a completely non-self-serving way, I'm sure. "Or, I don't know—like a shopping spree in Paris? We should go to Paris!"

I fold my arms over my chest and catch Oliver's eye. "You realize you're currently ineligible to receive the funds." I nod toward the glass in front of him.

Oliver breathes out loudly.

"There are ways around that," Jase says.

Tennyson pulls a face. "I don't think there are…"

"Also," I say to Jase, "you do remember that the only condition Dad made was that his alcoholic son maintained his sobriety—like, surely we as his family would want to encourage him down that path."

Oliver squints at me. "Feels a little rich, you talking about how family should treat each other."

"I'm not talking about how family should treat each other—our family infamously treats each other like shit. I'm talking about trying to keep you alive."

"Ignore her, Oli," Maryanne chimes in. "She's just jealous—what with that weird little plot of land he left her? Like, what even—"

And they both start laughing quietly, but loud enough for the entire table to be privy to what's going on.

"Oliver." Vi shakes her head at him, stares at him like he's a stranger. "What has gotten into you?"

"Alcohol," I say softly to Violet specifically, but all right, fine—I'll admit it was intentionally un-soft enough for Oliver to hear it, and so sue me for making an inflammatory comment. His eyes rolled so far back in his head, I'm sure it must have caused at least a bit of strain for his levator palpebrae superioris.

"Georgia, shut up," Maryanne snaps, with Oliver backing it up with a "Yeah, Georgia, shut the fuck up." They laugh again, and I'm literally counting down the hours till Sam and I get to leave tomorrow. And I do mean literally. It's seventeen hours, eight minutes from this exact moment—and it's because I'm doing that math in my mind that I miss the shift in Sam's posture. I don't catch it until he's sitting up square in his chair, head tilted, jaw tight, nostrils a little flared—and if I wasn't doing my leaving-math, I would have known what was coming next. He told me last night that it was inevitable, and I told him it didn't have to be, and we'd figure it out, but he said he didn't think he wanted to.

"Hey, listen man," Sam says loudly as he catches Oliver's eye over the table. "I can't be your sponsor anymore."

The whole table goes silent for probably a full four seconds.

"What?" Oliver whispers quietly.

Sam repeats himself. "I can't be your sponsor anymore."

Oliver sniffs this laugh that I think is meant to sound like it's made out of disbelief, but there's something in the exhale and the way his inner brow rises that tells me that actually, he's kind of devastated. "You're"—and then he does air quotes—"breaking up with me."

Sam sighs, shaking his head as he tries his best to rein in his frustration. "Don't call it that—"

"Why?" Oliver shrugs, and he's just being plain petulant now.

"Because." I do it unconsciously, but as best as I can in these chairs, I shift in front of Sam. "It's not a breakup, Oliver, and you fucking know that. A breakup implies something that you never were."

"Oh!" Maryanne lets out a dry laugh. "You're going to tell him what his own relationships mean to him now, are you?"

I barely look at her as I say, "Relationships are a two-way street, and I know what theirs wasn't."

"Do you?" she says, crinkling her nose patronizingly.

I raise an eyebrow. "Do I know that my boyfriend was in neither a sexual nor a romantic relationship with my brother? Yeah." I nod. "I do know that."

"Is it because of her?" Oliver asks Sam without looking at me, with just his chin jutted in my direction.

"Yep." Sam nods unapologetically.

And I hate the way Oliver's face looks before he asks, "You're picking her over me?"

It hurt him to ask it—I don't know why he asked it. It makes me feel a bit sick how sad his eyes look.

Sam's face strains—this is hard for him, and it wasn't a choice he made lightly. "I wish so bad that I didn't have to, mate, but yeah."

Maryanne tilts her head at Sam and plasters a manufactured kind of concern on her face. "Isn't that reckless and irresponsible to abandon him when he's in such a precarious headspace?"

"Yeah." Sam nods again, pretending to be impressed by her. "A very good and valid question, Maryanne, and while I don't fully believe you actually give a shit, sure, I'll bite." Maryanne's face drops. She's not used to being spoken to like that by many people. Sam keeps going. "In some ways, it is undeniably reckless and irresponsible, and I feel terrible about that, but considering the unique set of circumstances and the position I've found myself in—"

"Georgia knows all about positions," Maryanne whispers to Oliver, who sniggers, and Sam says nothing, just watches them quietly, waiting for them to stop speaking as though they're like, these terrible, ill-mannered children, and eventually their laughter awkwardly subsides. It's horrifyingly humbling and it's not even happening to me.

"Considering the position I've found myself in," Sam says again, and he gives them a look that basically says, "I fucking dare you to laugh," and believe you me, they do not. "I no longer feel able or equipped to support Oliver in that same way." Sam stares Maryanne down. "Unfortunately, it would be reckless and irresponsible to continue the other way too."

Oliver's face now, it's wrought with emotion—I think he's finally faced with the reality of everything he's losing and choosing to lose—and he stares across the table at me, his usually bright eyes all dim, which is how they are when he goes like this. They stare at me, ragged and full of resentment. "God, you fuck everything up."

"Oliver—" I start, but he cuts me off.

"I'm allowed to be fucking pissed about this!" Oliver yells.

Sam nods emphatically. "Yeah, mate, you are. But at me, not at her."

Oliver rolls his eyes. "How do you figure?"

"Because she begged me not to do this," Sam tells him as he points his thumb at me. I feel Oliver's eyes on me, but I don't want to meet them, so I just stare up at Sam, who keeps going.

"I told her I was going to break it to you last night, and she asked me not to, but I can't be what you need me to be, man." He shrugs like it's a puzzle he can't solve. I guess it is. "And I don't know how to reconcile being what she deserves me to be for her and who you need me to be for you. I don't think they can coexist."

"Yes, they can!" Oliver says, his tone a bit urgent now.

"How?" Sam shrugs again. "You've been a fucking prick to her, bro. Since the second you saw us together... But just to her, not to me, and I did it too." Sam pauses, thinking to himself. "Actually, I think I kissed her first."

"You did," Savannah and I both say in quiet unison.

Sam smiles and Tennyson swats one away.

"She's been fucking tortured this entire time at the prospect of hurting you," Sam tells Oliver, "and you're out here taking a swing at her every chance you get."

Oliver drops Sam's eyes when he says that, as though he's a bit ashamed. Sober Oliver would be, but he's not here right now. Just flecks of him, at best.

"And while she doesn't need anyone to do shit for her—she's more capable than all of us combined at—fuck—like, everything?—she does deserve a partner who can tell her brother to fuck on off when he's being an arsehole, and I can't say that to you when I'm your sponsor. But I need to as her boyfriend, so something's gotta give, Ol, and it's never going to be her."

Sam gives my brother an uncomfortable and sorry sort-of smile, and then I lean over and kiss Sam's perfect cheek.

"I love you," I tell him with this swelling feeling in my chest that's a bit like when you've been lying on the sand at the beach on an overcast day, and the sun finally breaks through and the warmth of it drenches you to the bone.

"Yeah." Sam kisses the tip of my nose. "I know."

"Wow," Maryanne pipes back up. "That is so sweet of you to flaunt your stupid love in front of our brokenhearted brother—"

And I take a big breath, ready for round two with Maryanne, but before I can say anything, my mother jumps in. "Maybe you should go, sweetheart."

"Margaret," Vi says in this sort of quiet, horrified voice. "Don't—"

"No." I catch my aunt's eye. "It's fine. I'm ready to go."

I peer up at Sam, and ask him without asking him whether he's ready to go too. He nods once, and that's enough for me. I push back from the table and stand up.

Tennyson starts shaking his head. "But you don't fly out till tomorrow."

"We have flexible tickets," I tell him. "There's nothing direct from Charleston to London anyway."

"Good," my mother says, nodding to herself. I can tell she believes she's doing the right thing by (sort of) sending me away (again), and I realize in that moment, I think it'll always be easier for her if I'm the problem.

People who aren't self-aware, people who haven't lived their lives in the pursuit of truth, find that the truth is confronting if you don't want to hear it. I think I represent to her a myriad of uncomfortable truths she just can't afford to lean into, because her whole life depends so heavily on a false reality. People don't tend to want those ruptured.

"I'll take them," Clay tells Vi, standing up.

"I'll come too," Violet says quickly. I think she's eager to leave, and same.

I turn to Tennyson, whose eyes look heavy now. I pull him a little to the side.

"I don't want you to go yet," he tells me with a frown.

I try to make it light, shrugging playfully. "But just think how easy life will feel for you once I am..."

I can tell in the way his brows go he doesn't believe that to be true, and then he pulls me in for this big bear bug, and when he lets me go, both of us are glassy-eyed, which makes me feel embarrassed in front of so many people, so I throw my arms around Savannah.

"Come visit us." I glance between them. "Both of you."

"We will." She nods.

Tennyson offers Sam his hand. "Look after her."

Sam flicks him a little smile. "On it."

"This has been the weirdest fucking couple weeks," Tennyson says, glancing between Sam and me, and I laugh. "And it should have just been shit," he keeps going, "but I had so much fun with you. I'm sorry for—"

I swipe my hand through the air and hope it dismisses his worries. "We're good," I tell him.

Tens lifts his eyebrows. "Yeah?"

"Yeah." I smile. "So good."

I turn to look at Maryanne, who's still sitting at the table between Jason and Oliver, looking unimpressed for—whatever, I've lost track of why she's pissed off now.

I take a big breath. "Maryanne." She lifts an eyebrow, waiting. "God, please delete my number. Don't contact me again."

Her jaw drops open, but I don't give her emotions even a second of airtime before I turn to Oliver. His eyes are flickering between Sam and I—angry, offended, hurt—at both of us now, at least.

Sam gives him a gentle, maybe even hopeful smile. "When you're ready, Ol, I'd love to help you find a new sponsor..."

"Yeah—" Oliver shakes his head. "I'm good, thanks."

"You really aren't," I tell him, and Sam flicks me a look. "Oliver." I grab his eyes and don't let them go. "I'm so sorry for how this all happened. Really, I am. I love you so much, and I'm so sorry I did something that hurt you. I wish it didn't, but I know that it did. I can't take it back. I wouldn't take it back if I could though, because—I don't know, at another point in our lives, you would have been so happy for me with Sam—"

"Stop talking," Oliver says, looking away, arms crossed over his chest now, a physical barrier between us.

"No." Now I shake my head. "I'm sorry I hurt you."

"Oh, great," he says sarcastically. "Now it's all better."

"If you need anything," I offer quietly, and I mean it, but he turns away all stubborn.

"I won't."

"Call me."

Oliver's mouth tugs downward. "I won't."

"I love you," I tell him anyway, and he just stares at me.

"Come on, I'll walk you out," my mother tells Sam and me, putting a guiding hand on my mid-back. It almost sounds maternal, except that she's guiding me away. Away from her, away from her other children, away from the life she's constructed and needs so badly to be real.

Clay and Vi go to pull up the car, and then it's just Sam, my mom, and me standing there awkwardly on a street corner.

Mom glances at Sam, giving him an uneasy smile. "Thank you for all you've done for Oliver."

Sam gives her an unsure look.

"I know he can be a handful," she says with an apologetic shrug. "So can she." She points at me with a laugh.

Sam smiles at her patiently, how he has this whole time with her. He gives her a kind wink. "I like handfuls."

That charms her a little. "It was a pleasure to meet you."

"You too." Sam nods. "And again, I'm so sorry for your loss."

She turns to me now and puts her hand just below my shoulder. "Goodbye, sweetheart," she says as the car pulls up in front of us.

I try my best to smile at her. "Bye, Mom."

She opens her arms, gingerly moving toward me for a hug, because I guess that's what mothers do? I don't know. But while we're hugging, when her mouth is close to my ear, she pulls back a little and looks up at me with nervous eyes.

"What's he like?" she whispers quietly.

And I'm completely caught off guard. I blink at her, our faces closer than they've ever been.

"What's who like?" I whisper back.

"The man," she says, "in New Orleans. Who saved your father." Her eyebrows are very up. "Is he—what's he like?"

"Um." I blink six times before I say more—not my finest work. "He's French. Sweet. Well read. He's—kind?"

Something flickers over her face, but I'm too blindsided to really pick what. Surprise? Frustration? Why would she be frustrated?

"You liked him?" she asks.

And I'm thrown, because what the fuck? What if I'm misreading the subtext? Is she really asking me what I think she's asking me? Could she be? And if she is, how do I answer?

With the truth, I guess. I don't know; I don't feel like giving her the comfort of lying about this or being dismissive of someone who's already been so dismissed for so long.

I nod slowly, carefully. "Yes."

She nods back and pulls away. It feels conscious and decisive and, actually, I'm really okay with it.

"Speak soon, sweetheart," she says, and I climb into the car and say nothing back.

I don't feel like lying for these people anymore.

62

ABOUT TWENTY-EIGHT THOUSAND HOURS LATER, Sam and I walk out of the arrivals gate of Terminal 5 at Heathrow and are met with the grinning and spectacular face of Hattie Ramsey.

She charges toward me, tossing both her arms around my neck with total abandon.

"Oh my God, hi! You look perfect. I missed you." She pulls away from me the slightest bit, and God, I've missed her too. "Oh, hello—you're quite swarthy right now, aren't you?" Then she notices Sam hovering close by. "Oh my God, Georgia, don't panic. But there is an outrageously beautiful man standing very near you."

I bat away a smile. "I know."

"Hi." Sam flashes her a smile.

She looks at me. "Is he your carry-on?"

Sam pulls a face and nods at me. "I don't think she can really carry that much with those twig arms—"

"No, she can't." Hattie nods solemnly.

I peer between the two of them, unimpressed. "Yes, she can."

"She can't really open jars on her own," Hattie tells Sam, who gives her a knowing look.

"Couldn't lift her own carry-on up into the overhead either."

"But she can"—I give each of them stern looks—"solve a decades-old mystery and play poker so well that she's been banned from two casinos in Monaco."

Penny gives me a proud little wink before he offers his hand to Hattie. "I'm Sam," he tells her.

She shakes his hand with both of hers, staring at him in awe and fascination. "I'm sure you are—wow!—God, Georgia—" She tears her eyes away from Penny to scowl at me. "You couldn't flick me a text to give me a heads-up that you met Thor on the plane?"

"Sorry." I shrug at the same time Sam says, "We actually didn't meet on the plane—"

"No, don't be sorry," she says to me specifically, before she turns to Sam. "And what?"

I nod a couple of times. "Yeah, so—we actually have a lot to talk about…"

Hattie smirks, amused. "Do we just?" She grabs one of my suitcases and starts wheeling it toward the car park.

I flash Hattie a look that says, "I will tell you everything you want to know later, just behave right now," and she sort of rolls her eyes, but that's good enough for me.

"Hattie, Sam is my boyfriend," I tell her.

"Yeah, no—that tracks. I mean, I'm pretty into that leggy Belgian model I've been hooking up with and I think maybe *I'd* like Sam to be my boyfriend."

Penny pulls a face. "Sam is…flattered?"

Hattie nods regally. "Sam should be."

I clear my throat. "Can Sam stay the night?"

Her eyes flick from me to Sam, so then I tack on, "Or actually, ideally, many nights?"

"Okay, wait—" She suddenly stops walking, hands on her hips. "What the fuck happened on this trip?"

It's about a fifty-five-minute drive from Heathrow to Hattie's and my Marylebone Lane apartment, and Sam and Hattie chat away the entire time. She asks a million questions about how we met and how we got together, and about midway through, she remembers it's all because my dad died, so she does a wellness check to see if I'm okay, but when she realizes I am, it's back to a million questions about Sam and everything else.

She's riveted by the Alexis stuff—who I have texted a few times, by the way. We've arranged for a FaceTime next week. I don't know what we're going to talk about. I haven't worked out whether we have anything in common yet, more than that we both knew my dad—although one might argue I didn't really know him at all.

There is a curious form of grief that I find emerging within me, beyond that whole thing where my father died thinking I'd done something terrible to someone else, which is a thought that still feels like a knife twisting in my chest. But now as well, there's this strange little haunting of what could have been. What could have been if my father felt empowered to be his whole self, embrace who he'd spent his whole life hiding—what would it have been like if he left my mother for the man he loved when we were younger? Oliver would have gone with Dad for sure, and imagine how different Oliver's life might look if he had felt validated by his father the entire time. And Maryanne would have stayed with Mom, and no matter how little I might have been, I've always known that if Maryanne was one place, my best bet was being someplace else—so I probably would have gone with Oliver. Maybe none of the shit with Beckett would have happened. Maybe it still would have, but maybe they wouldn't have sent me away. And I'll never know, and as a general rule of thumb, I don't allow myself to dwell on the what-ifs of life, but this one, this particular path that could have been mine to wander down—where maybe I could have had two fathers instead of none?

There's still time, Sam has said more than once. There is a beautiful optimism to him that isn't born from sunny idealism or anything close to naivety, but rather a deep sense of hope that was forged in him as he climbed out of the flames of addiction.

"You're doing it again," Sam says as he unzips his suitcase on my bedroom floor.

I blink myself back into the moment. "What?"

"That thing where you stare at me for a long time and don't say anything, and it's not sexually charged or judgmental, but I can literally see the thoughts pinging around behind your eyes, so what's on your mind, Gige?"

He flicks me a look like he's impressed with himself, then waits for me to speak.

I squint at him for a couple of seconds. "It's just that you're...really here."

"Yes." Sam nods, trying to follow along, but falls to confusion. "What?"

I gesture at him. "What are we going to do?"

"Like, tomorrow, do you mean?"

I shrug, sort of aimlessly.

Penny pulls a face. "I mean, I'm anticipating we'll not sleep that well because jet lag this way is fucking brutal, so probably we'll get up pretty early tomorrow morning and go get breakfast or something. What's your favorite café here?"

I purse my lips, thinking for a second. "Granger & Co."

"Okay." Sam nods again. "So we'll go there, and then after, I'll probably call my old modeling agency—"

"What about visas?" I interrupt.

"Well I'm okay for now—as long as I don't get paid here. But I guess I'll eventually have to get one of those global talent ones." He thinks for a second. "Or just marry you and get residency."

I press my lips together and don't let myself smile at the M word. Instead I ask, "What about your cafés?"

"Well, I just own them—they have their own managers. I only make the coffees there sometimes for fun." He gives me a golden-retriever smile.

"But you'll miss it," I tell him.

Sam shrugs. "Yeah, but I'll make you coffees for fun now."

"So you're really here?" I cross my arms over my chest. "Like, here-here?"

Sam glances around, as though he's not tracking. "I'm…so confused as to what you thought was happening until now?"

"I don't know," I groan. "I guess I thought maybe you'd get here and change your mind—and I wouldn't be angry if you did!"

"Well, firstly"—Penny gives me a stern look—"you should be. A man is only as good as his word. I said what I said. I meant it. And it's worth you remembering, Gige—it's my mind to change. It doesn't happen separate to me. We are in agreement that love isn't a feeling, right?"

I nod resolutely. "Correct."

"Lust is a feeling and awe is a feeling, and both things I have for you at the minute in fucking spades, but I'm self-aware enough to know they'll probably go away at some point or another—"

"I hope not," I tell him.

Sam gives me this look, like I know better than that.

"Feelings change, Gige. They ebb and flow—I know you know that. You've been the primary support person for an alcoholic for the last six years, and you were what you were for Oliver out of love, not because of how you felt about him." Sam raises his eyebrows knowingly. "I guarantee there were days where you were what you were to him despite how you felt about him in the moment…"

I nod again. "Yes."

Penny pushes some hair behind my ear. "I'm not going to change my mind."

"Okay."

"Okay." Sam smiles at me, triumphant. "Now, can we order dinner from that Chicken Shop place? I've always wanted to try it."

EPILOGUE

SIX MONTHS LATER, SAM IS still living with Hattie and me. I think she likes him more than she likes me at this point, but there's such a blissful ease between us all—though we're wondering if, when our lease is up, we should move to a bigger place. TBC, I guess.

Sam's mostly been modeling, but he's been in talks lately with a friend he's made here who also loves coffee—I think they're going to open a café in Fulham.

Work and university for me, it's been good. I still love it; I'm still completely riveted by the faces of everyone I come into contact with, though I'll admit that now being loved back how Sam loves me back, I can never tell whether I love to feel seen how he sees me, or if it's sort of a pain.

Both, maybe.

I've only spoken to Mom a couple times since I left, and Oliver not at all—Tennyson said he's doing better though.

I have weekly calls with Alexis. He's going to come here soon, he says. I don't know whether he will actually come, but in my professional opinion, he at least believes that he'll see me soon.

It's about a week before my birthday, fairly early on a Saturday morning—Sam went to Third Space and I'm just having a lazy day reading in bed—when our bedroom door opens.

Sam pokes his head in, and I smile over at him.

"I have a surprise for you," he says.

I scrunch my face up. "I don't really like surprises."

"No, I know."

I put my book down. "So why'd you do it then?"

"Well..." He sighs. "It wasn't really my idea, I'm just enabling it."

My face pulls in confusion. "Okay?"

And then there's a knock at our front door.

Sam motions for me to open it. I groan because my lazy bed Saturday isn't off to a rollicking start, and he kisses my cheek as I walk past him.

"What is this?" I look back at him over my shoulder.

He shrugs mysteriously. "Special delivery."

I roll my eyes at him as I swing open the door to find Tennyson and Savannah.

"SURPRISE!" Savannah yells.

"Oh my God!" I gawk.

Tennyson throws his arms around me, and then Savannah wriggles into the hug herself. "We're going to Paris!" she tells me.

I look back at Sam, so happy now. "I love Paris!"

He sniffs a laugh. "I know."

Tennyson pulls back a little, catching my eye. "We brought you something, actually..."

A moment later, Alexis Beauchêne appears.

My mouth falls open. "Alexis!"

He pulls me out of the Tennyson hug and into one of his. "Hello, mon cherie." He gives me a smile. "I said soon, did I not?"

I nod at him, pleased. "Oui, tu l'as fait."

He lights up. "Incroyable. Votre français devient très bon."

I wave my hand at him, unsure. "Comme ci, comme ça."

He gestures to himself, Tennyson, and Savannah. "Is this okay?"

"So much more than okay," I say emphatically. "Did you all fly here together?"

"Yeah." Tennyson nods. "We had to go via LA to pick up something—"

And then Oliver steps around the corner and I sort of freeze. I don't mean to, I don't choose to, I just go still and look at Sam.

He gives me this look that makes me feel like it's okay, I'm going to be okay—I don't think he'd let me not be, actually.

Oliver gives me a gentle smile. "Hey, Gige."

"Hi," I say quietly.

"I have something for you," Oliver tells me as he reaches in the pocket of his Varsity bomber, then offers me whatever's in his closed fist.

Cautiously, I stretch out my hand, and then he drops in a four-month sobriety chip.

I stare at it for a few seconds, smiling at it like a weirdo, my eyes filling with tears.

I look back up at him and swallow heavily. "Did you do this by yourself?"

Oliver's eyes flicker over everyone—Tennyson, Savannah, even Alexis—then his eyes land on Sam.

"No." Oliver tosses Sam a smile. "I had some help."

I stare over at Sam and feel an overwhelming sense of gratefulness for him.

"So, you had the best help..." I nod toward Penny.

"No." Oli shakes his head. "The best help would be in the form of my know-it-all little sister who actually, unfortunately, does know it all." He gives me a pointed look before he softens it again. "But I had a close second in the man who loves her."

Apparently, all this time, Sam had kept reaching out to Oliver, checking in, making sure he was okay. I don't believe Oliver was overly receptive at first, but once Maryanne realized there was no way around the sobriety clause, she faded out of Oliver's life quite quickly.

"The men who love her, actually," Tennyson clarifies, gesturing between himself and Alexis, and I could cry. Maybe I already am, actually.

"What do you think, Gige?" Oliver tilts his head, eyebrows all up and hopeful. "A long overdue family trip to Paris?"

I glance at Sam, who gives me a perfectly charming, lazy smile, then back at Oliver. I nod.

"Great." He claps his hands together and moves into the apartment. "I'm going to start packing for you," he calls back to me.

"Wait—" I look between the others. "When are we going?"

"We need to leave in an hour," Oliver calls again from somewhere in the house.

Savannah laughs and trails in after him, followed by Tennyson and Alexis, and then it's just me and Sam Penny in the hallway.

"So." He walks toward me, smiling, a bit pleased with himself. "How am I doing, first birthday as a boyfriend?"

I give him a measured and restrained nod. "Fine."

He squints at me playfully as he slips his arms around me. "Am I fucking it up?"

I get on my tiptoes and press my mouth against his.

"Actually..." I scrunch up my face as I try to work out the logistics of the sentence I'm about to try to say. "I think you're unfucking the greater 'it' up."

He laughs. "Just so you know, you are still, easily, the most complicated person I've ever met."

I smile up at him. "Thank you."

Acknowledgments

Emmy, my creative partner and OG BFF, I love you forever, and I love that every cover we do we love more than the last. I love that you paint and draw and sketch and color the way I want (and hope) my words to feel.

Benja, you are the hardest worker I know. You are the best man, the kindest man, the soundest man. Thank you for everything you've done for me and our family.

To Rachel and Maddi, this season would have been literally physically impossible without you. For everything you both do, for all the ways that you've facilitated me to be released in this manic season, for how well you love me, my kids, my husband, and my pets...thank you. I love our full house.

Bill and Viv, for all the ways you have shown up for me when I needed you, allowed me to be and focus when I needed to, and all the ways you've been there for my kids and loved them as much as you do, thank you.

Bellamy and Junie, you are the most wonderful, patient, releasing, gracious little people. I am so proud to be your mum.

Hellie, I know I talk so much, and I feel like there's always some sort of little fire somewhere, but there's no one I'd rather put them out with.

Caitlin and Alyssa, Hilary and Nicole, thank you for everything you do for me and for how hard you work.

Christa, you loved this story the second you heard of it. Thank you for carrying it so well and for being such a safe place for me and for fighting for me and my books in ways that most people will never know about, but I know about.

Emad and Sarah, this is our seventh book together, which is sheer madness. Thank you for always being excited, always saying yes, and jumping on board no natter the ship.

Amanda George, Scarlett Curtis, Sarah Mitchell, Bronte Ford, Kenzie Elizabeth, Connar Franklin, Madie Conn, Taylor Tippett, Han and Luke and Adam Moore, thank you for always being safe and supportive places for me.

And lastly, you. Thank you for loving my books and my characters and me. Thank you for welcoming us into your homes and letting us sit on your shelves and in your heart. It's been the honor of a lifetime.

About the Author

Jessa Hastings is an Australian native who now lives in Tennessee with her husband, two children, her beautiful, clingy dog, and three cats, which is one more than the last time she wrote one of these. She spends a lot of her time in London, which is still her favorite city in the world. Other current favorites are: Bluey, Jenni Kayne cardigans, Galaxy Minstrels, and Gracie Abrams's "The Secret of Us" album. *Magnolia Parks* was her debut novel and is the series that changed her life and made way for all this. She is very grateful.